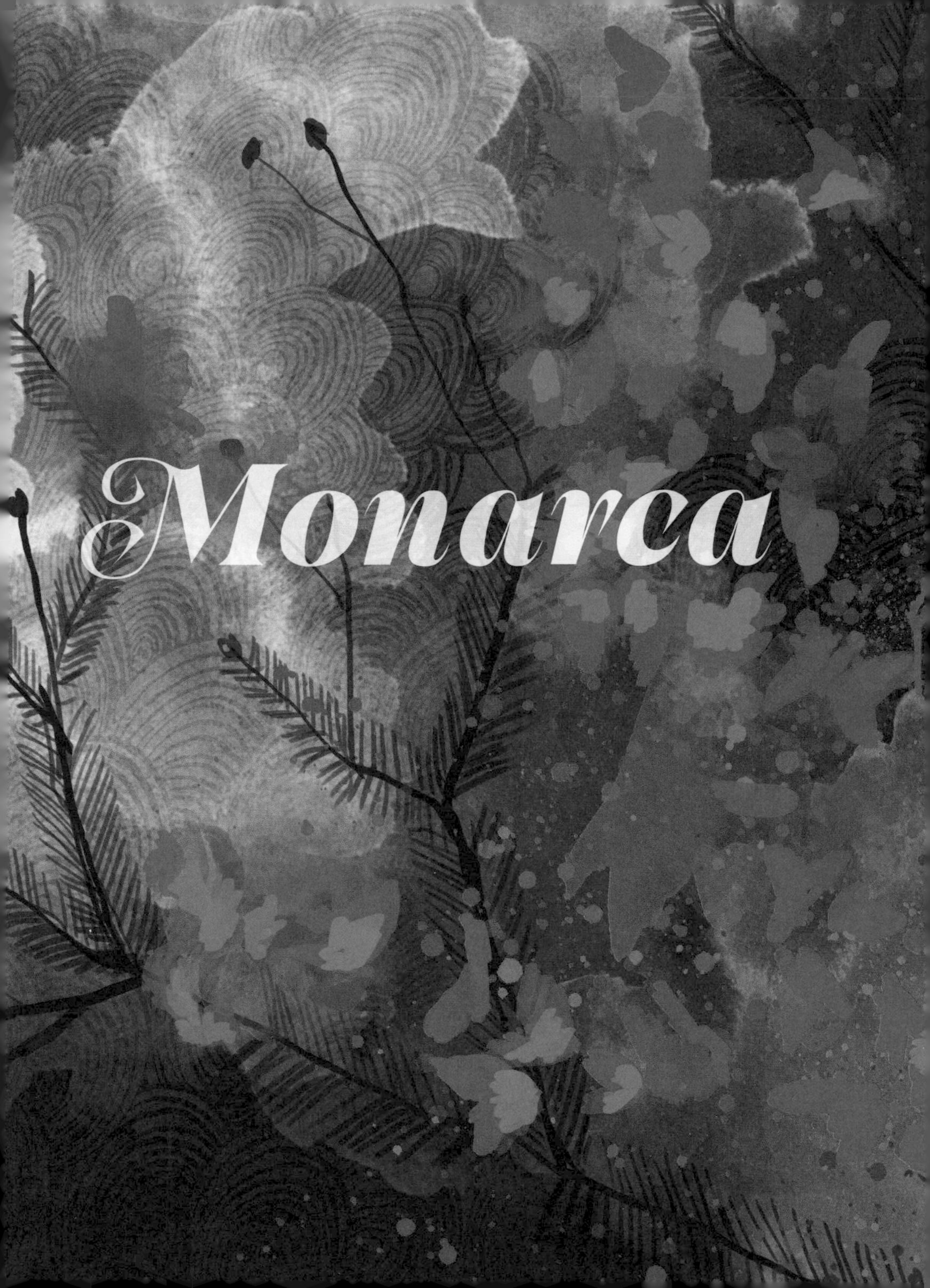
Monarca

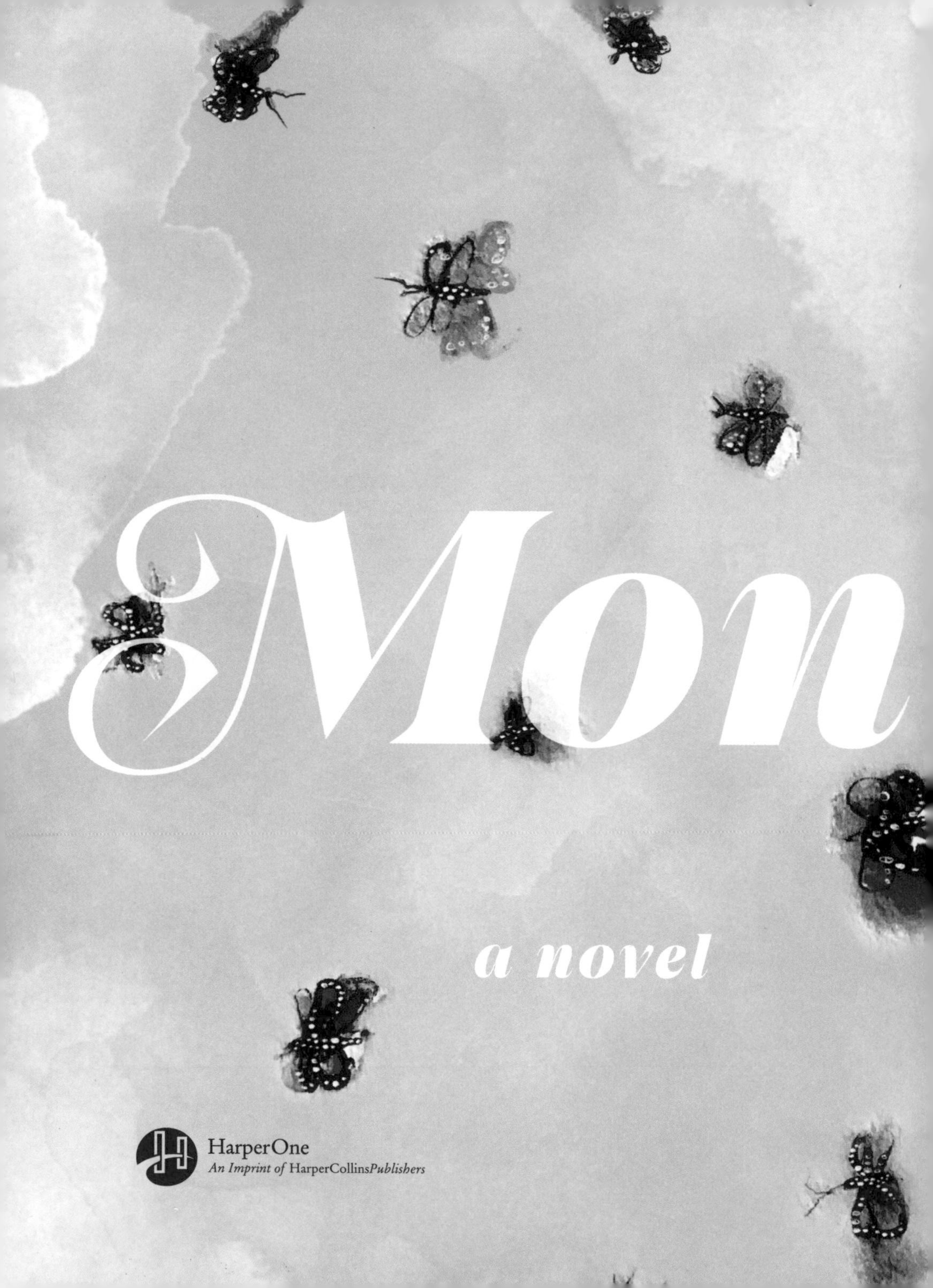

Mon

a novel

HarperOne
An Imprint of HarperCollins*Publishers*

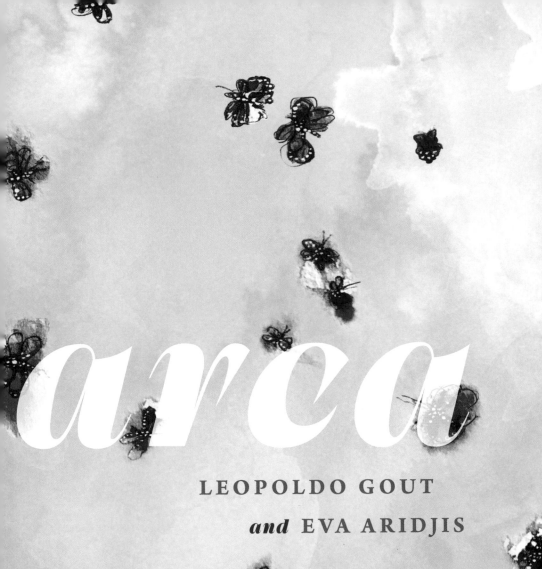

arca

LEOPOLDO GOUT
and EVA ARIDJIS

HarperCollins books may be purchased for educational,
business, or sales promotional use. For information,
please email the Special Markets Department at
SPsales@harpercollins.com.

FIRST EDITION

Designed by Janet Evans-Scanlon

Co-illustrator: James Manning

Library of Congress Cataloging-in-Publication Data
has been applied for.

ISBN 978-0-06-305733-3

22 23 24 25 26 TC 10 9 8 7 6 5 4 3 2 1

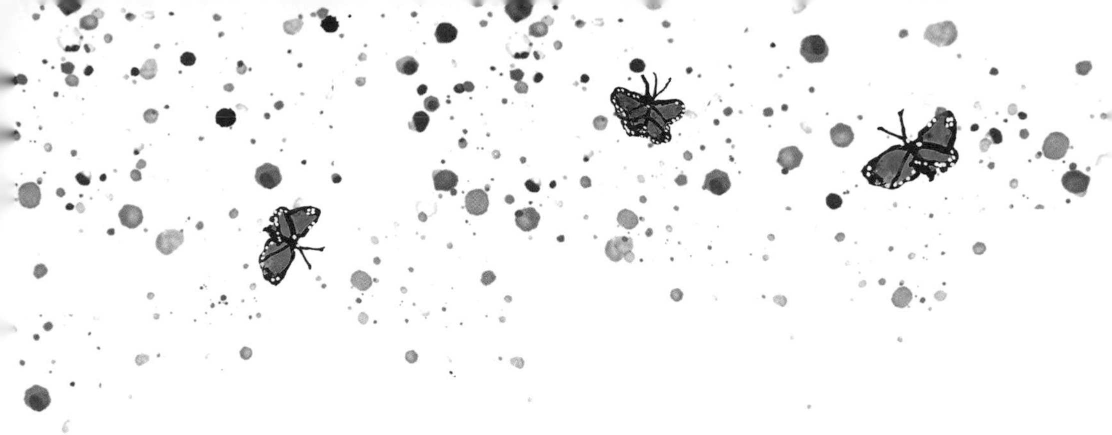

To Josephine,
my monarch butterfly–loving daughter,
and to Homero,
my monarch butterfly–protecting father.

This book was inspired by both of you . . .

—E.A.

To Inés Celestia.
We've been dreaming of this story since
that beautiful butterfly landed on your head
in México, at the very beginning of your
own magical journey . . .

—L.G.

contents

Monarca

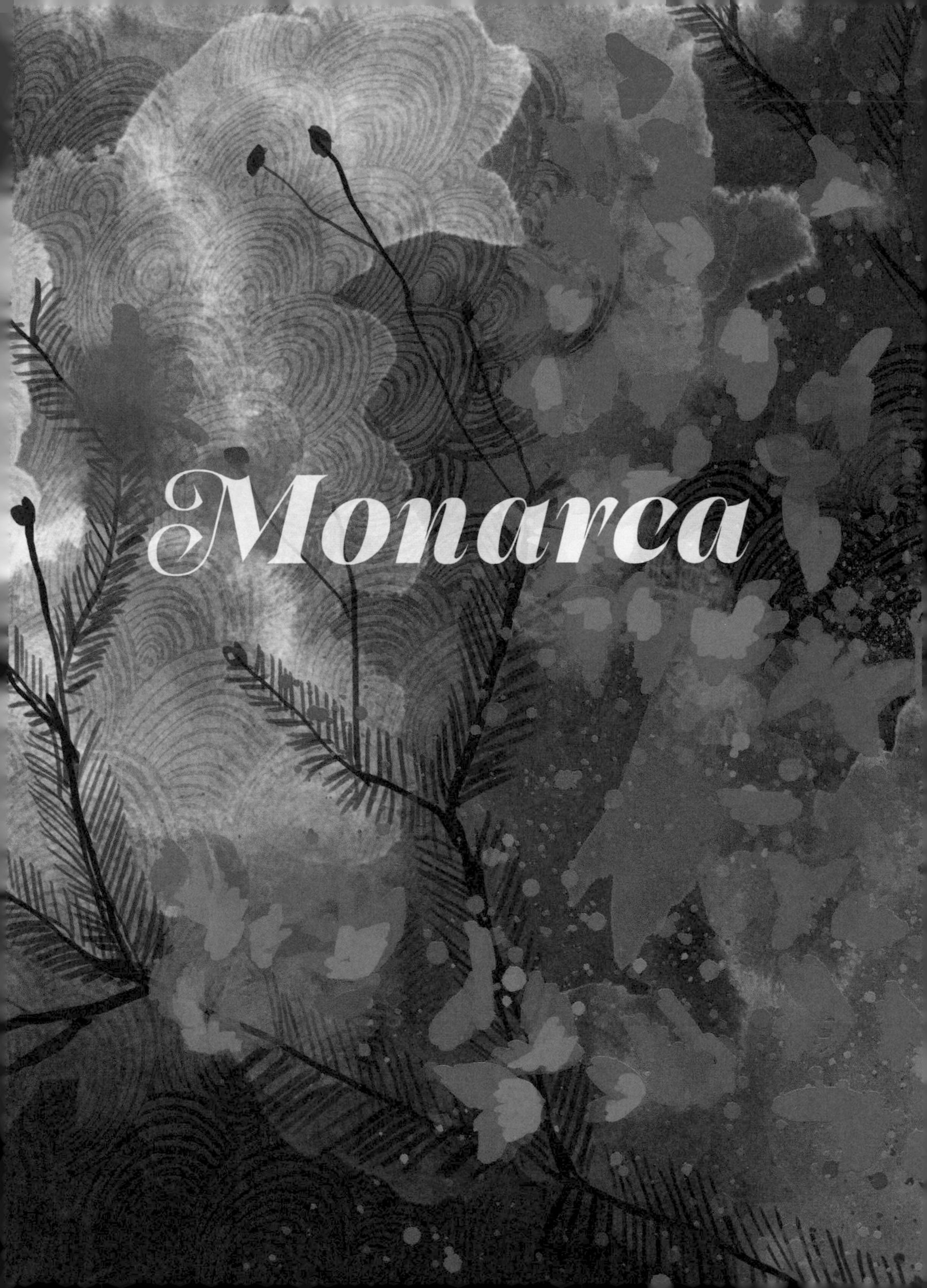

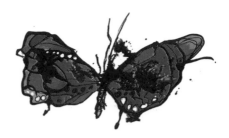

prologue

Just as every landscape on our planet undergoes seasonal transformations each year, so too do all living creatures undergo several transformations in their lifetime, both internal and external. The external transformations are usually dictated by an individual's age or by where they find themselves in their life cycle. But the internal transformations are far more erratic, taking place at unexpected times and in unexpected ways. They are not predictable like the four seasons, but they are comparable to the seasons in that they have four parts to them—the egg stage, the larva stage, the pupa stage, and the butterfly stage. The four stages of a monarch butterfly's life can be used to track the four stages of inner transformation: the egg, which represents the beginning of an experience; the larva or caterpillar stage, which represents the gathering of knowledge; the pupa or chrysalis stage, which represents processing that knowledge to transform into a new being; and the butterfly, which represents the final, enlightened stage.

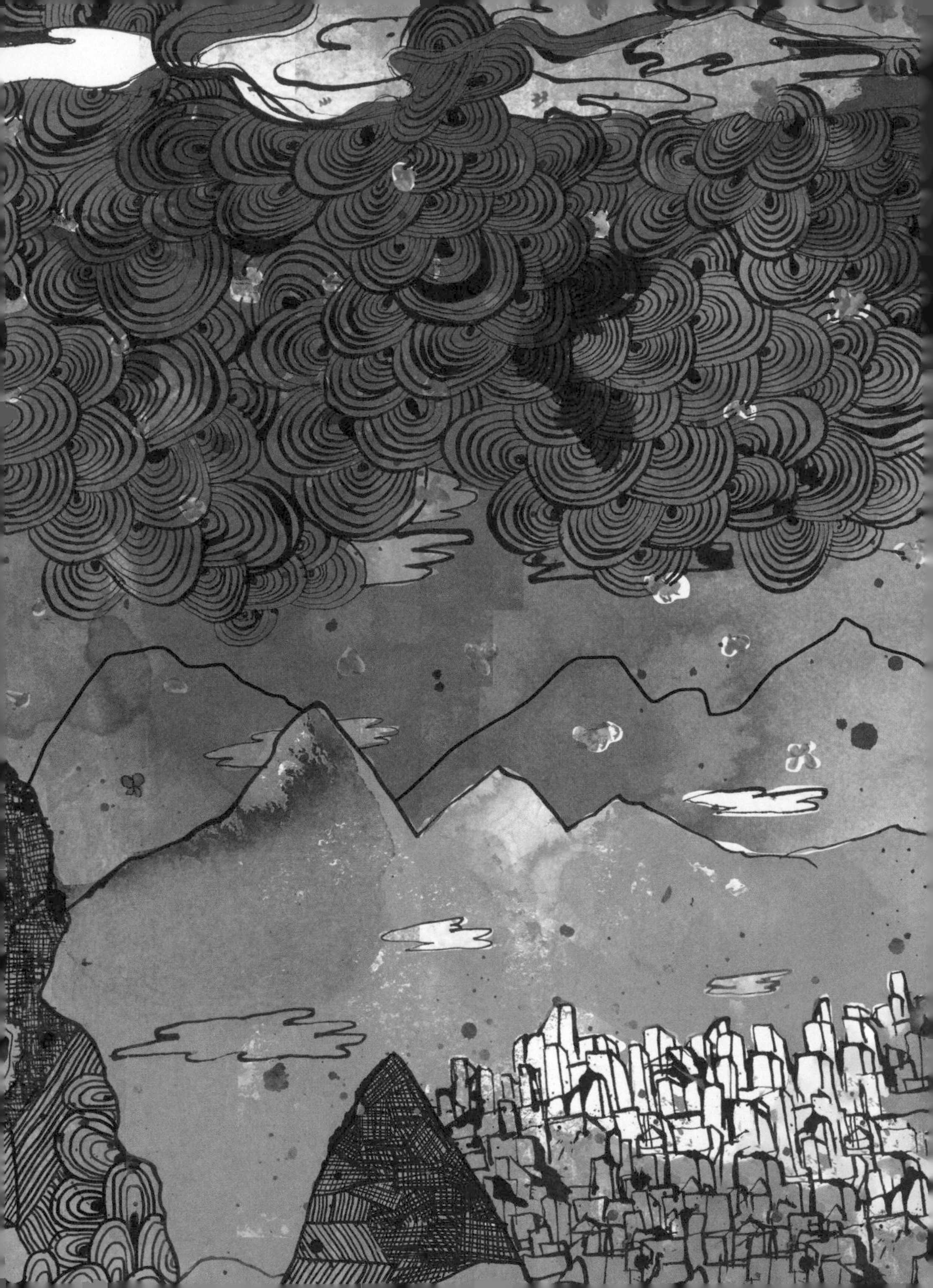

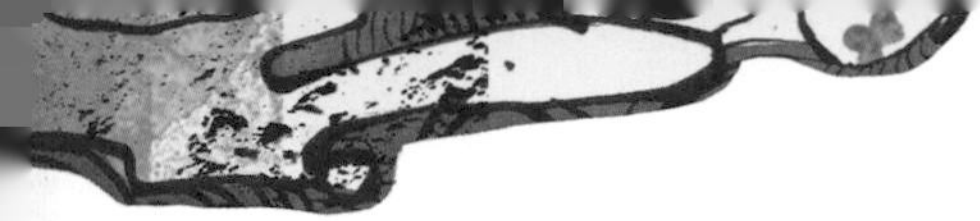

Inés was sitting on her favorite knoll overlooking the park,
sports fields, backyards, and sloping rooftops of her hometown.
Behind her, a wood full of green transitioning to red, orange,
and yellow announced the changing of the seasons. It was late
September and, as had recently become her custom, Inés was
spending the last hours of the afternoon escaping the hum of
human activity by retreating to this quiet spot. Each day she
would climb the hill, sit on the same patch of soft grass, and fill
her lungs with the crisp air. Then she would turn her gaze up

toward the clouds,

or down toward the town,

and
let mind spirit
her and drift.

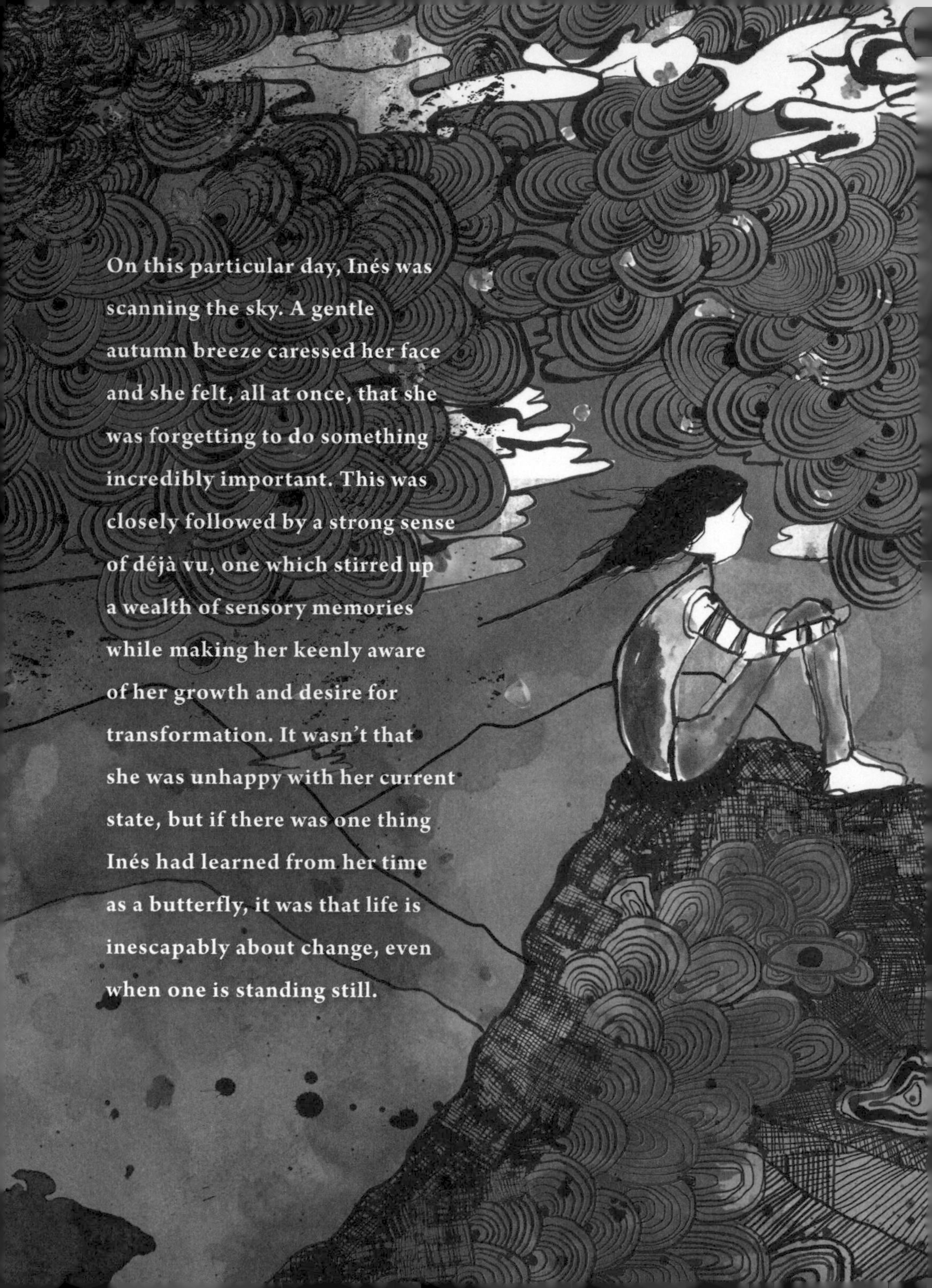

On this particular day, Inés was scanning the sky. A gentle autumn breeze caressed her face and she felt, all at once, that she was forgetting to do something incredibly important. This was closely followed by a strong sense of déjà vu, one which stirred up a wealth of sensory memories while making her keenly aware of her growth and desire for transformation. It wasn't that she was unhappy with her current state, but if there was one thing Inés had learned from her time as a butterfly, it was that life is inescapably about change, even when one is standing still.

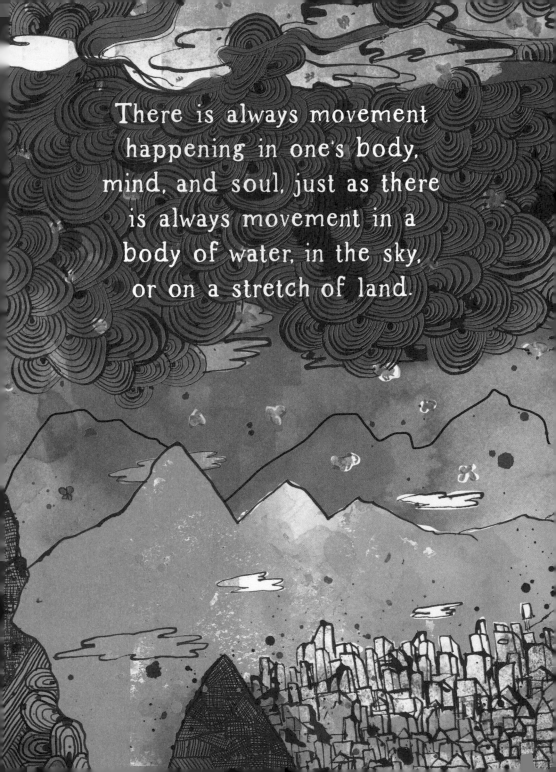

There is always movement
happening in one's body,
mind, and soul, just as there
is always movement in a
body of water, in the sky,
or on a stretch of land.

Inés had just turned fourteen
and her childish desires were
being replaced by those of a
young woman, while her human
impulses still remembered her
butterfly ones.

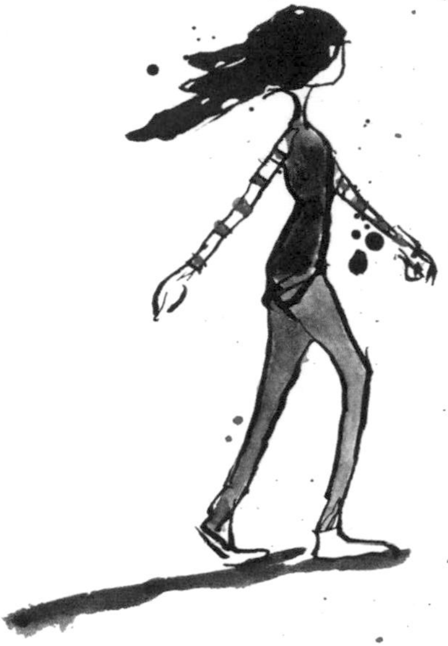

And now, as the breeze strengthened into a gust of wind, she was overwhelmed by a strong urge to take flight, to let a current carry her to distant lands, to embark on

a new adventure.

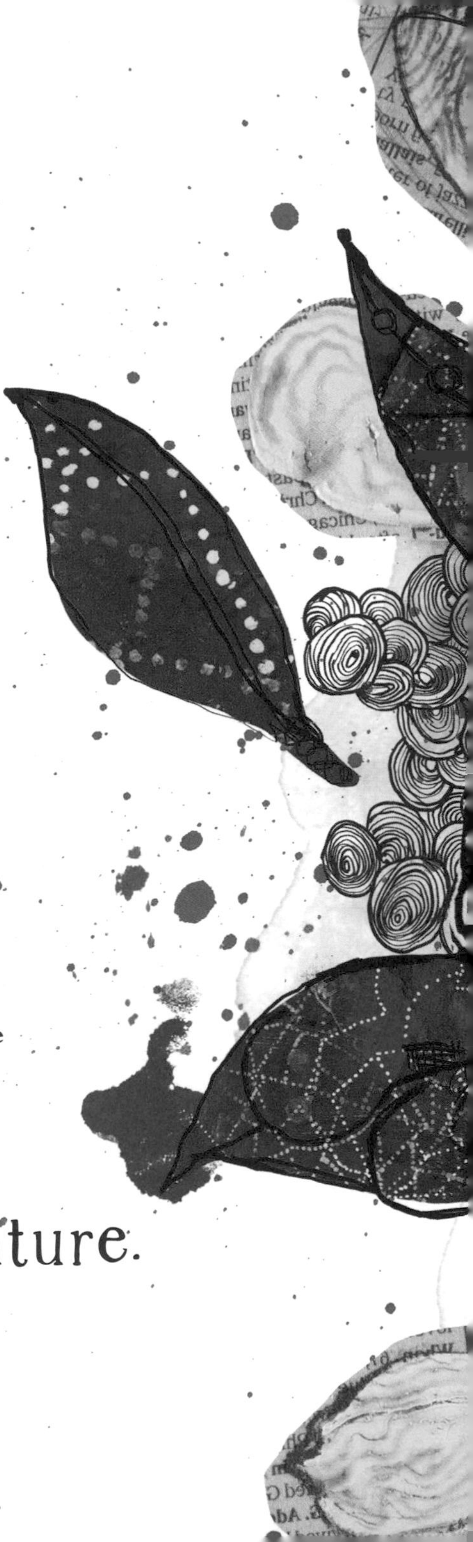

A clump of fallen leaves

was propelled

into the air

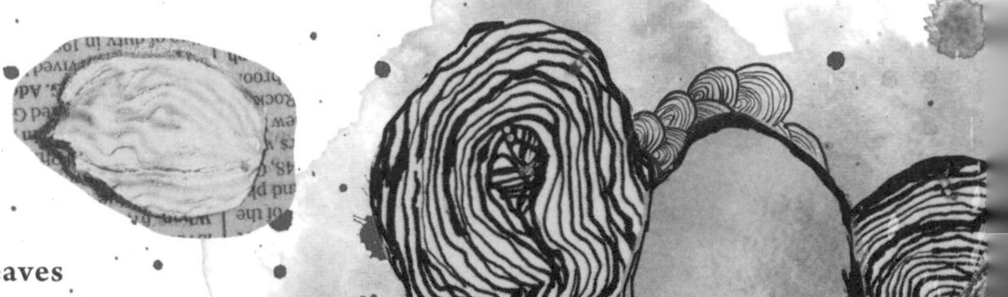

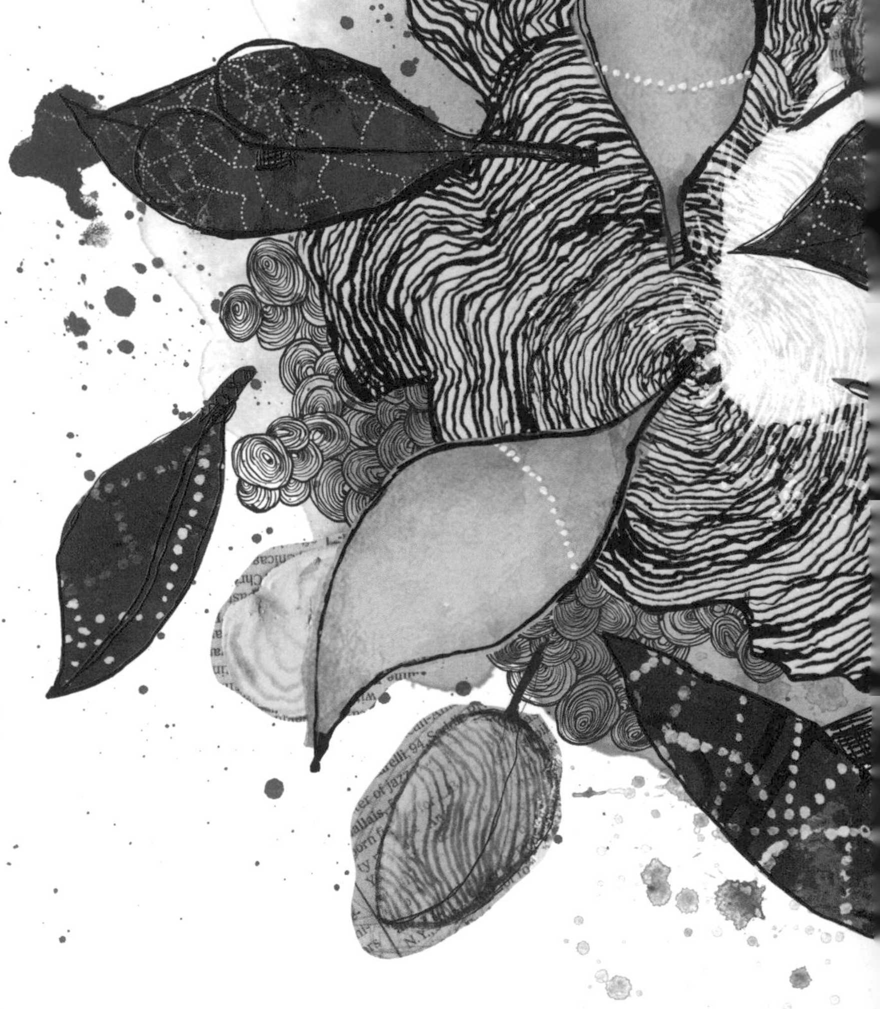

and swirled past her,

then floated
back down to

the ground.

But one leaf
defied gravity
and continued to

dance in the air,

spinning around
an invisible center
like a kaleidoscope
of orange, black,
and white.

Inés watched it closely,
immediately recognizing it
as a monarch butterfly.

She could even hear its wings flapping—
or at least she imagined she could—and
it was a familiar and comforting sound.

The monarch came to rest on a fallen branch in the grass near Inés's feet, and Inés concluded that it was a female due to the absence of black spots on its hind wings. The late afternoon sun cut through the air like a shard of glass, and its rays gilded the edges of the butterfly's wings and shone through their stained-glass patterns as they would through a cathedral's windows. And indeed this explosion of orange tempered by stark black lines and adorned with white diamonds had a similarly spiritual effect on Inés as she admired it: the natural world was her church, and this and every monarch butterfly's wings were her portal to it.

The butterfly proceeded to sunbathe by gently stretching her wings, which absorbed the sun's heat through thousands of overlapping scales that were rather like tiny solar panels. As a monarch, Inés had done this many times herself, and she recalled how the rays had filled her body with tremendous energy, great strength, and an intense desire to fly. It was proof that the sun's fire was at the center of all life on earth, and Inés now became aware of the sun's warmth trickling along her human skin as well, slipping into every pore and filling her body with renewed vigor. Inés was starting to remember a language she had almost forgotten, and she wished to communicate with the butterfly. But she decided not to disturb it, for she knew it would soon be embarking on a very long journey—the adventure of its lifetime—and it needed all the energy it could get.

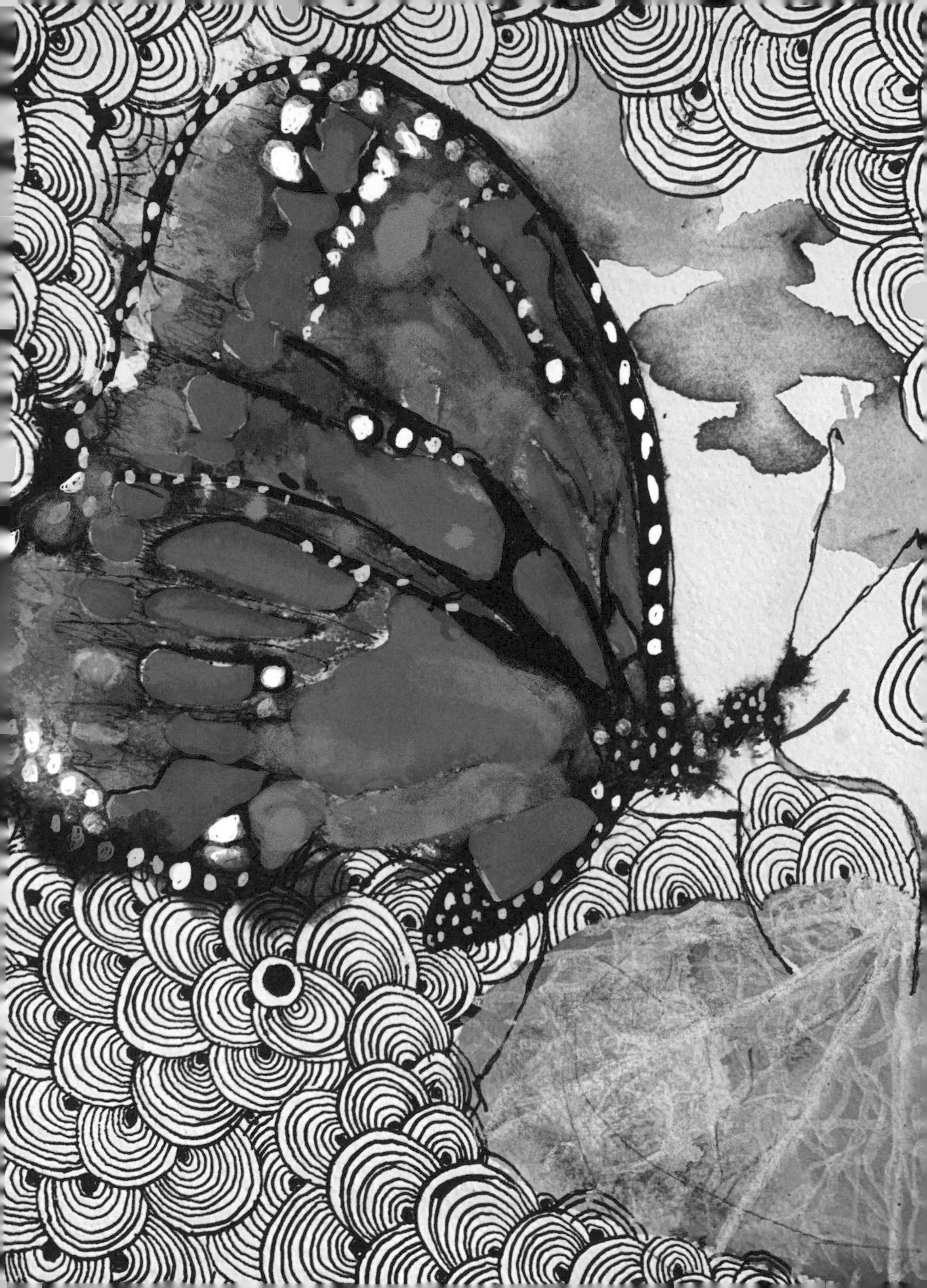

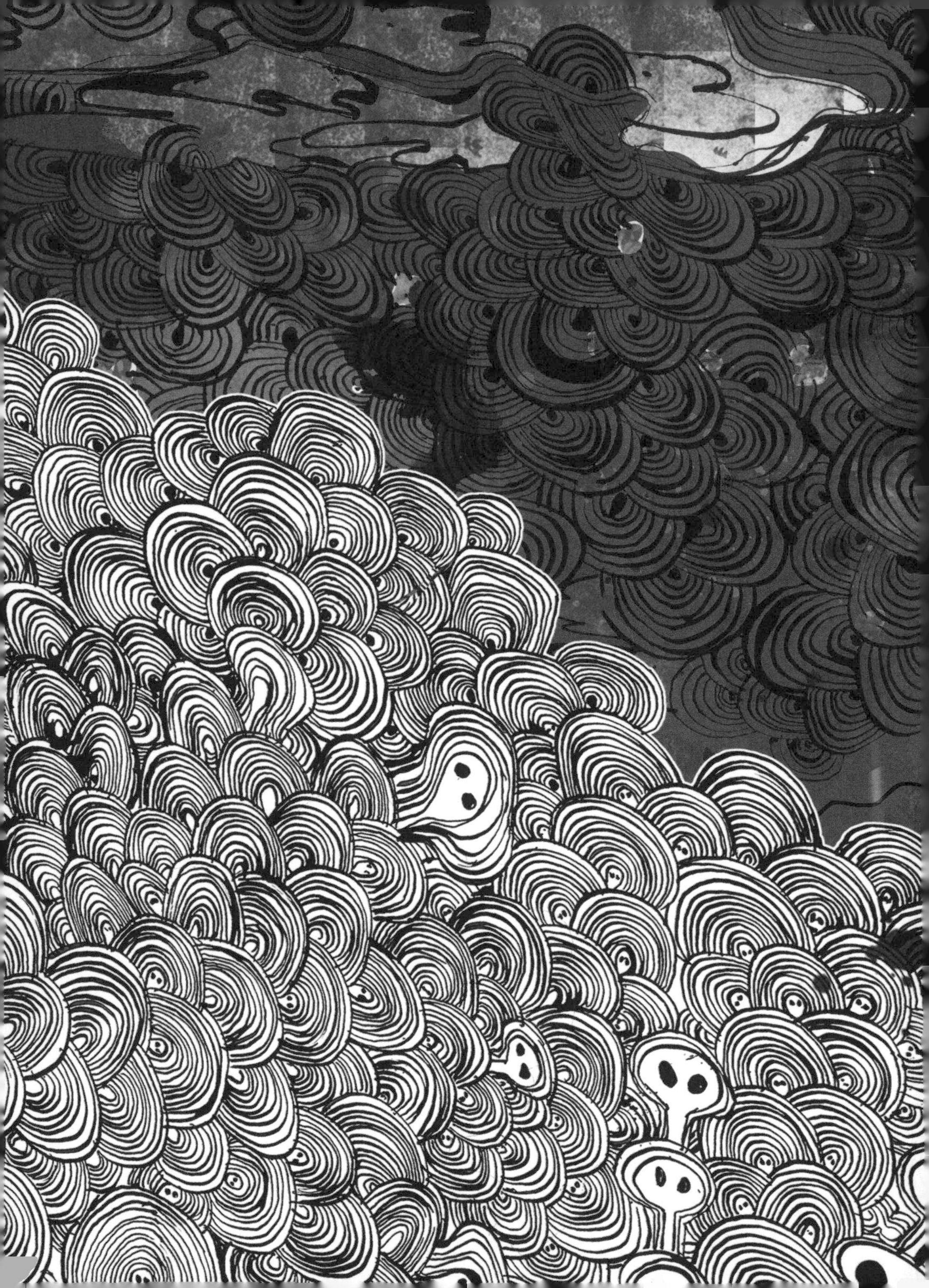

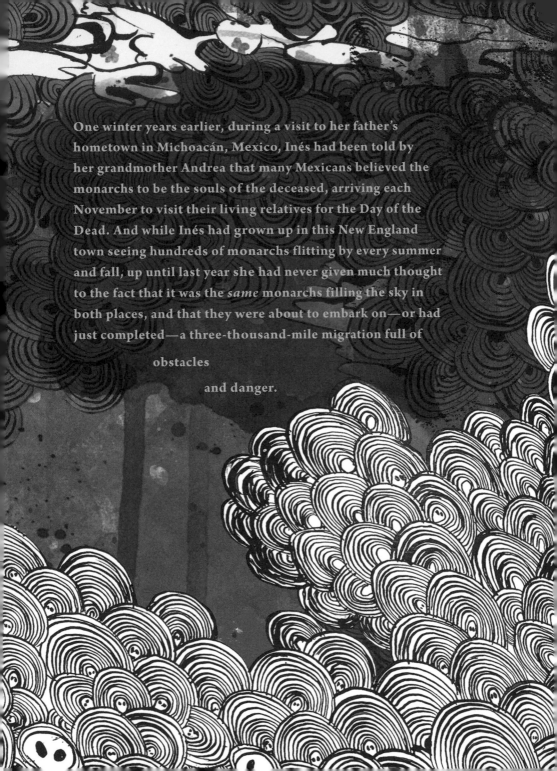

One winter years earlier, during a visit to her father's hometown in Michoacán, Mexico, Inés had been told by her grandmother Andrea that many Mexicans believed the monarchs to be the souls of the deceased, arriving each November to visit their living relatives for the Day of the Dead. And while Inés had grown up in this New England town seeing hundreds of monarchs flitting by every summer and fall, up until last year she had never given much thought to the fact that it was the *same* monarchs filling the sky in both places, and that they were about to embark on—or had just completed—a three-thousand-mile migration full of

obstacles

and danger.

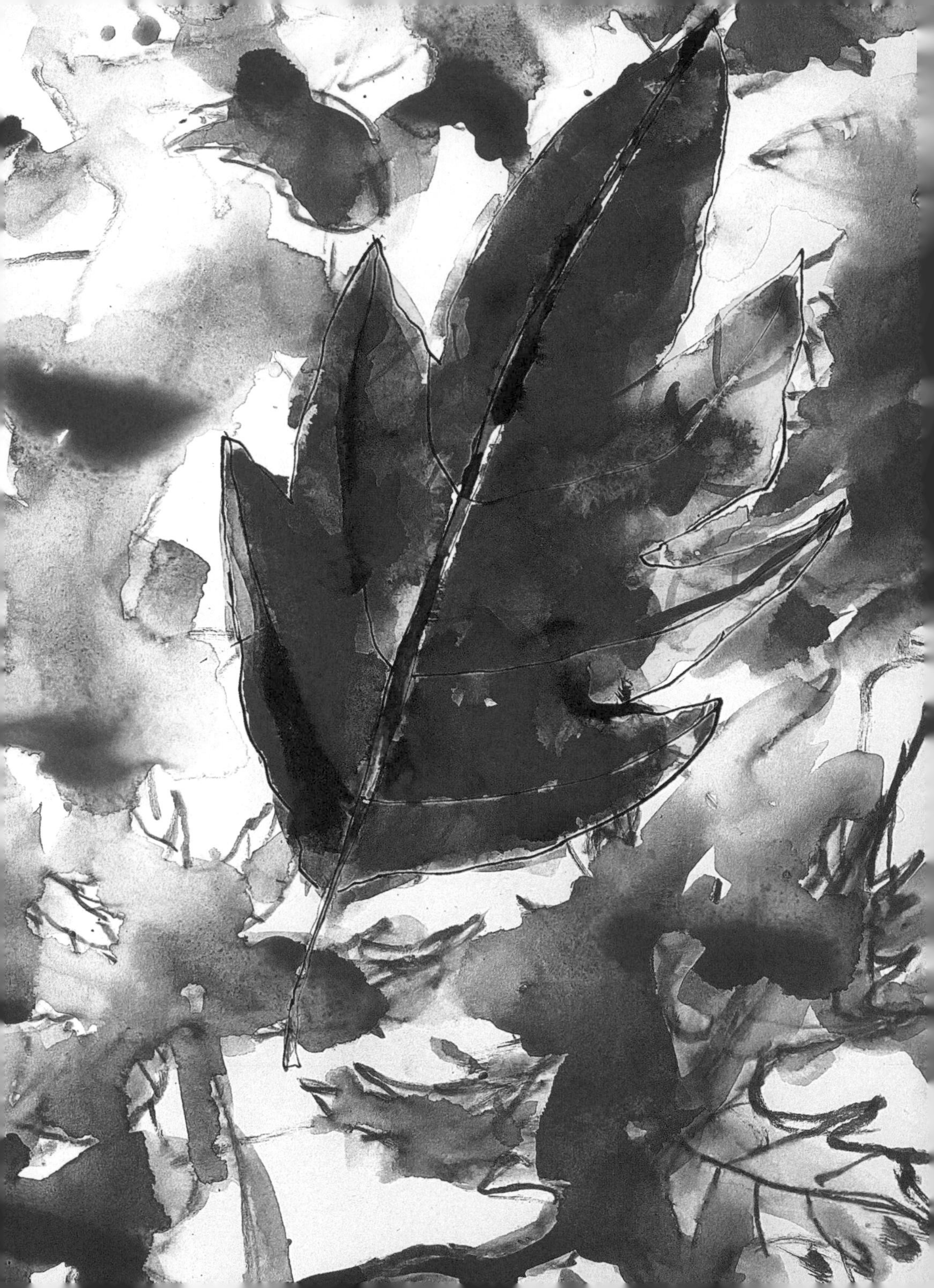

There was a sudden

drop

in the air's temperature

and Inés was flooded with sensations that
broke down all the barriers between her body
and its surroundings. The landscape exploded
in a symphony of patchwork colors, and it
pained her to realize she had almost forgotten
about these ultraviolet contrasts, invisible to
the human eye. Vibrant streaks and waves of
light were now visible in the sky, while the smell
of fertile soil, faraway flowers, and cool, damp
creeks filled her nostrils. She could *definitely*
hear the butterfly opening and closing its wings
now, through delicate vibrations in the air.

Inés stared at the monarch on the branch and
felt like she knew her. But how could she? Most
of the monarchs making their way through the
town were only a few days old, except for the
ones coming from Canada, who were at most a
few weeks old.

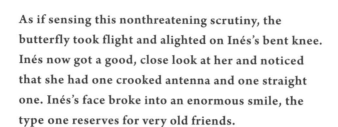

As if sensing this nonthreatening scrutiny, the butterfly took flight and alighted on Inés's bent knee. Inés now got a good, close look at her and noticed that she had one crooked antenna and one straight one. Inés's face broke into an enormous smile, the type one reserves for very old friends.

"Hello there. I think I know who you are," said Inés.

"I was born only three sunsets ago, so how could you know me?" responded the butterfly.

"Sometimes we recognize someone we haven't actually met before. Have you ever heard of magic?"

The butterfly shook her head. She hadn't been lying when she'd said she was new to the world.

Inés explained: "Well, magic is the energy that animates all living things, as well as the cords in space and time that connect those living things to each other. Most humans can't see those connections, but monarch butterflies can."

The butterfly looked around her. "You mean those colorful lines in the sky?"

"Exactly," Inés replied.

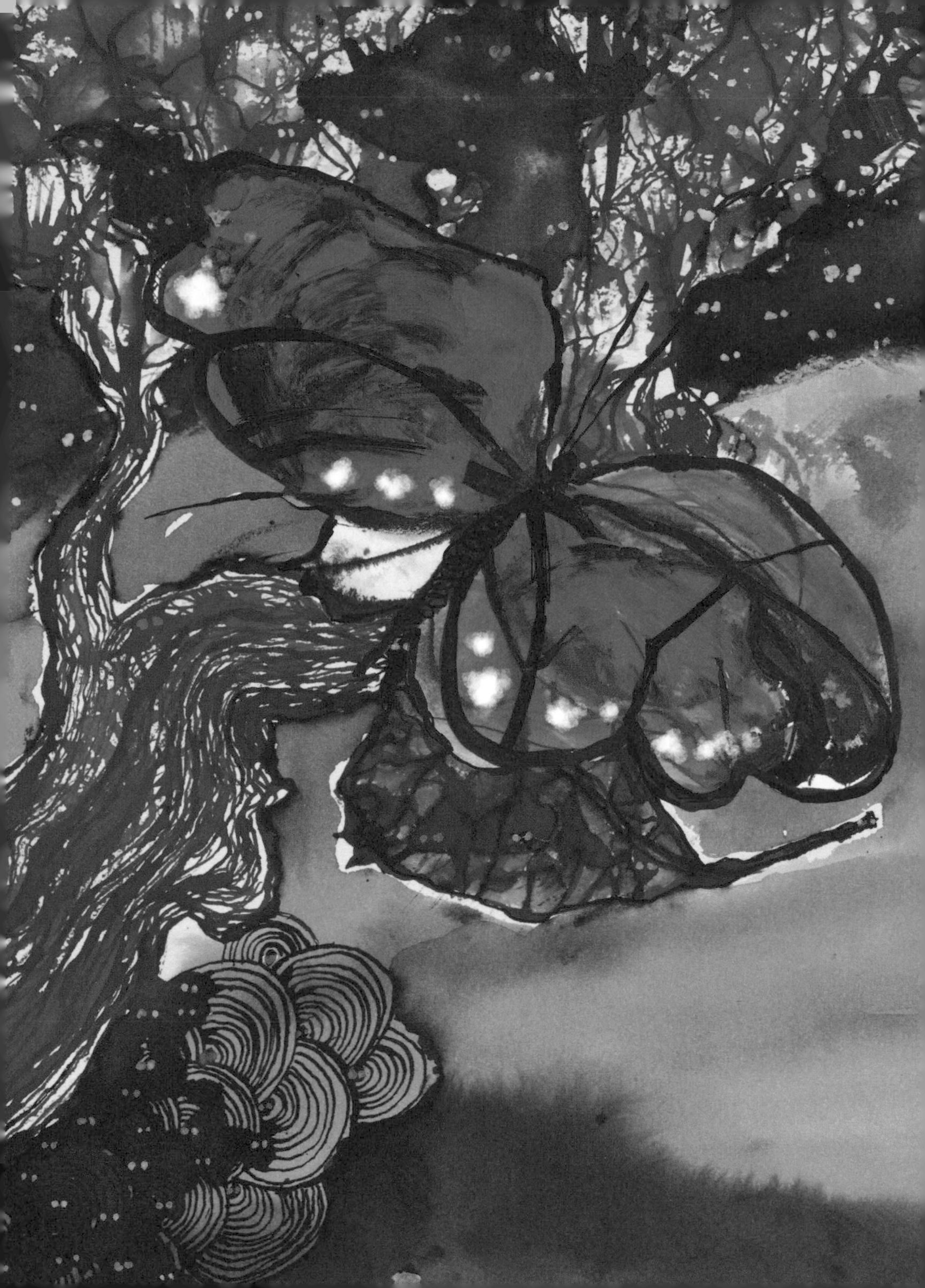

"Those lines are magical.

As are the flowers you feed from, the milkweed leaves you ate as a caterpillar, and the different animals you meet. We all pass energy around to each other, an energy that's constantly moving and changing and keeping the world alive. Magic is the sun that guides the monarchs south and the moon that guides your cousins, the moths. Magic is what just led *you* to land on *my* knee."

The butterfly smiled. "I think I understand. Magic is two living things meeting, in the same place and at the same time."

"Yes, but they can also meet *without* being in the same place at the same time. We're all connected to the other life forms we share this planet with, but we're also connected to our ancestors and descendants, through genetics and ancestral memory. It's because of genetics that I know who you are, because you look *just* like your great-great-grandmother Josephine. You both have the same wonky left antenna," Inés added, raising a curved finger to her forehead.

18

The butterfly looked startled. "How do *you* know about Josephine?" she asked.
"I was told that I'm related to her, and that she was a hero."

"Josephine was my best friend," replied Inés, "and she was a very special butterfly indeed. You're lucky to have her as your ancestor. What's your name, little butterfly?"

"My name is actually Josephine too, but you can call me Jo-Jo."

"Well, my name's Inés, and Josephine and I met in this town exactly a year ago. And then we traveled down to the sanctuary in Michoacán together, just like you will."

"Me? How do you know this?" asked Jo-Jo with surprise.

"Because you're the fourth generation, and the fourth generation is the one that migrates down to Mexico. You'll fly thousands of miles to get there, fleeing the cold air and following a trail of blossoms, and you'll have many adventures along the way. And then you'll spend the winter there."

"But how will I know how to get there? Or when it's time to leave?" asked Jo-Jo.

19

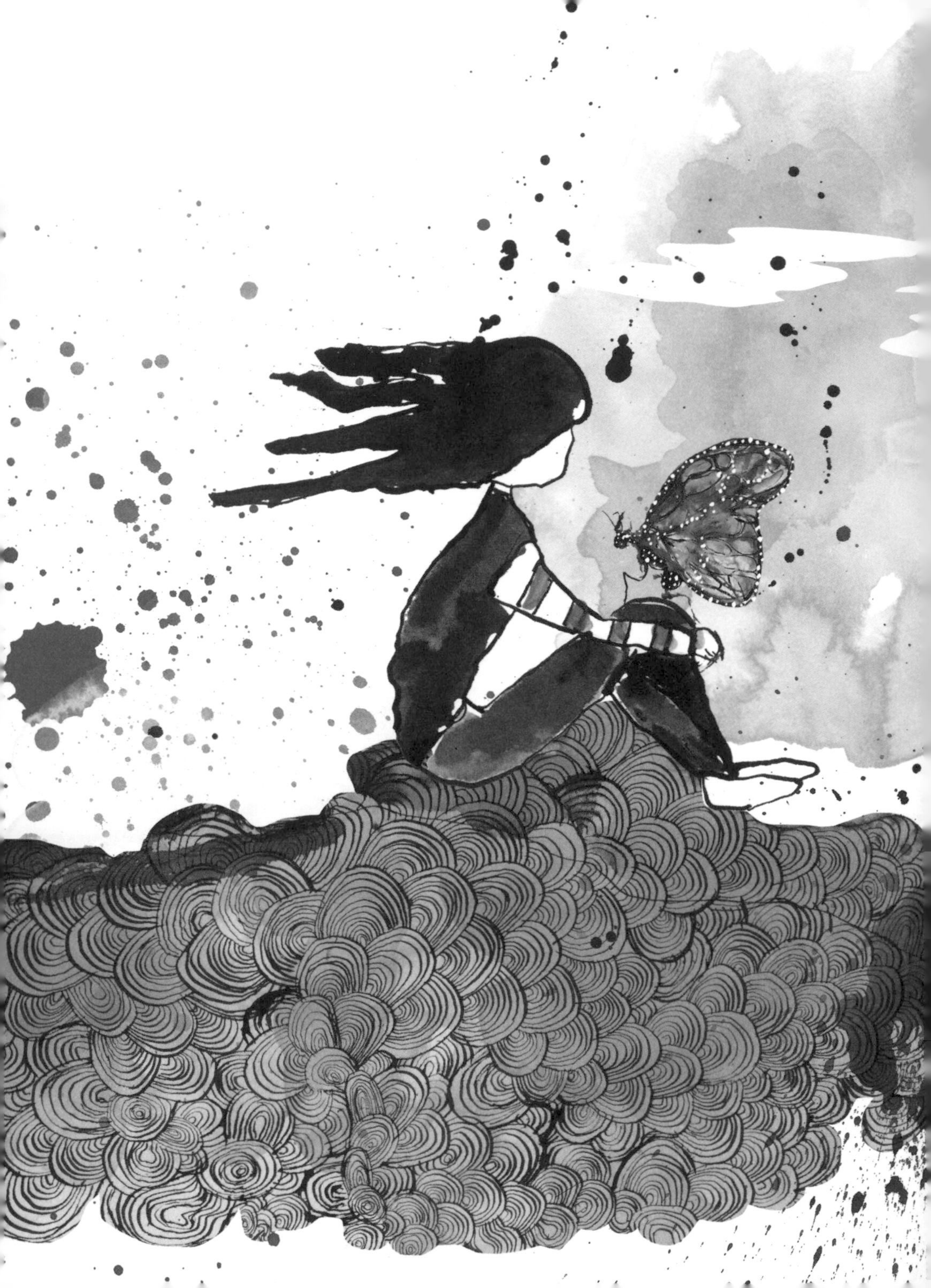

"You just will. For every important experience or decision in our life, there are four stages we must go through: the egg, the larva, the pupa, and the butterfly. You've already reached the fourth stage, so all the knowledge and experience you collected in your past forms—as well as the ancestral wisdom of the monarchs that came before you—will guide you. And in terms of when to leave . . . well, you'll suddenly feel a current of air which whispers to you that it's time to go."

Jo-Jo looked around with a worried expression. "But I like it here, and I'm frightened. How can a small butterfly like me undertake such a huge journey?"

Inés gently caressed Jo-Jo's head with her finger.

"You are wiser and more powerful than you could ever imagine.

I was also scared before I left here. In fact, I was terrified! But I made it to Mexico safely, and the experience completely transformed me."

"But you probably went by choice. And you're a human."

"Well, I didn't go as a human, or by choice. You see, I'm also a fourth generation, just like you. I had to go to save my family. Your great-great-grandmother and I, we saved them together."

"What do you mean?" asked Jo-Jo.

"If you can spare an hour or two, I'll tell you the story," offered Inés.

"Of course! I'd love to learn about the migration and the world from you," replied Jo-Jo.

Inés shook her head. "It's the other way around, Jo-Jo. If this story had a title, it would be *What Inés Learned from the Butterflies.*"

And once they had both settled in comfortably, Inés began . . .

The Egg

chapter

1

The egg:

A tiny, off-white butterfly egg is stuck to the under-side of a milkweed leaf, waiting for its tenant to emerge. A female monarch will lay hundreds of eggs during a two-week period, but usually only one per leaf so that each larva will have enough to eat when it hatches. Milkweed leaves are the only thing a monarch caterpillar can eat. The egg will sit for an average of four days before the caterpillar breaks out. The egg is seemingly still, but inside it the magic of creation is manifesting a hungry being, building its form one cell at a time.

The egg represents the beginning—the beginning of a life, the beginning of a journey, the beginning of our story. The egg is preparation, expectation, the seed of an idea, a seed being planted. The egg determines where and when each journey will begin. The egg is a vessel, a birthplace, a launching pad for an individual or an experience. It represents infinite possibility.

One year before her encounter with Jo-Jo and one day before her birthday, Inés was in ballet class spinning gracefully but frowning as she did so. The audition for her town's production of *Swan Lake* was coming up in a few days' time and she still hadn't mastered her *fouettés*. She was determined to land the lead role this year, the first step in her plan to become the best dancer in her town, then in the state, and finally to join the New York City Ballet. Despite Inés being only twelve going on thirteen, her whole life was dedicated to dancing—to the study of it, to the practice of it, and to the incomparable feeling of freedom it gave her. She'd dreamed of being a ballerina ever since the age of three, when she'd opened up a music box and watched with fascination as a small figure in a tutu jumped up from a lying position and stuttered in circles to "Für Elise."

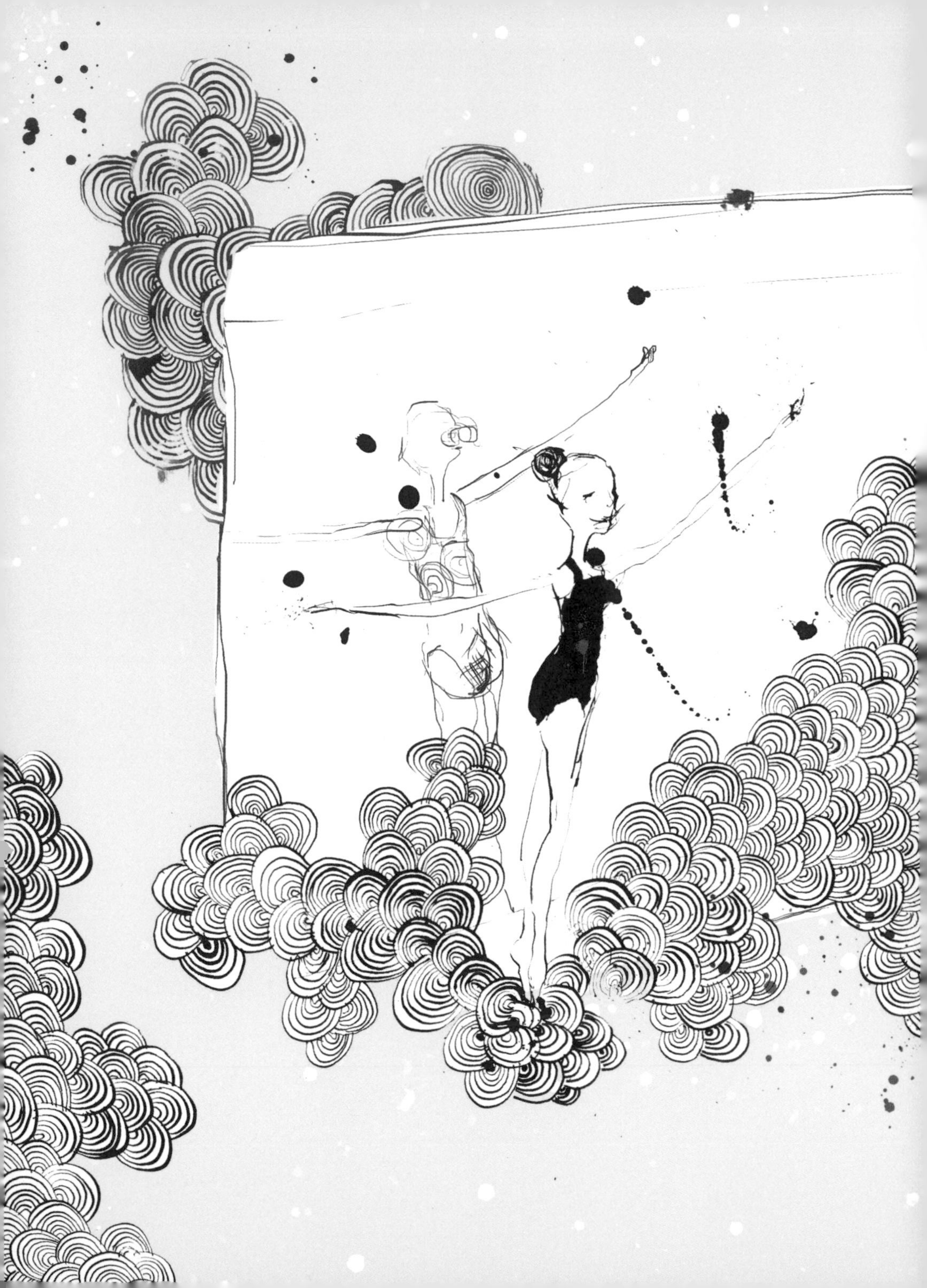

Her parents didn't think it was healthy for her to be so intensely focused on a single goal at such a young age. They supported Inés's passion for dance because they knew how

important
it was
to her...

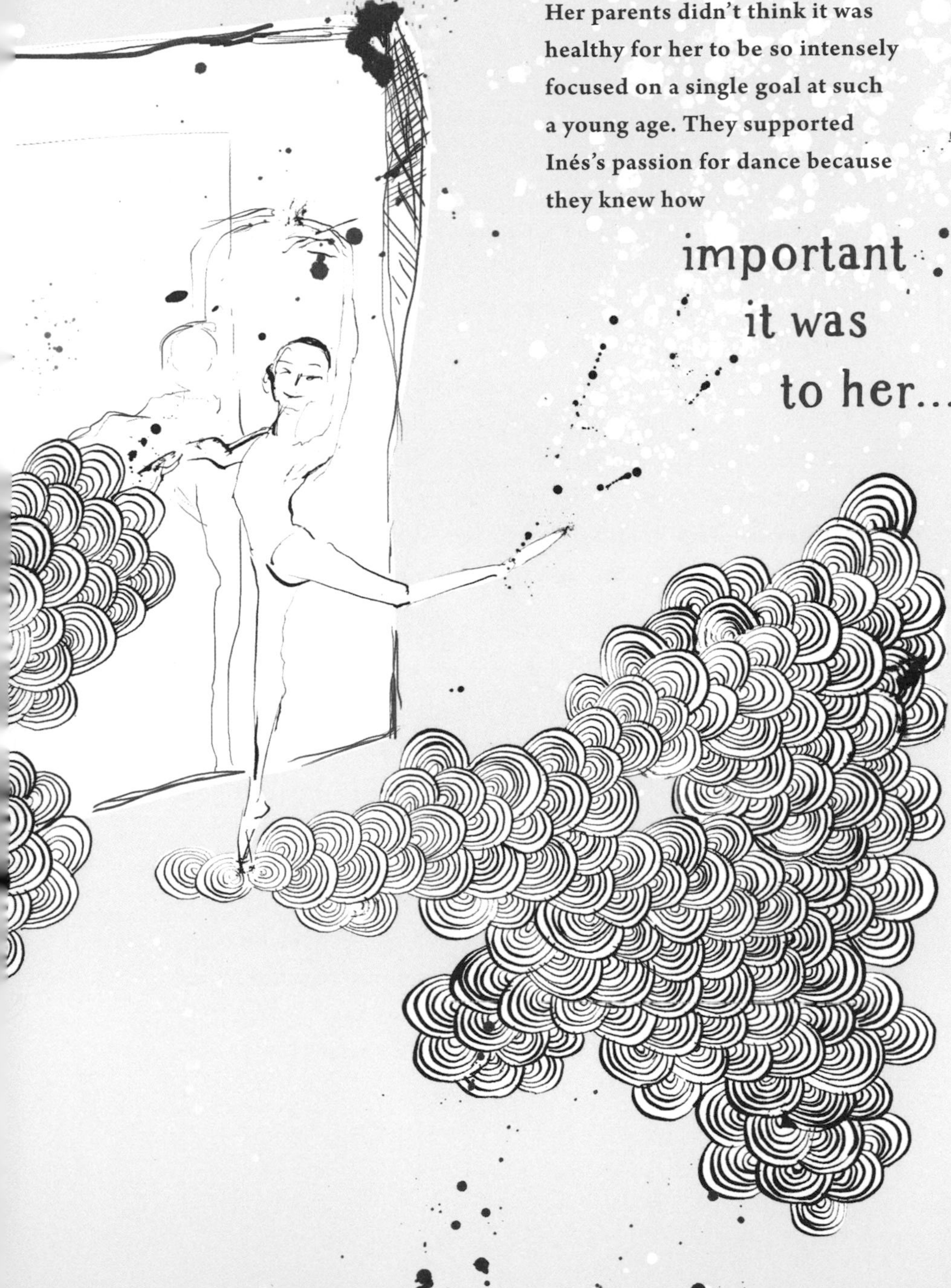

. . . but her Mexican father felt she should be spending more time with friends and family, while her American mother thought she should be concentrating more on schoolwork and cultivating her mind. They both agreed that she spent too much time indoors and should frequent the park more, or take walks in the woods. Meanwhile her older brother, Leo, spent his days skateboarding with friends and was an avid graphic novel and screenplay reader, aspiring to write his own one day. He had a level of ambition more suited to a teenager, while Inés spent her afternoons and weekends rehearsing, and evenings in her room watching ballet performances on the computer. She knew that practice can make perfect, but she didn't realize that her pursuit of success was distracting her from more important things and that the isolation and lack of time outdoors were taking a toll on her mind and body.

Inés felt misunderstood and frustrated, and she attributed these feelings to wanting and needing more than her surroundings could provide. She thought that her moodiness and restlessness were a result of not being able to express herself fully, and that her family and town were limiting when it came to her boundless potential and dreams. She was of course about to transition to adolescence—and an enormous and unexpected transformation was about to take place on top of that—but for now Inés believed that the need for change she felt deep in her bones was connected to the ballet production. If she could only complete two more *fouettés* without stumbling slightly to one side, she would get the role and her life would immediately improve.

Inés's class ended, and she
stepped outside and walked to
the curb to wait for her mother to
pick her up. She noticed that the
brisk fall air was having a strange
effect on her body today, making
her shiver but also filling her
with energy.

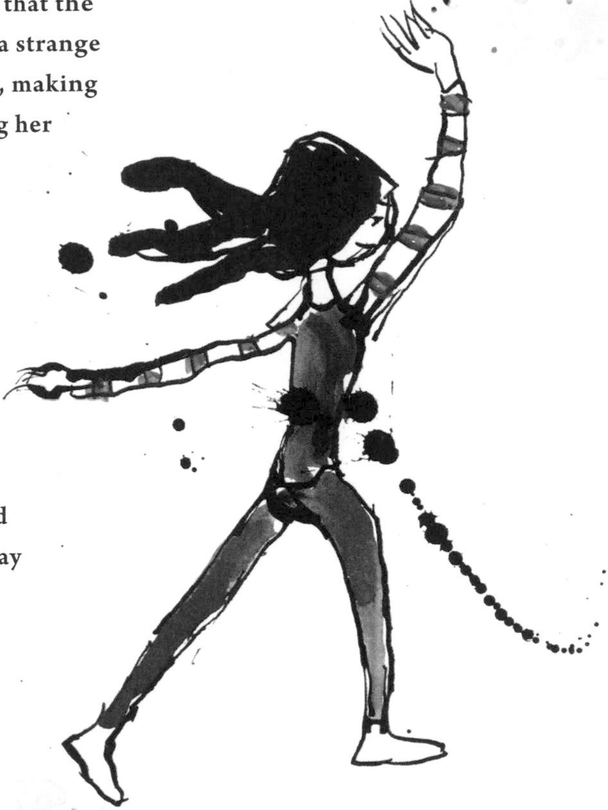

She felt like

running
down
the street

and contemplated
calling home to say

she would
walk instead,

but at that moment her
mother pulled up in her
white Volvo.

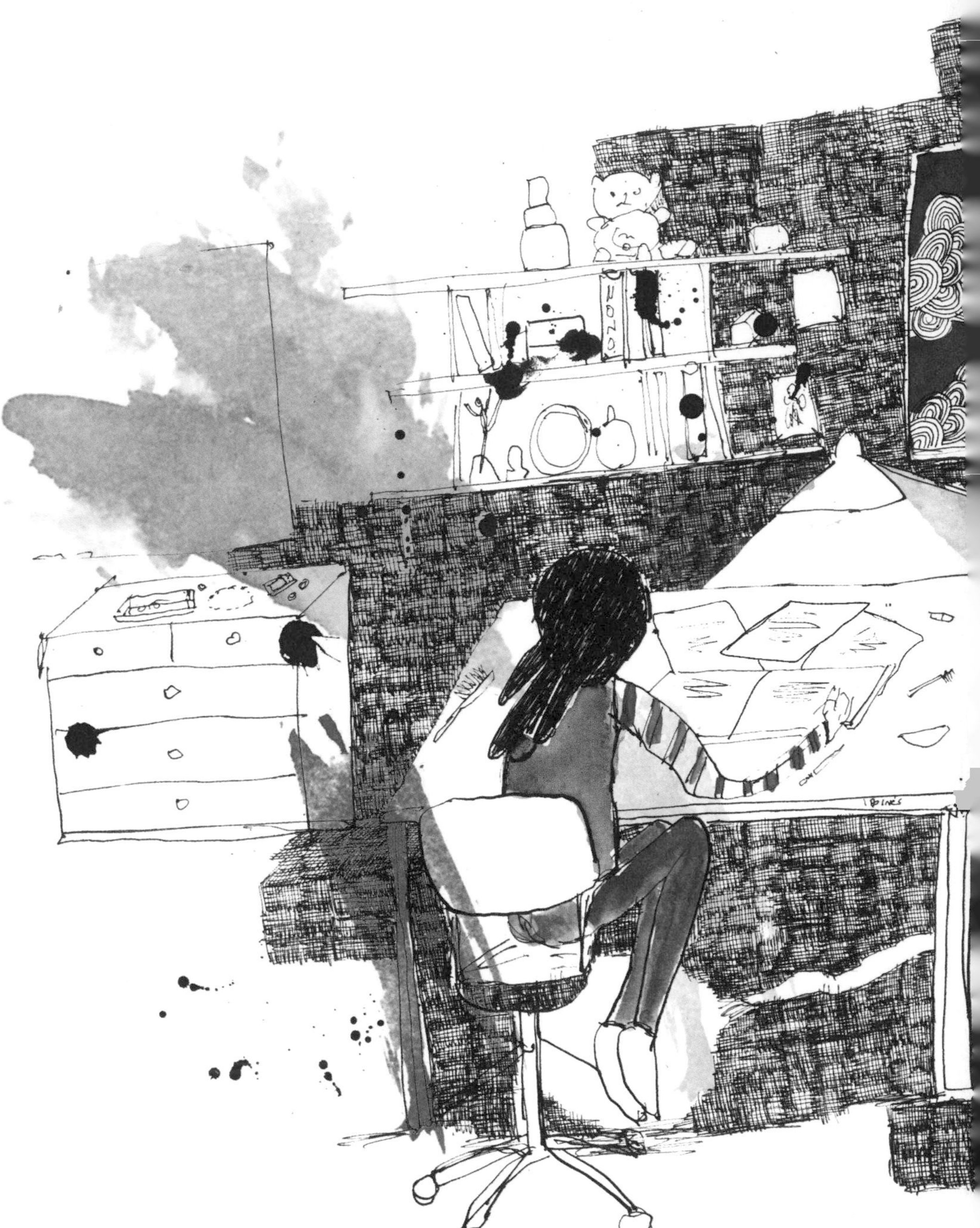

That evening Inés sat under a small pool of lamplight at her desk, staring disinterestedly at some pages containing her math homework and chewing on the end of a pencil. Her bedroom window was open and she could hear a soft rain starting to fall outside. Suddenly a strong gust of wind blew in, causing the curtains to flap violently and her homework to fly off the desk and scatter across the floor. Inés jumped up, closed the window, and picked up the pages. But as she raised her eyes, she spotted an enormous winged insect on the wall: a butterfly or moth with large, amber circles which resembled owl eyes on its wings.

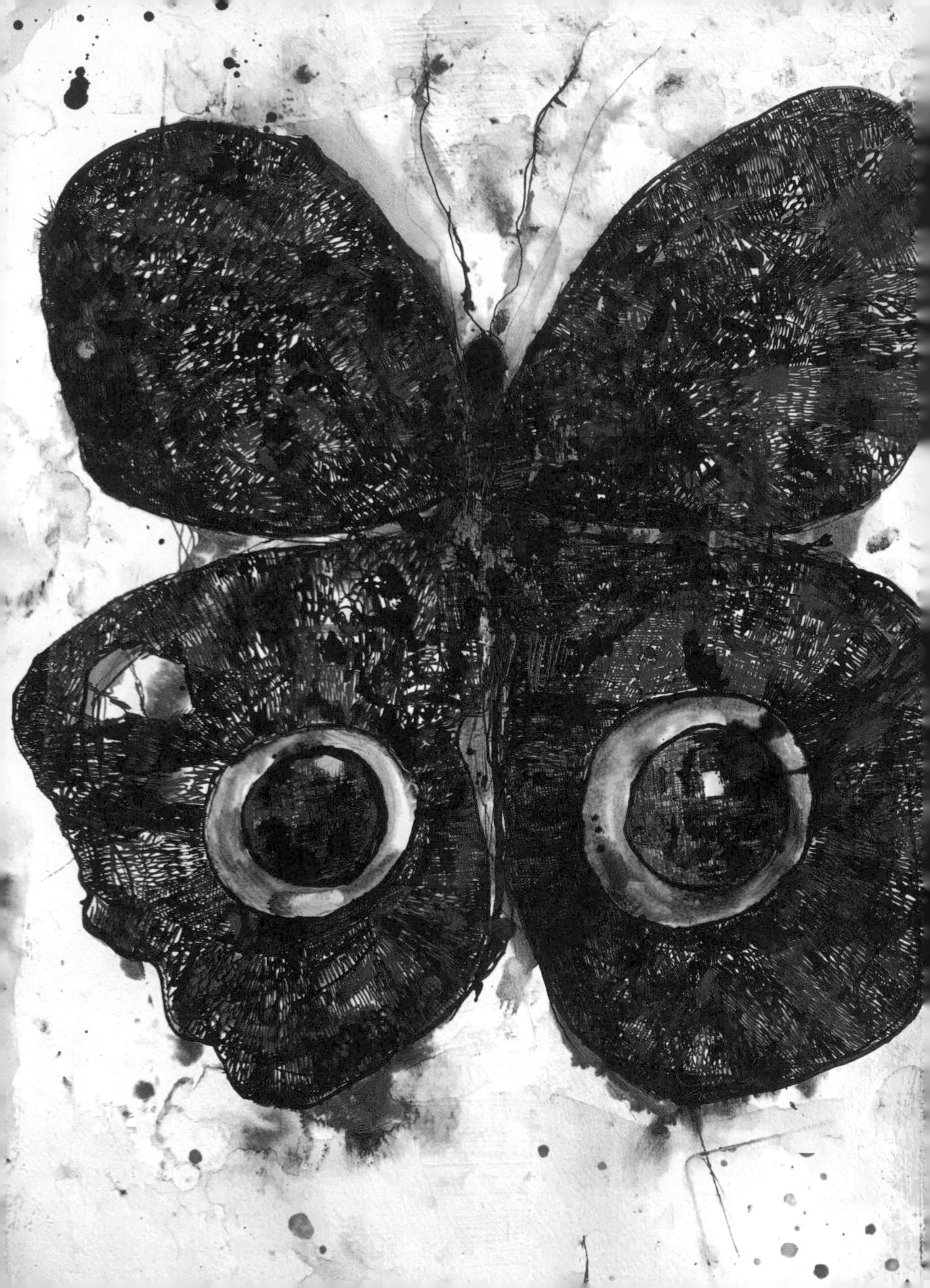

Inés screamed,

startled by the size and dramatic appearance of this unexpected visitor. Within seconds her brother could be heard stomping up the stairs, and then he opened the door with a skateboard under his arm and raindrops in his hair.

"What's the matter?" Leo asked. Inés pointed at the wall and Leo turned to look at the butterfly.

"What the heck is that?" he exclaimed, lifting his skateboard in the air to smash it.

"No, don't!" Inés cried, as Leo's skateboard came down on the wall with a thud.

The butterfly, spotting the dark and menacing shadow moving toward it, escaped just in time and drifted out the bedroom door. Inés pushed past Leo into the hallway and saw it heading toward the stairs. She hurried down the steps to get ahead of it and opened the front door to release it.

The butterfly flew
back out into the night,

deciding that a little bit
of rain wasn't so bad

when compared to
this teenaged boy

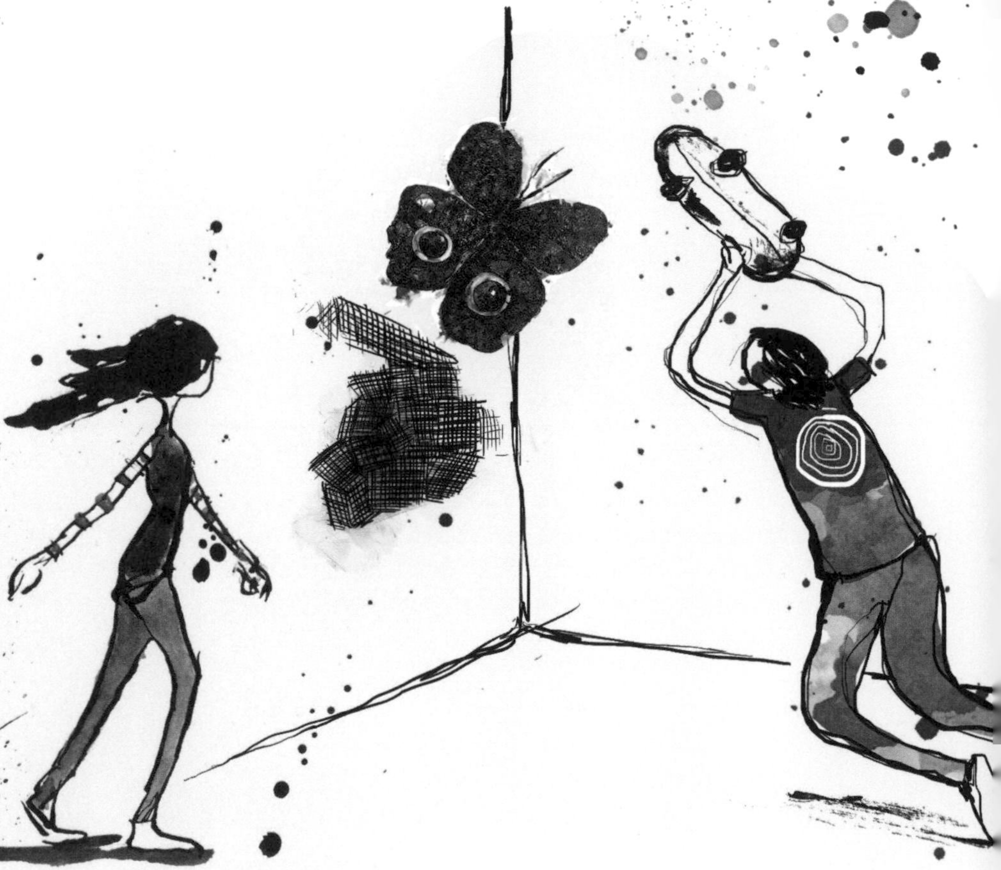

and his giant
flyswatter.

Inés watched as the creature's striking wings faded into the darkness, then closed the door and frowned at Leo.

"There's no need to kill insects *just because you can*. It only takes a moment to help them back outside."

"Well, you're the one who screamed like your life was in danger," retorted Leo.

That evening after dinner, Inés did an internet search for "moths with eyes on their wings" and discovered that her visitor had been an owl butterfly.

The encounter had left her feeling strangely unsettled

and, while she wasn't particularly superstitious, she did wonder whether it had been an omen of some sort that this peculiar creature had flown into her room two days before her audition and the night before her birthday. At least Leo hadn't managed to kill it, as that surely would have been bad luck.

Inés fell asleep thinking about portents and owl-eyed messengers and soon found herself in a terrifying dream: an enormous hawk was chasing her up and down the streets of her town, periodically swooping down to try and grasp her in its enormous talons. But just as it was about to seize her, Inés woke up, and she sat up to reground herself in reality. She turned on her bedside light and scanned the walls to see if the owl butterfly had somehow returned, but it hadn't.

Inés lay back down and stared up at the ceiling, suddenly harboring the terrible feeling that she wasn't going to get the role in the ballet. From her inability to do several *fouettés* to the owl butterfly to this bad dream,

the past day had made it clear that she was losing control over events.

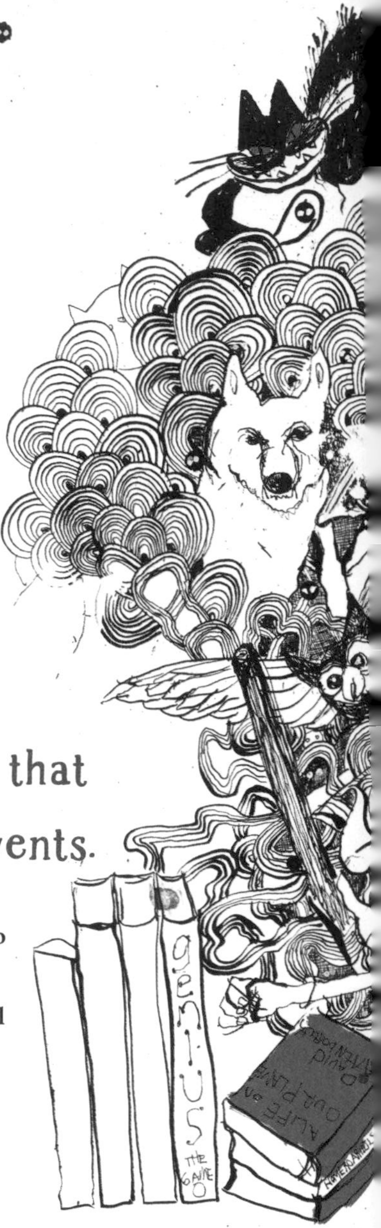
genius
THE GAME

And now she was having trouble falling back to sleep, so she would be sleep-deprived on top of everything else. Inés lay awake fretting until dawn, when she finally fell asleep, only to be awakened three hours later by her parents and brother bursting into her room.

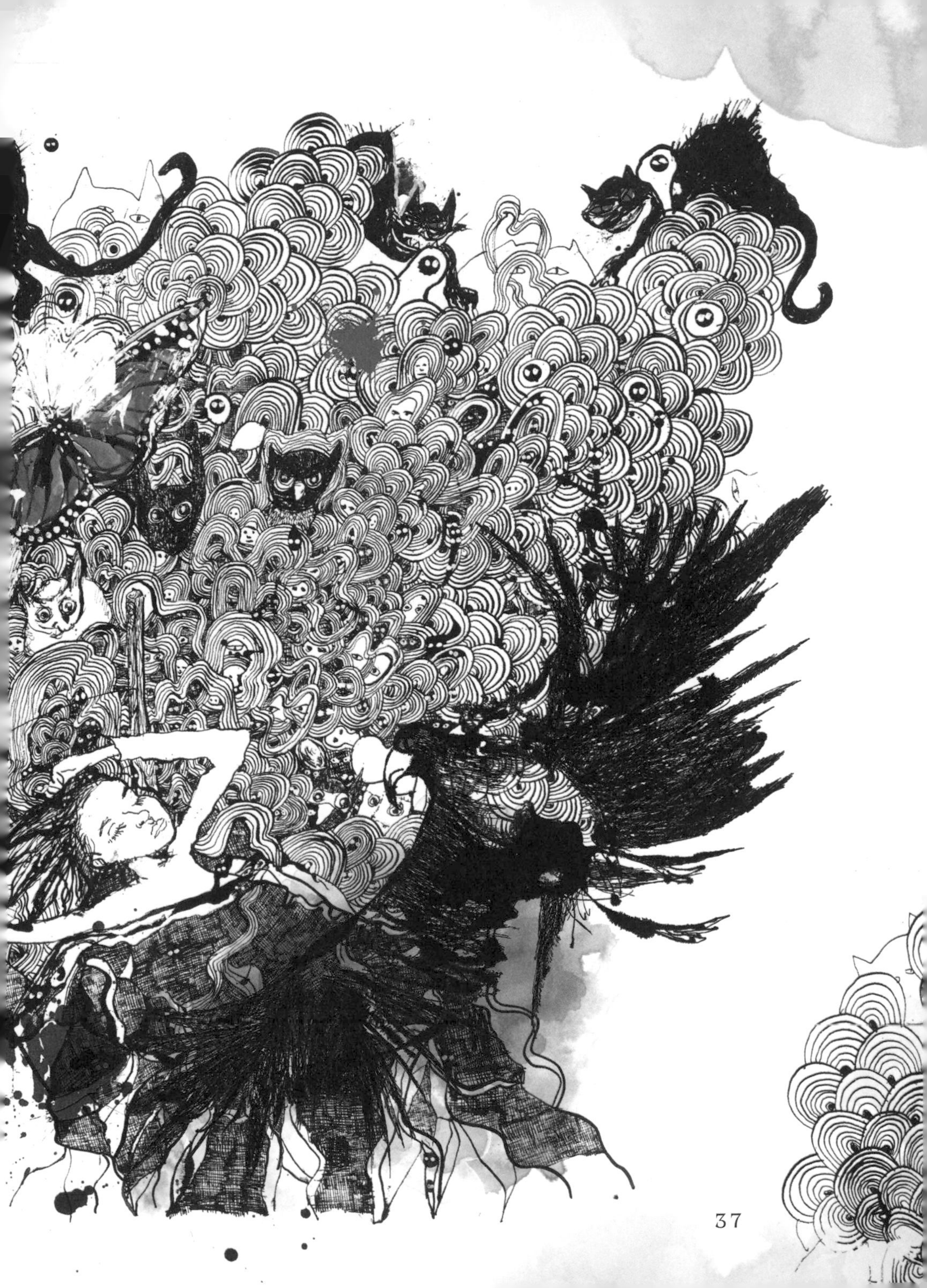

"HAPPY BIRTHDAY!"

her mother exclaimed,

carrying a stack of chocolate chip pancakes
with a lit *13* candle stuck into the top.

Her father and brother started to sing "Las Mañanitas" and Inés, exhausted, forced herself to sit up and smile. Her mother approached with the pancakes and Inés blew at the candle, wishing for the role in *Swan Lake*. But the candle flickered and didn't go out, and she had to blow a second time to extinguish it. "Another bad omen," she thought to herself.

Inés picked up a pancake with her fingers and took a bite. Her poor night of sleep had made her hungry, and the sugar and chocolate suddenly appealed to her. Her father stepped forward and held two small bags out. "These are from your grandmother Andrea. She gave them to me several years ago but insisted I wait and give them to you the morning you turned thirteen."

Inés put the pancake down and took the gifts from him. One was a black velvet bag tied closed with a piece of string, and the other was a plastic bag containing seeds that resembled small coffee beans. "What are these seeds?" Inés asked, holding the bag up to the light.

Her father shrugged and gestured for her to open the other one. Inés pulled the tie off the velvet bag and pulled out a jet-black stone carved into the shape of a butterfly, attached to a gold chain. She turned the stone over in her hand, feeling its smooth edges and glossy surface. The pendant felt weighty and warm in her palm, and she sensed an energy radiating from it into her skin. She examined the crude but expressive design on the butterfly, and saw her eye reflected in it.

"Your abuela says that obsidian necklace has been in our family since pre-Hispanic times, passed down from one young woman to the next. So take good care of it."

"It's beautiful," Inés's mother commented. "Make sure you call her to thank her."

"I will," Inés promised, although truthfully the heavy, clunky necklace wasn't her style. "I should get dressed for school now. Thanks for the birthday pancakes."

Her parents smiled and left the room. Inés put the necklace back in its bag and placed both bags on her desk. She opened her closet and pulled out a white T-shirt, black jeans, and a yellow, black, and white striped sweater.

Inés was getting dressed when her cell phone rang on her desk. She walked over and saw that it was her grandmother Andrea, calling for a video chat. Inés sighed, feeling obligated to answer even though she didn't have the time. So she accepted the call, and Andrea's kind and weathered face promptly filled the screen. Andrea was holding her phone way too close, giving Inés a macroscopic view of the deep creases around her eyes and mouth, created by a lifetime of smiles. "Hi, abuelita," Inés said. "Thank you so much for the gifts."

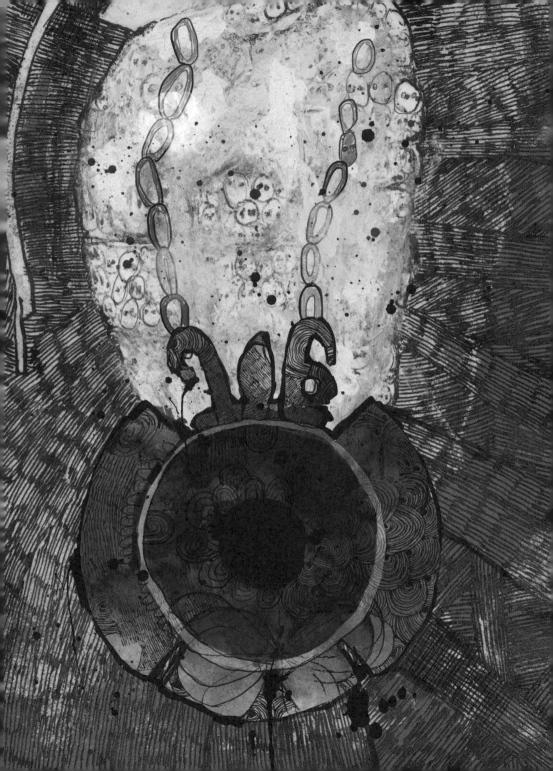

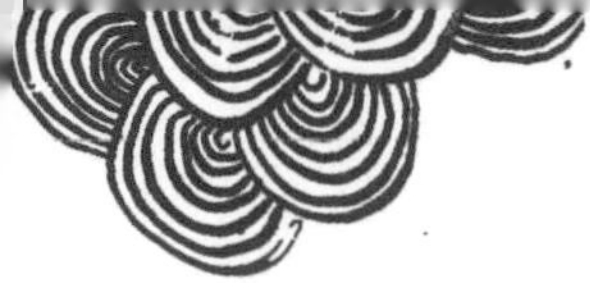

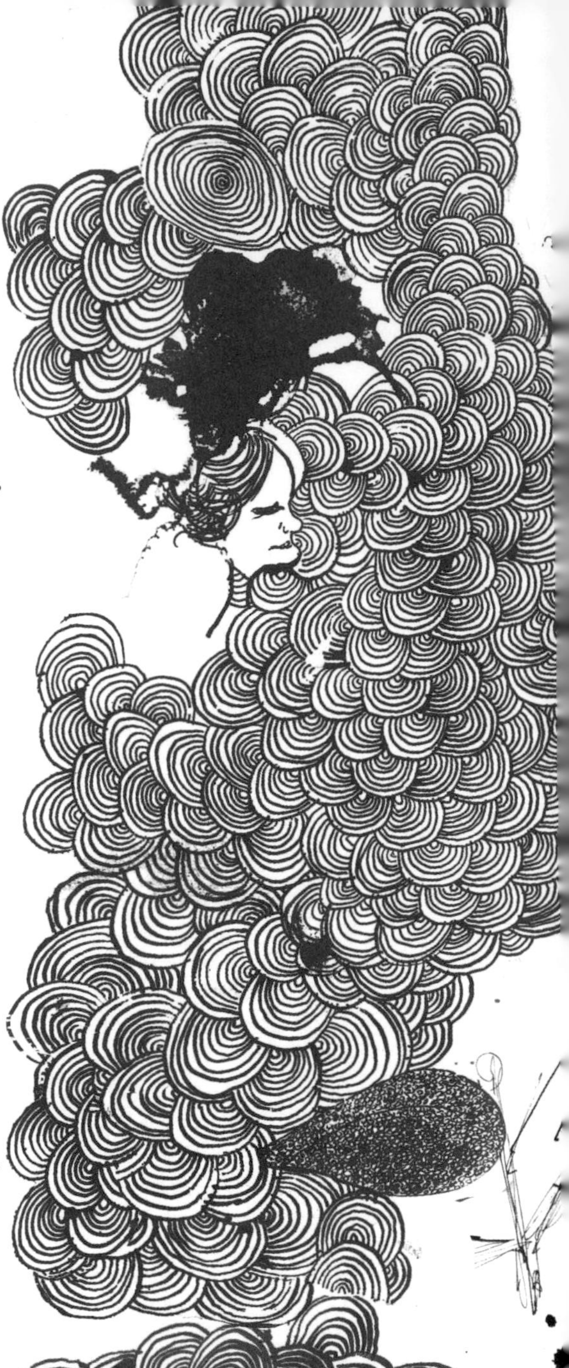

"Feliz cumpleaños, mi amor," answered Andrea. "Ya te pusiste el collar?"

Inés reached for the black velvet bag and put the phone down while she slipped the necklace around her neck. Then she held the phone up to show her grandmother. "See?"

Andrea nodded approvingly. "Muy bien. Ahora no te lo quites, ni siquiera para bañarte o dormir. Ese collar es tu vínculo al pasado, al futuro, y al presente eterno." Inés's Spanish was not perfect, but she understood Andrea's request that she not take the necklace off, not even to bathe or sleep, and then something about the past, the future, and an eternal present. Inés thought to herself that there was no way she was going to wear this necklace all the time, but she did appreciate that her grandmother had gifted her a family heirloom,

and she'd certainly

wear it today.

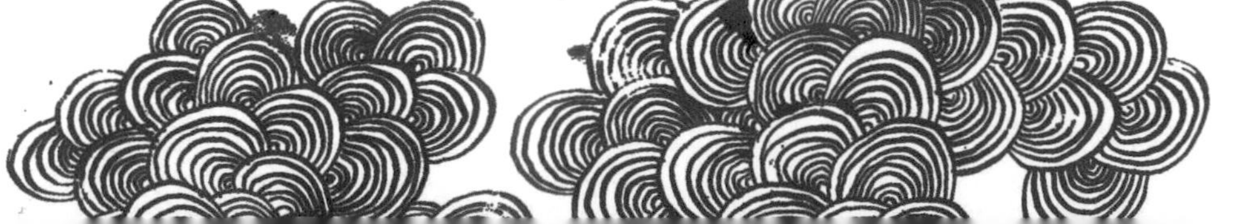

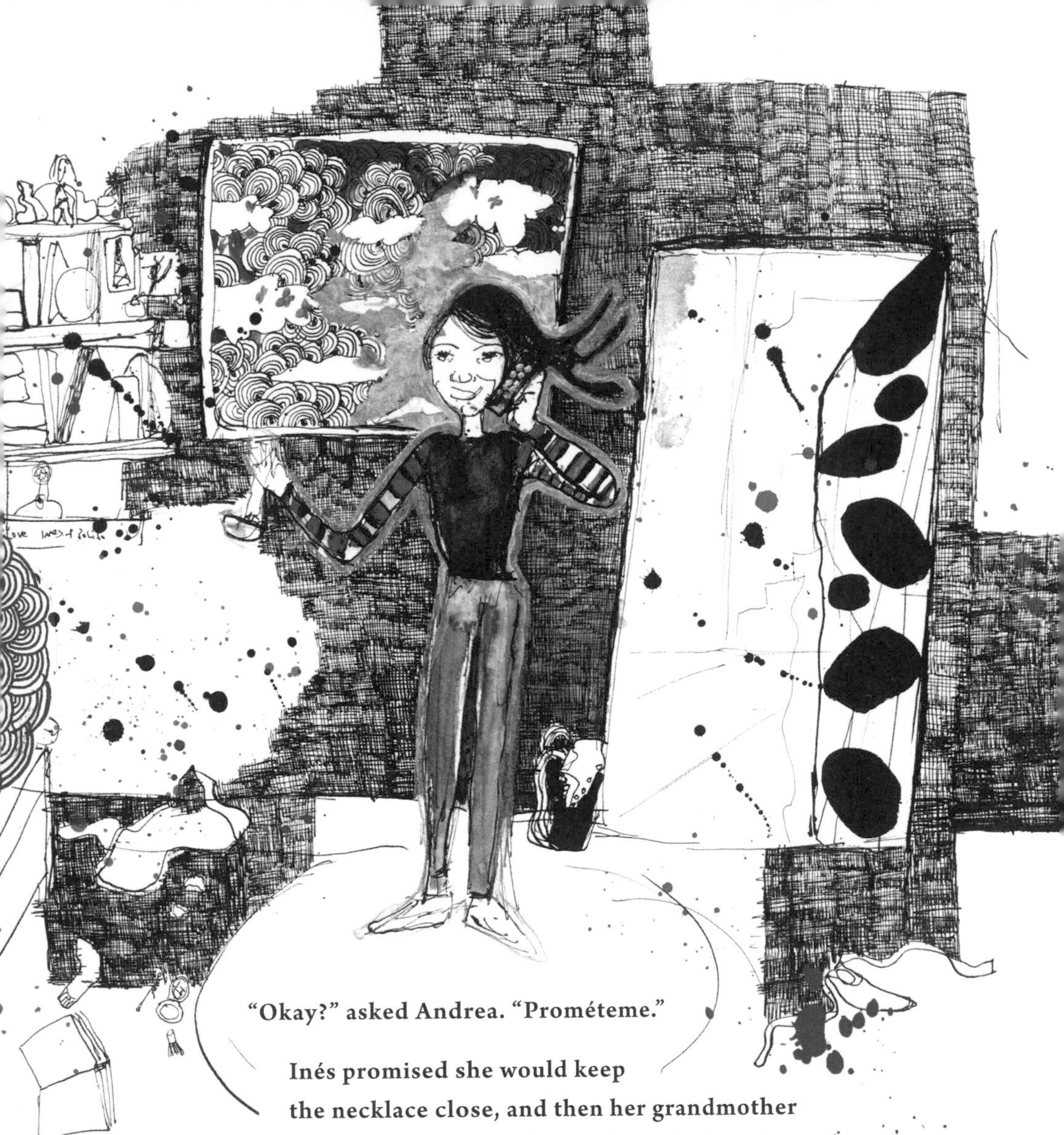

"Okay?" asked Andrea. "Prométeme."

Inés promised she would keep the necklace close, and then her grandmother ordered her to go to the garden and plant the seeds she'd sent.

Inés felt annoyed;
you don't tell people what to do on their birthday,
and she had to get to school.

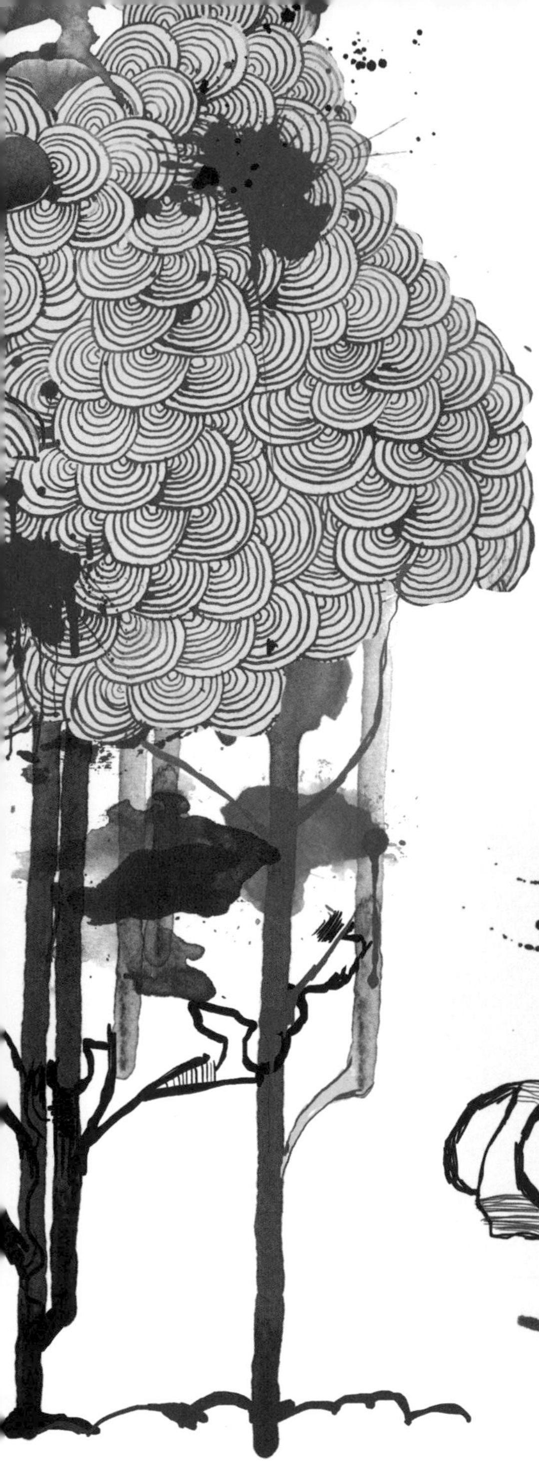

"Later, abuelita; I'm running late for school. I'll call you this weekend!" Inés blew her grandmother some kisses—making them as big and dramatic as possible to make up for the guilt she felt at not chatting longer—and hung up. She grabbed her backpack and sweater, dashed down the stairs, and sprinted out the front door, the butterfly pendant bouncing uncomfortably against her chest.

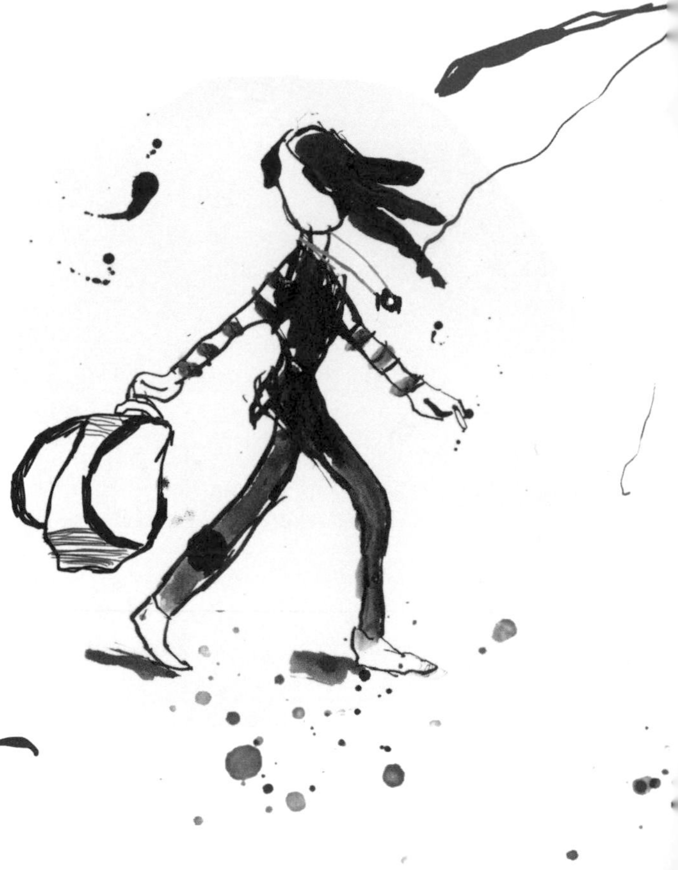

It was a beautiful fall day, and the golden morning light illuminated both the treetops and Inés's youthful face.

As she waited for a car to pass so she could cross the main street, Inés observed that the town looked remarkably different.

The colors
of the trees,
buildings,
and cars

had taken on
a deeply vivid,
almost

electric quality.

She closed her eyes for a few moments, letting them rest, then opened them again. The colors were just as radiant as before, and in the sky she now noticed long wisps of colorful clouds. Perhaps the lack of sleep was affecting her weary eyes.

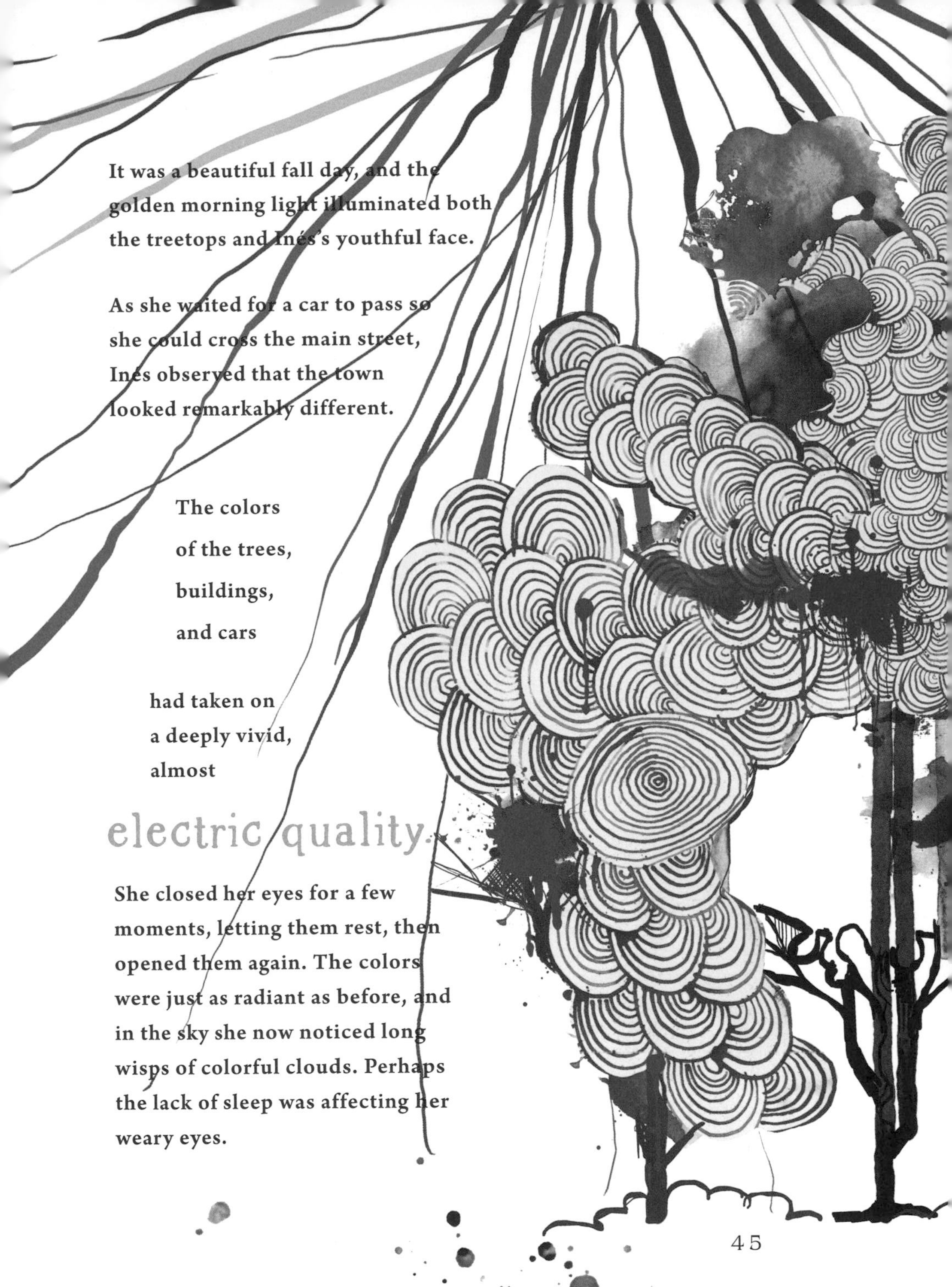

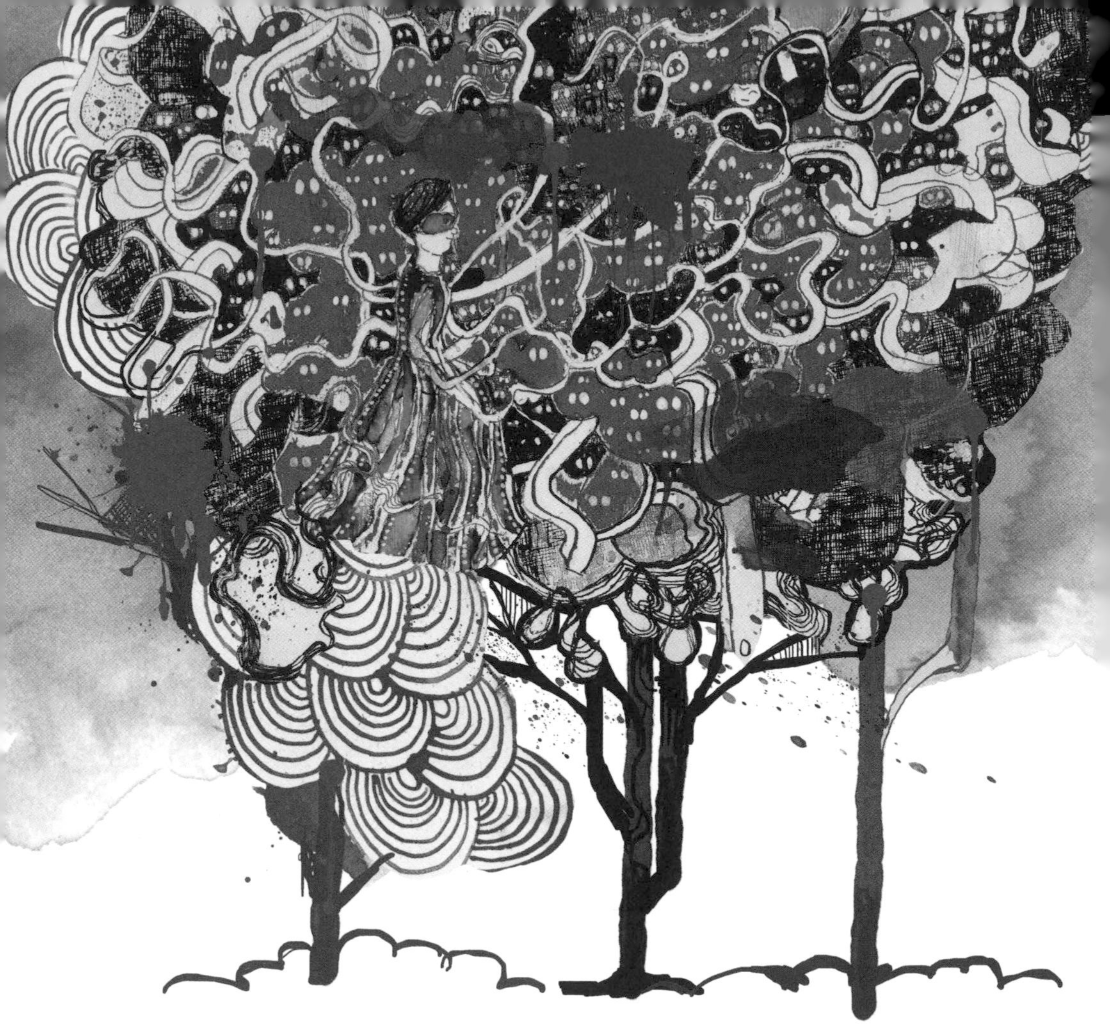

Inés tried to cross the street, but in addition to the assault on her vision,

she was now hearing strange sounds.

Alarmed by her surroundings becoming so distorted, she decided to head back home. As she approached her house, she heard low rumbles that resembled deep and ancient voices.

She turned in the direction they were coming from but saw only the row of trees that had always stood guard on the sidewalk. And then, as she got closer to the front door, she heard high-pitched whispers, seemingly emanating from the flower beds her mother had planted in the spring. Inés stepped inside and her mother asked what she was doing back home. Inés informed her that she'd suddenly felt sick and was going upstairs to rest.

Inés felt tremendous relief when she finally reached her room and kicked off her shoes. She pulled the curtains closed, swept the covers to one side, and climbed into bed. Her room was dark and quiet now, and she looked forward to a long, nightmare-less nap. As she lay her head down on the pillow and closed her eyes, the events of the past day swirled around in her mind. Images and ideas slowly started to lose their edges and blend together, morphing into the incoherent thoughts and mysterious shapes that often precede sleep.

But sleep wasn't to be. No sooner was her body sinking into slumber than she heard a light tapping at her window. Inés tried to ignore it—it wasn't a loud sound and she could probably sleep through it—but quickly her conscious mind took over and demanded to know: *What* is making that noise? She could sleep through a fire truck blaring down the street, the loud and nasal sound of the neighbor's lawnmower, and even Leo's music thumping next door, but she could filter those sounds out because she knew what they were. But this tiny tapping at the window, a few feet from her bed—she had no idea what was causing it. Annoyed, Inés stood up, shuffled over to the window, and pulled the curtain aside.

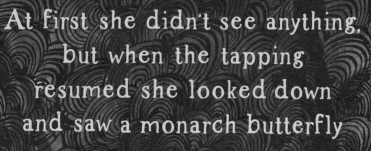

At first she didn't see anything,
but when the tapping
resumed she looked down
and saw a monarch butterfly

resting on the outside of the window, toward the
bottom. It lifted one little leg and tapped again,
and Inés couldn't help but smile. She always loved
this time of year, when the monarchs made their
way through her town, and this beautiful butterfly
was surely a better omen than the sinister owl-eye
variety. She leaned in to get a closer look and could
see that the butterfly's left antenna was crooked,
although its right one was straight.

The butterfly gently flapped its wings, and Inés now
became aware of hundreds of other butterflies in
the background—resting on tree trunks, perched
atop cars, sitting on mailboxes, drifting past in
the air. This group was about to start migrating,
apparently, and they were congregating outside her
house of all places.

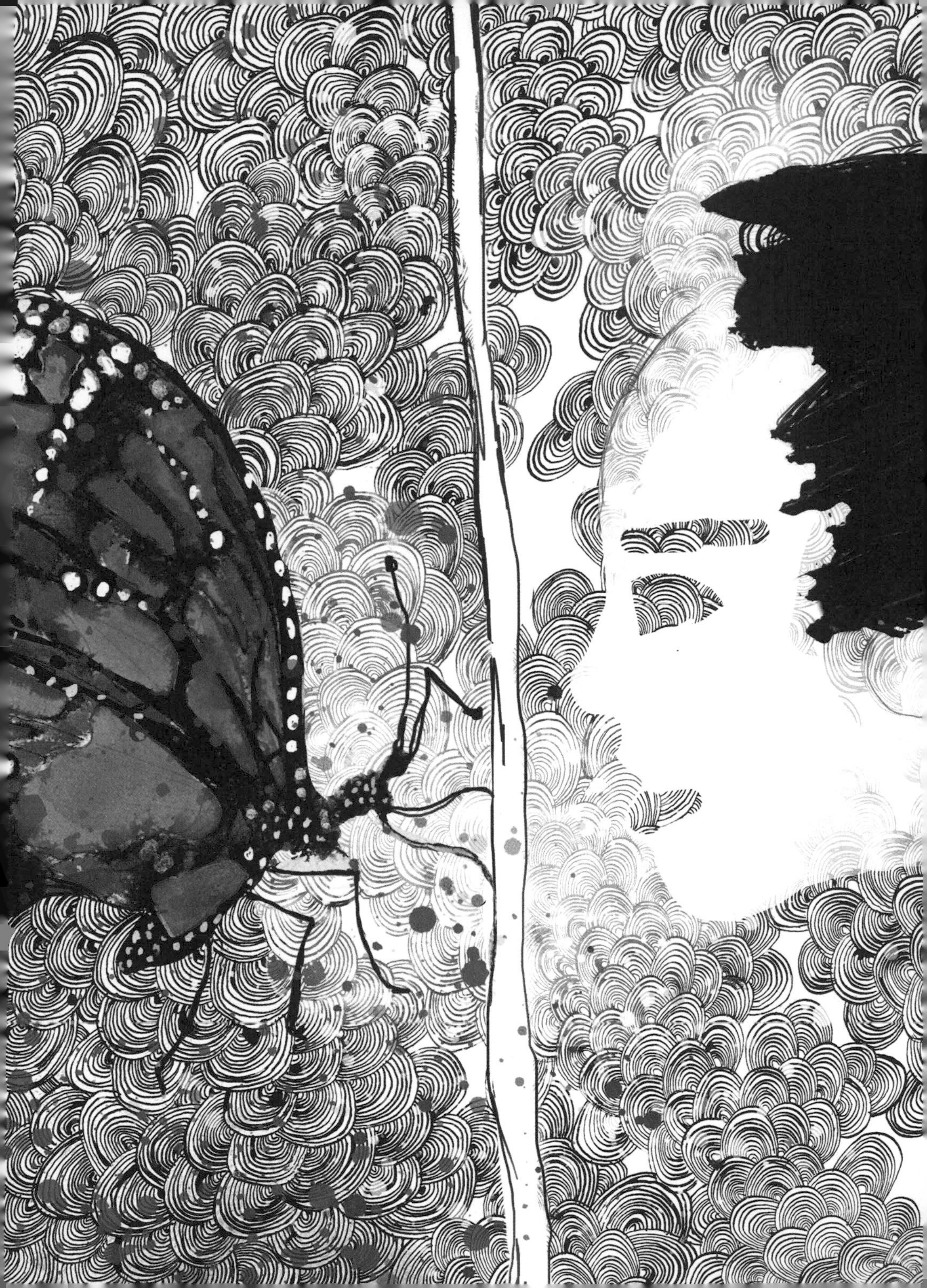

Inés was once again overwhelmed by the vibrancy of color before her: the orange and yellow of the monarchs, the streaks in the sky, and the many shades of green in the trees and grass, all unusually bright today. Suddenly, all the butterflies started to flap their wings in unison, and the street shimmered with the movement of their wings and with thousands of specks of golden dust filling the air. Inés could hear and feel the myriad wings *swoosh-swoosh-swooshing* like a deafening heartbeat, and she felt dizzy and nauseous.

Inés stumbled back to bed, feeling breathless and like she was trapped inside of something she needed to break out of. It was almost like she was being born again, and had to push her way up and out of an invisible womb or egg. A weight pressed down on her head, while an external force called out to her. An idea was clamoring for attention, an experience was begging to be had, an unfamiliar landscape was longing to be explored. She felt a sense of urgency although she didn't know for what, and then a blinding light spilled forth and she grimaced and closed her eyes.

chapter 2

The Larva, or Caterpillar

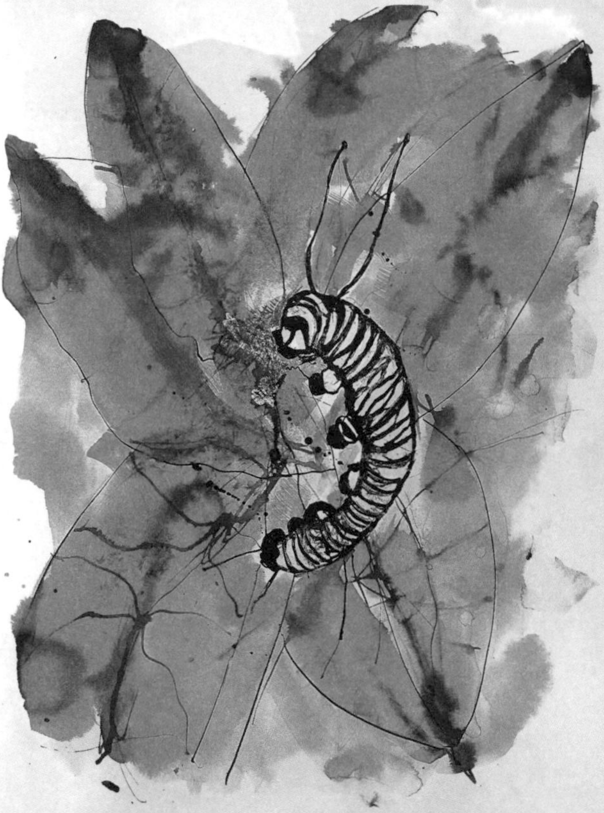

The larva,
or caterpillar:

When the being inside a monarch egg decides it is time to enter the next phase of its life, a caterpillar bursts out, headfirst. And just as a newborn mammal immediately gravitates toward its mother's breast, the first thing the caterpillar discovers as it emerges is the milkweed leaf its mother laid its egg on. It promptly starts to feed, consuming both the eggshell and the leaf. A monarch caterpillar grows at a startling rate—from three to four millimeters to thirty to forty millimeters in just over two weeks—and in order to grow it must shed its skin, or molt, multiple times. Every stage in between molts is called an instar, and a monarch caterpillar goes through five of them.

The caterpillar is all appetite—it is hungry for milkweed leaves, hungry for experiences, hungry for life. But the caterpillar doesn't march off on its many legs to have adventures right away; it's not ready for that, and its terrible eyesight keeps it grounded. For now it must simply eat and grow. The caterpillar is about ingestion and consumption, about watching and listening, about nourishment. The seed that was planted is receiving water and light. A caterpillar must gather strength for its body and collect knowledge for its mind. The caterpillar represents learning as much as possible about the world, a situation, or oneself.

When Inés opened her eyes again her vision was blurry, but as soon as it cleared she realized she was on the outside of her window looking in. She could see the butterfly pendant gleaming on her bed, as if she had simply vanished from that spot and the necklace had been left without a wearer. Inés lifted her hand up to push at the window, but instead a thin black leg rose up in front of her. A deep feeling of dread opened up in the pit of her stomach; she felt uneasy and sick. With mounting confusion, she lowered her gaze and saw that she now had six legs, a furry black body with white spots, and four monarch butterfly wings sprouting from her thorax. In a panic she tried to run but immediately hit the window and slid downward, startled and dazed. She heard a good-natured laugh coming from her left and turned to see the butterfly with the wonky antenna, who was still standing in the same spot she'd been when Inés had heard her tapping.

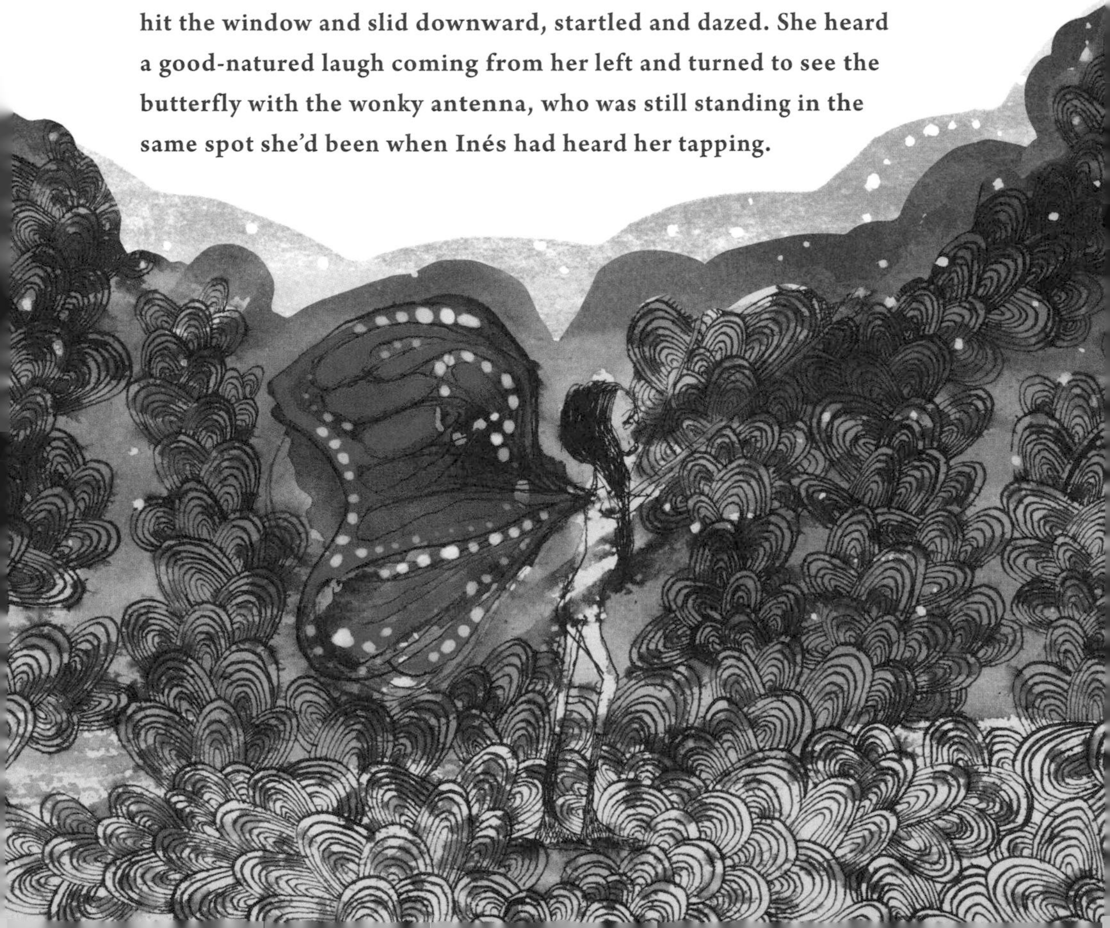

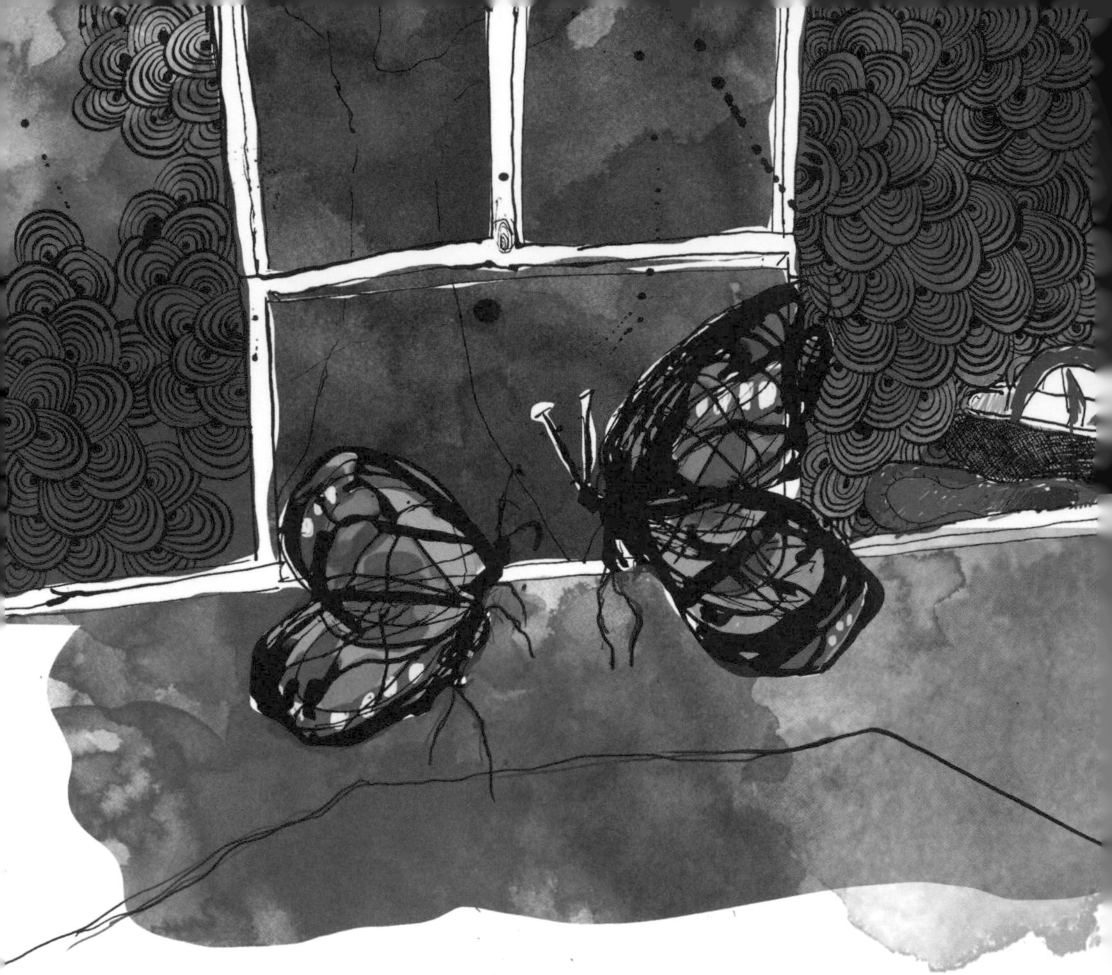

"I was also overwhelmed when I first emerged from my chrysalis, but you'll get used to your new form soon," the butterfly said. "My name is Josephine; what's yours? Caligo the seer instructed us to come get you, but he didn't mention your name."

"It's Inés," Inés replied feebly. She closed her eyes and opened them again, trying to wake up from this psychedelic dream. Not only had she turned into a butterfly, but she was conversing with one too.

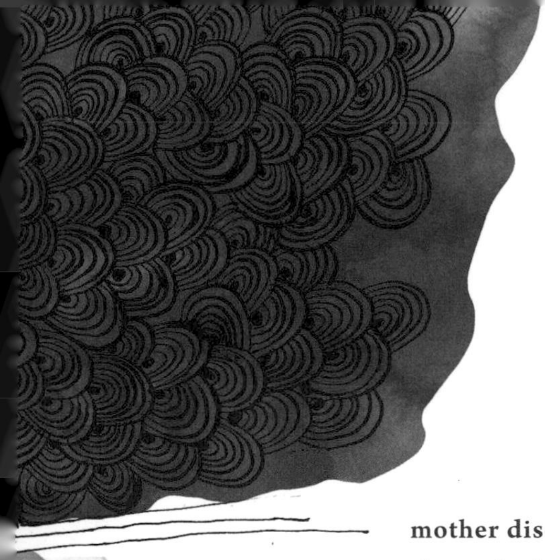

There was movement
in her room

and Inés watched
through the window

as her mother came in to
check on her. When her

mother discovered that she was missing,
she rushed out again, calling out her name
with alarm.

"Do you want to try flying a little?"
Josephine asked.

"We need to embark on our migration soon, so perhaps you should practice using your wings."

Inés heard her name being called from the front of the house now, and without thinking twice she flew off the window and around the corner, where she spotted her mother looking up and down the street with worry. Inés swooped down and hovered in front of her mother's face. "Mom, I'm here!" she shouted, but her mother gently swatted her to one side and marched back inside. Inés landed on the kitchen window and looked in; her mother was making a phone call.

Josephine joined Inés on the kitchen window, as did a male butterfly. "This is Valerio," Josephine said. "He's part of our group." Inés glanced over at Valerio briefly, then refixed her gaze on her mother.

A car was heard approaching, and Inés turned to see her father pulling into the driveway. "Papá! Papá!" Inés called out, but he couldn't hear her either. He got out of his car and walked toward the house so quickly that Inés had to jump out of the way in order to not get injured by the force of his body.

"Why are you so concerned with these people?" Valerio asked as he hovered nearby. "You should be focused on meeting the swarm and preparing for the journey ahead!" This caught Inés's attention, and she finally turned to Valerio and got a good look at him. He had two black circles on his hind wings (as all male monarchs do), exceptionally large and buggy eyes, and black fuzz sticking up at the top of his head that resembled a mohawk.

"I'm not going on any journey," Inés replied.

Josephine and Valerio looked at each other, then back at Inés.

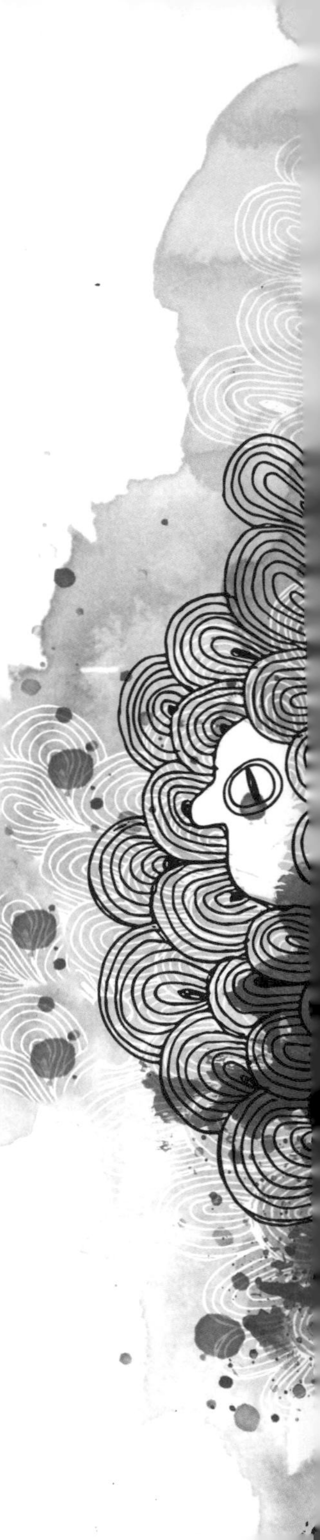

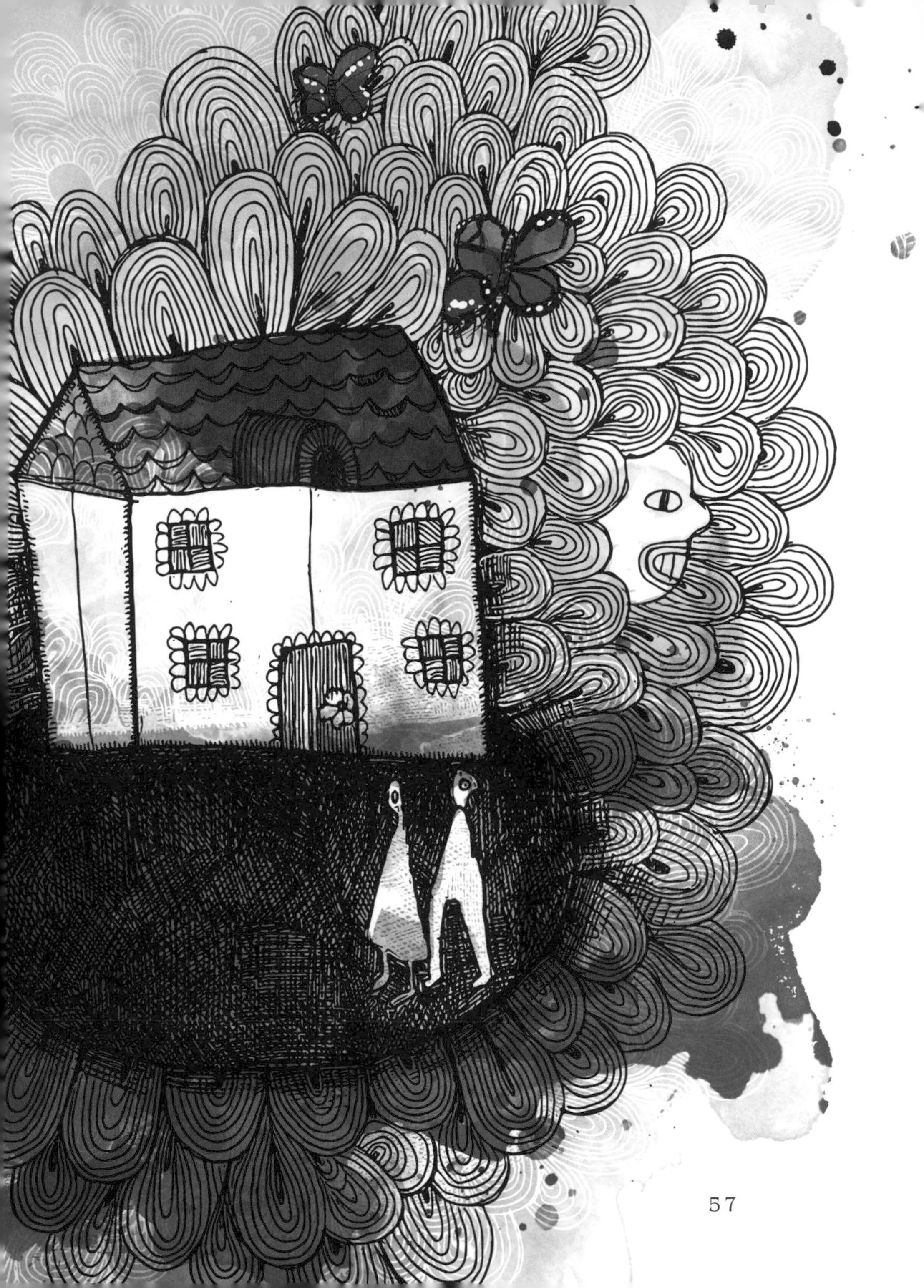

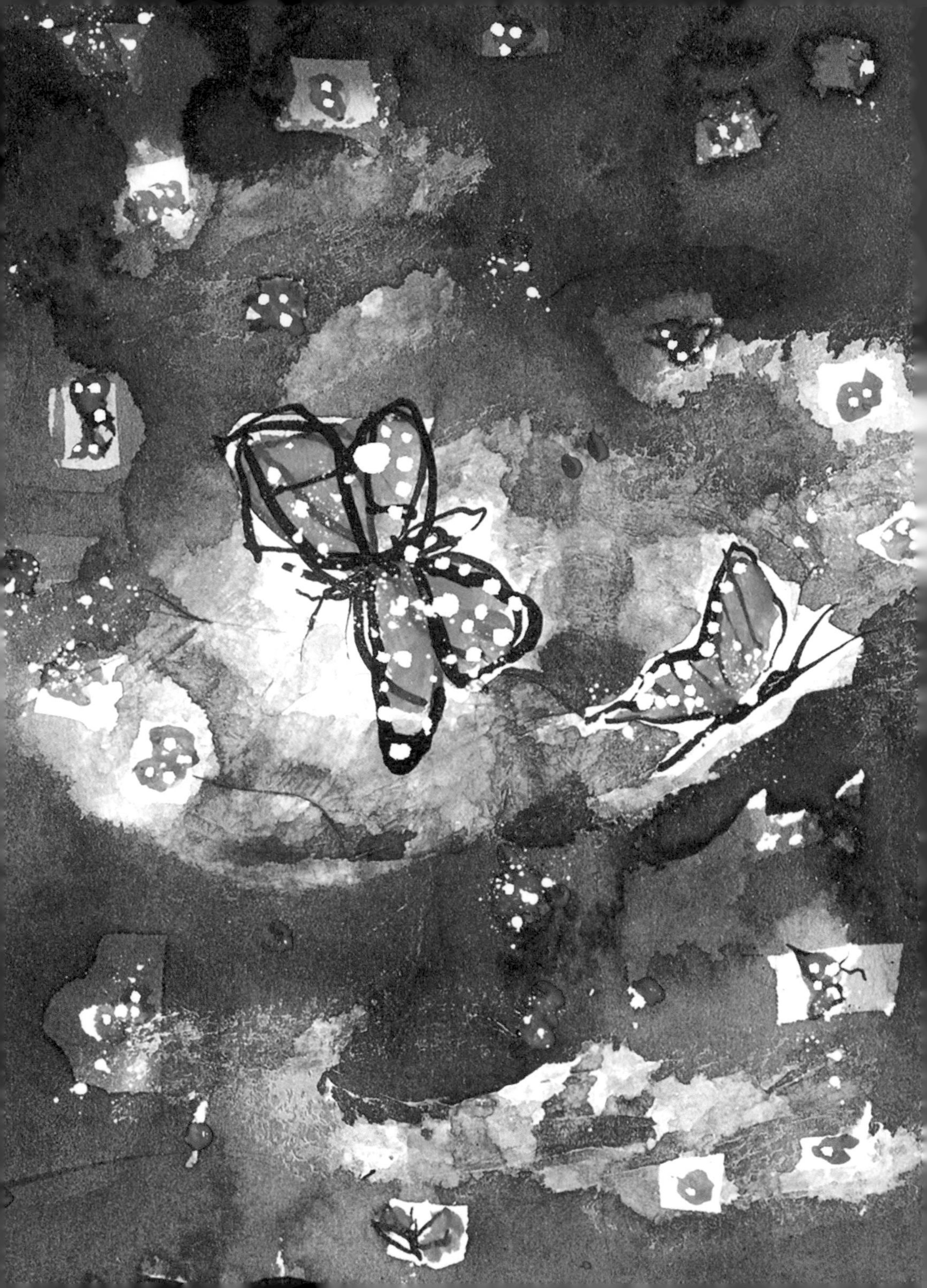

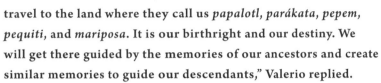

"We're all going to Mexico,

just as our great-grandparents did last
winter and just as every fourth generation
of monarchs has for millennia. We will
travel to the land where they call us *papalotl, parákata, pepem,
pequiti,* and *mariposa.* It is our birthright and our destiny. We
will get there guided by the memories of our ancestors and create
similar memories to guide our descendants," Valerio replied.

Inés of course knew about the migration, but her shock at
becoming a butterfly had led her to temporarily forget about it.
She looked around and saw that all the butterflies from before
were still in the vicinity. Some were resting on the trees in front
of her house, some were in the air, and now there was even a
group clustered on her father's car.

Inés's eyes filled with tears as she spoke. "I can't leave here. This
is my home, plus I have an audition tomorrow. I need to turn back
into a human. *Please,* tell me how this happened so I can undo it!"

Josephine and Valerio glanced at each other again. How could
this be the "very important butterfly" they had been instructed to
collect before embarking on their migration, when this butterfly
didn't even think she was one? A gust of wind suddenly blew them
toward the south, and Valerio shot up toward the sky and called
out to the other butterflies, "It's time to go!"

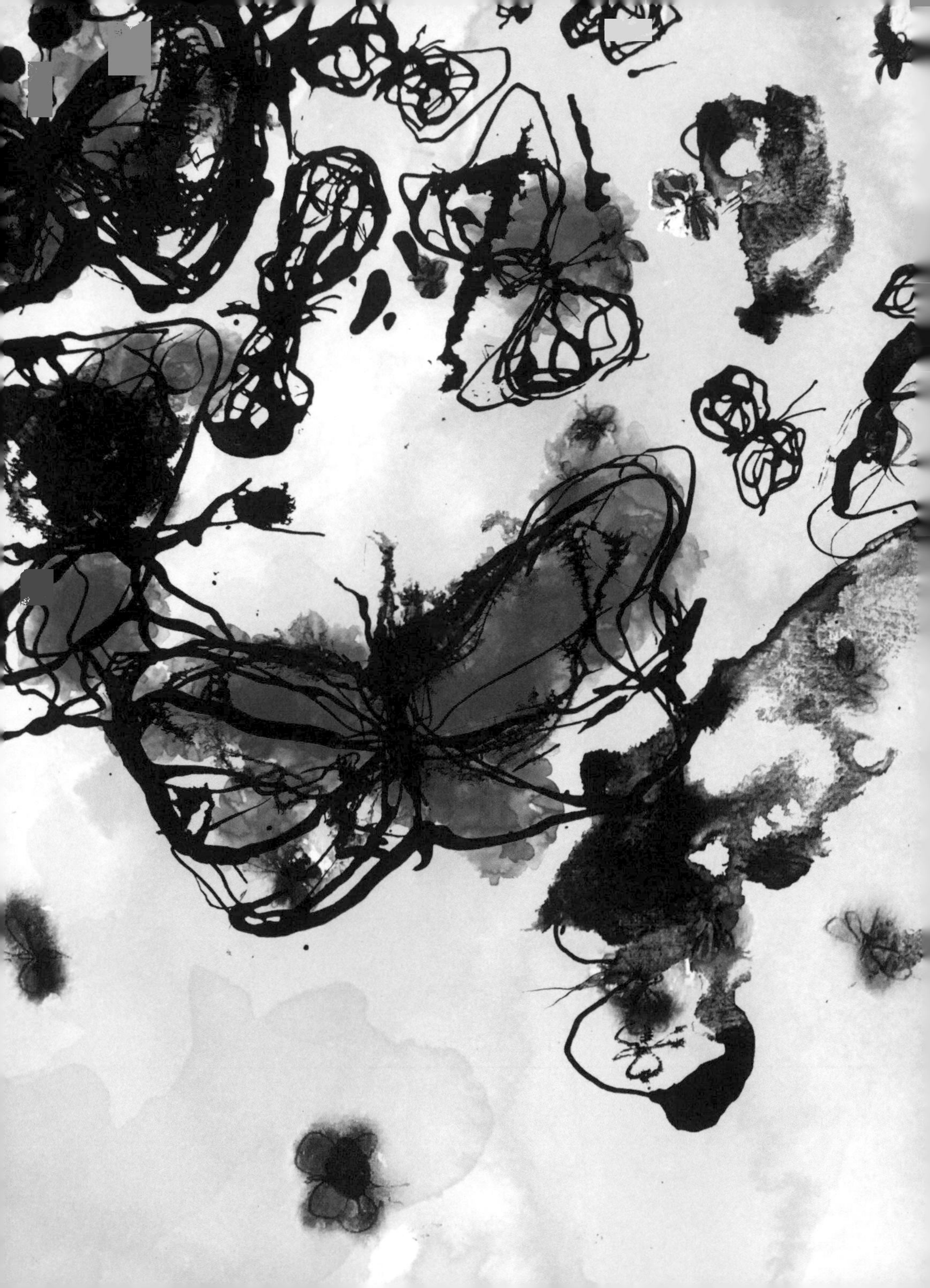

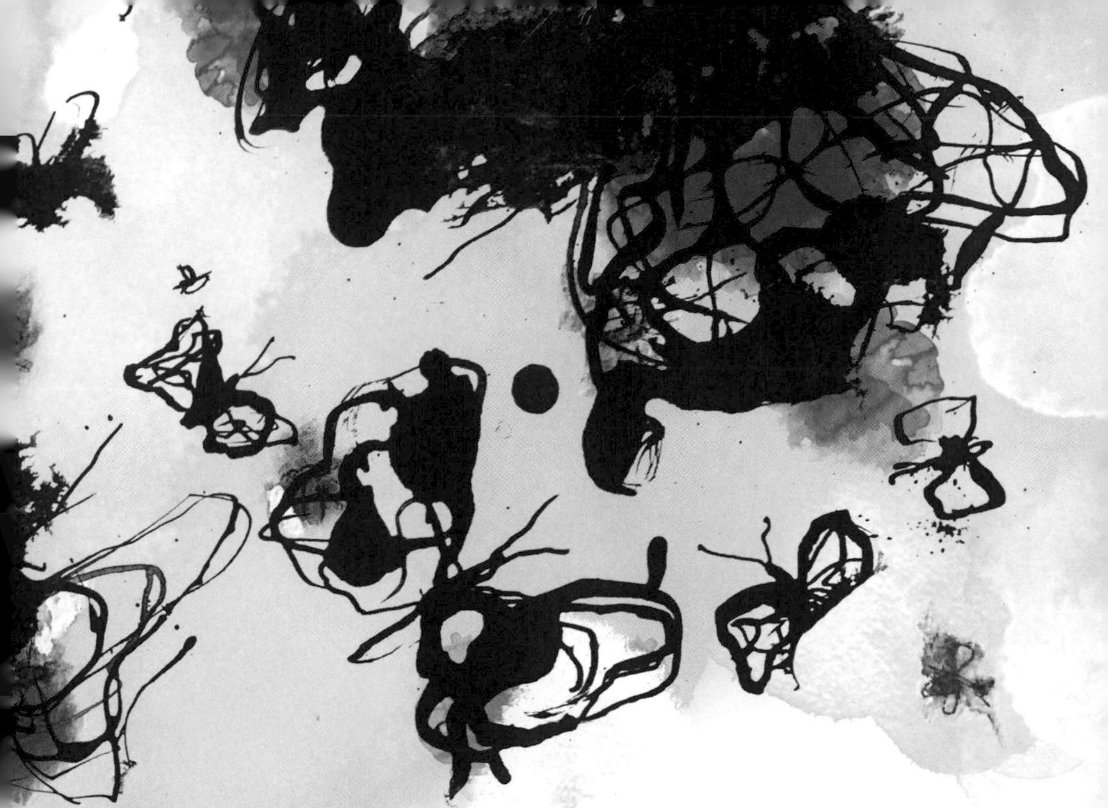

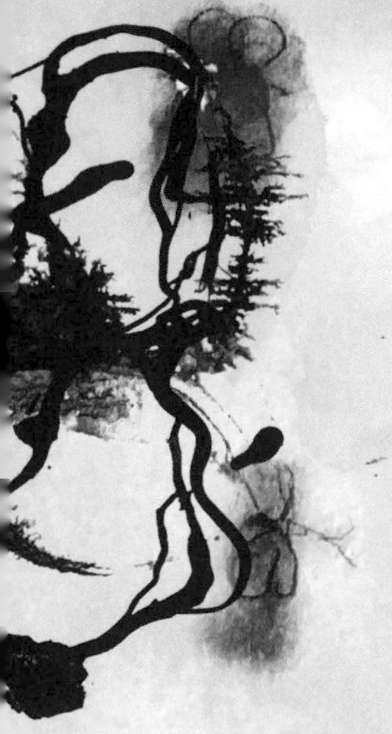

The monarchs started to peel off from their resting spots and joined Valerio in the air. Josephine turned to Inés and spoke to her in a maternal tone.

"Come with us, sweet wings. Don't be afraid."

But instead of accepting Josephine's invitation, Inés flew back to the kitchen window and proceeded to beat on it with her two front legs while frantically calling out to her parents. Josephine looked at Valerio, who looked at the clouds and shook his head. "If we wait any longer," he shouted, "we'll freeze to death." Valerio turned back to the swarm and called out, "Remember, everyone—if you get lost, just follow the lights!"

As the army of butterflies began to move southward, Inés turned to see what "the lights" were and was astonished to see a beautiful array of pink, orange, purple, and turquoise rays converging on a point in the distance, almost like a sunset but with vertical neon streaks instead of horizontal ones.

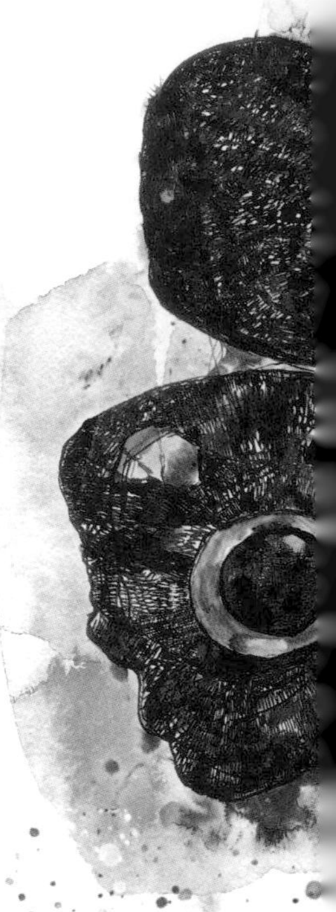

Josephine called out to Inés one final time, but Inés turned her back to the group and didn't budge. Josephine joined the swarm at its tail and flew with them, looking worried. She had failed Caligo, and Inés would surely die from cold if she stayed glued to that window all night.

After twenty seconds Inés turned to look over her winged shoulder, and she watched with growing unease as the cloud of butterflies shrank in the sky, the distance between them and her growing with each passing moment. And then her unease turned into panic, for not only was she inexplicably still a butterfly, but she was alone now too.

Or so she thought, because suddenly a booming and irritated-sounding voice called out from across the yard, "What do you think you're doing, Inés?"

Inés turned and spotted an owl butterfly resting on the trunk of one of the large trees lining the sidewalk. Was that who had just spoken to her? And was it the same owl butterfly from last night?

As if reading her mind,
the owl butterfly spoke again:

"My name is Caligo
and yes,
we met last night.

Thank you for saving me, and for being a human who realizes that all species matter."

Inés flew over to join Caligo on the tree trunk. "So you know of course that I'm really a human! Can you help me transform back? I don't know why or how, but I turned into a butterfly a few minutes ago."

"I know," replied Caligo. "But you will not be transforming back anytime soon. Once the egg has hatched, you cannot return to the previous stage. You are a caterpillar now, and it is time to feed. By that I mean it's time for you to learn as much as possible about the world around you. Instead of speaking, listen. Instead of showing, watch. Be open and do not resist your destiny."

63

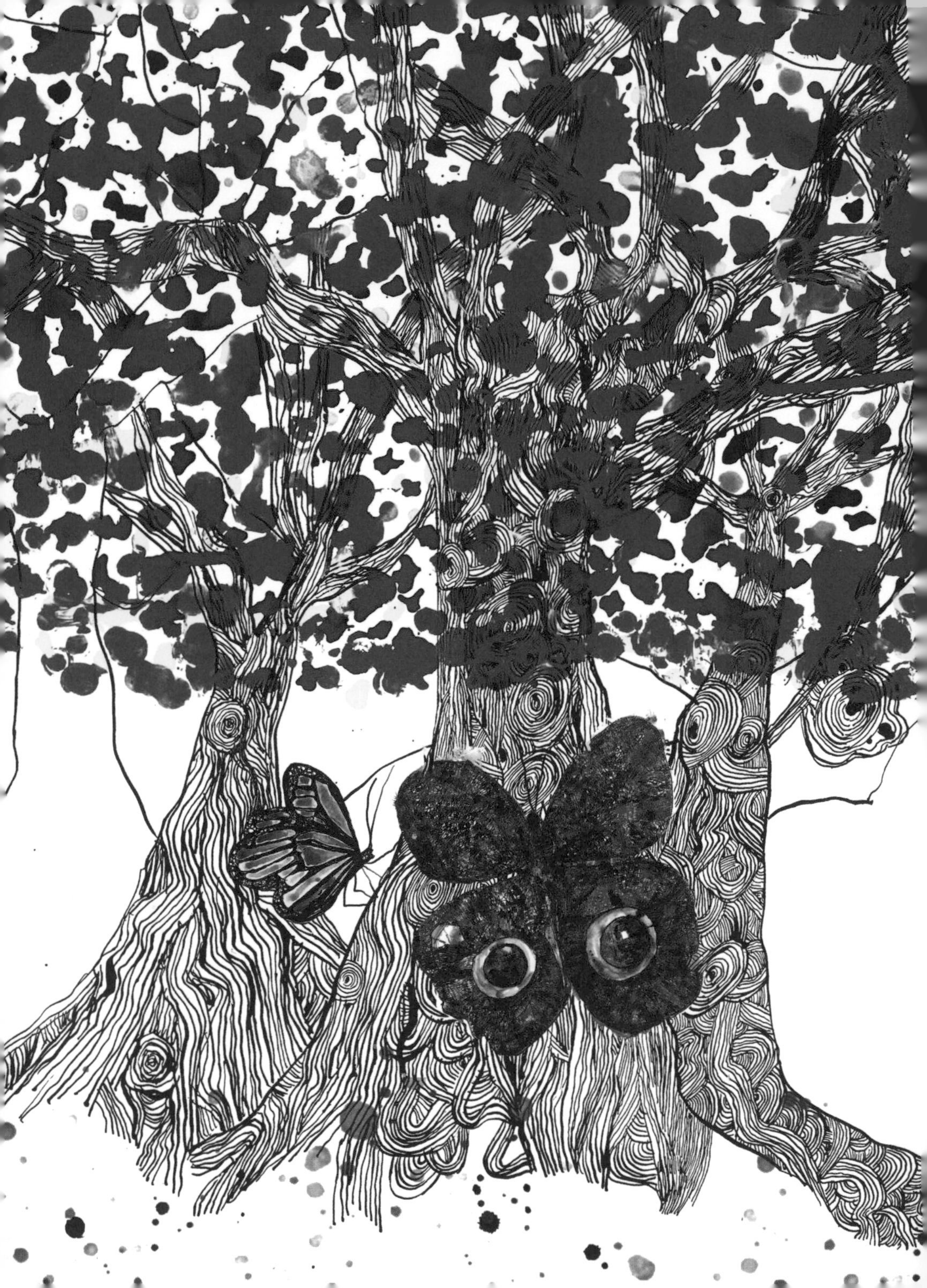

Inés felt very confused. Not only was she a human in the form of a butterfly, but this mysterious creature was telling her she was a caterpillar. Was it possible that he could not see, despite the enormous eyes on his wings?"

Again Caligo responded to her thoughts directly. "I am Caligo the seer, and I have four eyes—two on my head and two on my wings. I can see the north and the south, the east and the west. I can see the past, present, and future, and the place where the past and the future converge to create an infinite loop. I am also a messenger, and you must fly south and catch up with the other butterflies immediately."

Inés tried to wrap her head around his cryptic words, then shook her head. "There's no way I'm leaving my family. They're very worried about me, and I have my . . ."

"If you don't go, your family will die!" interrupted Caligo.

Inés turned to look toward her house with alarm. "What do you mean?"

"On the day the souls of the dead return to visit the earth, there will be a final battle for which you were chosen at birth. All the answers lie ahead, Inés. Now hurry, before it's too late." And with that the yellow eyes on Caligo's wings disappeared as if covered by invisible eyelids, and his shape evaporated and faded away, absorbed into the trunk of the tree.

Inés tiptoed over to where Caligo had just been, but there was no trace of him. She heard the front door of her house opening and saw her father rushing back to his car. She flew over and landed on the driver's side window, but when her father reversed the car into the street, Inés let go and flew back to the kitchen window. Her mother was now sitting at the table, crying. Inés's buggy eyes glazed over with a film of tears at the sight, and she screamed as loud as she could and pounded on the window with all her might. But it was no use: her parents couldn't hear her anguished demonstrations.

Inés gave up and stopped to catch her breath. She could feel the cold air permeating her body—*her butterfly body*—and in an instant she knew that she had to head south. Not only did she know this, but she now needed it and wanted it, just as any living being wants to sleep when exhausted or eat when starving. In the distance she could still make out the swarm, but its many members had become a tiny black shape silhouetted against the setting sun's rays of orange, pink, and red.

She stole one final
look at her mother,

then took flight.

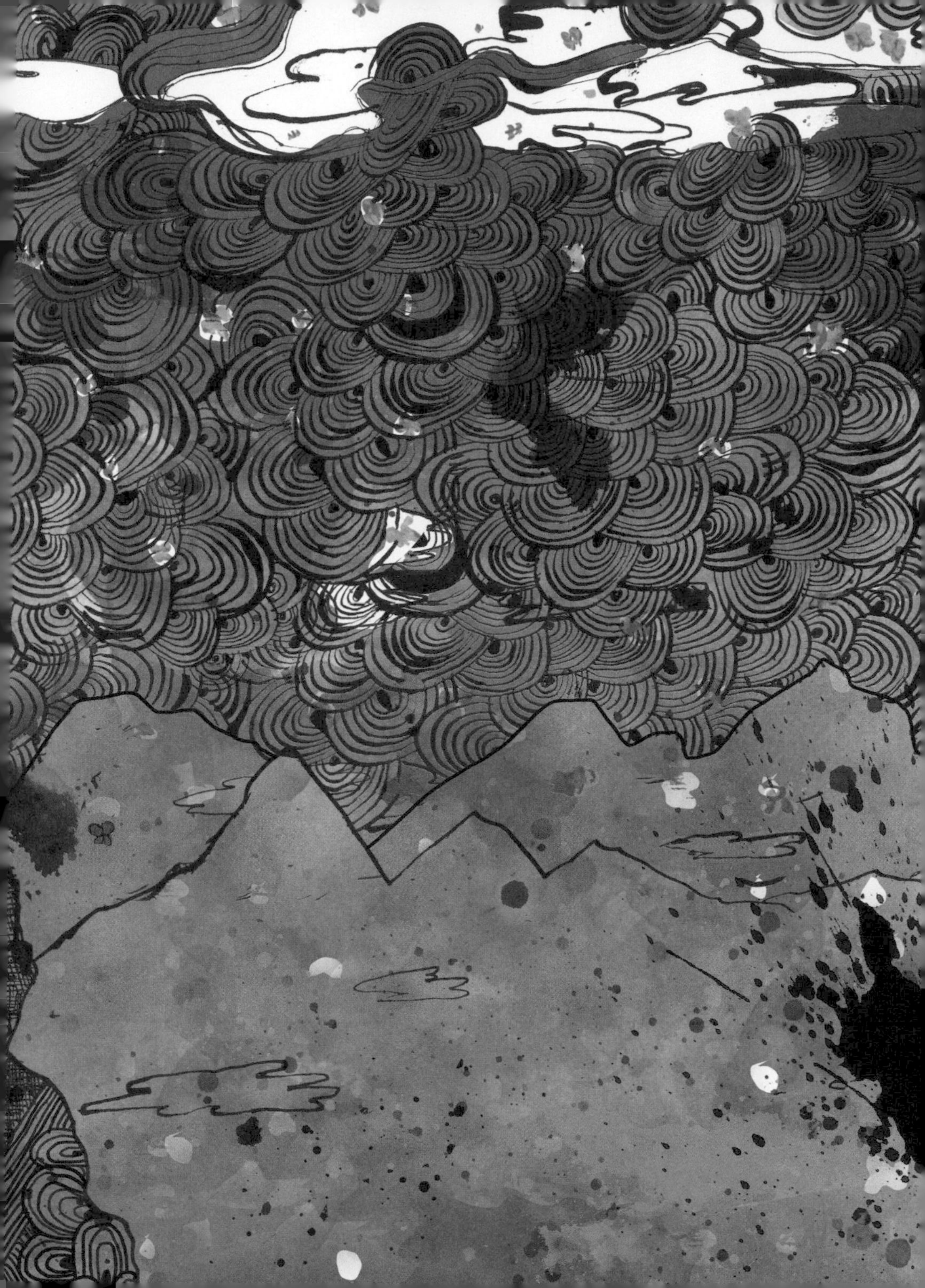

Inés could not deny that flying was
an incredible experience. She had
always loved dancing because it gave
her a sense of freedom, of defying
gravity and invisible barriers with her
leaping, twisting, and twirling body.
If singing was a voice expressing itself,
then dancing was the body's song. But
flying was like dancing without any
restrictions whatsoever—she could
go up, down, in any direction and for
any distance. She could float on a wind
current at an altitude of four thousand
feet, cut through a low-hanging cloud,
or simply drift, taking in the sights
around her. She saw industrious
bumblebees feeding on lavender below,
noted a flock of starlings alighting on a
lawn, and passed a crow in midair.

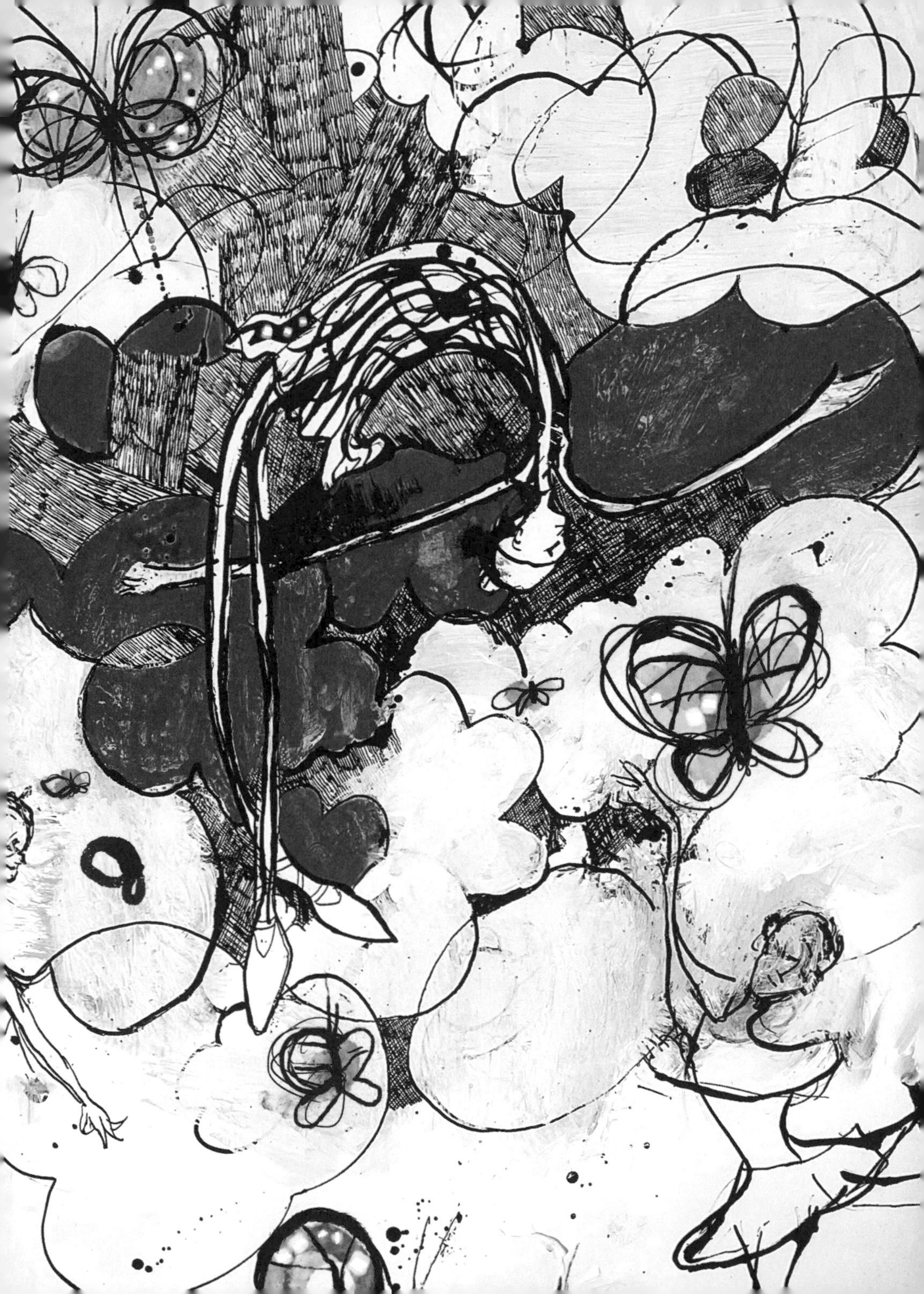

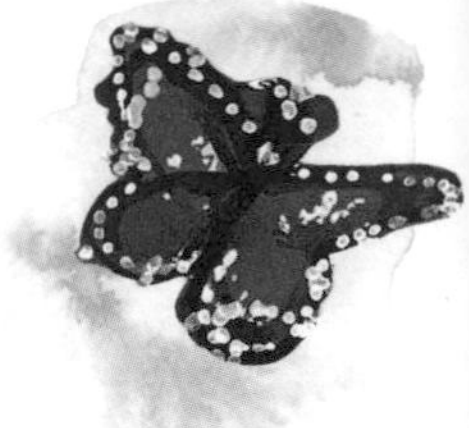

Inés longed to take her time—her body and spirit had been craving this type of unfocused outdoor activity—but instead she propelled herself forward as fast as she could, hoping to catch up with the others. And as she did, she looked down upon the streets below and saw myriad humans going about their business, walking dogs and driving cars and popping in and out of buildings. None of them ever looked up; it was as if they had a total lack of curiosity about what transpired in the world above them. Inés felt sorry for them, these people who thought they were so special but who were in fact tied to the ground by invisible anchors. Not only were they unable to fly, but they seemed to completely ignore the other spheres of life and activity taking place around them. "They're really missing out," Inés thought to herself. "Except for birdwatchers and astronomers, who tend to scan the skies."

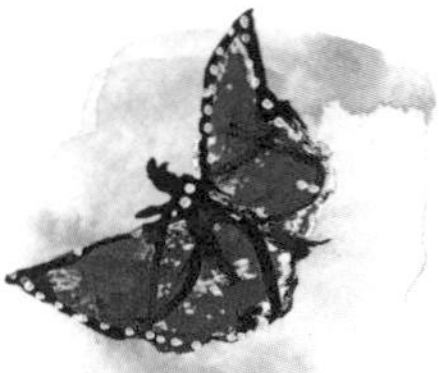

Inés refixed her gaze on the black speck that was the swarm, and as she drew closer it started to grow larger and reacquire its color. Eventually the one lone shape broke apart into more and more bodies, until at last she could make out hundreds of butterflies and she joined the group at its tail. Josephine was still there at the back—perhaps she'd been holding out hope that Inés would change her mind—and she greeted her with a warm smile.

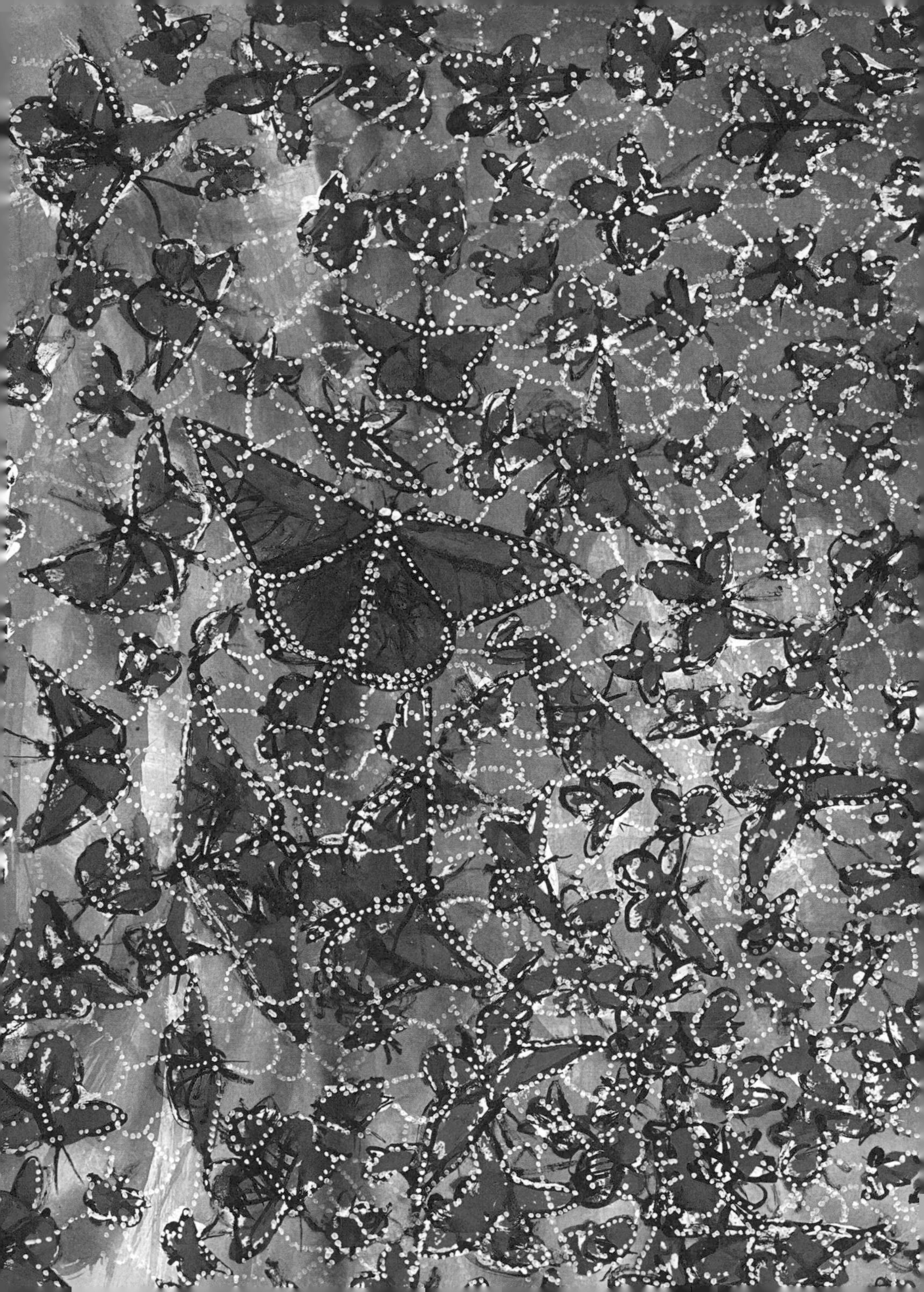

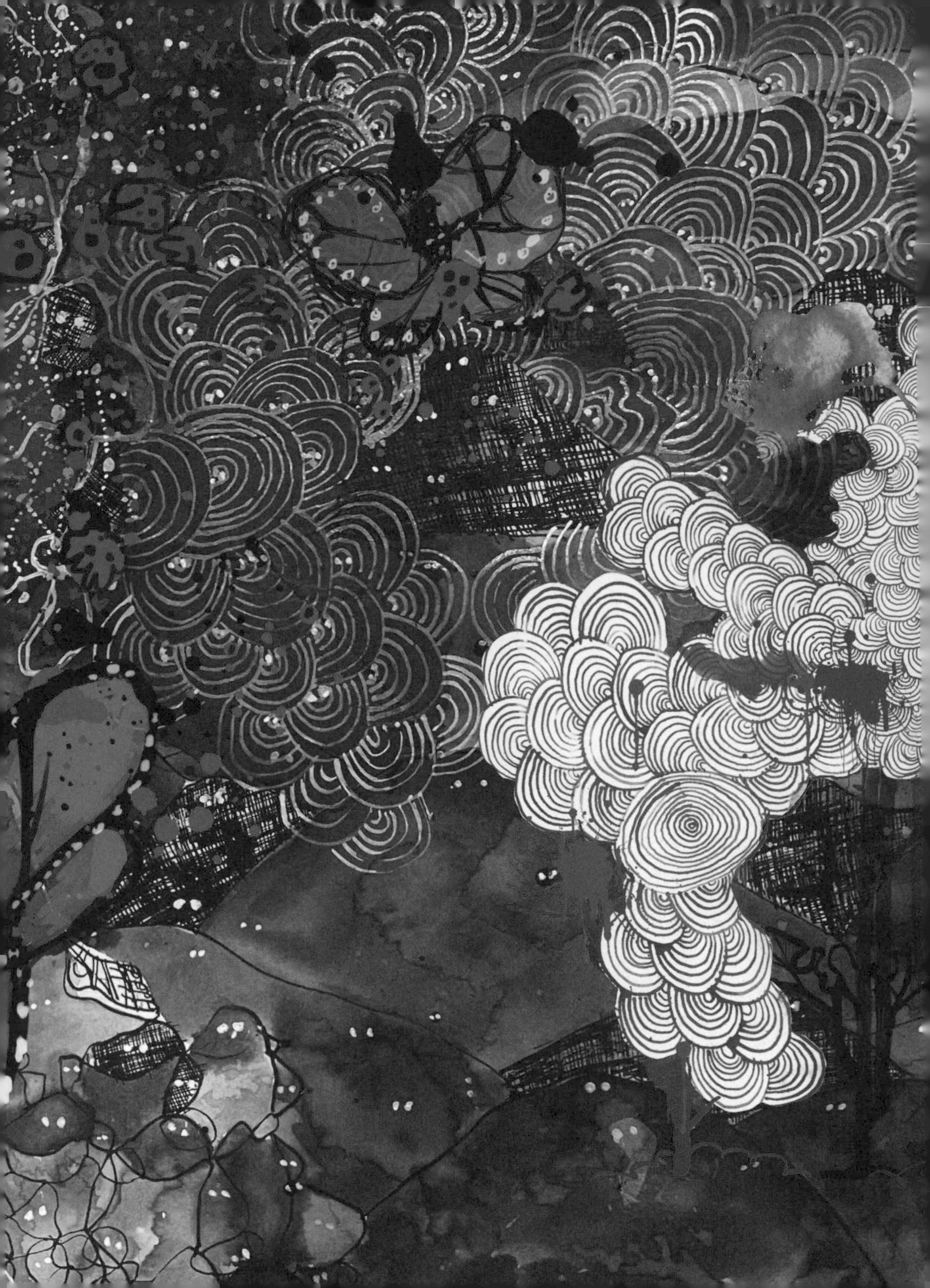

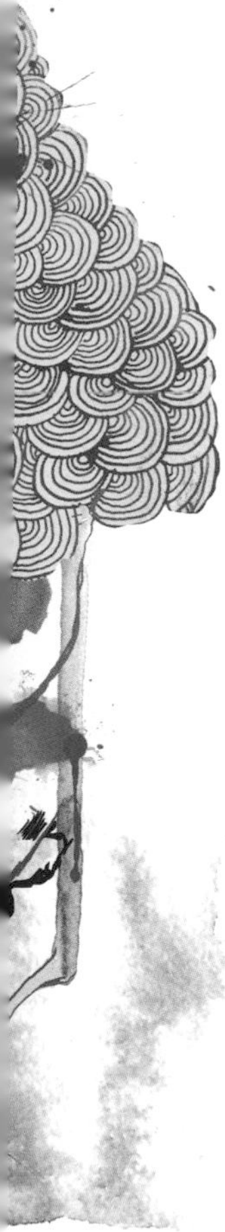

"Welcome!" Josephine shouted. And then, as if sensing that Inés was exhausted from the effort of catching up, she added, "We should be stopping any minute now; we don't fly at night!" And sure enough, within minutes the swarm started to dip downward, as one by one the butterflies descended onto some oak trees in a suburban park.

As dusk fell, there was a marked dip in the temperature and the butterflies huddled together in a single upside-down group on a branch, their bodies hanging side by side with their wings folded so as to make space for their neighbors. The undersides of their wings were a pale orange—almost white—and the vision of the butterflies clumped together like this was a dramatic one. They looked rather like an enormous bunch of pale origami grapes, and Inés wondered if the branch would snap from the weight of so many bodies.

Josephine positioned herself next to Valerio on her right and made room for Inés on her left. "Come," she said. "There's space for you here."

But Inés shook her head and walked to the opposite end of the branch, where there were no butterflies. "I'm going to stay over here, thanks."

Valerio frowned.

"There are two reasons
we all roost together—the first is warmth
and the other is safety.

If an oriole flies past here and decides it needs a snack,
who do you think it will eat? A small butterfly sleeping all
exposed on its own, or one integrated into a large group?"

Inés, still identifying as a human, scoffed at the idea that
she could be eaten by a bird. "I'm claustrophobic and prone
to feeling hot, so I think I'll take my chances."

Josephine looked at Inés and nodded.

"Valerio's right, you know.
We don't want to lose you."

Inés turned away without responding. She didn't plan on sleeping anyway—how could she when her whole universe had been suddenly and unexpectedly turned upside down? Like Gregor Samsa in *The Metamorphosis*, she'd opened her eyes to find herself transformed and was on a journey she'd had no intention of taking. Her parents must be even more worried now that night was approaching, and before long they'd be calling the police. And perhaps the most troublesome part of all was that she'd be missing the audition. She pictured her role being given to someone else and knew that everything she'd been working toward and dreaming about all year was definitely and completely out of reach now.

From one moment to the next dusk turned to night, and nothing was visible except for some treetops gently illuminated by the stars. Inés could no longer see the butterflies on the other side of the branch, but judging by the absence of rustling sounds, it seemed they were fast asleep. Was there a butterfly trick to falling asleep within seconds that she wasn't yet acquainted with?

There was, and it was exhaustion from flying coupled with circadian rhythm. Most living creatures rose with the sun and slept with the moon—unless of course they were nocturnal and it was the other way around—and it wasn't something that was questioned or tampered with. Insomnia was a human ailment brought about by an overactive mind, whereas butterflies and other creatures couldn't afford to not sleep when it was time to sleep, just as they couldn't afford to not forage for food, or to not migrate away from cold weather when winter approached.

Inés suddenly felt incredibly tired, and without closing her eyes—for butterflies don't have eyelids—she fell asleep. And she stayed that way for an hour or two, until she was awakened by her own body's shivering. A biting cold had set in and her thorax, legs, and wings felt stiff and achy. She reluctantly clambered over to the other end of the branch and inserted herself into the still-vacant space next to Josephine. Josephine woke up for a moment, saw that it was Inés and not a predator, and went back to sleep. And Inés now felt undeniably warmer and safer, and from that moment until the dawn her sleep

was peaceful, deep, and undisturbed.

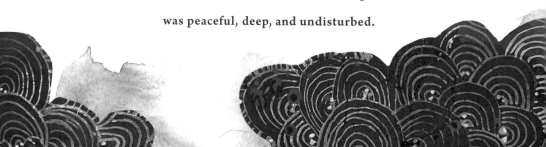

The first thing Inés did the following morning

was look down at her body.

Her heart seized up when she saw that she was still a butterfly and that it hadn't been a dream.

She also felt a pang of hunger, and she realized she hadn't eaten since her birthday pancakes twenty-four hours earlier. How she'd managed all that flying on an empty stomach was a mystery; perhaps it was something butterflies could do or perhaps she'd been driven by the thought of her family being in danger. And now, as she remembered Caligo's ominous words, she wondered exactly how flying south with this swarm of butterflies—*away* from her family—could possibly save them from any sort of danger. And what sort of danger were they in anyway? If Caligo hadn't spoken her name, and if all the events of the past day hadn't been quite so extraordinary, she never would have believed him. But this world had been imposed on her—a world she knew little about—and she didn't dare question its rules or the logic set forth by its longtime inhabitants.

"Good morning,"

Josephine said. "We spotted some zinnias to feed from, so prepare to take off soon." Inés nodded distractedly, trying to figure out what distance they'd traveled from her house and wondering if she should continue with the butterflies or attempt to make her way back. Just then Valerio called out, "It's time to go!" and there was a huge flutter of movement all around her. The butterflies headed toward a nearby yard and Inés, famished, decided to follow.

As Josephine and Inés flew toward a cluster of orange and pink flowers, it seemed to Inés that she could smell their sweetness through her antennae. And then, when she alighted on a large pink blossom with a dark center that seemed to call out to her, Inés could *taste* its sweetness through her feet. "How odd," she thought to herself. "Perhaps this lets butterflies know if something is safe to eat before they try it."

And while this "taste" had filled Inés with a strong desire to drink,

she realized she didn't know how.

Josephine smiled as if understanding her dilemma and demonstrated for Inés by uncoiling her tubular proboscis and inserting it into the flower. She then looked at Inés expectantly. Tentatively unfurling her own proboscis and placing it inside the blossom, Inés felt her antennae droop downward. Tiny sensors on her proboscis guided it toward the very bottom and she started to make sucking motions. Within seconds she was imbibing a sweet and delicious nectar, and she continued to feed hungrily. "Very good," said Josephine encouragingly. "With flying, feeding, roosting . . . your body should always know what to do. Just trust your instincts."

"It's like a straw," Inés replied, "only the straw is attached to my face."

Josephine smiled, but she clearly didn't know what a straw was. And why should she? There was no need for objects to aid with feeding in the natural world.

Inés resumed drinking and thought about what Josephine had just said about instincts. Humans were born completely helpless—they couldn't walk, feed themselves, or speak immediately after birth; in fact, it took them years to learn how to do these things. But other animals in the world—especially those hatched from eggs like reptiles and insects—simply emerged, completely unaided, and proceeded to move and feed on their own. Perhaps these animals were the most evolved . . . Had they not been the first to inhabit the planet?

Josephine and Inés finished the nectar and moved on to another blossom. Inés noticed that some pale yellow dust from the first flower had attached itself to her body and dropped onto the second one. And one moment later she realized with excitement that it was not dust, but pollen. "I'm pollinating!" she thought to herself. She then thought about humans feeding, and how they helped only themselves when they did so. But butterflies and bees performed a function in the service of all life on earth while eating, and they did so easily and organically.

The butterflies all fed in silence, then migrated a short distance to a sunny patch and proceeded to open their wings as wide as they could. They remained like this, and while Inés again imitated Josephine, she was confused. "I thought we were in a big hurry to escape the cold," she said. "So why have we stopped to sunbathe?"

Josephine smiled. "We're getting energy from the sun. The energy we need for flying."

Inés looked down at her wings and was suddenly aware of a current of energy—almost like electricity—running up and down them and filling each of their scales with power. She felt like the bride of Frankenstein being brought to life with zaps of lightning, only here it was simply the sun's energy—bountiful and unharnessed—which was the animator of life. And as she looked over at all the butterflies charging their wings in unison, she was profoundly moved by this communal activity, and by how clear and deep their connection to the sun was. It was no wonder that every ancient civilization had worshipped the sun, along with sun gods and goddesses.

And why did humans need so many things, anyway? Life as a butterfly seemed pretty uncomplicated so far: find a flower to feed from, use the sun to get energy, choose a tree branch to sleep on. Everything was out there for the taking, everything was free and renewable, and there was more than enough to go around. But at this point, truth be told, Inés had no idea how dangerous the migration to the sanctuary was going to be.

The butterflies soon resumed their journey south, and Inés continued to fly with them but stuck to the back of the group. The tail was the spot that was closest to home—even while she moved farther away from it with each flap of her wings—and this strategic spot would allow her to sneak off if necessary, the way sitting in the back row of a theater allowed one to exit a movie or play more discreetly.

Before long there was a commotion up ahead, but Inés couldn't see what was happening due to the cluster of butterflies directly in front of her. A minute later she realized that the swarm was flying over a four-lane highway packed with cars, and that many butterflies were flying so low that they were bouncing off car windshields, while others were

suffocating from the fumes
and falling to the road,

only to be run over.

As Inés and the others at the back approached the freeway she called out, "Up, up! Fly as high as you can!" and the butterflies within earshot all veered upward and crossed over safely. But as they did, Inés was deeply saddened to see about two dozen orange bodies on the road below, while an endless stream of cars drove over them as if their lives meant nothing. And she also felt guilty, because she knew how dangerous cars were while the other butterflies didn't, and if she hadn't been all the way in the back she could have spotted the cars and warned the others much sooner.

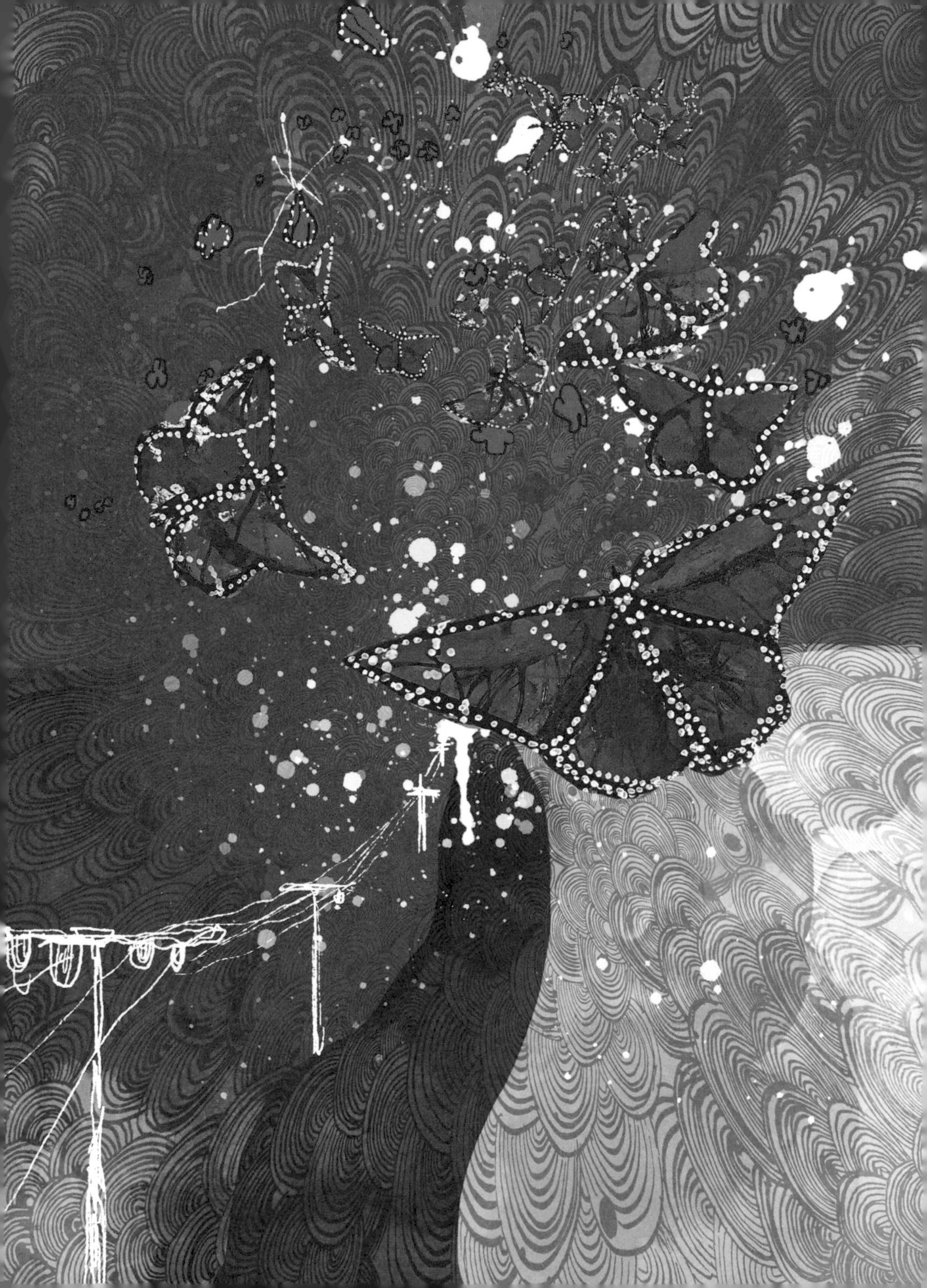

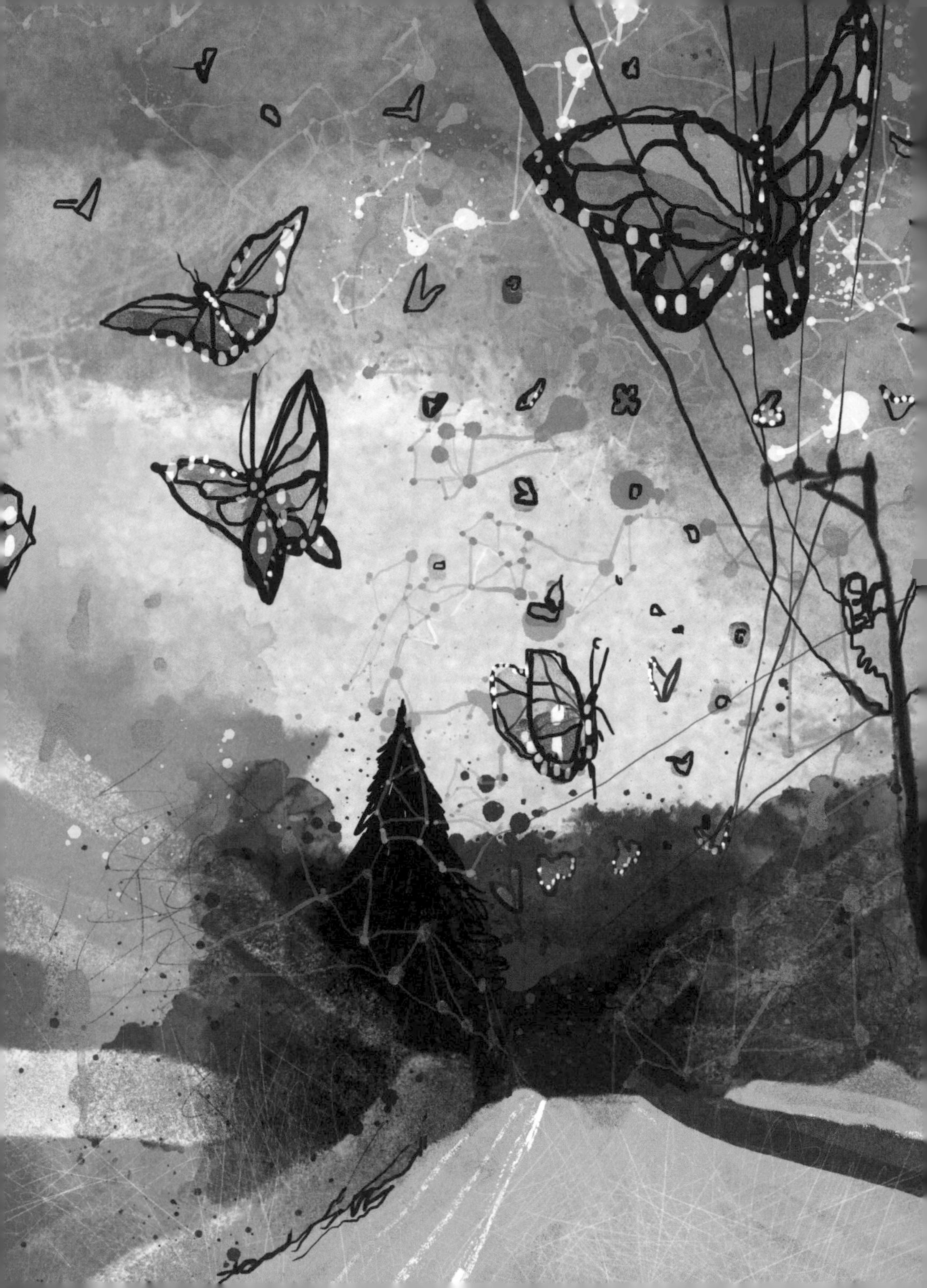

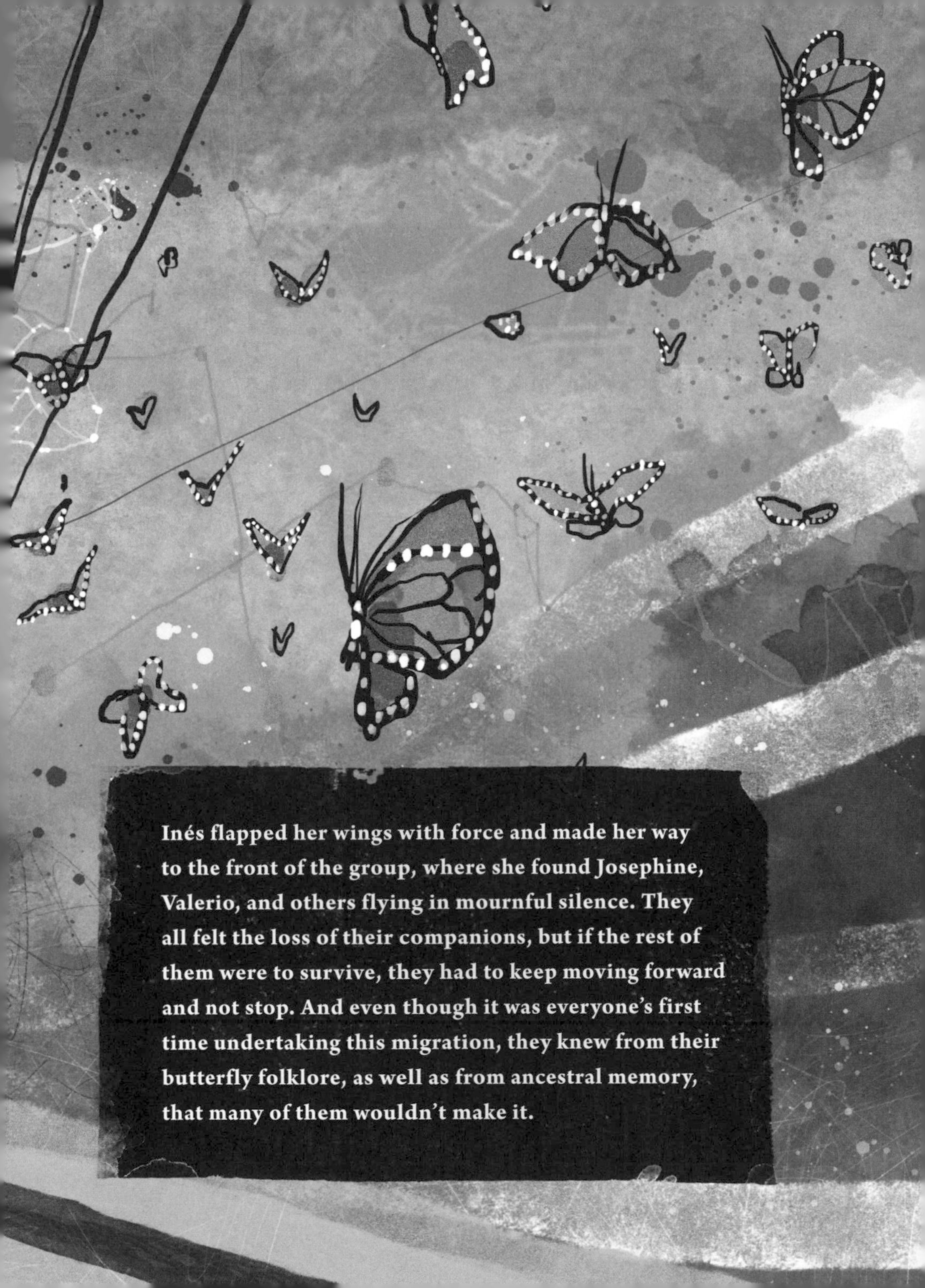

Inés flapped her wings with force and made her way to the front of the group, where she found Josephine, Valerio, and others flying in mournful silence. They all felt the loss of their companions, but if the rest of them were to survive, they had to keep moving forward and not stop. And even though it was everyone's first time undertaking this migration, they knew from their butterfly folklore, as well as from ancestral memory, that many of them wouldn't make it.

In the middle of the afternoon, somewhere over Pennsylvania, they came across a field of common milkweed next to a field of corn and descended on it hungrily. Inés again followed Josephine as she landed on the blooms, but just as she was preparing to feed, she spotted a bright yellow crop duster parked at the edge of the field. Inés could see that the plane had the word MONPLANTO printed on its body, and also that it had a small mirror jutting out on each side. Curious to know what she looked like as a butterfly, Inés slipped away without Josephine noticing.

Inés landed on one of the mirrors and was truly shocked when she saw her reflection.

Of course she *knew* that she had turned into a monarch butterfly, but somehow she'd expected her head and face to still be human. Instead, her face was black and fuzzy, with enormous, buggy compound eyes, a curled-up proboscis where her nose and mouth used to be, and two antennae sprouting from her head. Inés uncoiled her proboscis, then rolled it back up. Suddenly she heard an engine start, and before she realized what was happening, the plane had lifted off the ground and started flying toward the field.

Terrified, Inés tried to take flight, but the air pressure pushed her body down and she couldn't move. She turned to look into the cockpit and saw a young man sitting there, grinning to himself as he surveilled the ground below. How could she not have noticed him before? Inés then turned to look toward the field and saw the monarchs below, a tapestry of orange triangles feeding on the milkweed. The plane swooped down toward them and started to spray pesticides, but the butterflies looked up just in time to take flight and avoid the deadly fog. The butterflies flew around the field in a panicked loop, and when the plane veered around to pursue them, Inés realized with horror that the pilot was *purposely* targeting them. She called out a warning, but the sound of the engine was so deafening that she couldn't even hear herself. She tried to take flight again and managed to get off the mirror, but she became stuck to the windshield instead.

As the plane attempted to spray the butterflies a second time—and they were able to avoid the poison once more—Inés couldn't help thinking about the film *North by Northwest*.

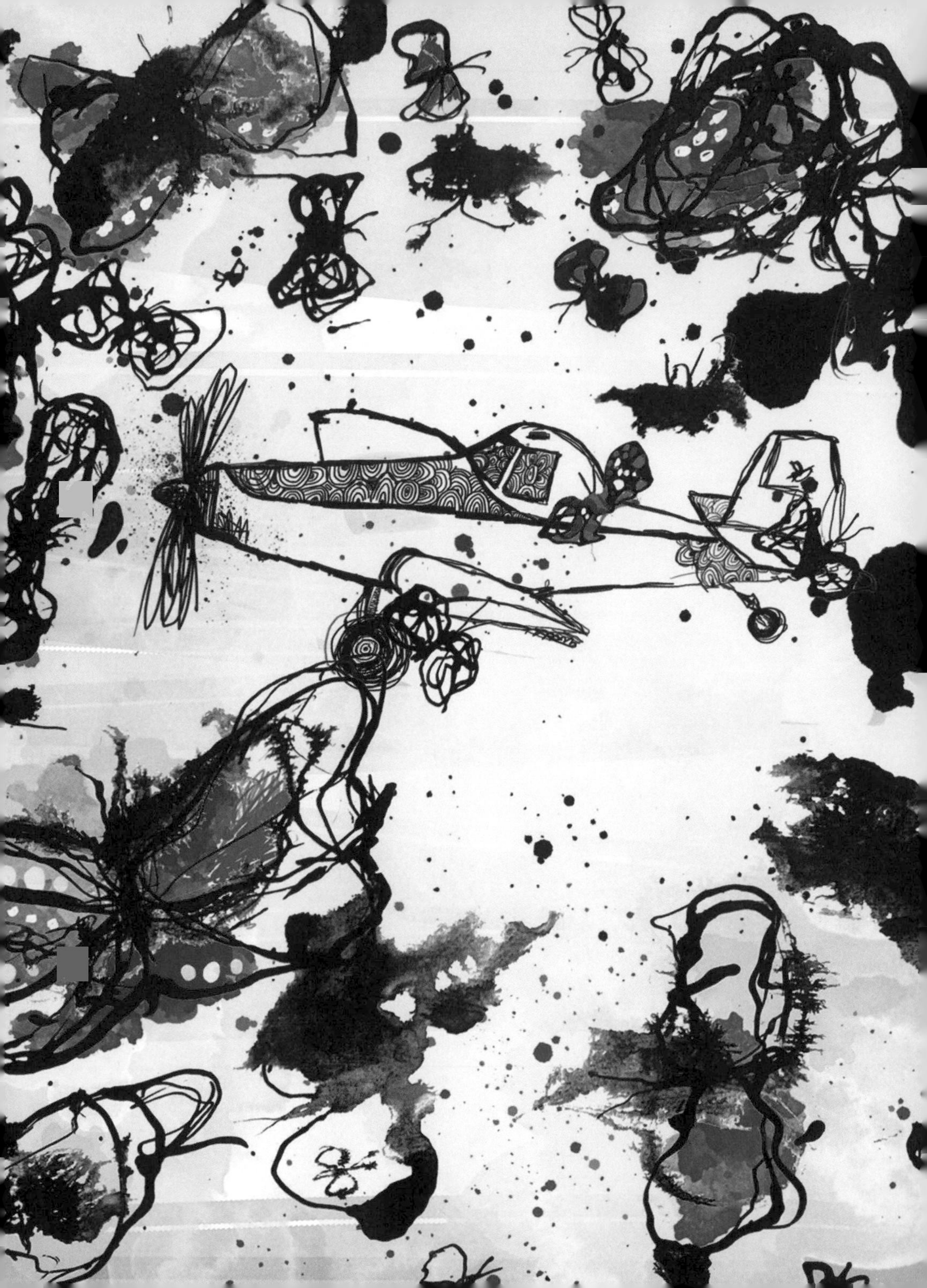

Only here the intended victims were butterflies instead of a man in a suit, and this was reality, not a movie. Inés knew that pesticides and herbicides were responsible for the devastating collapse of insect populations all over the world, including bees and monarch butterflies. Many of these highly toxic substances killed every insect or plant they came into contact with except those genetically engineered to resist them, and were extremely harmful to the humans harvesting and consuming the tainted crops as well.

The butterflies headed en masse toward a nearby forest, but when Josephine looked back for Inés, she saw that her friend was stuck to the plane's windshield. Josephine flew over to Valerio to alert him, and he directed the entire swarm to do a U-turn and head back toward the plane, narrowly avoiding collision with its enormous metallic body by flying upward and hovering above it.

Inés looked up at the butterflies and tried to unpeel herself, without success. A cluster of fifteen butterflies flew downward to try to assist her, but they too got stuck to the windshield as their bodies were flattened by the wind. Seeing this, Josephine had an idea and called out:

"Everyone, do what *they're* doing!"

The monarchs all flew to cover up the windshield, and within seconds the pilot was forced to crash-land his plane, his visibility and light completely blocked by the blanket of butterfly bodies. Just moments before impact the swarm took flight and fled toward the forest, while the crumpled plane emitted a plume of smoke behind them.

The butterflies found a clearing in the woods and landed on the branches of some trees. They were pleased with their successful rescue mission and relieved by the destruction of the plane that had tried to kill them. Inés smiled with the others and thanked them for rescuing her, but then she noticed that Valerio was *not* smiling. He landed next to her, looking angry. "What were you doing on that plane, all on your own?" he demanded to know.

"I . . . I was looking at myself in the mirror," said Inés. "Because I'd never seen what I looked like before. As a butterfly."

"So you put all of us in danger, just so you could look at your reflection?" Valerio asked. "We could have flown straight here—to safety—but instead we flew *toward* that flying monster to rescue you. You left the swarm, and we all could have died as a result of that!"

Inés felt terrible. Of course she'd never imagined that her going to look in the mirror would endanger the others, nor that there'd be a man inside the plane who intended to fumigate them to death. But it was true that they'd all risked their lives to save her, even though she was just one tiny part of the group—one butterfly. "I'm sorry," Inés responded. "I promise I won't leave the swarm again."

Inés now heard a human voice shouting at the edge of the forest, and as she listened she realized it was probably the pilot. She wanted to know why he'd targeted them, and turned to Valerio for guidance. "I hear a man speaking and I want to get closer to make out what he's saying. Will this put the swarm in danger?"

Josephine overheard these words and alighted next to them. "As long as you stay in the forest and don't let him see you, it should be fine. Why don't I come with you?"

Inés and Josephine flew back to the edge of the forest where, sure enough, the pilot was pacing back and forth and shouting into a cell phone. They landed on a branch above him and listened.

"No, I wasn't able to stop them; instead, the damn insects made me crash my plane! And you still owe me for the pesticides I sent to your avocado farms last month!" There was a pause while the person on the other end of the line spoke, and finally the conversation concluded with the pilot shouting, "I'll be sending you the bill from the mechanic, and I won't be spraying any more swarms until you pay me every cent!" The man then stabbed at his phone to end the call, stuffed it into his pants pocket, and turned to look at his damaged plane.

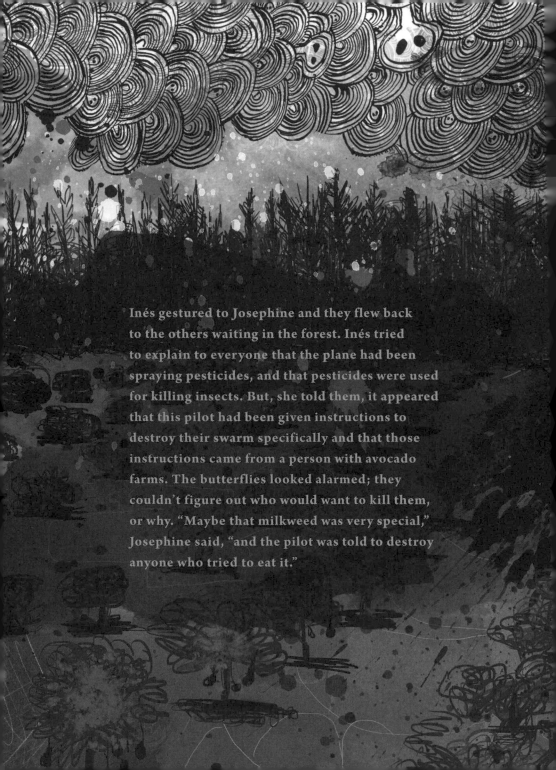

Inés gestured to Josephine and they flew back to the others waiting in the forest. Inés tried to explain to everyone that the plane had been spraying pesticides, and that pesticides were used for killing insects. But, she told them, it appeared that this pilot had been given instructions to destroy their swarm specifically and that those instructions came from a person with avocado farms. The butterflies looked alarmed; they couldn't figure out who would want to kill them, or why. "Maybe that milkweed was very special," Josephine said, "and the pilot was told to destroy anyone who tried to eat it."

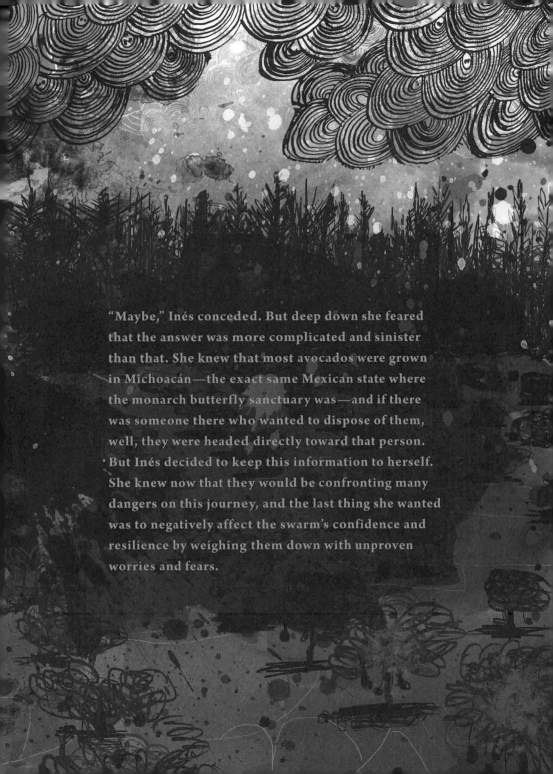

"Maybe," Inés conceded. But deep down she feared that the answer was more complicated and sinister than that. She knew that most avocados were grown in Michoacán—the exact same Mexican state where the monarch butterfly sanctuary was—and if there was someone there who wanted to dispose of them, well, they were headed directly toward that person. But Inés decided to keep this information to herself. She knew now that they would be confronting many dangers on this journey, and the last thing she wanted was to negatively affect the swarm's confidence and resilience by weighing them down with unproven worries and fears.

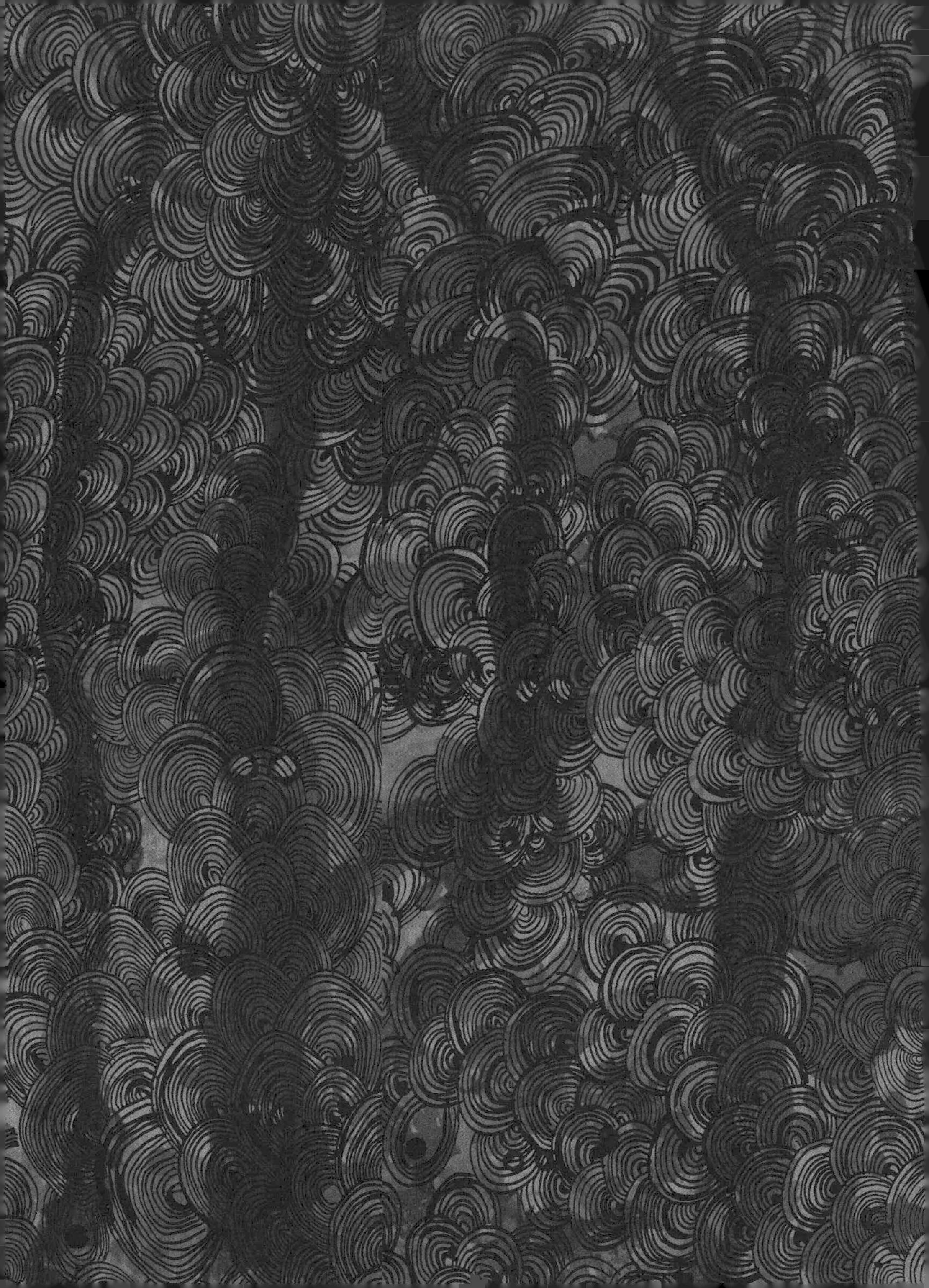

The butterflies decided to spend the night in the forest since they were exhausted from their challenging day. As Inés settled down to roost next to Josephine, she thought about the lessons she'd learned that day. She'd learned how to feed and sunbathe, but most importantly she'd learned about community.

For better or for worse, she was part of this swarm now,

and in order to survive, they each had to put their individual needs aside and operate as a unit. She could have helped the whole group cross the freeway but hadn't because she was purposely hanging back, and then she'd endangered everyone by going off to look at her reflection. Feeling ashamed of herself and grateful for the kindness and forgiveness the butterflies had shown her, Inés was determined to do better by them going forward.

The next day they were off bright and early, and they'd already been flying for several miles when they came across a large picnic table in a garden, with several plates of sliced oranges, strawberries, and bananas laid out on it. It seemed the fruit had been abandoned, so the butterflies descended upon it hungrily. Inés landed on a wedge of orange and started to feed. Even as a human she loved oranges, but as a butterfly this was the best thing she'd ever tasted. As she sipped the sweet juice from the succulent fruit, she felt her body filling with energy.

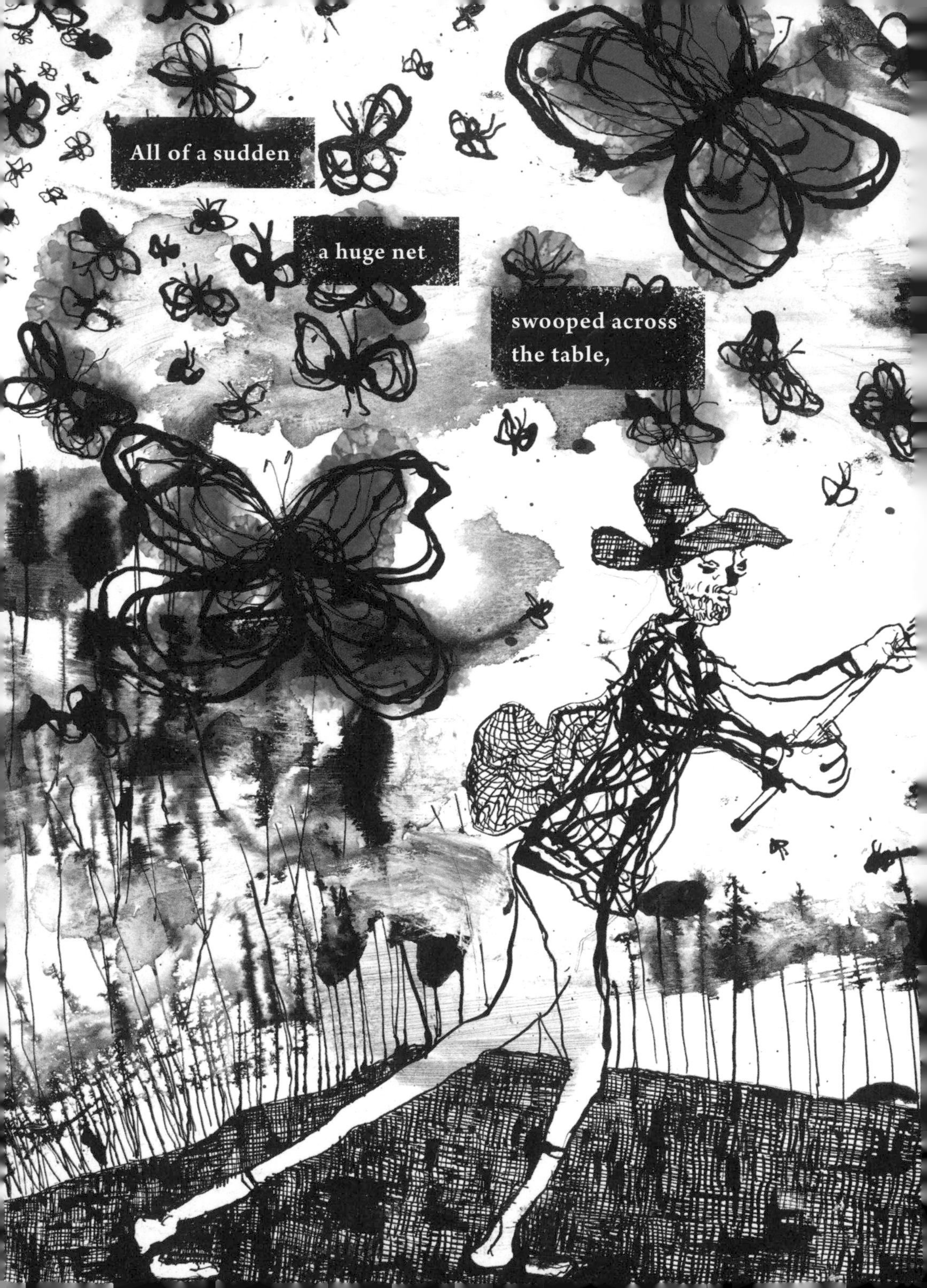
All of a sudden
a huge net
swooped across the table,

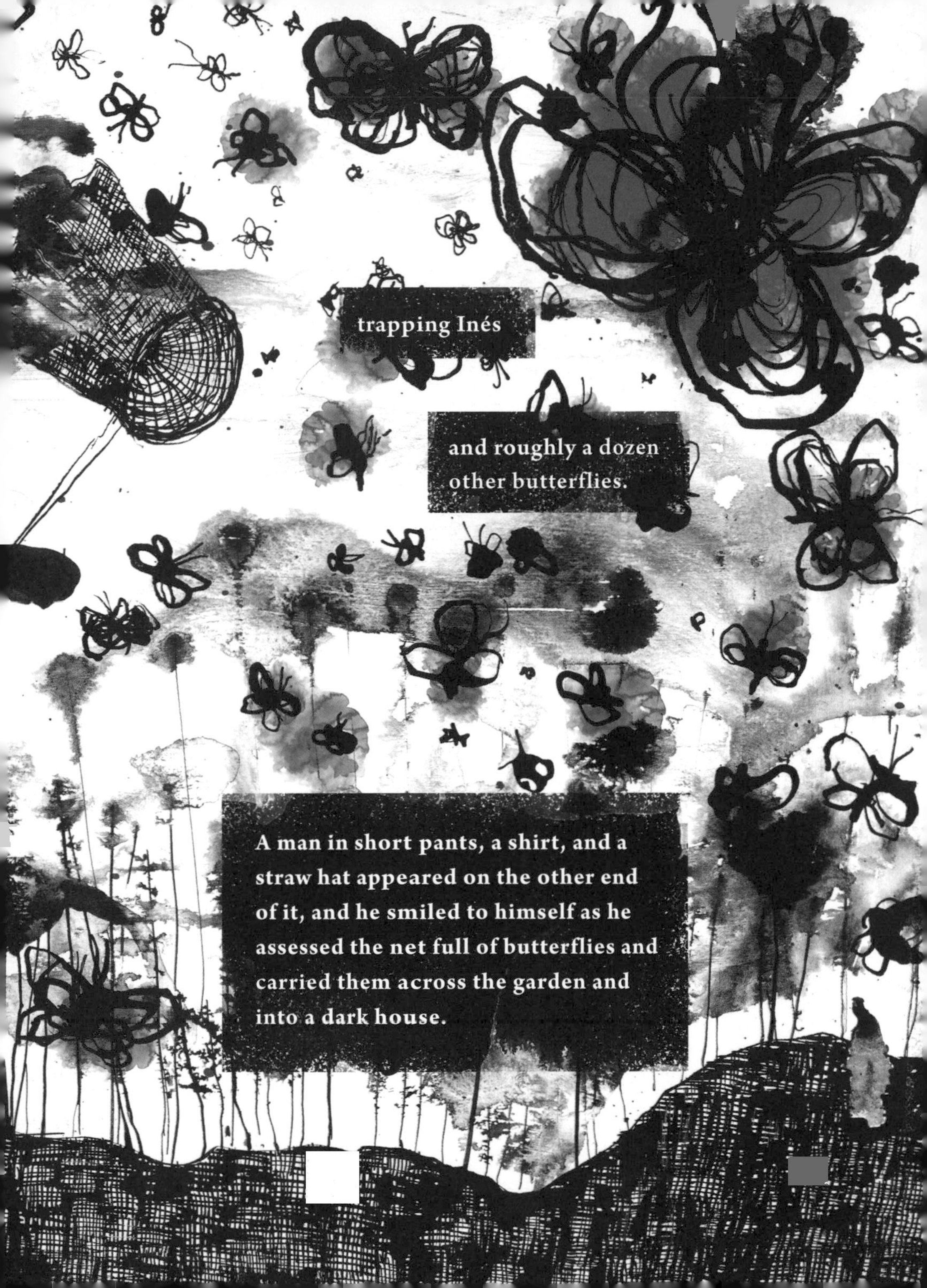

trapping Inés

and roughly a dozen other butterflies.

A man in short pants, a shirt, and a straw hat appeared on the other end of it, and he smiled to himself as he assessed the net full of butterflies and carried them across the garden and into a dark house.

Inés could feel the other monarch bodies pressed up against hers, and she pushed her face against a hole in the netting to breathe. As the man walked down a corridor, Inés scanned the walls and was horrified to see frame after frame of mounted butterflies of different species, their beautiful dead bodies pinned to white boards. This man was a butterfly collector.

The man turned into a room that was clearly his workshop, and Inés surveyed its contents with alarm: there were several tables covered with killing jars, boards, rulers, box cutters, magnifying glasses, and boxes of pins, pencils, and pens. In a bookcase were dozens of books about butterflies, and on the wall hung a poster featuring all the different North American butterfly species.

The man put the net down on a table and started to fill killing jars, grabbing two butterflies at a time and popping them into a jar before screwing the lid closed and moving on to the next one. He put Josephine and Valerio into one together, and then Inés in another one with a butterfly she'd never spoken to.

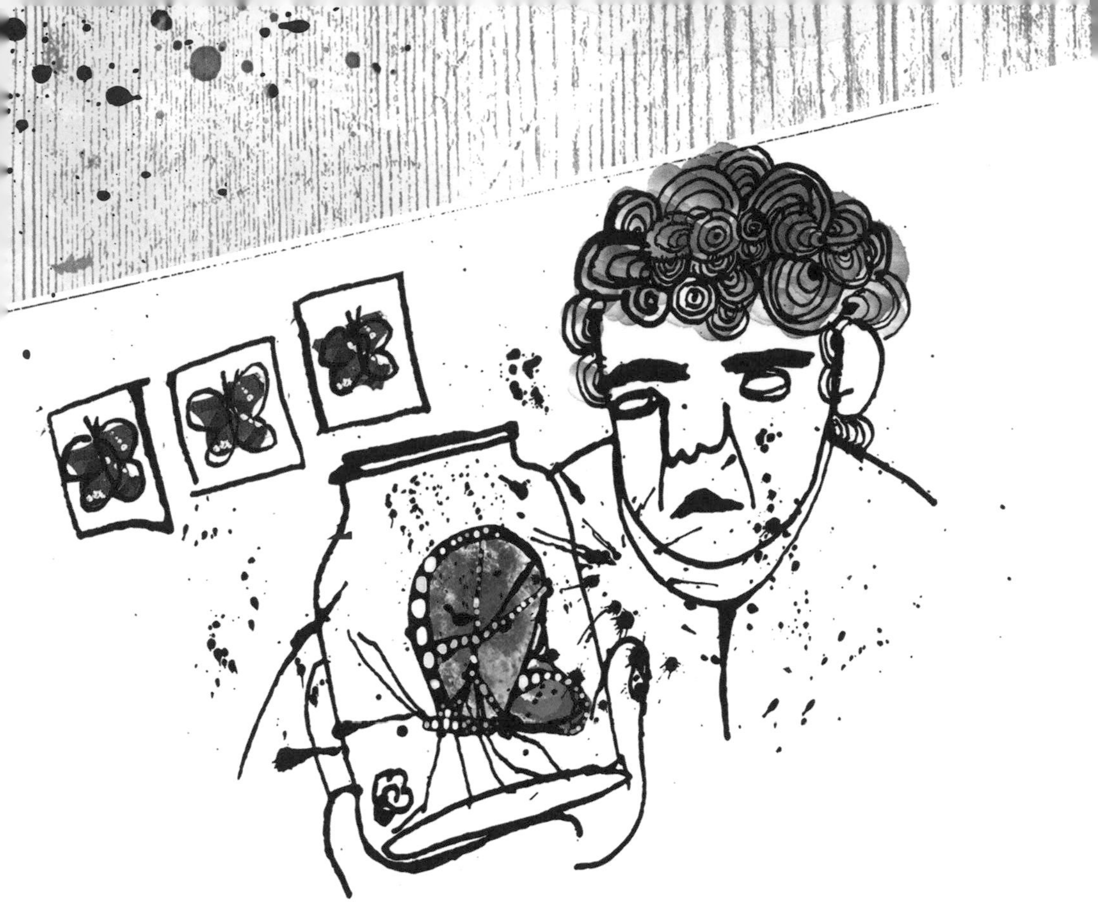

Inés immediately became aware of the scent of chloroform, and she gazed out through the glass with dread as the man stuffed the last two butterflies into a jar

and left the room with his net,

intent on catching more.

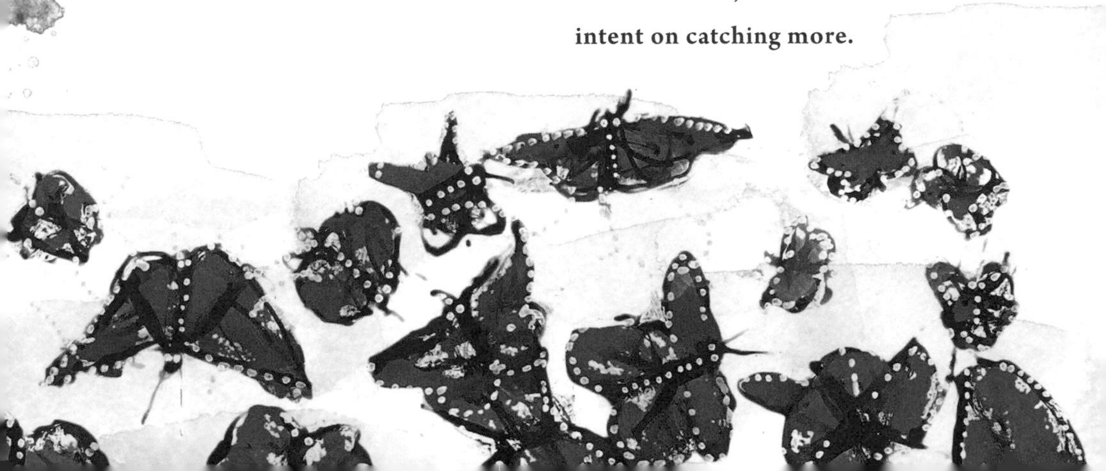

No sooner did the man exit the room than an orange cat sauntered by in the hallway, and Inés made a loud meowing noise to try to get its attention. When the cat glanced into the workshop with curiosity, Inés made enormous movements—the biggest ones she could muster—with her wings and legs. She waved her legs around and jumped from one side of the jar to another, encouraging her jar mate to do the same. Within seconds the cat was at the jar, swatting at it. Inés struggled to keep up the jerky movements, as she was starting to feel dizzy and weak from the chemical fumes. She delivered one final dramatic tap on the inside of the jar with a front leg, and the cat lifted its paw and batted at it, knocking the jar to the ground. It broke open with a loud crash, and Inés and the other butterfly zoomed out.

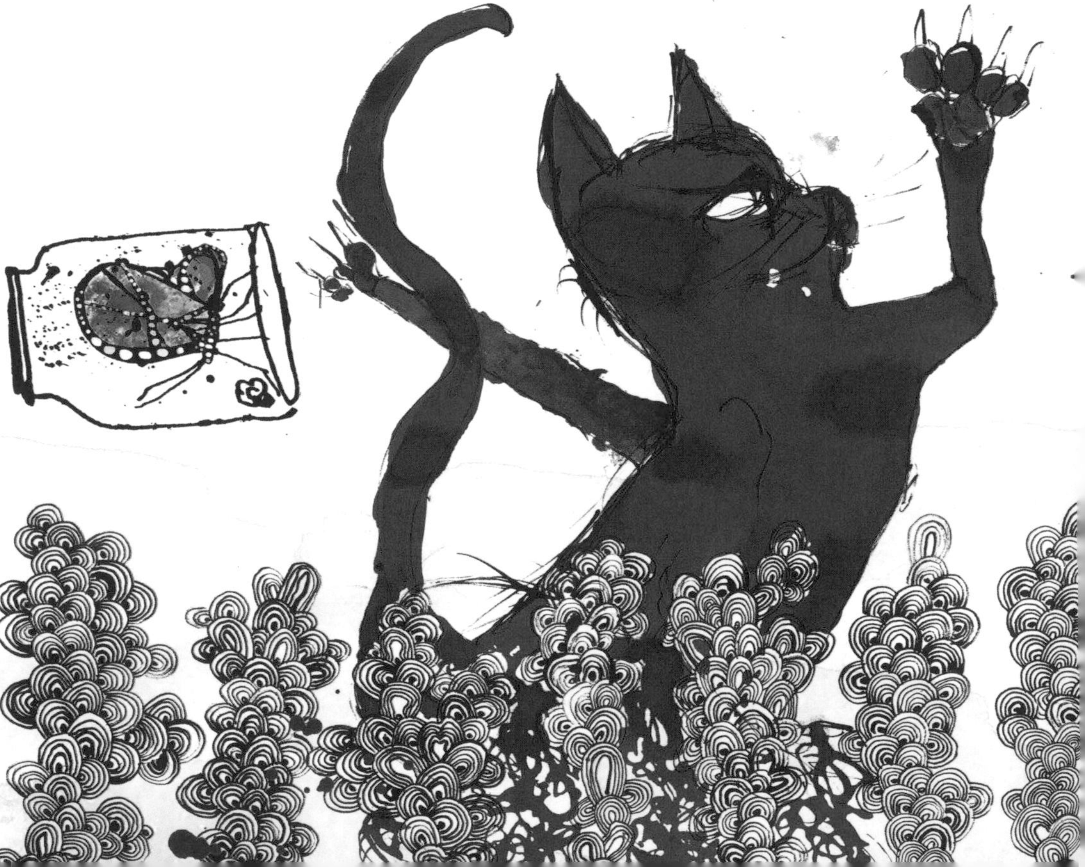

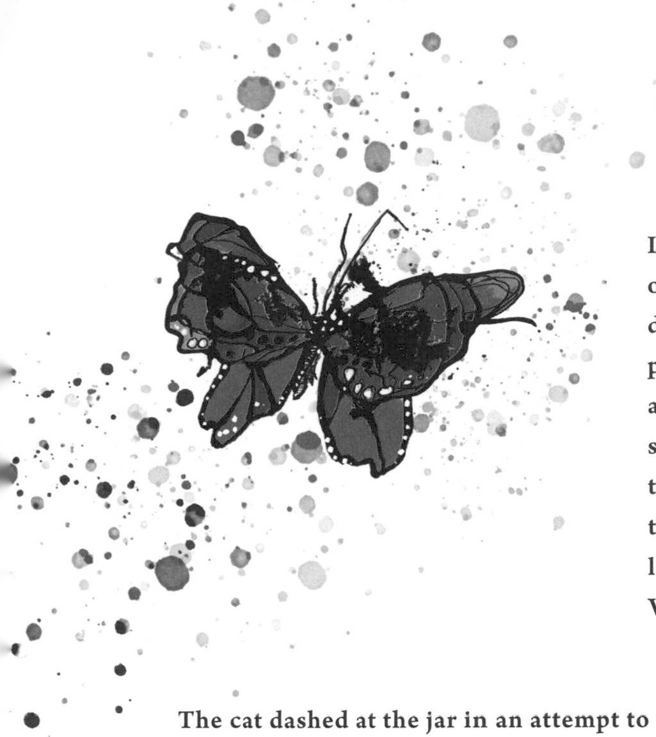

Inés beckoned to the other butterfly and they descended upon the cat, pulling its tail as hard as they could. The cat swung around angrily and tried to bite them, but they flew into the air and landed on the jar holding Valerio and Josephine.

The cat dashed at the jar in an attempt to catch them, but they flew off it at the last moment and the cat knocked the jar off the table. It too broke, freeing Valerio and Josephine, and then the four of them proceeded to taunt the cat. And in this fashion the butterflies were freed two by two, with the growing group of rescued butterflies joining forces to enrage the cat until all six killing jars lay smashed on the floor. The butterflies then escaped to freedom through a small open window in the corner of the room, and found their friends waiting anxiously in the trees outside. The swarm sped away as quickly as it could, desperate to get away from this murderer and his gallery of butterfly corpses.

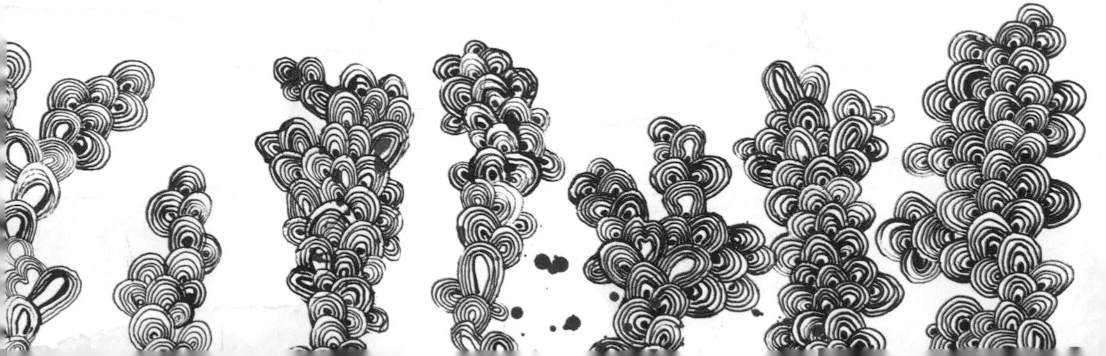

The butterflies flew for hours without stopping, still terrified by what had been another near-death experience. Inés was starting to feel embarrassed about her association with humans, now that she was seeing the world from another species' perspective. All the dangers that the swarm had encountered so far were human-made and involved people: the freeway full of cars, the crop-dusting plane with its malevolent pilot, and now a man who killed butterflies as a hobby.

But no sooner had Inés completed this thought than a *natural* danger presented itself: the sky above the swarm darkened and rumbled angrily, and a steady rain began to fall on the monarchs, beating down on their backs and wings. The butterflies rushed to take cover under the nearest vegetation they could find: bushes lining the parking lot of a suburban mall. They spent the night there huddled together for warmth, and the next day they emerged at dawn and spread their wings, allowing the last of the moisture on their bodies to evaporate in the sun, and filling their bodies with vigor and strength.

The butterflies traveled for several days without incident. Inés tried to steer the swarm away from highways, and if they did have to cross one she made sure everyone flew as high as possible. One day they encountered an elderly couple in Virginia who had planted the monarchs' favorite flowers in their garden and laid out fruit for them, but this time the butterflies studied the premises before declaring the site a safe haven for everyone. And indeed it was, for it was the garden of famed entomologist and monarch butterfly specialist Lincoln Brower and his wife, Linda, and these humans always made sure their garden was a bountiful feeding and resting spot for any monarchs passing through on their long and exhausting migration. Inés was relieved to encounter people such as these and thought about how simple it was to help the weary monarchs, although so few people actually did.

One evening, while flying over the swamps of Louisiana, the butterflies were alerted by falling air pressure to a heavy rainstorm that was approaching. They took cover under a bald cypress tree (which despite its name was not lacking foliage) and spent the night there. They fell asleep to a chorus of frogs and heard the grunty calls of a tricolored heron at dawn. The butterflies then sunbathed on the trunk of the tree, and Inés watched a roseate spoonbill wading in the swamp, dipping its aptly named beak in the water and attempting to catch minnows and small crustaceans.

Shortly after taking flight, the monarchs came across a group of alligators resting in the mud below. Inés was surprised to see some of the butterflies—including Josephine—fly downward and alight on the reptiles' backs and heads.

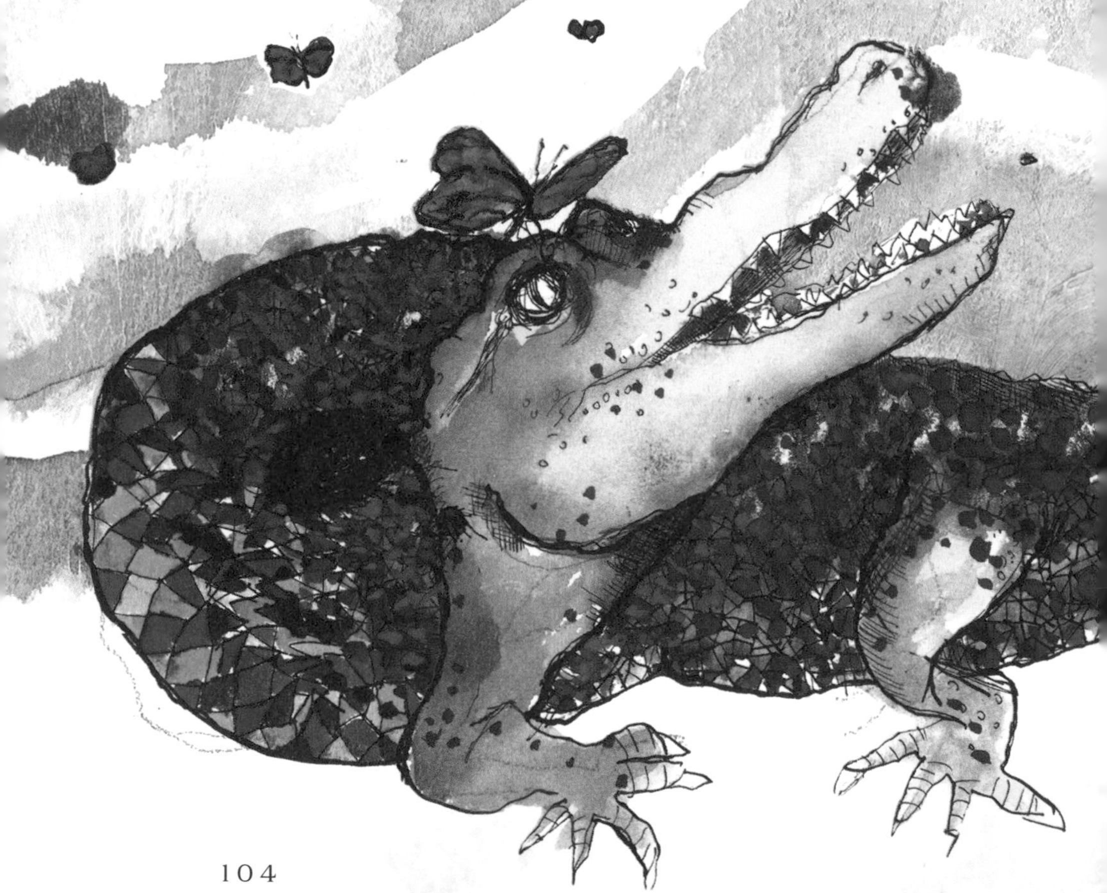

Inés landed on the ground nearby and watched with alarm as Josephine clambered along the snout of a small alligator, which remained completely still but followed her with a roving eye. "Don't go near its mouth, Josephine!" Inés cried out. "Alligators are extremely dangerous!"

Josephine laughed good-naturedly and said, "They're not interested in eating *us*; in fact, we're going to get some nutrients from *them*." And then Josephine proceeded to walk to the alligator's left eye, stick her proboscis into a glistening tear, and drink from it. "I actually think they enjoy this," she added, as she sipped from the salty tear and made space for a second butterfly that arrived to join her. And indeed the alligators were all grinning and showing off their sharp teeth now, a group of scaly, muddy beasts who suddenly found themselves caressed and adorned by a fluttering of winged orange jewels.

Inés chose to get her sodium from a puddle of mud instead, but as she watched the alligators she thought about how humans vilified them, even though it was clear they could be gentle creatures when they wanted to be. And perhaps they were aesthetes too, able to appreciate the beauty of the butterflies or feel beautiful themselves with some monarchs on their heads. And then Inés thought about how alligator tears and mud provided the swarm with salt, and how the fulfillment of *every* creature's biological needs really did seem to lie somewhere in the natural world.

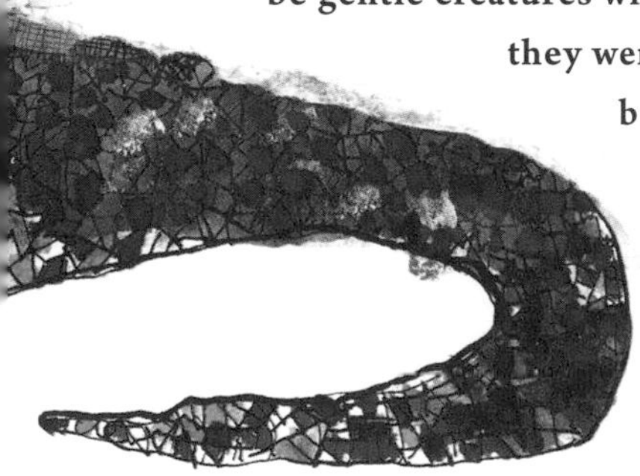

A day or two later the landscape below them changed to desert and Inés realized they were flying over Texas. She could see horse ranches below, as well as enormous feedlots full of cattle. Some of the cows raised their heads to watch the butterflies as they flew by and Inés felt terrible for them, suspecting that they'd never known any sort of freedom or happiness and never would. Inés knew from her short time as a butterfly that each and every one of them was an individual with its own personality, mind, and spirit, just as every butterfly in her swarm was an individual too.

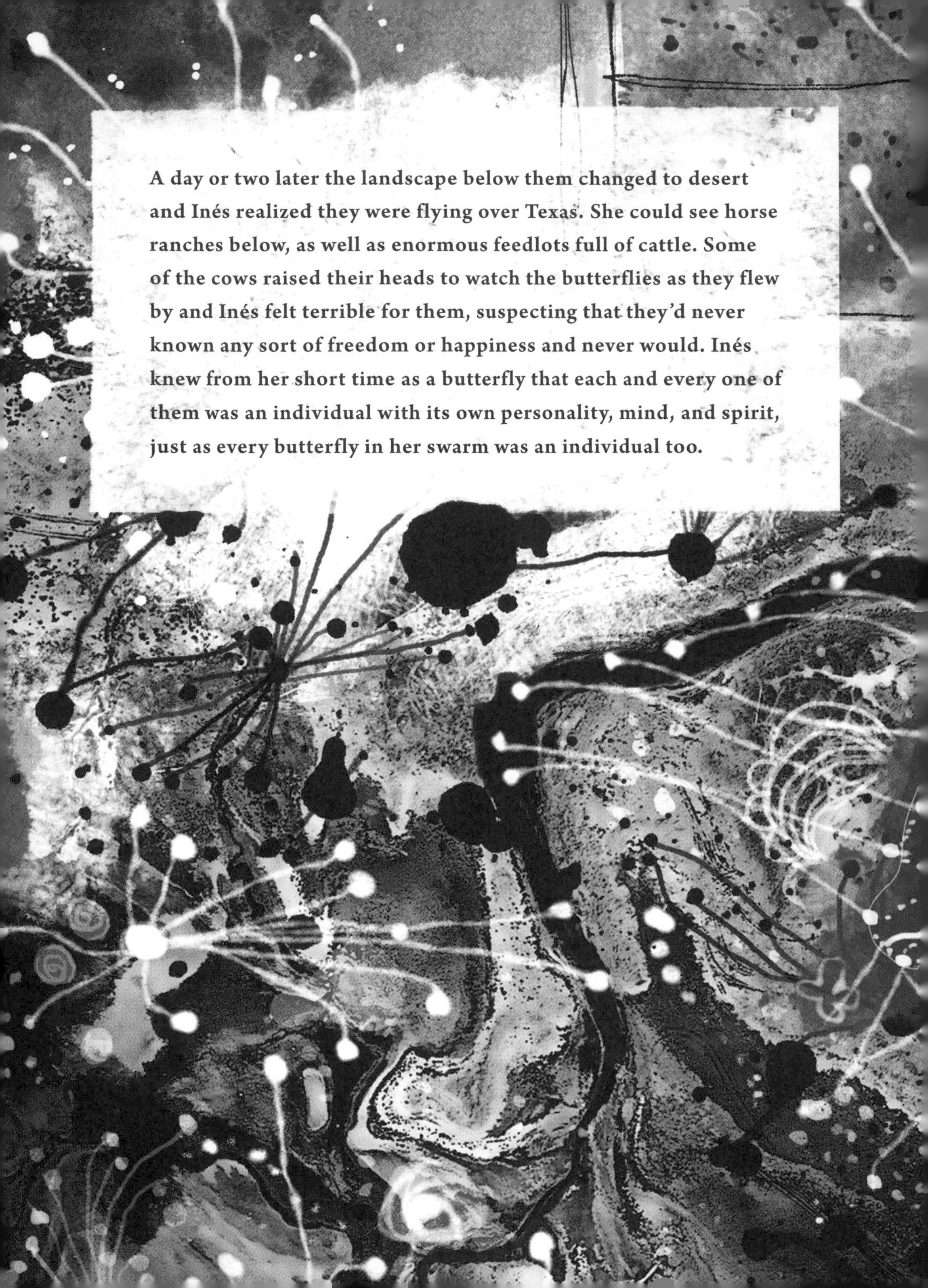

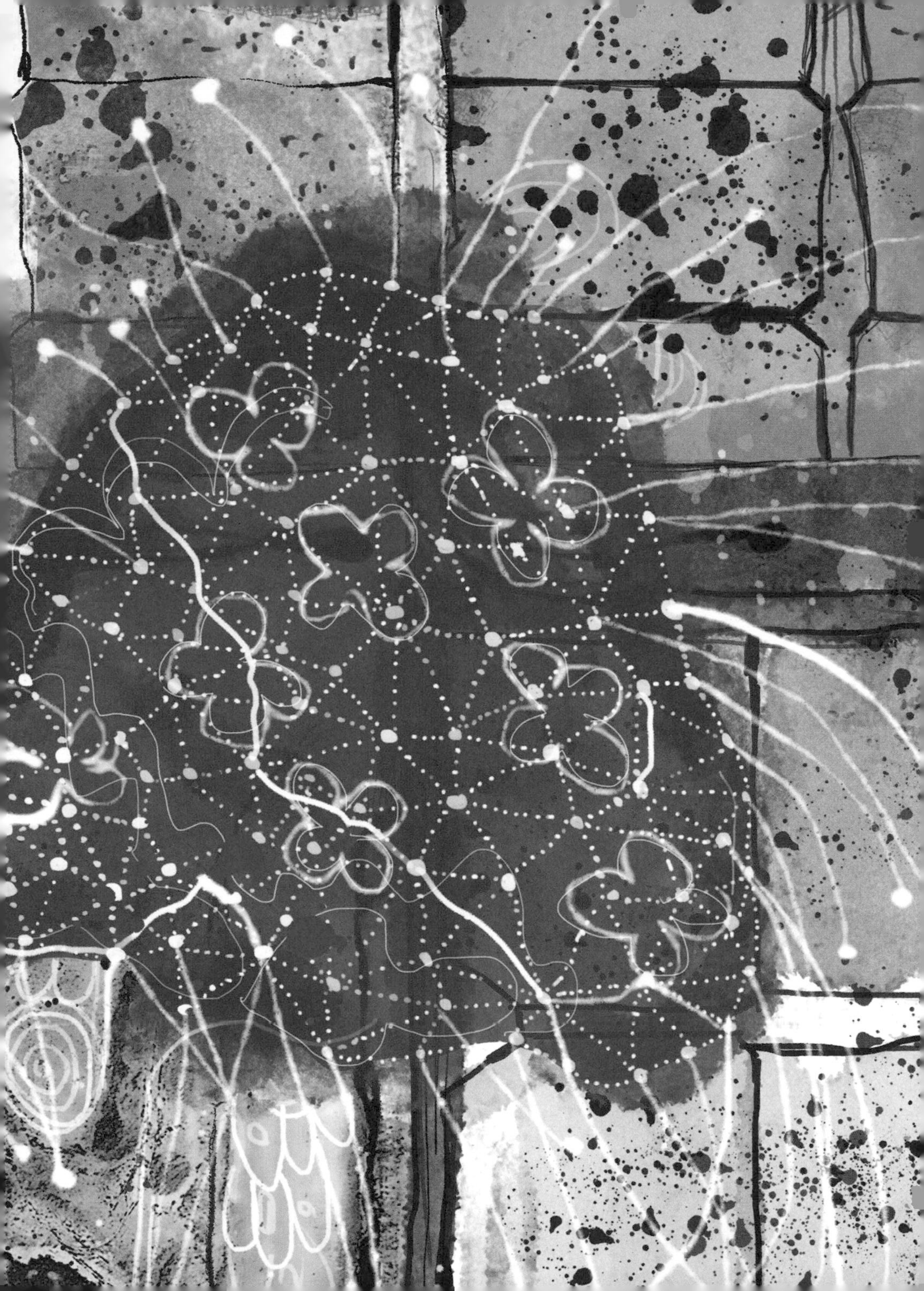

A couple hours later the butterflies in front of her began to chatter excitedly. Inés flew up to investigate and saw two large clouds heading directly toward them—one from the west and one from the north. A minute or two later these clouds revealed themselves to be two other swarms of monarchs, swarms that had traveled just as many miles as they had, only they'd originated in different states and taken different routes. It seemed as if the three groups would crash into each other, but in the same instant they all swooped to the south and converged. And they flew over Eagle Pass— also known as Butterfly Alley—as one giant glittering and fluttering golden cloud. Inés's heart filled with joy and excitement, and she cheered with the others as they flew over the border into Mexico together.

chapter

3

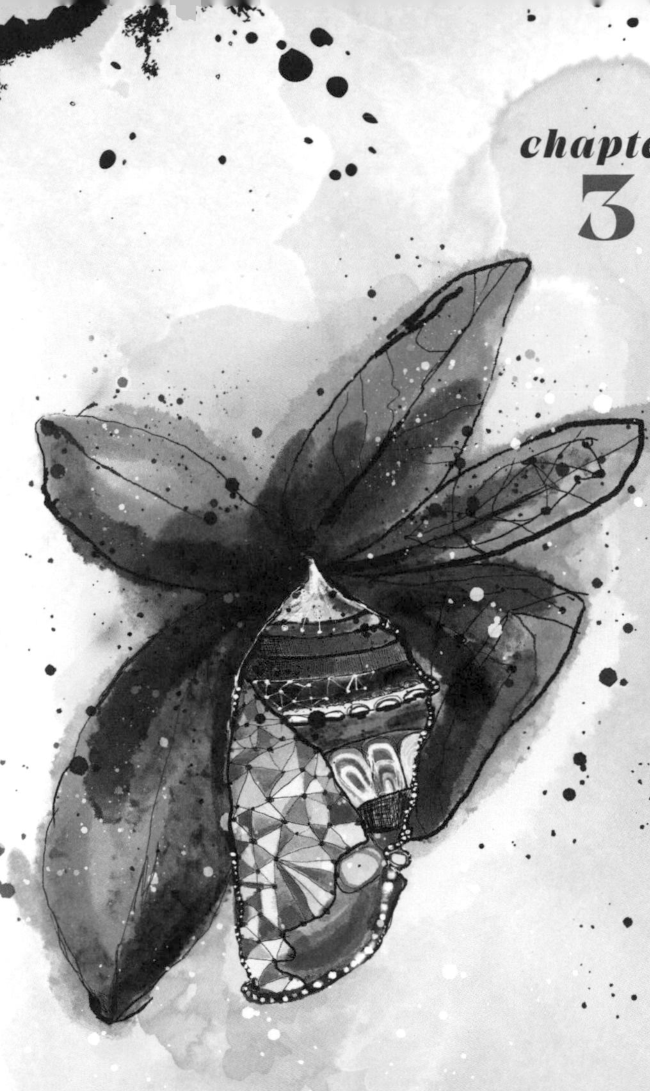

The Pupa, or Chrysalis

The pupa,
or chryalis:

The monarch caterpillar has nourished its senses and mind and is now ready for true transformation, or metamorphosis. But first it must set the stage for this metamorphosis and surrender the time required for it to take place. The caterpillar leaves the milkweed plant, crawling twenty to thirty feet away in search of a safe place to pupate, and lays down a silklike mat. It then attaches itself to this mat with a hook near its tail and hangs there for a day. Finally it sheds its skin one last time, revealing an inch-long jade-green casing underneath: the chrysalis. For the next ten to fourteen days, the caterpillar will stay inside this chrysalis, which from the outside appears immobile. But inside there is a magical alchemical process taking place. The caterpillar's body is breaking down into a soupy substance, and is reforming into that of a butterfly. The caterpillar's chewing mouthparts are becoming a proboscis, as it will only drink from now on. Its eyes are growing larger, and its eyesight will improve dramatically. Reproductive organs, which were absent in the larval stage, are forming. The emerging butterfly will have three pairs of legs instead of eight, and wings.

The pupa or chrysalis stage is about meditation, reflection, and stillness, but also about recreation and regeneration. In contrast to when it was inside the egg, the caterpillar has now seen and heard things; it has tasted the world; it is conscious of itself. The caterpillar will shed everything that no longer serves it; it will grow wings and become what it wishes to be. The seed has sprouted and a shoot is growing. The chrysalis represents clarity and enlightenment—the moment when one takes all the knowledge one has gathered, wraps oneself up in it, and emerges a different being. The chrysalis is about understanding and embracing one's true form, about becoming one's true self.

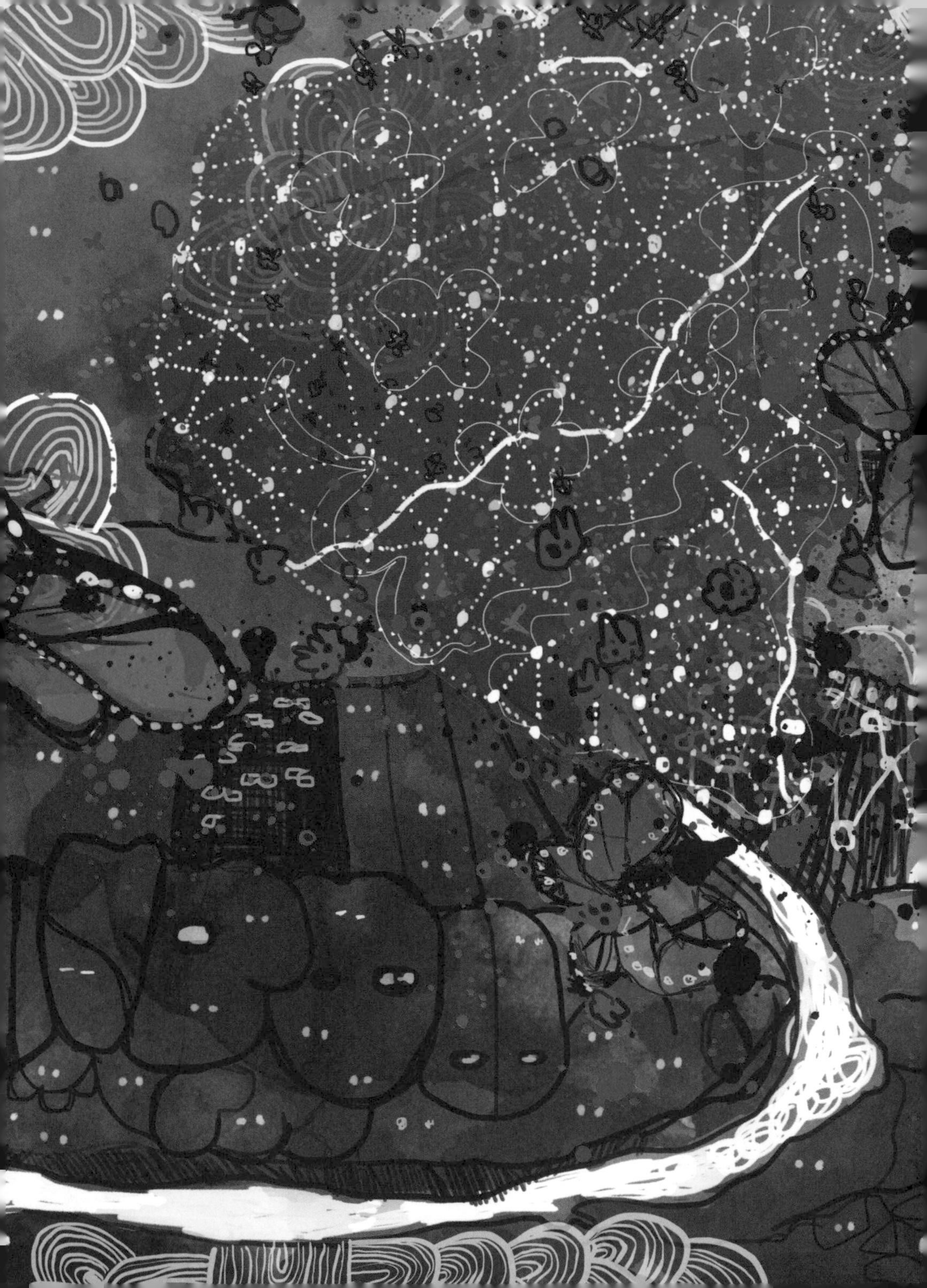

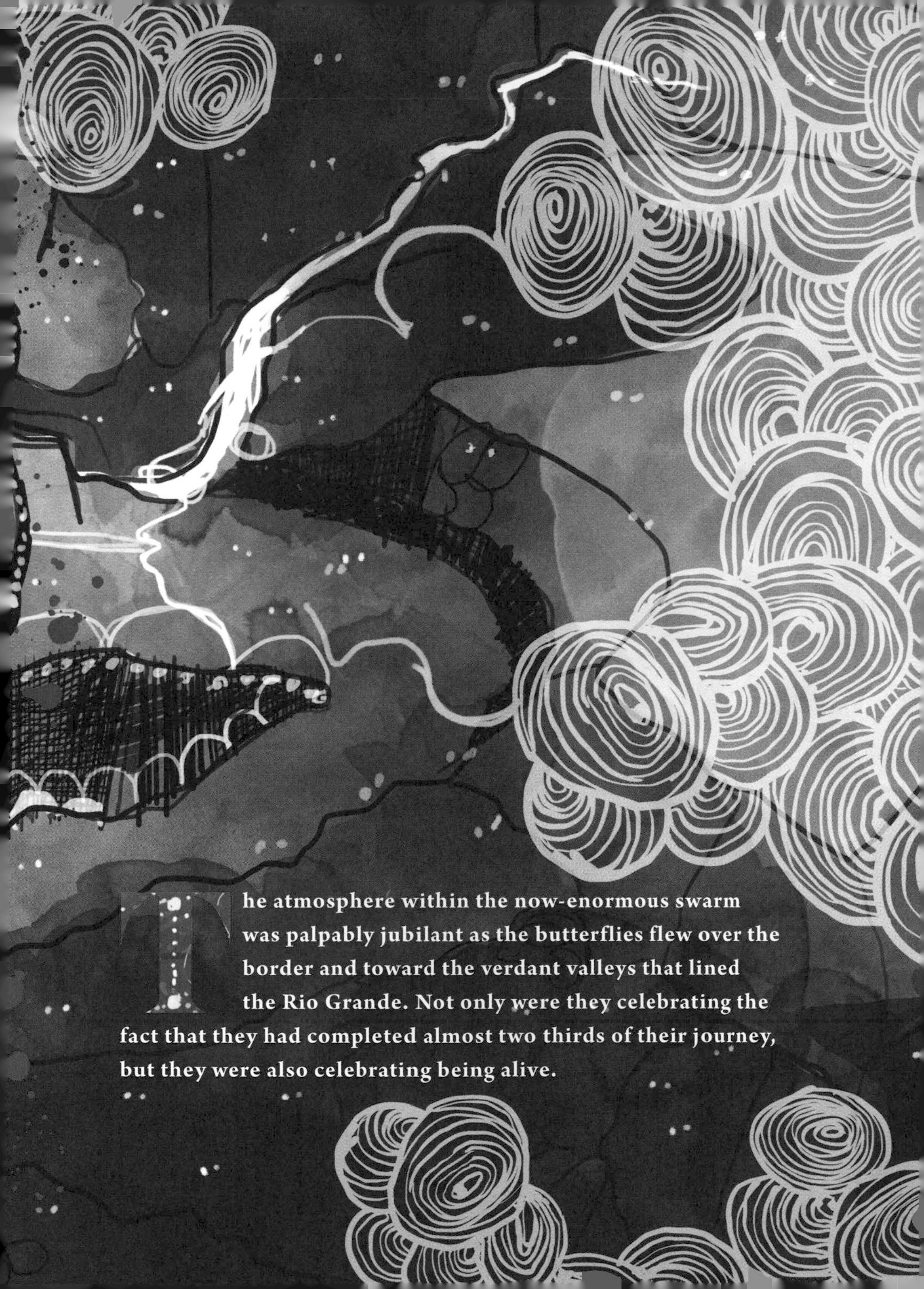

The atmosphere within the now-enormous swarm was palpably jubilant as the butterflies flew over the border and toward the verdant valleys that lined the Rio Grande. Not only were they celebrating the fact that they had completed almost two thirds of their journey, but they were also celebrating being alive.

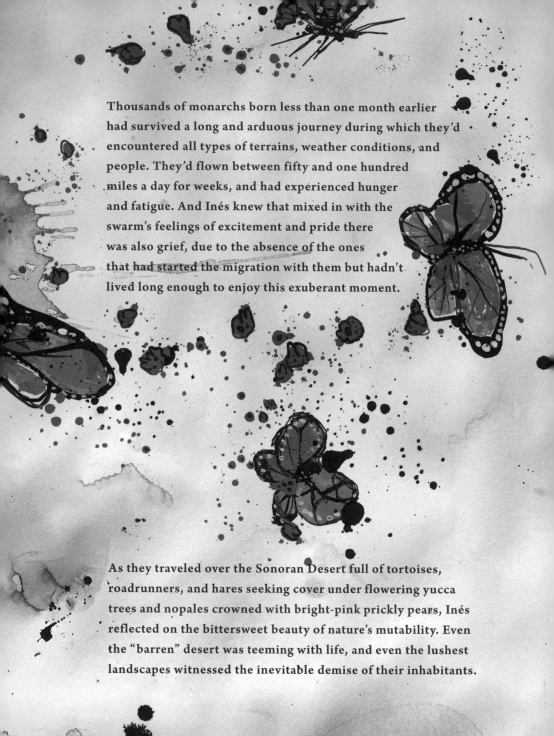

Thousands of monarchs born less than one month earlier had survived a long and arduous journey during which they'd encountered all types of terrains, weather conditions, and people. They'd flown between fifty and one hundred miles a day for weeks, and had experienced hunger and fatigue. And Inés knew that mixed in with the swarm's feelings of excitement and pride there was also grief, due to the absence of the ones that had started the migration with them but hadn't lived long enough to enjoy this exuberant moment.

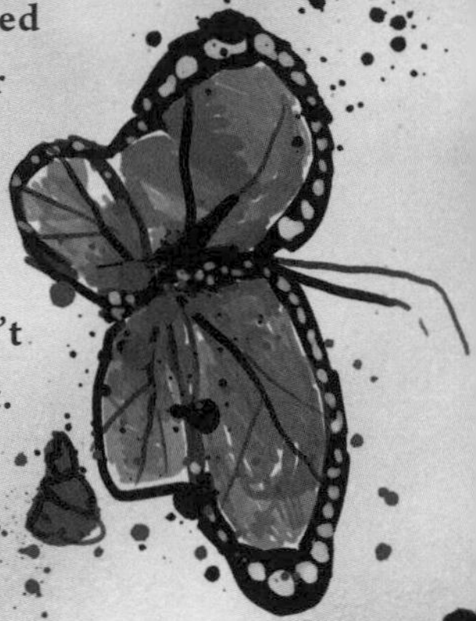

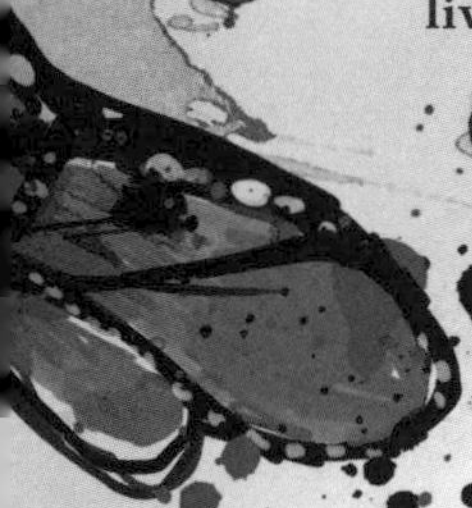

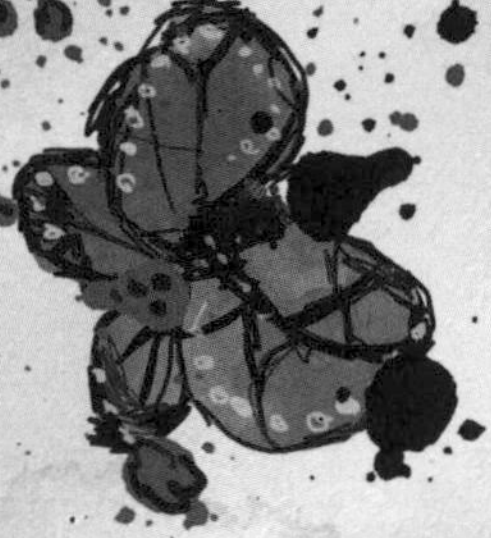

As they traveled over the Sonoran Desert full of tortoises, roadrunners, and hares seeking cover under flowering yucca trees and nopales crowned with bright-pink prickly pears, Inés reflected on the bittersweet beauty of nature's mutability. Even the "barren" desert was teeming with life, and even the lushest landscapes witnessed the inevitable demise of their inhabitants.

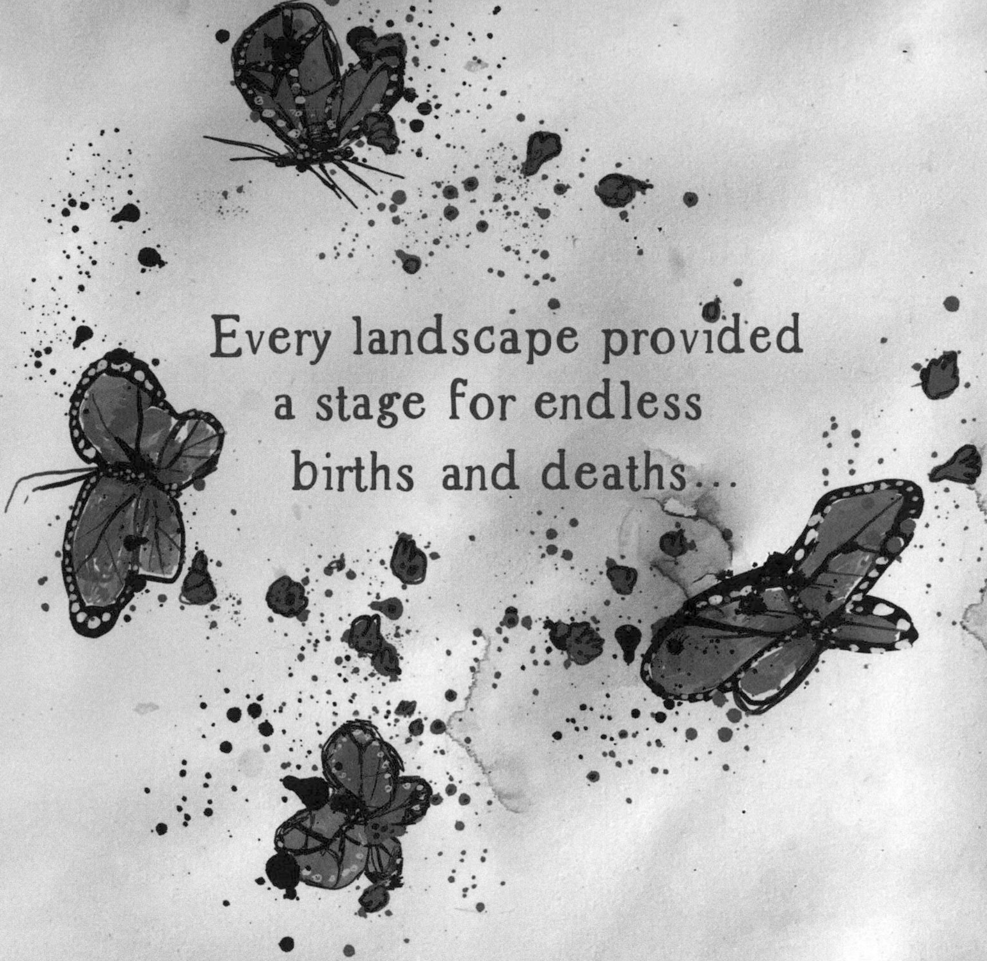

Every landscape provided a stage for endless births and deaths . . .

. . . like a theater to which different productions and performers arrived, acted out their dramas, and then departed again, making way for the next crop. And in the end it appeared it was the flora that enjoyed the longest lifespan, for it was the trees and other plants that saw the seasons come and go, each one bringing with it a cast of characters composed of various mammals, birds, insects, flowers, and fruits. And every fall this desert saw millions of monarch butterflies flying through it, but did the cacti standing guard under the blazing sun realize that the individuals were completely different from last year's?

Inés thought again about the dozens of butterflies her group had lost along the way,

but she felt that those individuals now lived on through the swarm.

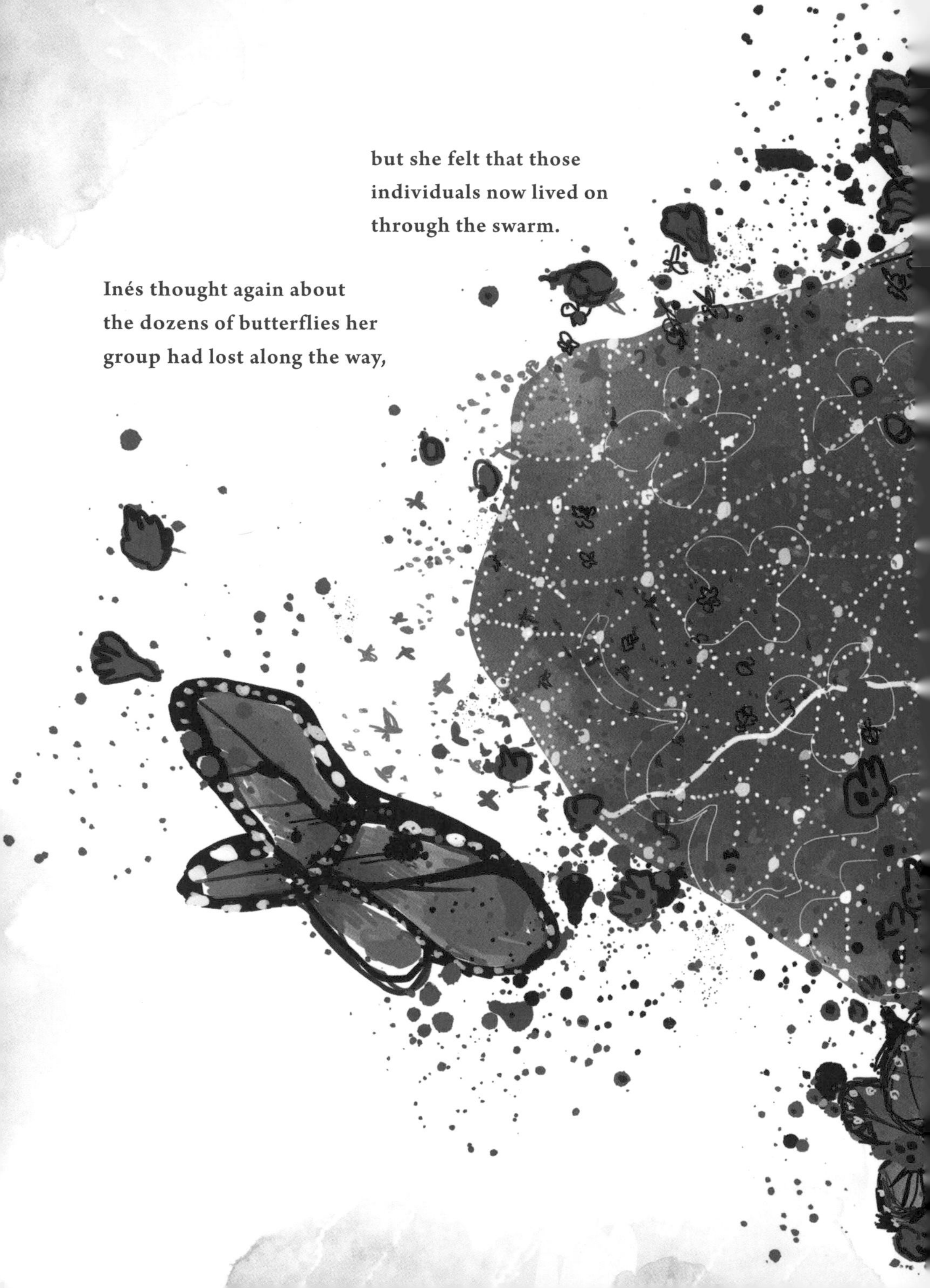

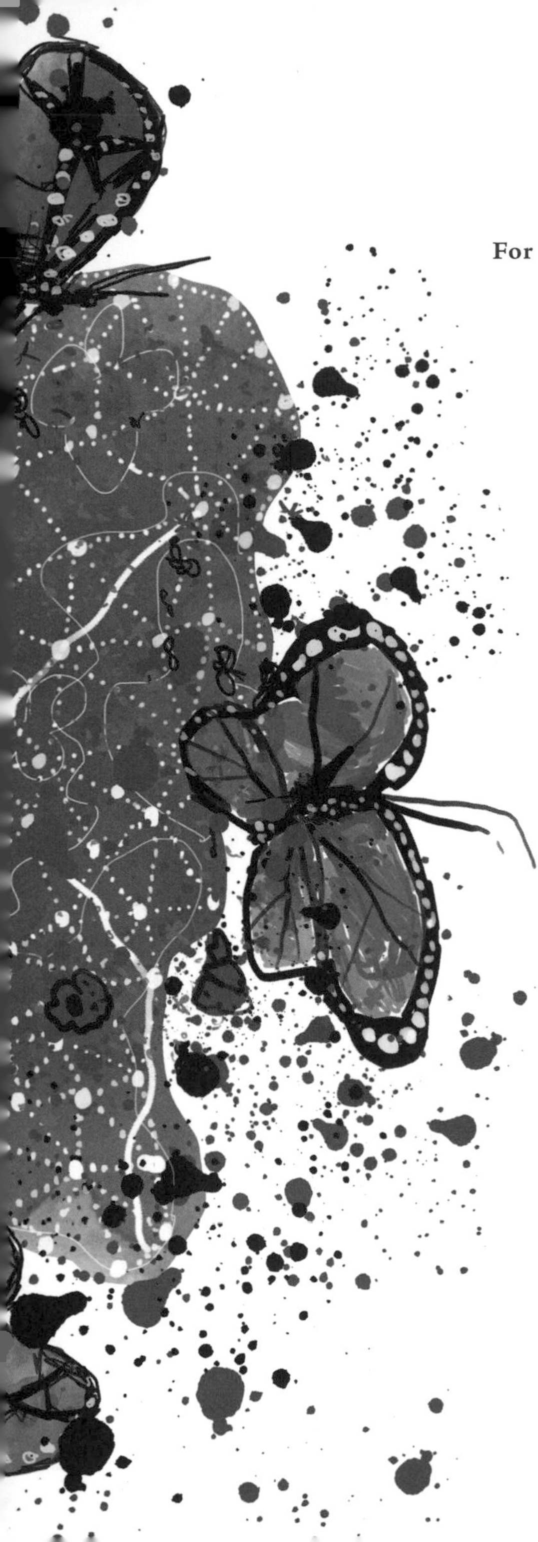

For they shared a common ancestry,

a common destination,

and a common fate,

and no matter how many butterflies there were in a swarm, the word

swarm

would always be a singular word, indicating one unit.

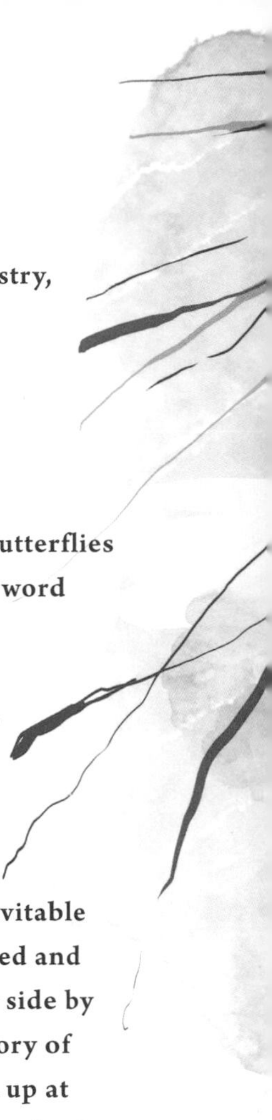

Death and loss were an inevitable part of life, and the deceased and the living would always fly side by side in the collective memory of the monarchs. Inés looked up at the lights in the sky—those glowing tendrils that connected the swarm to the world—and realized that they were shining brighter than ever. Perhaps the spirits of their lost had become energy and light and were now helping to guide them forward.

Inés and her swarm flew for hours in the windless heat, now part of a giant caravan of migrating butterflies. Suddenly someone announced that there was a patch of desert milkweed up ahead, but there were also humans—lots of them—and the monarchs were wary of people now. Inés braced herself for yet another human-related danger, and flew to the front of her swarm to investigate. There was indeed a large group of people walking in the distance and heading in their direction, and Inés could see that there were men, women, and children amongst them. She knew there was only one thing these families could be doing in the middle of the punishing desert, and she turned to her fellow butterflies to calm them.

"They won't bother us," she assured them. "It's safe to land on the milkweed."

Valerio looked skeptical. "I don't know, Inés. We were almost killed by just one person twice, and look how many of them there are."

"I know we've had bad experiences with humans, but there are many good humans in the world too. These people are migrating, just like us. They're tired and hungry, just like us."

"Migrating humans?" Josephine asked.

"We're escaping the winter by heading to a country where there's warmth and food for us, and they're escaping poverty and violence by heading to a country where there are opportunities for them. In the end we're just the same—living beings trying to survive and protect our families."

The monarchs didn't understand the words poverty and violence, for thankfully these were not concepts in the butterfly world, but they trusted Inés and were desperate to rest and feed. They started to alight on the milkweed shrubs—even as the large group of migrants moved closer to them—and Inés sighed with relief. She was famished and exhausted too.

It was the children who spotted the butterflies first. Inés heard their excited cries of, "¡Mira las mariposas!" and "¡Son mariposas monarcas!" And perhaps the entire group took this encounter with the swarm to be a good omen, for they too decided to stop and rest, settling down only a few yards away from the butterflies.

As Inés fed on milkweed, she examined some of the human faces and could see fatigue and worry there. One family in particular caught her attention: a man who was carrying a boy on his shoulders and a woman holding a little girl's hand. The family of four approached a spot a few feet from Inés, and the man leaned over so the boy could climb off him. The woman laid out a sheet and they all sat down on it, then the man pulled some peaches and bottles of water out of a knapsack and passed them around. Inés felt her heart tighten as she thought about her own family back home—a mother, father, sister, and brother just like this family.

Josephine noticed Inés watching them and caressed her back with one wing. "I believe you when you say that you used to be a human, and that the people in that house were your family. I saw you as a girl in your bedroom; I just didn't realize that the butterfly that then appeared next to me was *you*."

Inés turned to look at Josephine and smiled sadly. "Thank you, Josephine. I miss my family very much. But you're my family too now—the whole swarm is. And ever since I started to see the world from a nonhuman perspective, it looks very different. If I ever become a girl again, I'm going to dedicate my life to helping other species.

120

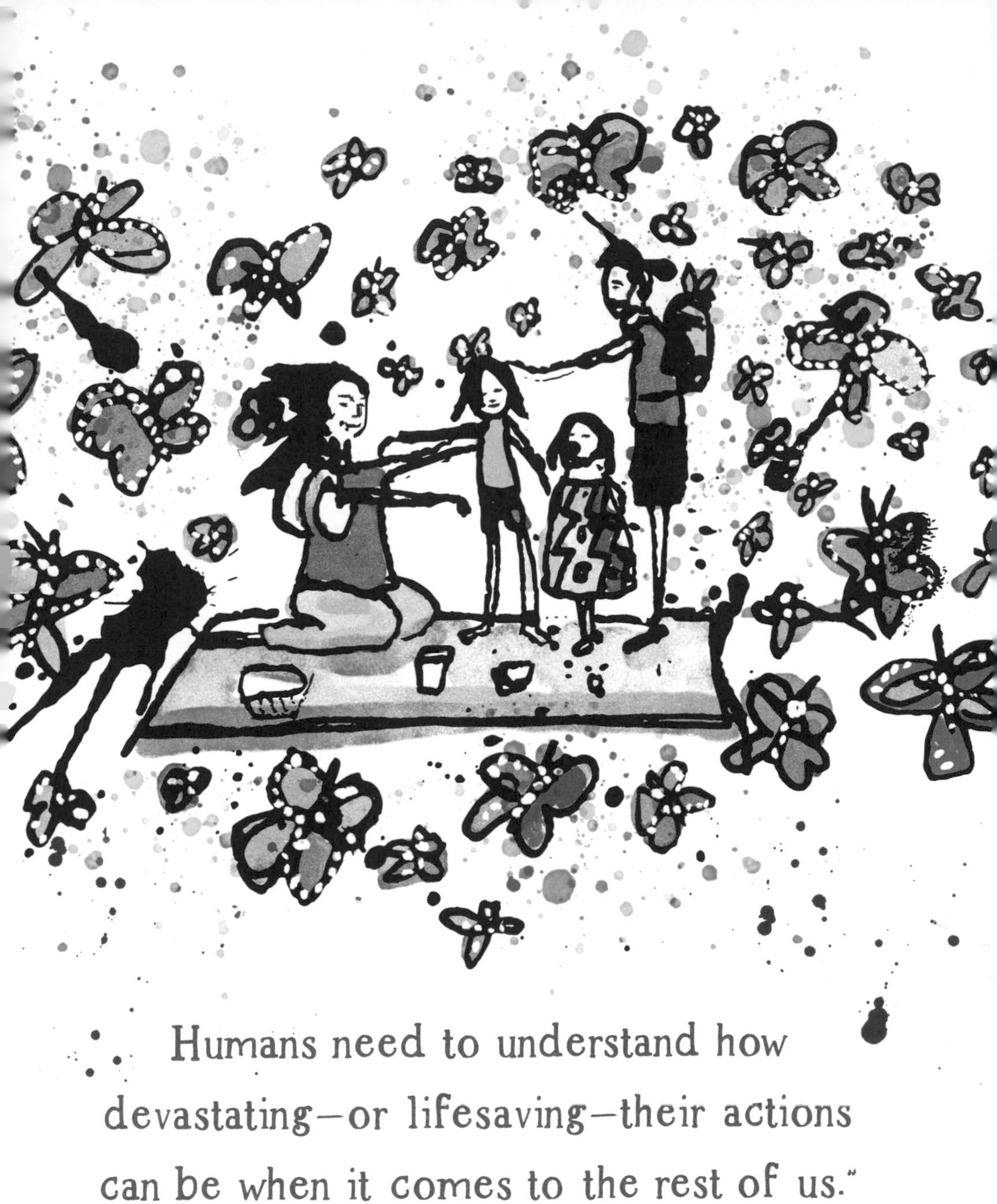

Humans need to understand how devastating—or lifesaving—their actions can be when it comes to the rest of us."

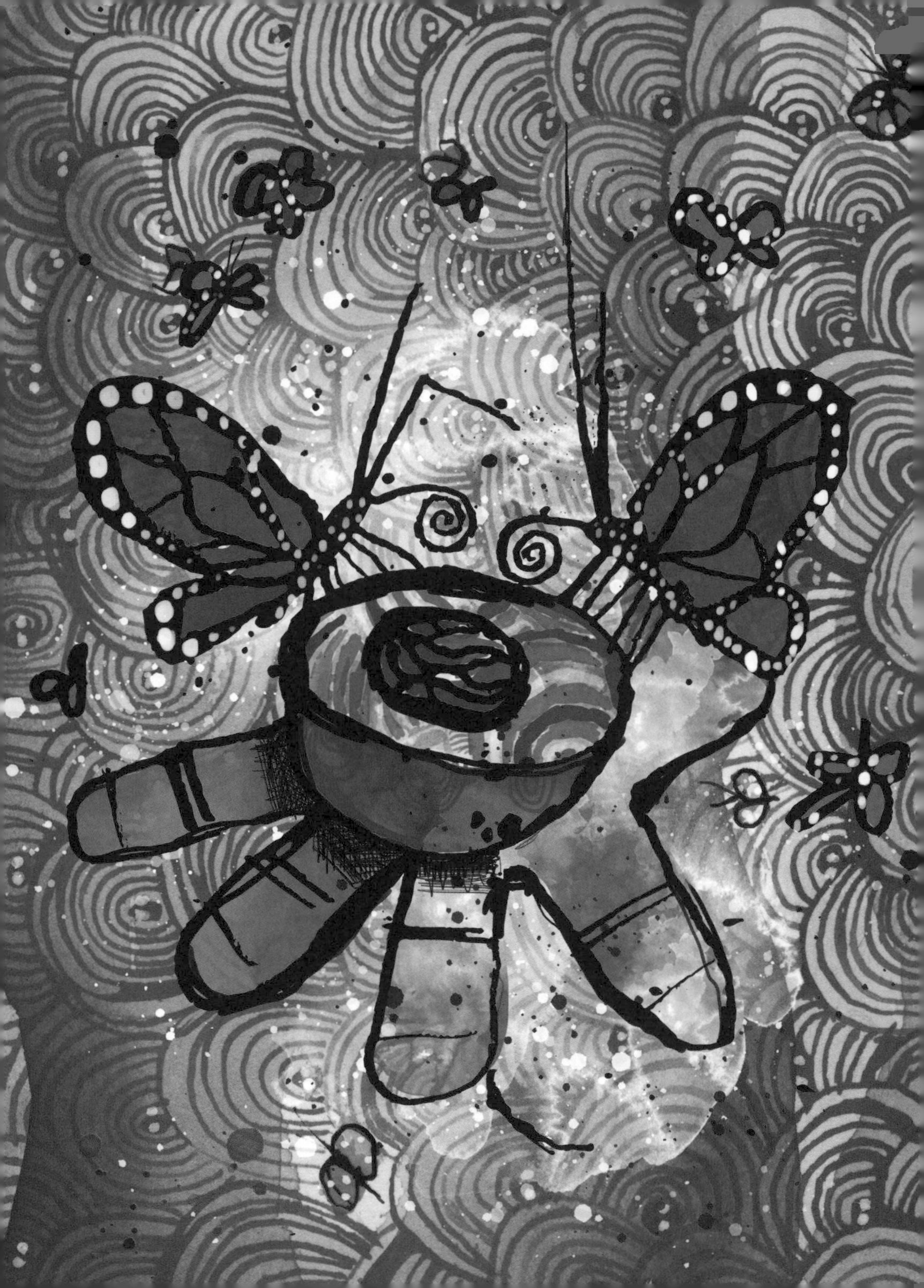

Almost as if he had understood Inés's words, the boy looked over at the butterflies and then down at his peach. "¿Les puedo ofrecer un poco a las mariposas?" he asked his parents. His mother replied that yes, he could offer the butterflies some, but who knows if they'd eat it.

The boy placed half a wedge of peach in his palm and held it out toward Inés and Josephine. Inés nodded to Josephine reassuringly, and the two of them flew over and landed on the boy's hand. As they imbibed the fruit's sweet and delicious juice, the boy's eyes widened and shone with delight. The boy's mother and father and sister were all grinning from ear to ear, and Inés noticed that all the migrants were observing the swarm as they ate. She could sense how welcome and uplifting this encounter was for them—it seemed the natural world had the capacity to instantly lift the human spirit. Perhaps people had forgotten they were a part of it, but when immersed in it they felt a sense of belonging again.

And so the two groups of migrants crossed paths in the middle of the desert, sharing this brief moment of communion in time and space. They parted ways some twenty minutes later—one flying south and the other marching north—and Inés looked over her winged shoulder to get a last look at the humans. She could still see some smiles lingering on their sunburned faces, and the group seemed more energized now, radiating warmth and strength. For both groups of travelers the greatest challenges lay ahead, but each individual had placed their faith in their community, knowing they were more likely to succeed together than alone.

The desert eventually gave way to the oak- and pine-covered mountaintops of the western Sierra Madre and, as the late-afternoon sun bore down on them, the weary butterflies stopped to rest in a cool, green forest. But no sooner had they settled in clusters on an oak tree than a group of around fifteen black-headed grosbeaks and black-backed orioles—birds whose orange, black, and white coloring was not unlike their own—descended upon the butterflies hungrily. The birds' arrival was so swift and unexpected that it took mere seconds for each bird to grab a monarch in its beak and begin to consume its abdomen,

letting the disembodied wings

flutter lifelessly

to the ground.

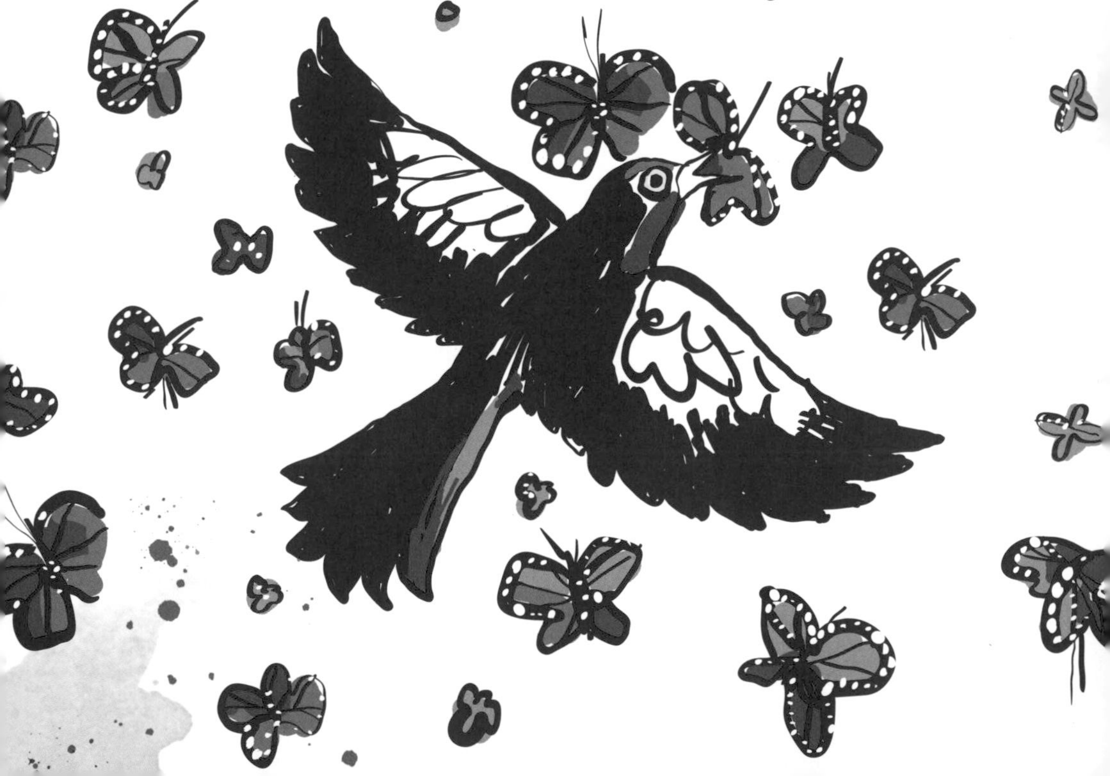

Inés and Josephine, perched next to each other on a branch, watched with terror as the birds darted about and pecked at butterflies around them. A grosbeak jumped from another branch onto theirs and regarded them with an enormous, shiny brown eye. Its beak was not particularly pointy or sharp, but to Inés it resembled a giant pair of pruning shears. Inés and Josephine instinctively felt it was better to stay still than to fly away, and the bird quickly moved on, choosing a nearby male as its meal instead.

A few minutes later the birds had had their fill and took off as suddenly as they'd arrived, allowing the surviving monarchs to resume stirring and breathe a collective sigh of relief. They took stock of their losses and discovered that the birds had taken around sixty males, who were less toxic to the predators than the female monarchs. The butterflies decided to move on rather than spend the night in this forest, as the birds would surely return seeking breakfast in the morning.

The butterflies settled in another forest and hoped for the best. That evening Inés thought back on the bird attack and marveled at how terrifying birds were if you were an insect. But at the same time, Inés knew that the birds had preyed on them out of necessity, and they'd taken only the amount they needed to survive. That was certainly different from humans, some of whom ate animals three times a day when they didn't need to eat them at all, and ate animals who'd never had a taste of freedom or a chance at survival, the way the consumed butterflies had.

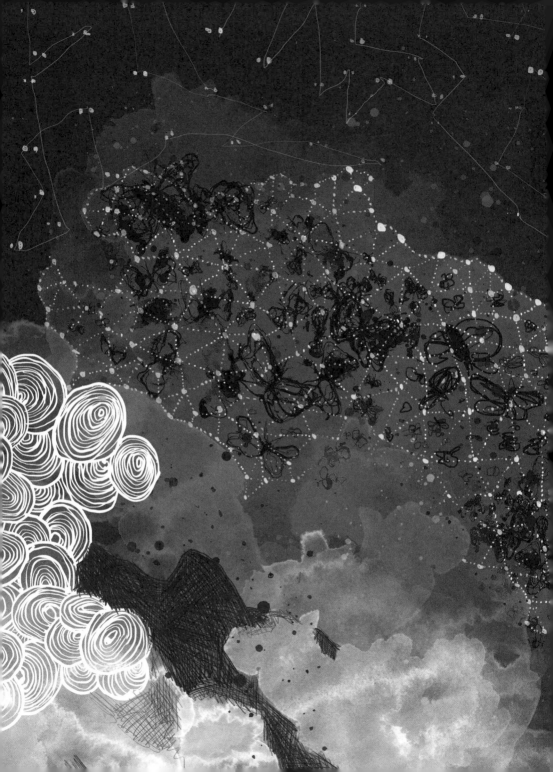

The swarm glided south on a thermal—an upper air mass—which helped them conserve energy as they continued to travel over the Sierra Madre and on toward the Sierra Gorda. And then finally a few days later, as they approached the state of Michoacán, the butterflies noticed that the lights in the sky were bursting with color and converging on a mountain range in the distance that stood two miles above sea level and contained the swarm's final destination: the monarch butterfly sanctuary.

Nestled in the cool, subtropical hills of the Trans-Mexican Volcanic Belt, this place was the monarchs' El Dorado, providing them with treasure in the form of its *Abies religiosa*—the oyamel fir trees that would protect them from the winter for the next four months. It was their Jerusalem, their Ganges, their Mecca, the ancient homeland from which their species spread out millions of years ago, and the sacred spot where they could commune with the spirits of their ancestors and Mother Nature in her purest and most complete form. And it was the place where, at the end of the winter, many of them would find a mate to create the next generation with.

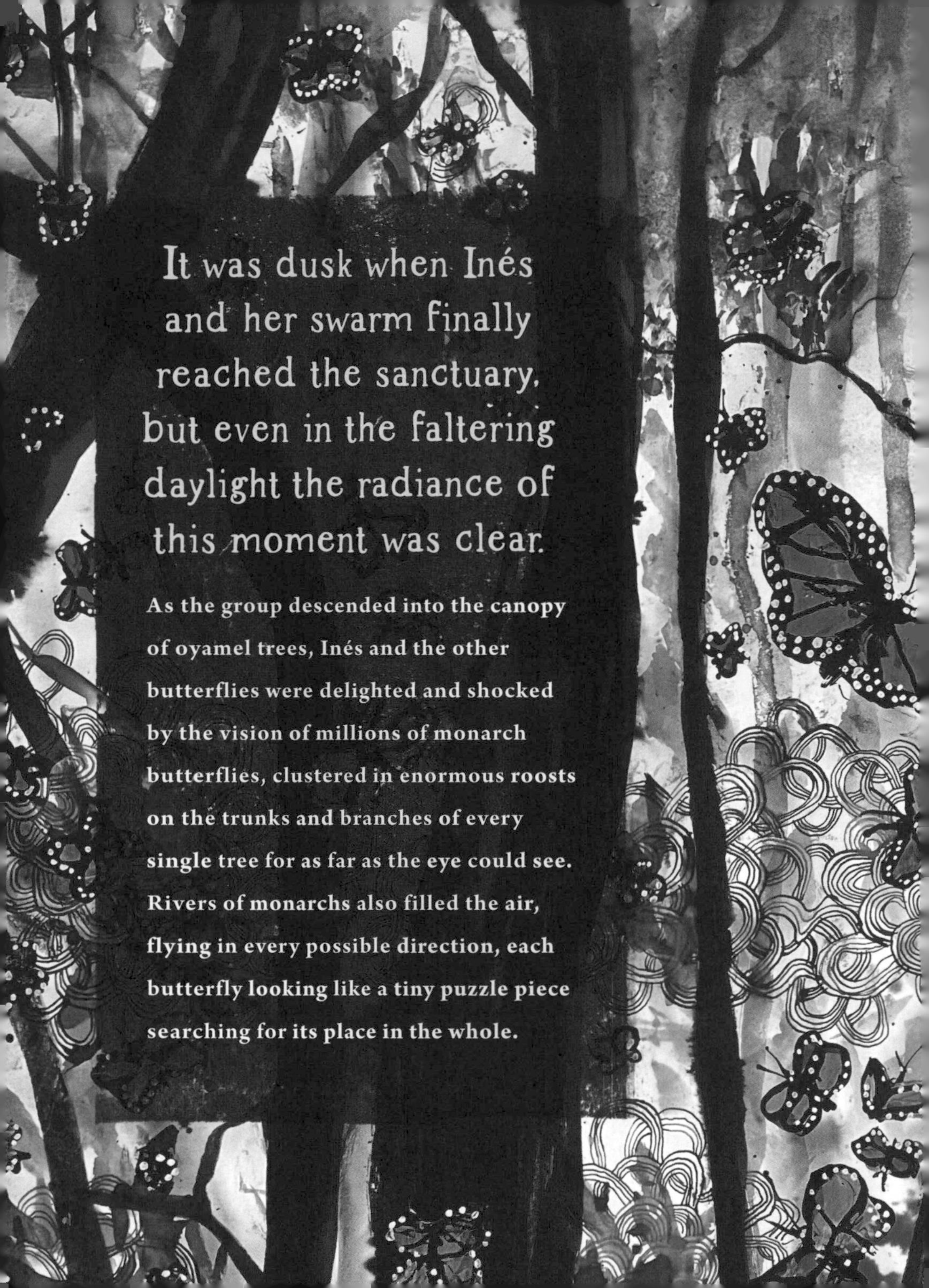

It was dusk when Inés and her swarm finally reached the sanctuary, but even in the faltering daylight the radiance of this moment was clear.

As the group descended into the canopy of oyamel trees, Inés and the other butterflies were delighted and shocked by the vision of millions of monarch butterflies, clustered in enormous roosts on the trunks and branches of every single tree for as far as the eye could see. Rivers of monarchs also filled the air, flying in every possible direction, each butterfly looking like a tiny puzzle piece searching for its place in the whole.

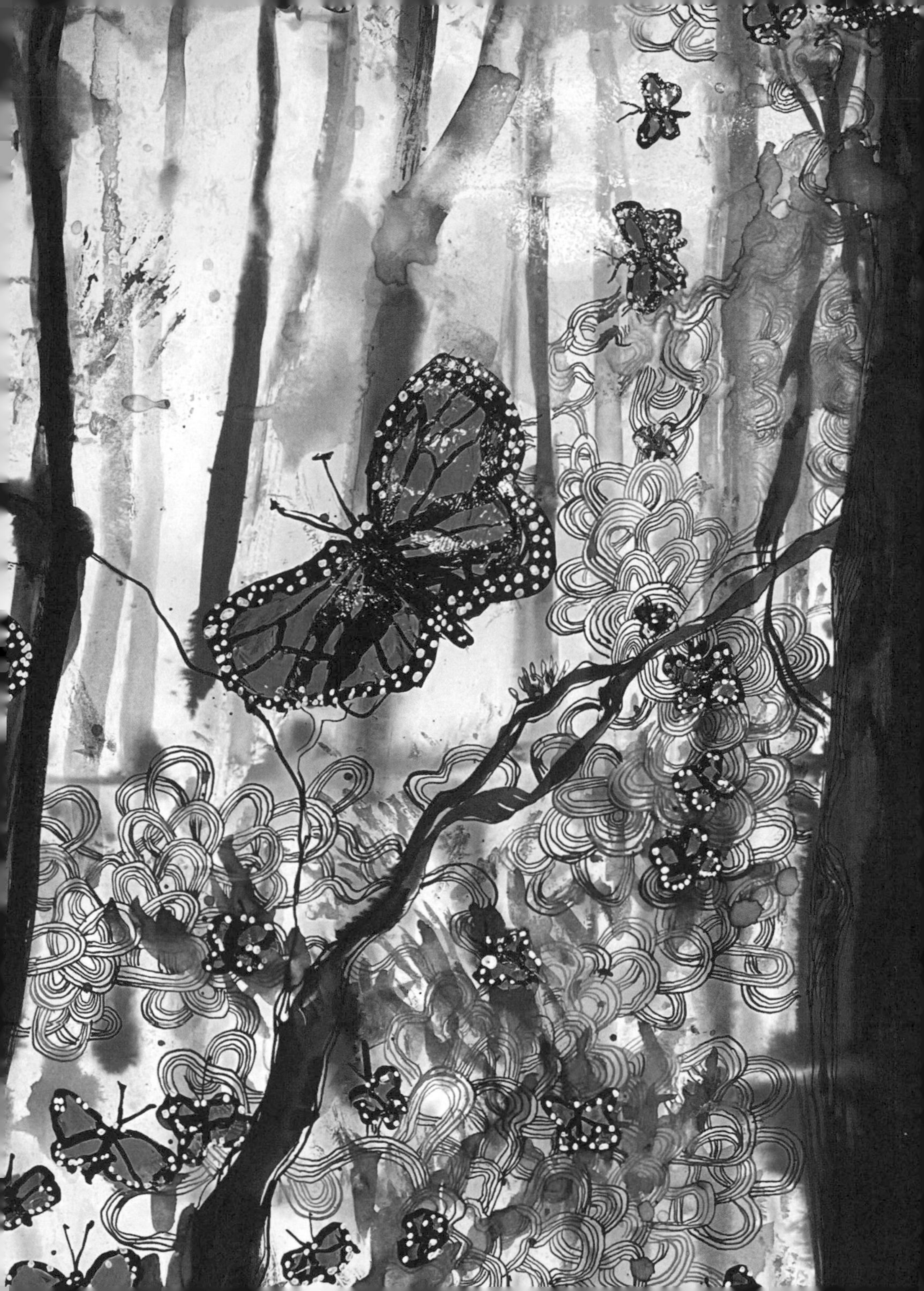

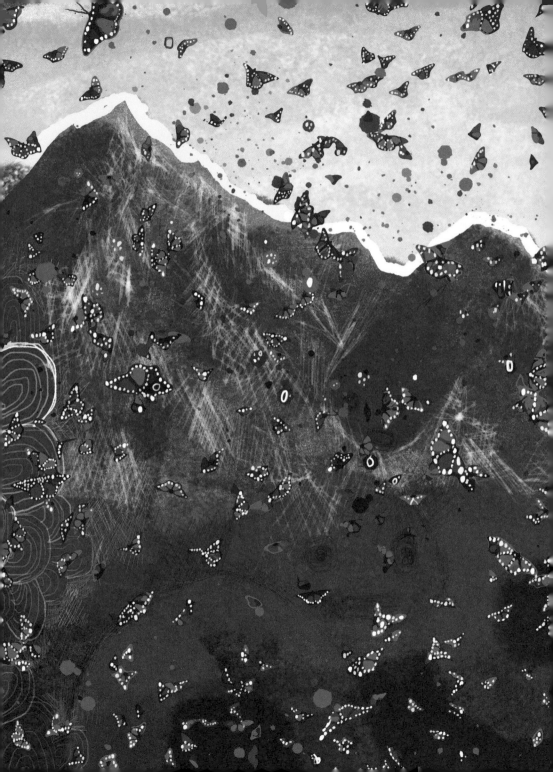

The monarchs who had preceded them rejoiced at the arriving swarm, for the more of them there were, the better it was for them as a species, the greater chance each individual had at survival, and the more options they had for mating. Each and every one of them had just concluded an immense and exhausting journey, and now it was time to relax and celebrate. It was like a gigantic gathering for relatives who'd never met, but whose main purpose since the day they'd been born had been to arrive here, at this family reunion. The fourth-generation monarchs all shared this common destiny, and reaching this sanctuary had, up until now, been their sole purpose. Their bodies and spirits had been propelled forward by a mysterious need and desire that guided them to this home, which was both familiar and comforting, yet entirely new.

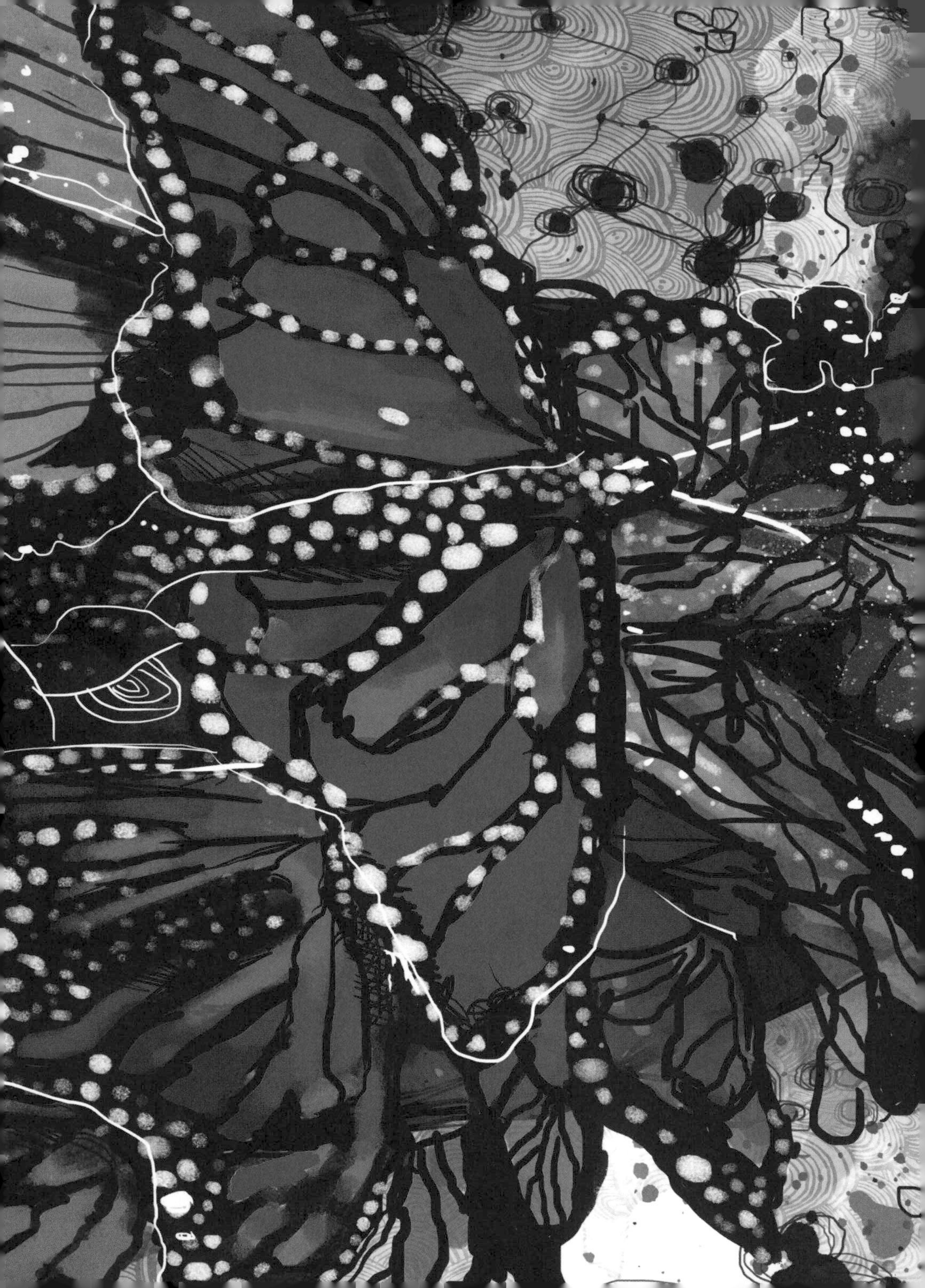

Before long it was dark and Inés found a spot on a tree with Josephine and Valerio—whom she had been careful to stay close to—and hundreds of others. Before she fell asleep, her thoughts returned to Caligo's ominous declaration and to her family in the United States. Were they safe now that she was here? And what was the battle he had referred to? Was it their close encounter with the airplane, their escape from the butterfly collector, or the bird attack? And lastly, would she ever turn into a human again? She knew that her father's village, where her grandmother Andrea still lived, lay at the base of this very mountain. Wanting to hear news about her family, Inés decided that she would go in search of Andrea the following day.

Inés was ruminating on these thoughts when she heard the motors of several vehicles ascending the mountain, followed by the voices of men speaking Spanish. She unpeeled herself from the huge cluster of butterflies she was in and flew down to investigate.

Inés watched with alarm as six men wearing headlamps climbed out of three flatbed trucks with chainsaws in their hands. They approached six oyamel trees that stood at the edge of the forest—trees that were completely blanketed in sleeping monarchs—

and turned on their chainsaws.

A seventh man with a mustache and a hawk on his shoulder got out of a van and gave orders; he was clearly the leader of this clandestine and illegal operation. Inés knew that this forest was protected—she had learned about it in school— and if the men were coming at night, it was because they wished to hide their actions.

The six men proceeded to slice through the tall but slender trunks of their chosen oyamel trees. Inés thought she could hear each tree emitting a faint but distinctive wail as its body was severed. Before long the trees crashed down onto their sides, with many of the butterflies managing to fly off but others being crushed between the trees and the forest floor. The men then cut the trunks up into smaller pieces and loaded the logs onto the back of their trucks.

After about an hour they finished their work and got back into their vehicles. As the trucks pulled away, followed by the van, Inés noticed a logo painted on the smaller vehicle's side: an avocado wearing a sombrero above the words "Aguacates Don Pascual." Inés felt a chill run through her body as she recalled the phone call between the pilot in Pennsylvania and the mystery person on the other end of the line—the one whose avocado farms the pilot had sent pesticides to. As the vehicles made their way down the side of the mountain, Inés flew to a tree near the road to see where they were headed.

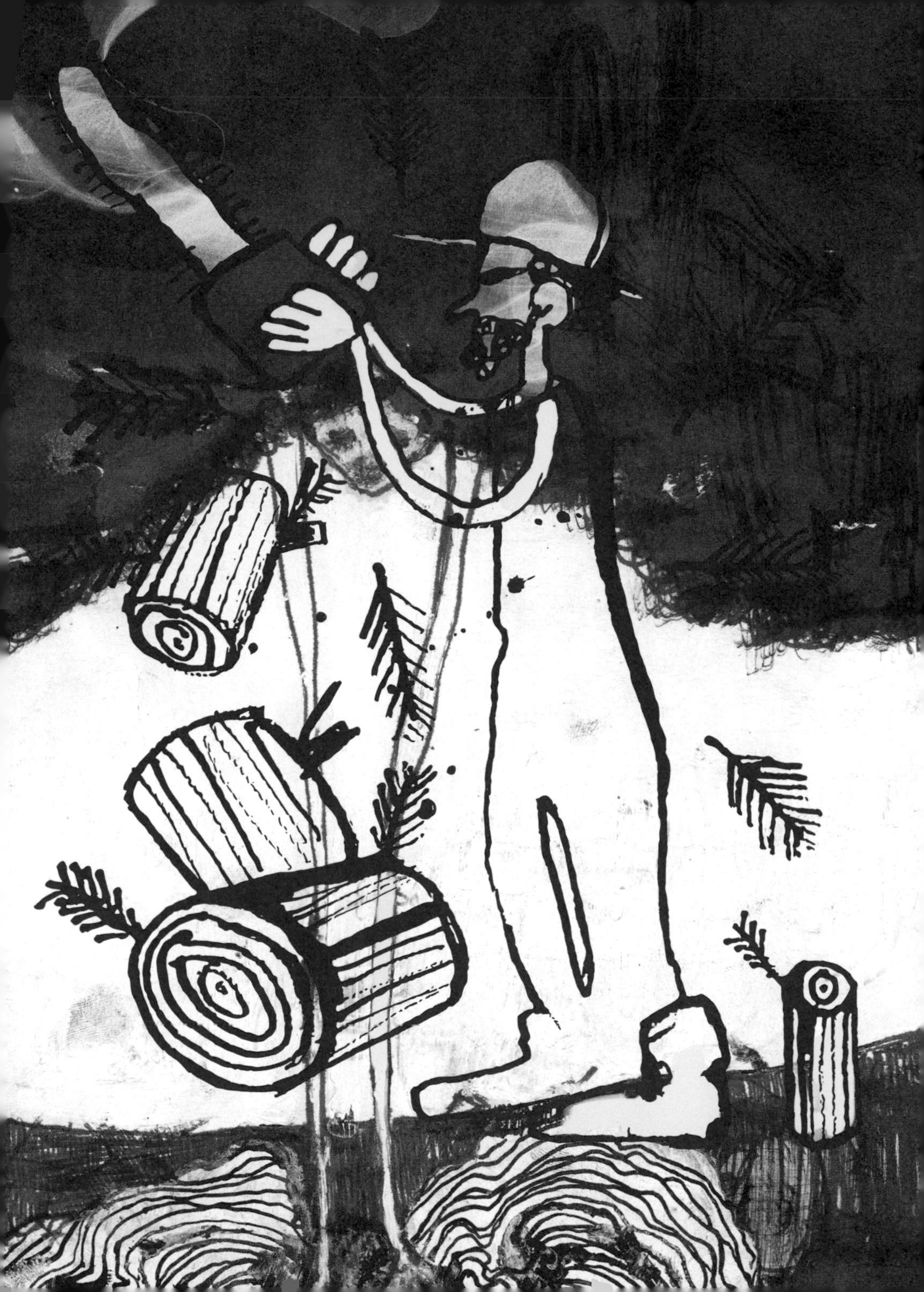

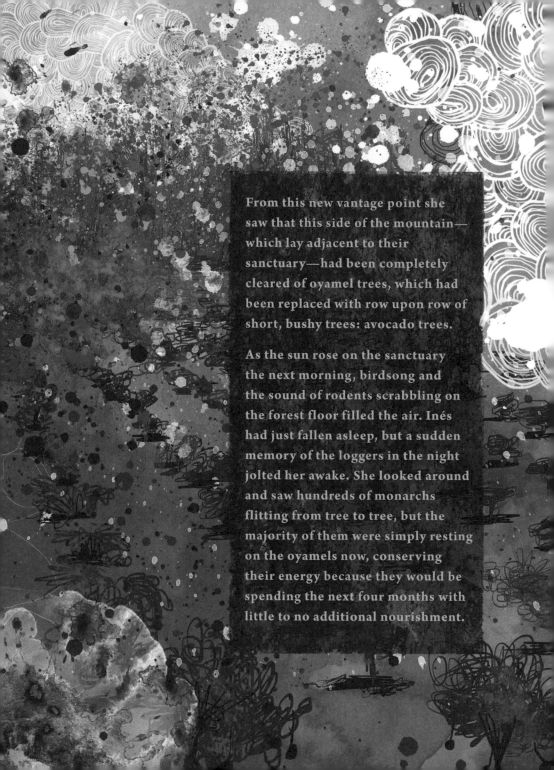

From this new vantage point she saw that this side of the mountain—which lay adjacent to their sanctuary—had been completely cleared of oyamel trees, which had been replaced with row upon row of short, bushy trees: avocado trees.

As the sun rose on the sanctuary the next morning, birdsong and the sound of rodents scrabbling on the forest floor filled the air. Inés had just fallen asleep, but a sudden memory of the loggers in the night jolted her awake. She looked around and saw hundreds of monarchs flitting from tree to tree, but the majority of them were simply resting on the oyamels now, conserving their energy because they would be spending the next four months with little to no additional nourishment.

Inés heard whistling and footsteps and looked down to see a grade-school boy making his way up a path with a large sketchpad under one arm and a tote bag hanging from the other. He stopped when he reached the top of the hill and walked over to the stumps of the trees that had just been cut down. Inés heard him curse with anger, but then he squinted up and saw the majestic tapestry of monarchs in the many trees that still remained, and his expression softened. He smiled contentedly before sitting down at the base of an oyamel and leaning his back against the trunk.

The boy pulled a box of pencils out of his bag and started to sketch some monarchs that had landed on a stone a few feet away. Inés flew down to watch and was impressed by his work: despite his young age, the butterflies were drawn with the right proportions and with scientific attention to detail. Inés flew to the tip of his shoe and looked at him expectantly, trying to figure out a way to communicate with this person who clearly appreciated them. When the boy noticed her, he started to draw her instead, flicking his eyes back and forth from Inés to the page. He pressed a little too hard on his pencil and the tip broke off, causing him to exclaim softly and pull another pencil out of the box.

Inés followed the pencil tip with her eyes as it landed on the ground nearby, and suddenly she had an idea. She flew over to the tiny piece of lead, picked it up with her front legs, and flew over to land on the boy's sketchpad. She then dragged the pencil tip up and down on a corner of the page, writing clear letters as the boy's eyes widened with amazement. She wrote the words "Doña Andrea" and then turned to look at the boy expectantly.

"¿Te refieres a Doña Andrea, la viejita que vive en el pueblo?" the boy asked. Yes, Inés was asking about the old lady named Andrea who lived in the village. The boy then asked if she wanted him to go find her, and Inés wrote "Sí" with the pencil tip. The boy nodded excitedly and promptly stood up to embark on this incredible mission—fulfilling a monarch butterfly's request. He headed back toward the path leading down the mountain, and meanwhile Inés rushed to where Josephine and Valerio were still roosting and asked them to come with her immediately. The three of them flew to catch up with the boy, landed on his shoulder, and hitched a ride there down to the village. The boy walked slowly and carefully, not wanting to disturb the butterflies.

When they entered the bustling village and Inés looked around, she quickly realized that it was November 2nd, or the Day of the Dead. They passed a cemetery where people were busy sweeping graves and adorning them with brilliant orange marigolds, while grinning sugar skulls and *pan de muertos* beckoned from every bakery window. None of the people they encountered seemed to notice the boy walking by with three butterflies on his shoulder, but Inés figured that three monarch butterflies probably weren't that enthralling in a village whose inhabitants had seen millions upon millions of them.

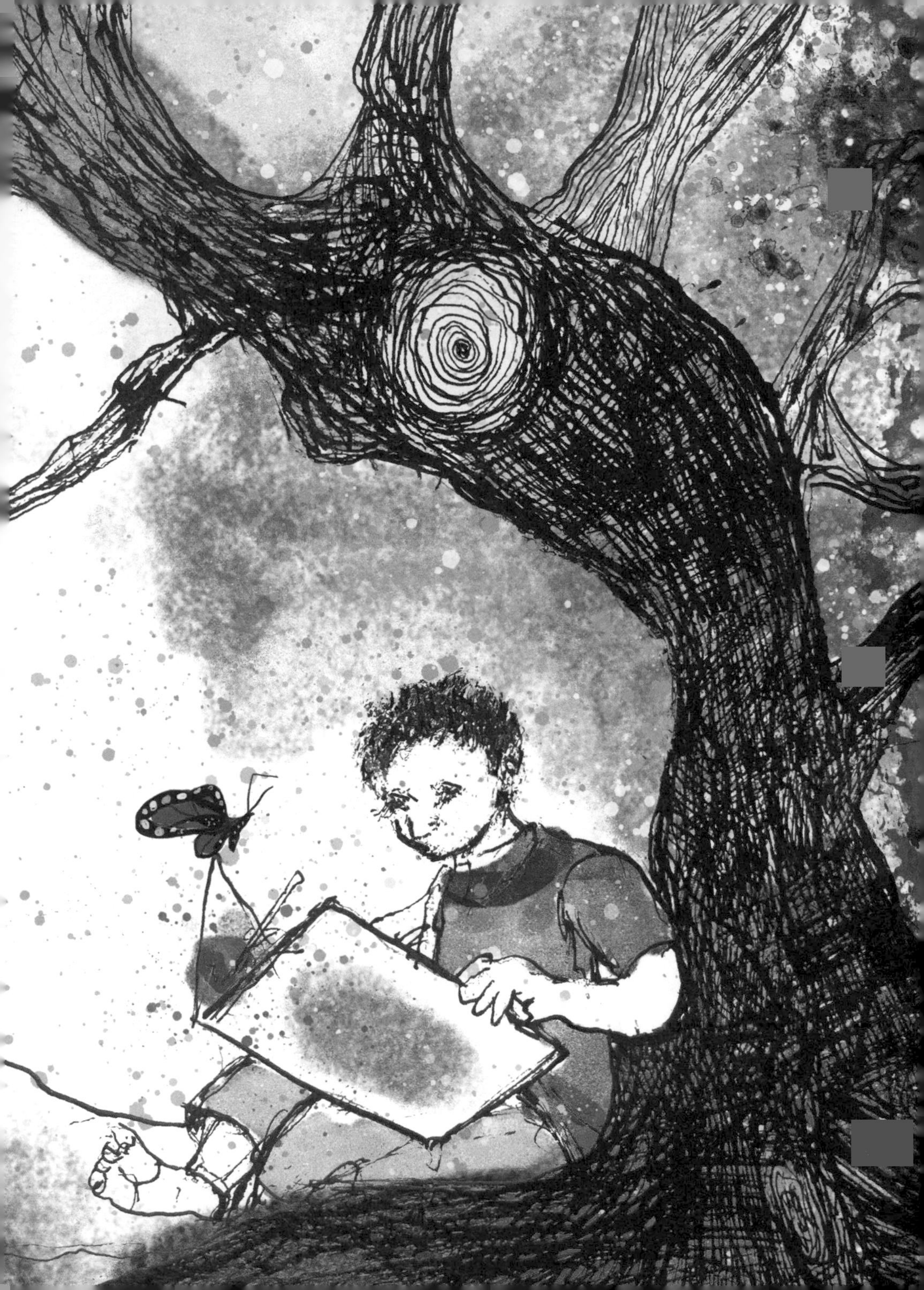

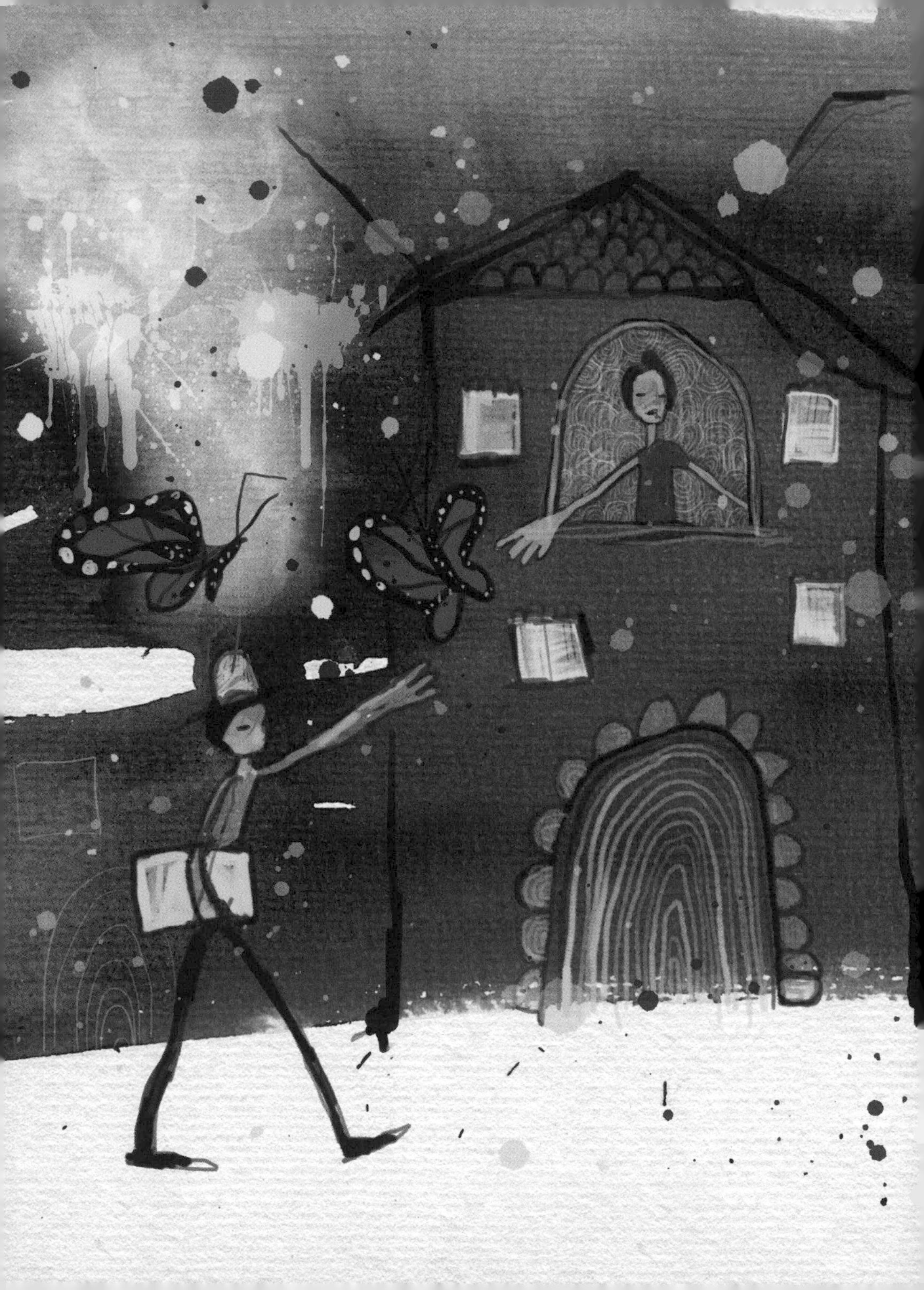

But there was one person who definitely noticed, and that was Inés's grandmother Andrea. As the boy approached her small, royal-blue house, she peered out her open kitchen window and cried out, "Homero! What is this wonderful gift you're bringing me today?"

Homero smiled and explained to her that he'd been up on the cerro drawing the butterflies when one of them—the female with two straight antennae as opposed to the female with a crooked one—had somehow picked up his broken pencil tip and written Andrea's name with it. Andrea seemed very pleased with this information, but not at all surprised. Nodding as if it were the most natural butterfly behavior in the world, she insisted that Homero and the monarchs come inside.

As they entered her grandmother's house, Inés recognized the smell of the wonderful green mole made with fresh chayotes that Andrea always made. She flew off Homero's shoulder and landed on Andrea's open palm, and her grandmother looked her squarely in the eye and said,

"I'm so proud of you for completing the migration, Inés, and grateful that you knew to come and find me."

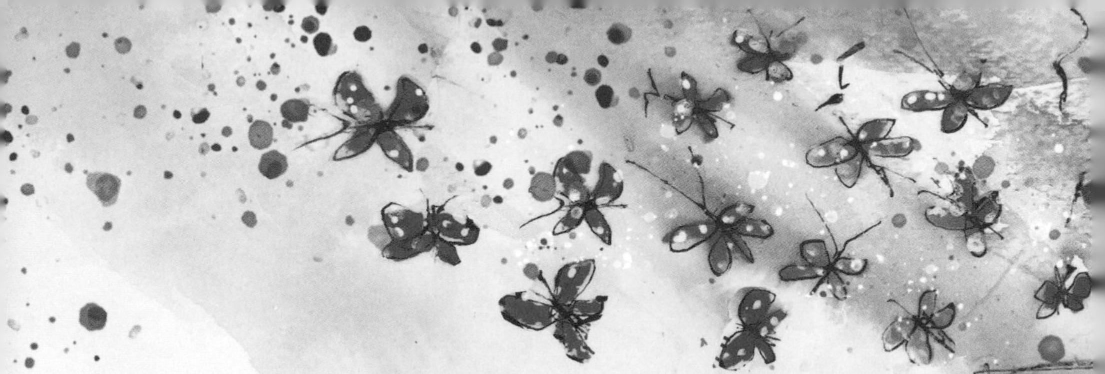

Inés immediately felt immense relief, for she was surely safe now that she was with a loving family member who knew who she really was. "But *how* did she know?" Inés wondered.

Andrea invited everyone to take a seat at the kitchen table, and when Homero had sat on a chair and the butterflies had settled on the embroidered tablecloth, Andrea turned to look at Josephine and Valerio. "What are your names, dears?"

Josephine and Valerio introduced themselves, suddenly realizing that Andrea could understand their words and they could understand hers. "So you speak butterfly?" asked Josephine.

Andrea chuckled. "I do, but it's not a language I had to learn. I was born knowing how to speak it, as was Inés. I'm very happy to see that Inés made good friends during her migration here, and I want to hear all about the adventures you've had. But I'm afraid these stories will have to wait for another day, as right now there's an urgent danger facing you."

"Are you referring to the men cutting down trees in our sanctuary?" asked Inés. "Who I believe are avocado cultivators? I saw them last night, when they came to cut down six oyamel trees."

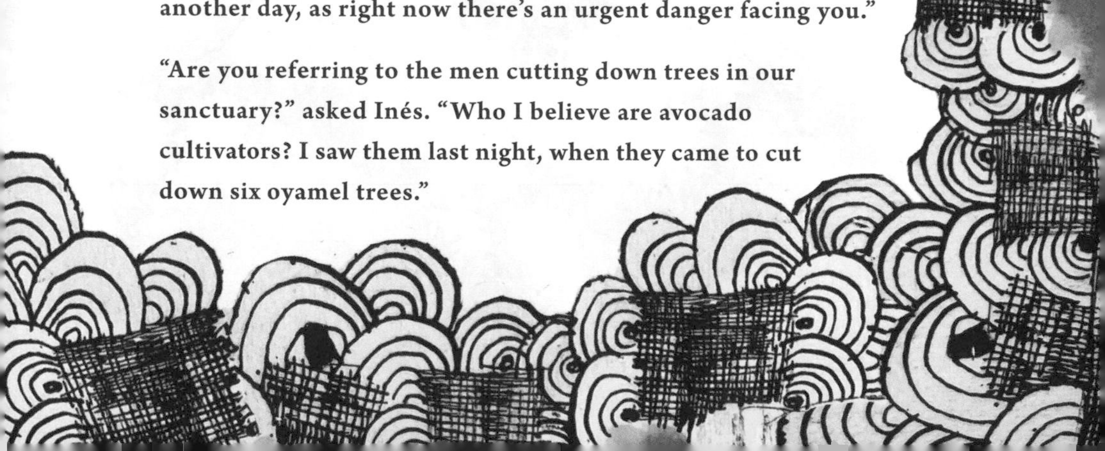

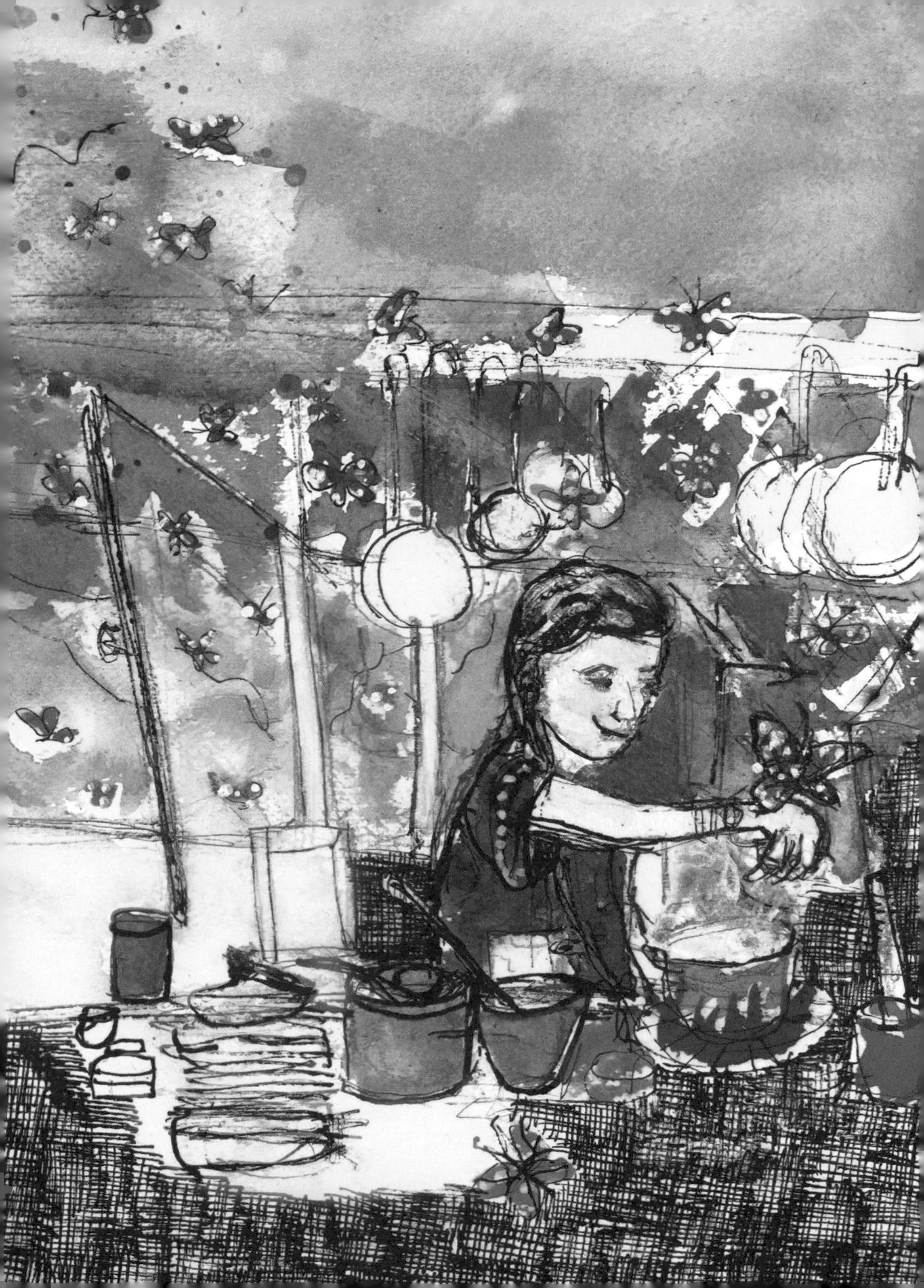

Andrea nodded gravely. "That is indeed what we need to discuss, but first I want to tell you *why* you turned into a butterfly, and what your role in this life-or-death matter is." Inés looked at Josephine and Valerio with alarm, then turned her attention back to her grandmother.

"Butterflies have been around for over two hundred million years," Andrea began, "and when they were first created by Mother Earth, she bestowed magical powers on them. It is these powers that allow you to see the threads connecting all of the living things in the world, and to sense the energy of life all around you. As small individual butterflies, you cannot change much. But if enough of you with the same collective goal flap your wings in unison, you can make tremendous things happen."

"There were dozens of butterflies flapping their wings when I transformed into one," commented Inés.

"That's exactly what I'm talking about," continued Andrea. "And this also happened hundreds of years ago, but the other way around. You see, the monarchs began migrating north and then back down to Mexico around two million years ago, so this was already the case in pre-Hispanic times. And the Purépecha Indians—who still live here in parts of Michoacán but who back then populated the entire state—well, they considered the monarchs to be the souls of their deceased and offered them fruit and water every winter. The two communities were always very close, and the monarchs of course appreciated the warm welcome and support they received from the Purépechas every year, when they arrived here after their long and exhausting migration."

As if suddenly remembering that these butterflies had also just completed a very long and exhausting migration, Andrea stood up and uncovered a plate of fruit that lay cut and ready on a counter in the corner. She brought the plate over to the table, and the butterflies fed hungrily. Andrea smiled, beckoned to Homero to help himself to some as well, and continued her story.

"So in the year 1420—exactly six hundred years ago— a swarm of migrating monarchs observed a scary scene below while en route here: an army of fierce Aztec warriors were conquering villages in the neighboring territories and taking the children prisoner, and everybody knew that the Aztecs sacrificed their prisoners to the gods. So when the butterflies arrived here, they wanted to warn their Purépecha friends about the approaching danger, only they had no way of making themselves understood. In their desperation, all the butterflies started flapping their wings at the same time, and suddenly one of the female butterflies—Parakata—magically transformed into a thirteen-year-old Purépecha girl. Parakata was able to warn the Purépechas of the imminent Aztec invasion, and this prompted them to fortify their villages and resist the attack. In fact, the Purépechas were one of the only Indian tribes to never be conquered by the Aztecs.

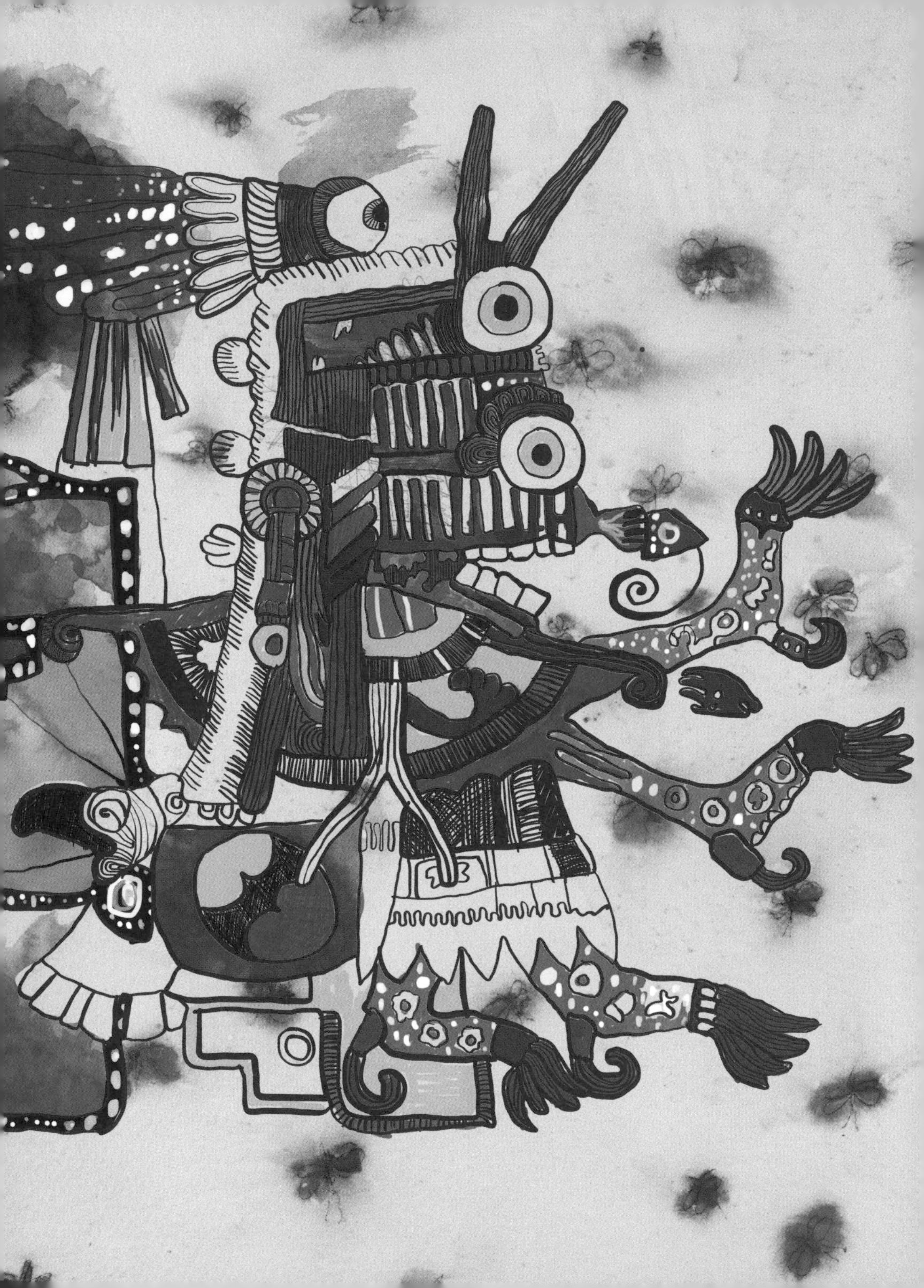

"Forever grateful to the butterflies, the Purépechas started to worship a butterfly goddess and carved large stone sculptures of her.

They also vowed to protect the butterfly forests from all invaders in the future, including the Spaniards who would arrive one hundred years later. Parakata herself remained in human form and went on to have many children with her artisan husband, who made her the obsidian pendant I sent you for your birthday. That pendant has been passed down from one female in our family to the next, and every fourth generation the girl receiving it transforms into a monarch butterfly, in order to commune with our ancestors and offer the living swarm assistance, just as the butterflies offered us humans assistance on that fateful day six hundred years ago."

"So I'm the fourth generation, and meant to help the butterflies?" Inés asked.

"You are a daughter of the sun—that's what the Purépechas called these girls—and you need to protect the sanctuary from its imminent destruction. The fate of not only your swarm but the entire species hangs in the balance."

Thinking back on Caligo's words, Inés now realized what he'd meant when he said her family was in danger. He'd been referring to her *butterfly* family, not her human one. "But how can *I* stop those men?" Inés exclaimed. "I'm just a tiny butterfly. If you could tell me how to transform back into my human self, I'd have a much better chance at helping."

Andrea shook her head and smiled. "I'm afraid you need to do it as a butterfly, my beloved Inés, but you won't do it alone." Andrea motioned to Josephine and Valerio. "Your friends will help you. Not just these two, but all the butterflies up on that mountain. You've now completed your time in the pupa—meaning you've absorbed the secrets and truths of the chrysalis—and now it's time for action. It's time for you to embrace and manifest your butterfly self, and for you to save your species."

Andrea turned to Homero and spoke to him in Spanish. "Homerito, you've seen the gradual but relentless destruction of the sanctuary, and we both know of Don Pascual's plans to turn it into an avocado plantation. We know that he's paid off local government officials to turn a blind eye to the logging and that he's planning on deforesting the entire sanctuary. The soil

under the fir trees is rich and fertile and sacred to all the life it sustains. The reserve is one of the wonders of the natural world, and all the monarchs who arrive here every winter will die without the oyamel trees. I am old and cannot even climb the mountain, but you are young and I know you love the monarchs. So I'm asking you to stay close to the butterflies and help them in any way you can."

Homero immediately nodded in agreement, then turned to admire the butterflies. He hadn't understood the story Andrea had told Inés in the butterfly language, but he knew there was something magical and urgent taking place, and he was eager to offer his assistance and be part of it.

Andrea's face cracked into a warm smile and she turned to Inés again. "Are you ready?"

Inés took a deep breath and exhaled. "I think so."

"Good. When you return to the sanctuary, the first thing you must do is warn the others of the approaching danger. And then you must figure out the right way and time to defeat Don Pascual. You must also avoid Chaneque."

"Who's Chaneque?" Inés asked.

"He's the hawk who sits on Don Pascual's shoulder. Don Pascual has heard the legend about a group of monarch butterflies who will fight hard to save their sanctuary from humans, so he's trained Chaneque to scan the skies and be ready to warn and assist him should the need arise."

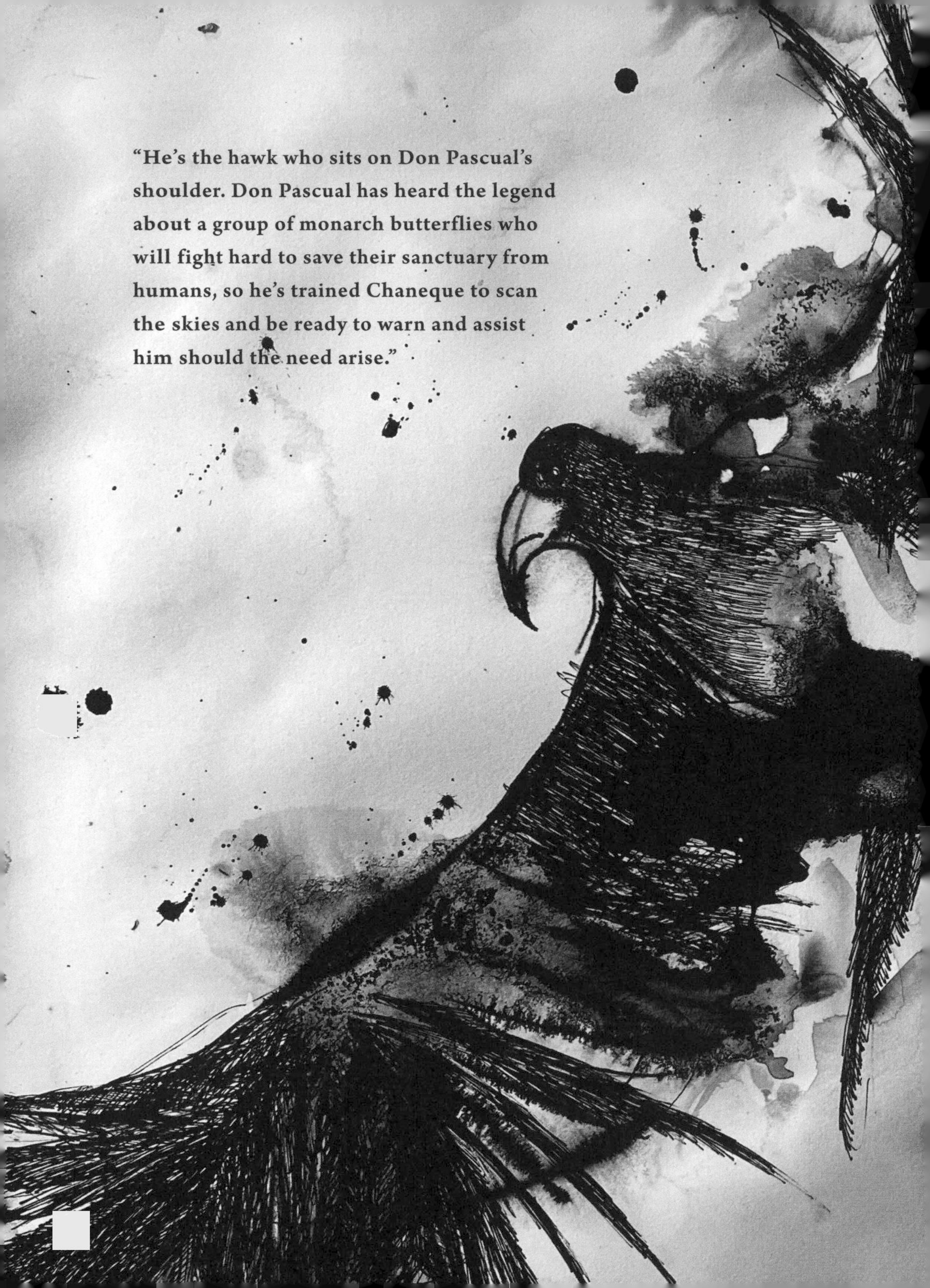

Inés thought back on Caligo's words about her being chosen for a battle, and she realized that *this* was the battle he was referring to. Suddenly her heart seized up and she exclaimed, "Caligo told me I had been chosen for a great battle since birth,

on the day the souls of the dead return to the earth."

Andrea's face hardened. "That means Don Pascual's assault will be taking place this very evening! He is doubtless planning to take advantage of the Day of the Dead celebrations in the village and may go ahead and destroy the sanctuary completely. You must go *now*, Inés, before dusk descends. The loggers are surely starting to gather in preparation for tonight's destruction."

Andrea stood up and helped the butterflies back onto Homero's shoulder. As she accompanied them to the door, she spoke to Inés: "Remember, you're not a human pretending to be a butterfly, nor a butterfly pretending to be a human. You are both, and you're right where you're supposed to be. You flew down here thinking it would save our human family; now use that same resolve to save our butterfly family. After that you will become a girl again."

As Homero walked hurriedly back toward the mountain, Inés turned to look at her grandmother, standing in her doorway. Andrea's eyes shone with pride and worry, and she called out, "Good luck, Inesita—you are a daughter of the sun! Good luck, Josephine, Valerio, Homero!"

As they headed back through the town and toward the mountain, Inés observed all the townspeople preparing feasts and decorating altars to honor their dead. The dead relied on the living to keep their memories alive, just as the living owed their lives to the dead who had come before them; for if our ancestors hadn't existed, neither would we. And in a similar way, if the natural world ceased to exist, then so would the human world. Every time humans destroyed a part of nature, they were destroying themselves as well.

Inés now lifted off of Homero's shoulder and flew toward the sanctuary with renewed purpose. She would protect the forest for the sake of all the animals who called it home, for the sake of the monarchs, and for the sake of humanity. She would give all of her butterfly self and all of her human self to achieve this—and if she failed, she would die trying.

chapter 4

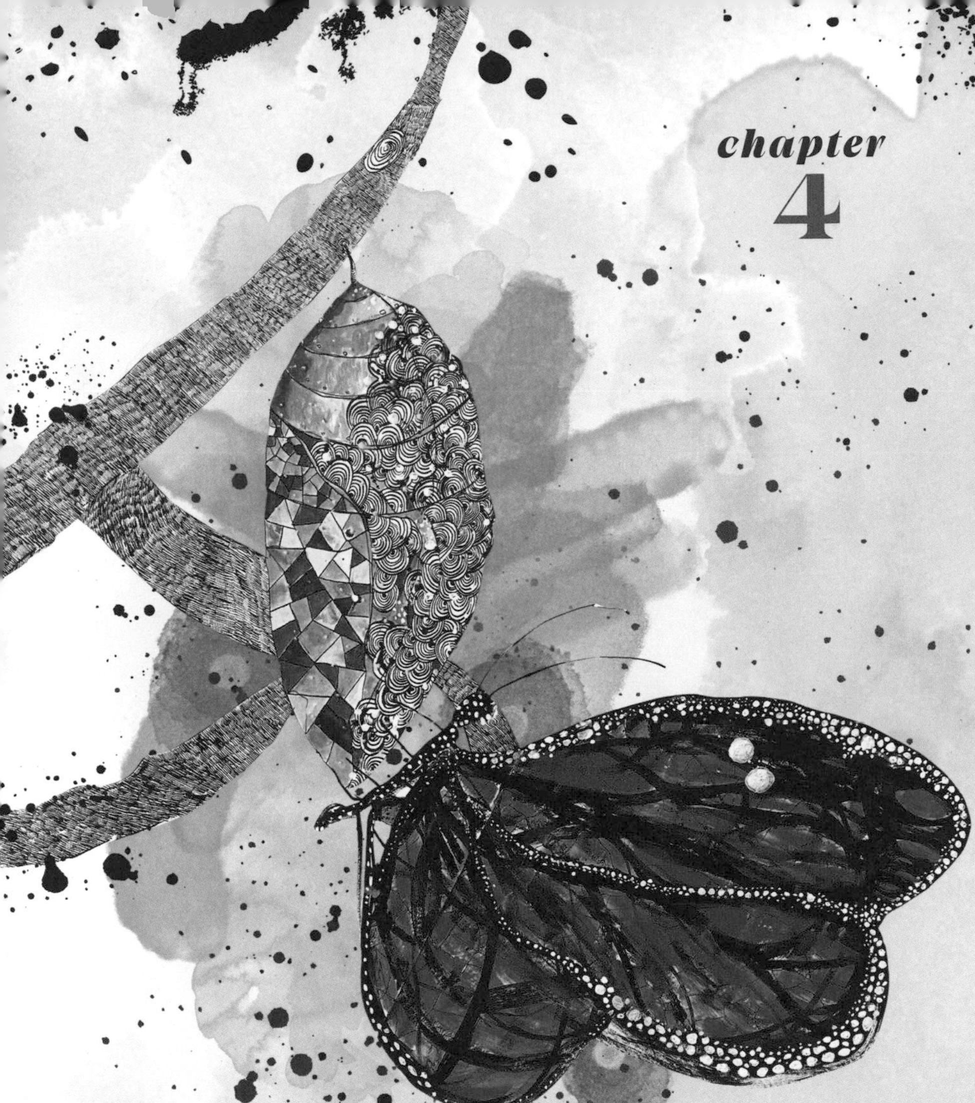

The Butterfly

The butterfly:

About ten days after the caterpillar enters the chrysalis, its transformation is complete and it is ready to emerge as a magnificent butterfly. The pupa's casing, which up until now has been a brilliant green adorned with golden spots, turns clear and reveals the orange, black, and white patterns on the wings folded up inside. This sudden transparency means the butterfly's emergence is imminent, and a monarch will usually push its way out midmorning. Once free of the structure that hosted its metamorphosis, the butterfly will take a few moments before expanding its wings and will then wait an hour for its wings to dry. Finally it is ready for action, and it takes flight . . .

The fourth stage in a monarch's life and in our parallel process is about pursuing one's dreams, doing what one knows is right, and loving others. It is about teaching, creating, and reproducing, about passing on gathered knowledge and experience and making one's mark on the world. The monarch butterfly is a pollinator, so every time it feeds, it spreads life. The shoot that emerged from the seed has turned into a full-grown plant or tree; it is now ready to host other life forms on its leaves or branches and to provide regenerative nourishment to them without perishing in the process.

The monarch butterfly trusts its instincts, for they are based on messages and secrets learned from past incarnations and ancestors. The butterfly has the power to change the world with its wings, despite its small size and apparent fragility. The butterfly is the final stage in a monarch's life; once reached, it will last until the monarch's death. The sooner one reaches this enlightened stage, the longer it will last and the more that can be accomplished.

Just as the butterfly has four wings, its form is the sum of the four parts of its life; one could not exist without the others. For us humans, these four parts are our physical, emotional, psychological, and spiritual lives. The butterfly represents knowing oneself while being open to the world and its gifts. It is a unique individual, but also part of a community that in turn is part of the natural world. When the time is right, the butterfly embarks on its migration, which will last for the rest of its life. The butterfly knows which way to go; it has tuned in to the natural world, its ancestors, and its inner compass.

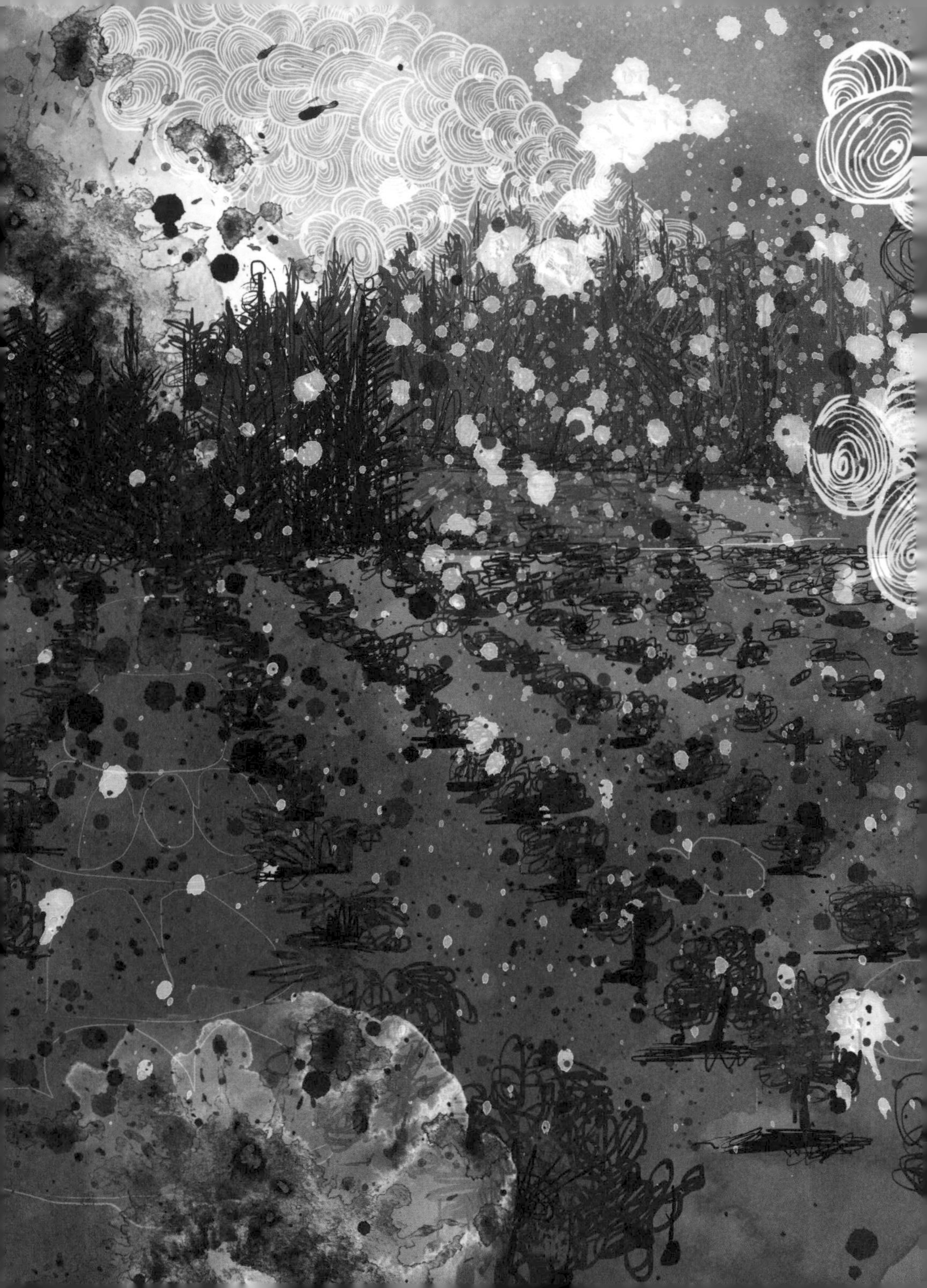

Inés fluttered toward the top of the mountain, while Homero kept pace with Josephine and Valerio on his shoulder. "Conserve your energy!" Josephine called out to her, but Inés was too preoccupied to sit passively while the boy did the walking. A long hour later, as they approached the outer edge of the sanctuary and were able to look down the other side of the hill to where the avocado farms lay, Inés was horrified to see an army of flatbed trucks and a few diggers surrounded by dozens of loggers standing around talking, presumably waiting for dusk to fall.

Inés, Josephine, and Valerio had to warn the others of the impending danger, but how could they warn millions of butterflies roosting on hundreds of different trees and flitting in the air in every possible direction? And what should they tell them? If they told the butterflies to evacuate, that would leave the trees completely exposed and make it easier for the loggers to cut them down. And where would the butterflies go? This place was their sanctuary for a reason: only the oyamel forest's unique microclimate could shield them from the winter, and the butterflies had to conserve their energy to make it through the next several months, during which they'd have very limited access to food, if any.

They had to stay and fight for their sacred home, and that of their ancestors, and of all the generations of monarchs still to come.

Inés, Josephine, and Valerio spoke individually to a few butterflies on each tree, and in turn those butterflies alerted the ones next to them, so that the urgent message rippled upward and outward on each oyamel tree like a collective shudder. The sleeping butterflies were roused from their slumber, and before long millions of tiny bodies were standing upright and on guard, their antennae reaching toward the sky. Dusk fell too quickly that evening, and soon the butterflies felt the vibration of the vehicles creaking their way up the side of the mountain. Inés, Josephine, and Valerio positioned themselves on Homero's shoulder again as the boy moved to the entrance to the reserve and they waited for the trucks to appear, feeling both terrified and defiant as the sound of the motors

drew closer

and closer.

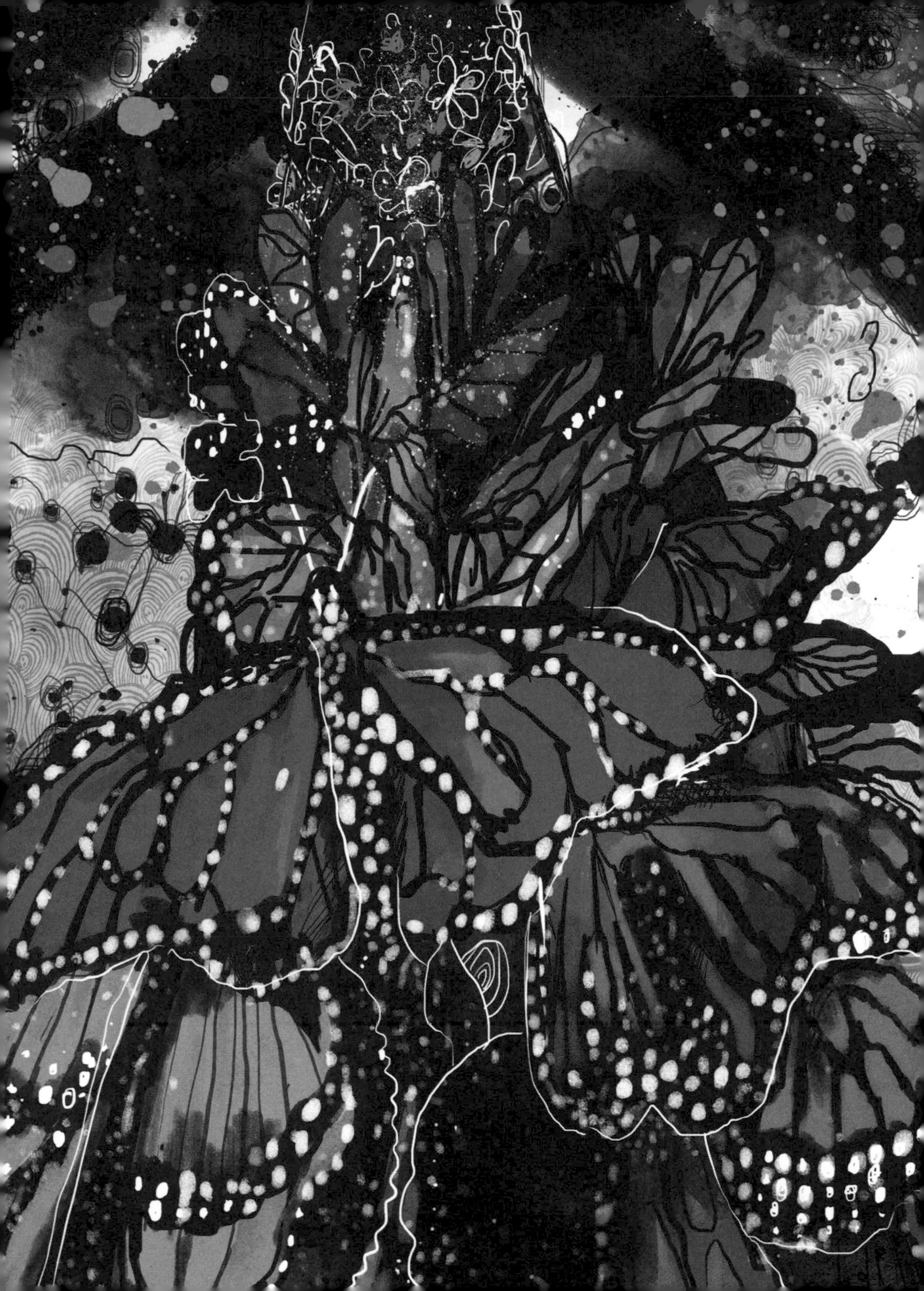

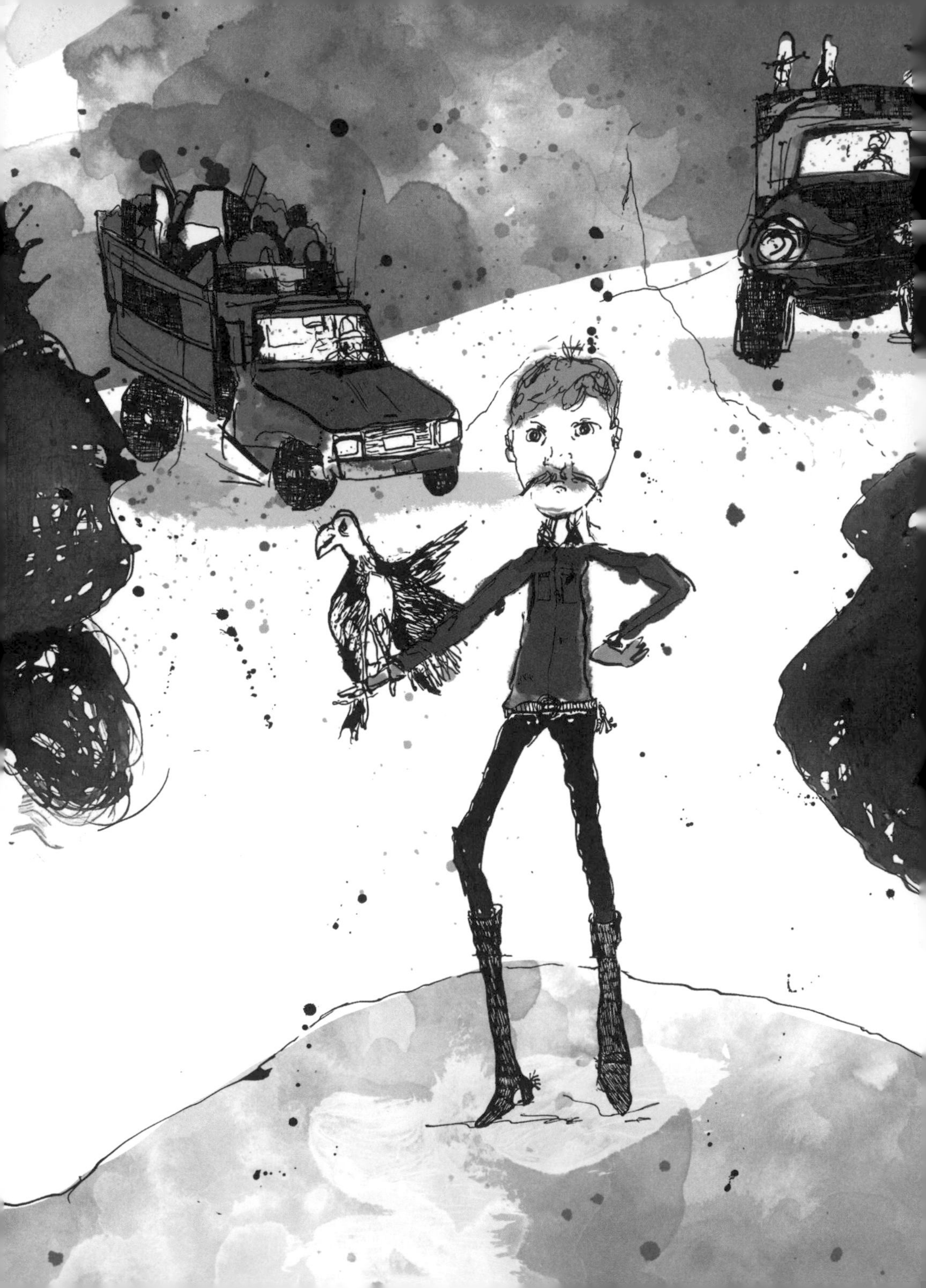

A few minutes later, the first vehicles arrived at the outer edge of the sanctuary. At the front of the ominous caravan was a dusty red car, and Don Pascual emerged from it with Chaneque on his bent arm. Inés surmised that he'd chosen to leave his van behind to avoid it being spotted by a villager and tied to the destruction of the sanctuary. But there were no villagers in sight, and Inés could see rivers of flickering candlelight, hear the music of harmoniums and mariachi bands, and smell the burning *copal* wafting up from the cemeteries below.

As the trucks continued to arrive and the loggers descended from them with chainsaws in hand and lamps attached to their heads, Don Pascual surveyed the treetops with a large flashlight and pointed to particular trees that he wanted the men to cut down first. His eyes then fell on Homero standing a mere five feet tall in front of them, and Don Pascual's face broke into a perverse smile. "What are you doing here, boy? Get back down to the village, to honor your dead relatives."

Homero shook his head.

"I'm not going anywhere. I am here to protect the butterflies and their forest. *My* forest."

Don Pascual laughed heartily. "Okay, boy. Don't say you weren't warned." And then Don Pascual's smile evaporated, and Inés suspected that he was worried about Homero witnessing what was about to occur. Sure enough, he added, "If you say anything about what's about to happen, you and your family will be very, very sorry." Homero didn't respond, but Inés could feel his body tense up at the thought of his family being harmed.

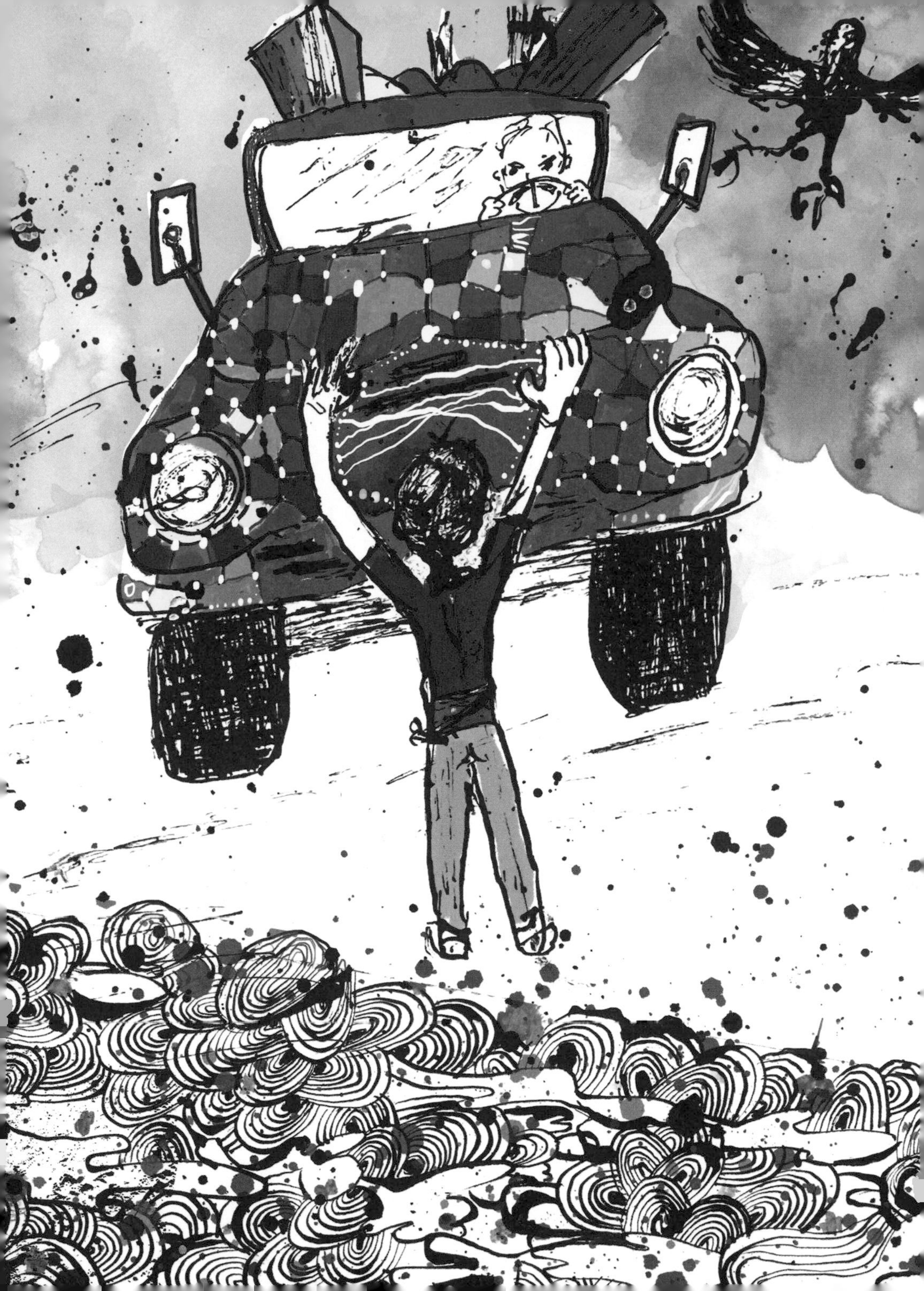

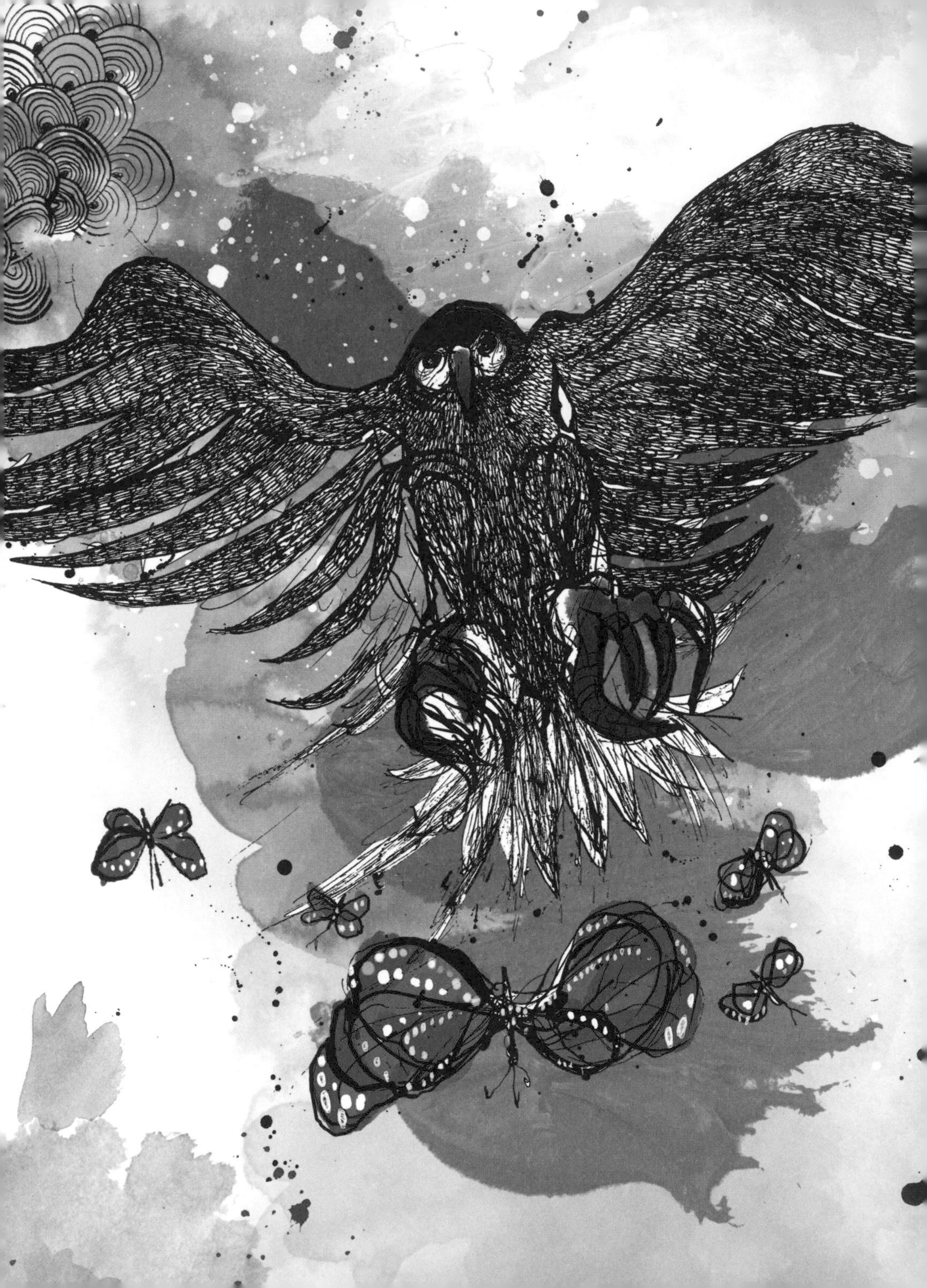

Don Pascual went back to speaking to the loggers, and from within the dusk Inés became aware of a sharp and threatening gaze directed at her and her two best friends: Chaneque's. The hawk was staring at them with piercing, amber-colored eyes—eyes that seemed to devour the trio with their scrutiny and which were calculating and cold, devoid of empathy or emotion.

Suddenly Chaneque emitted a shrill cry

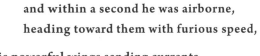 and within a second he was airborne, heading toward them with furious speed,

his powerful wings sending currents into the air as they flapped.

Inés, Josephine, and Valerio all took flight and dashed toward the interior of the forest. The three of them then veered in different directions, and it was Inés that Chaneque chose to follow. Inés darted around the forest in panicked loops with Chaneque a mere few feet behind her. At this point the other butterflies had taken up defensive positions on the trees, meaning that the air was free of butterflies and Inés was easy to keep track of. Chaneque was getting closer and closer; suddenly he swooped toward Inés and attempted to grab her in his enormous talons, but she swerved to the right around a tree and Chaneque had to keep flying forward for a few moments before he could loop around and resume his pursuit of her. Inés now remembered the nightmare she'd had back home about a hawk chasing her down the street and realized it had been a vision.

165

With Chaneque once again directly behind her and gaining speed, Inés tried to think of ways of outsmarting him. She had to bring this chase to an end quickly, because she could hear the chainsaws slicing through tree trunks and the trees again crying out and moaning in anguish as their bodies were mutilated. But she simply couldn't think straight. Turning to look over her shoulder, she saw Chaneque's huge, outstretched talons moving in to seize her. She saw her life flash before her eyes and took what she thought would be her last breath, but to her astonishment Chaneque did not grab her. Instead he quickly descended to the forest floor, and Inés landed on the closest oyamel tree and quickly hid amongst the hundreds of monarchs already standing on it. Turning her gaze downward, she saw why Chaneque hadn't killed her.

Chaneque was busy destroying another butterfly—

one that had deliberately flown into the hawk's talons at the last minute to take Inés's place. Even from the height of the tree, Inés could see that the butterfly's wings had enormous owl-eye markings on them, and her heart sank as she realized that Caligo had sacrificed himself for her. At that moment Chaneque noticed that he'd caught the wrong butterfly and looked around suspiciously, searching the air for Inés; but she was now camouflaged in the blanket of monarchs, and his night vision was not strong. Annoyed and confused, the hawk dropped what remained of Caligo's body and flew back to rejoin his master, Don Pascual.

166

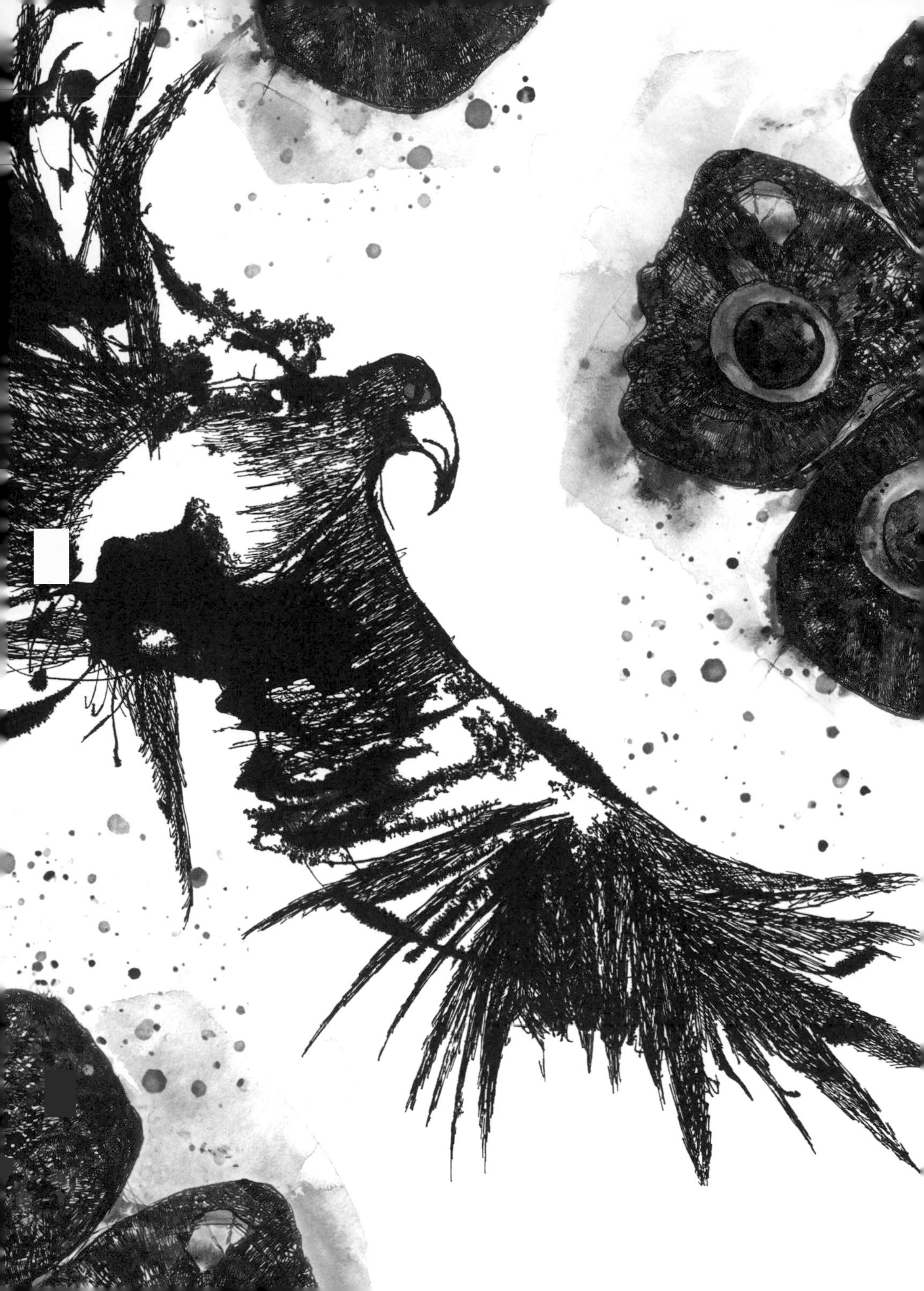

Inés stared at Caligo's lifeless wings on the ground, but she couldn't mourn his death for long: he'd given his life so that she could help save the sanctuary, and the battle for its salvation had begun. Inés heard more trees crashing to the ground and saw thousands of distressed monarchs who'd previously been resting on them fluttering about in the air, not knowing what to do. She rushed back toward the edge of the forest and was horrified to see the army of loggers in the midst of a full-fledged assault. Ten oyamel trees were being attacked at once, while Homero stood shouting in front of them, only to be violently shoved aside by one logger after the other. The sound of the chainsaws and the screaming of the oyamels was unbearable now, and Inés could sense the roots of the trees convulsing and shriveling up in the ground as the bodies they kept anchored were ravaged.

Inés dashed from one oyamel to the other, crying out to the butterflies that it was time to attack. And then hundreds of thousands of butterflies took flight and descended upon the loggers, crowding their heads and swarming in their faces so that the loggers had to stop what they were doing. No longer able to see anything, the loggers cursed the insects and waved their chainsaws wildly in the air, slicing through the bodies and wings of many butterflies. Suddenly one logger accidentally slashed another logger on the arm, and the injured man howled in pain. The other loggers quickly turned off their chainsaws, and now the only sounds in the forest were the loggers yelling profanities and the butterflies flying, which resembled a light and steady rainfall.

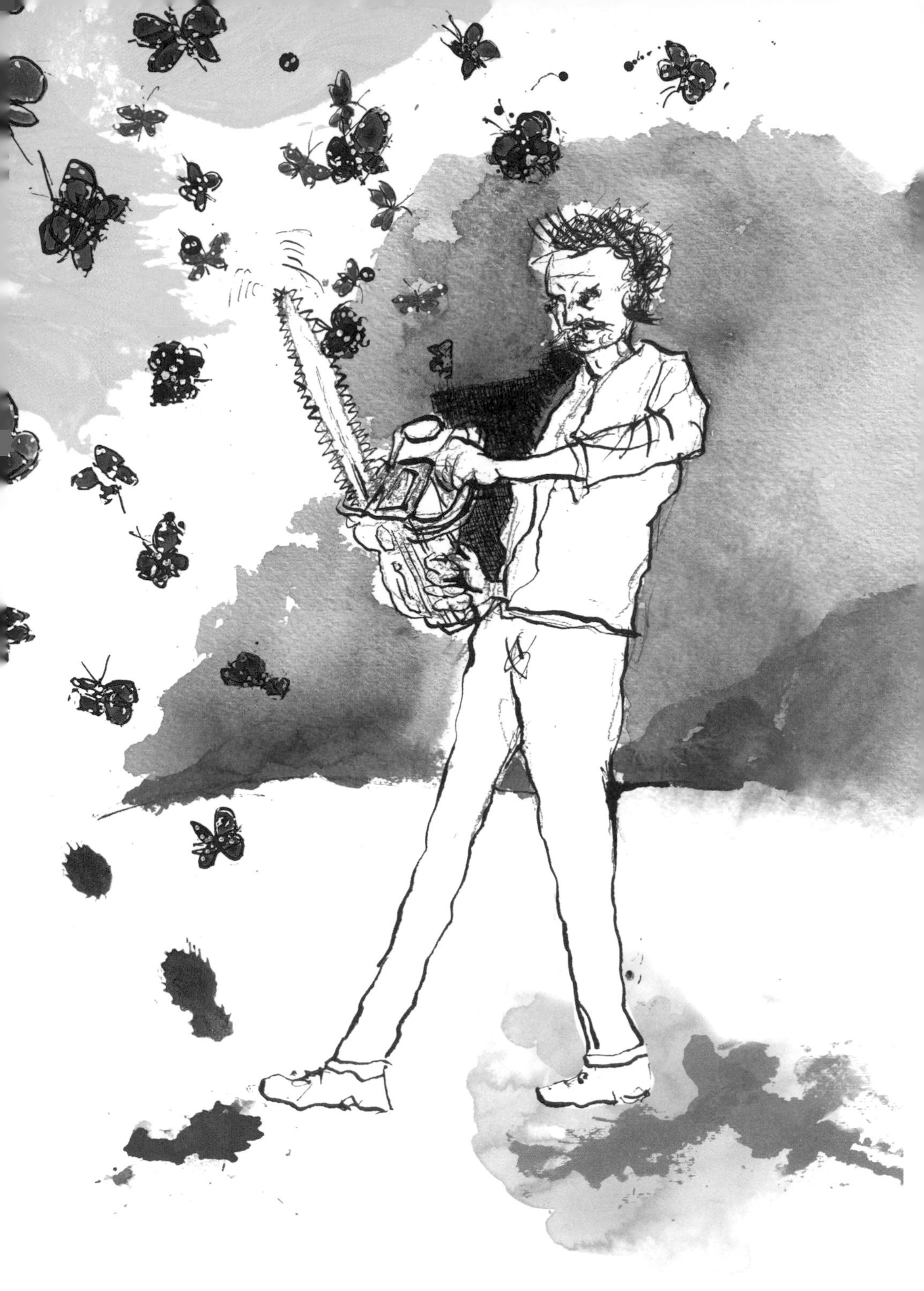

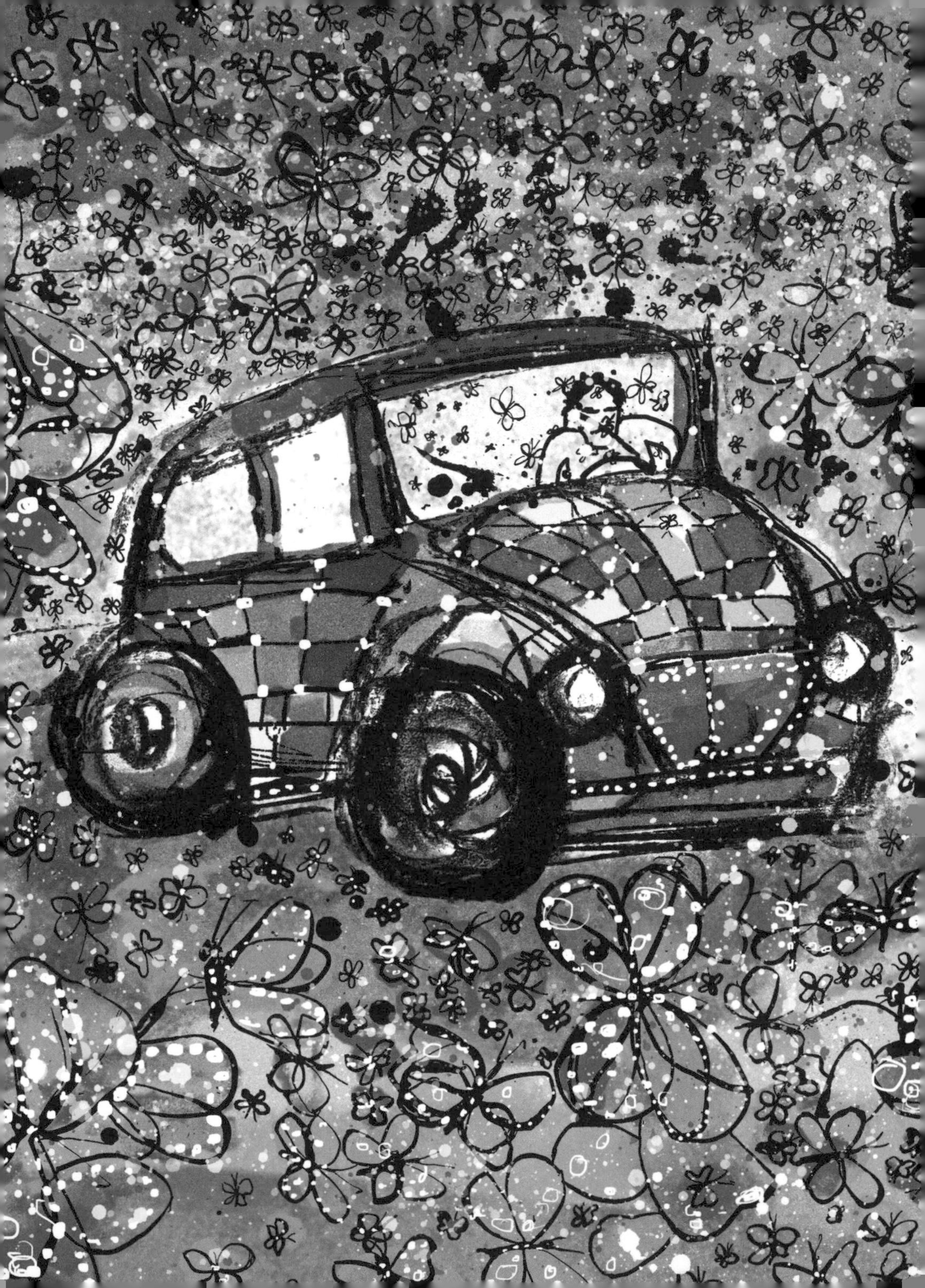

Inés looked around for Don Pascual and discovered that
he'd retreated to his car with Chaneque. The two of them—
man and hawk—were watching events unfold through the
car's windshield. Don Pascual lowered his window an inch
and yelled out at the loggers,

"Come on, you useless cowards! Are you
really scared of these filthy insects?
If you don't get back to work immediately,
I'll fire you!"

Some of the loggers turned on their chainsaws and attempted
to move toward the trees again, but—like blindfolded
children swinging sticks at a piñata hoisted out of reach—
they were unable to locate the oyamel trunks and terrified
of getting sliced by a fellow logger's blade. The beams from
their headlamps cast jumpy spotlights all around the forest,
like a chaotic outdoor laser show.

Don Pascual cursed in frustration and jumped out of his
car and into one of the diggers, while Chaneque alighted on
the cab of a flatbed truck to watch. Don Pascual started the
digger and proceeded to barrel toward a tree, and Homero
bravely ran to stand in front of it. But Don Pascual did not
slow down, so Inés darted in front of the digger and flapped
with all her might in Don Pascual's face. He swatted at her
violently, managing to grab her and crumple her in his fist
before throwing her out toward the forest floor.

Inés lay on the ground dazed and unable to move. When she tried to stretch her wings, she felt a deep pain searing through her thorax. Feebly turning to look at her wings, she could see that they were bent and torn beyond repair. Meanwhile Don Pascual was demolishing a tree with the digger, while Homero clung to the sides of the vehicle, trying to stop him. Inés felt like a failure: she hadn't come close to saving the forest, and now she would surely perish. Josephine and Valerio swooped down to land on either side of her and stared at her with alarm.

"Oh, Inés!" exclaimed Josephine when she saw the condition of her wings. "Please don't put yourself in any more danger. Whatever it is we need to do, just tell us, and Valerio and I will try to do it!" Valerio nodded in agreement, looking anxious and upset.

"But I have no idea what we're supposed to do!" replied Inés. "I fear this whole thing was a terrible mistake: all of you putting this blind trust in me and thinking I could help save our sanctuary. And Caligo isn't here anymore to advise me." Feeling desperate, Inés began to cry.

Josephine caressed her with an outstretched wing.

"Please don't give up, sweet wings. I *know* you can do it. Look inside your heart—and into the depths of your wisdom. *Please.*"

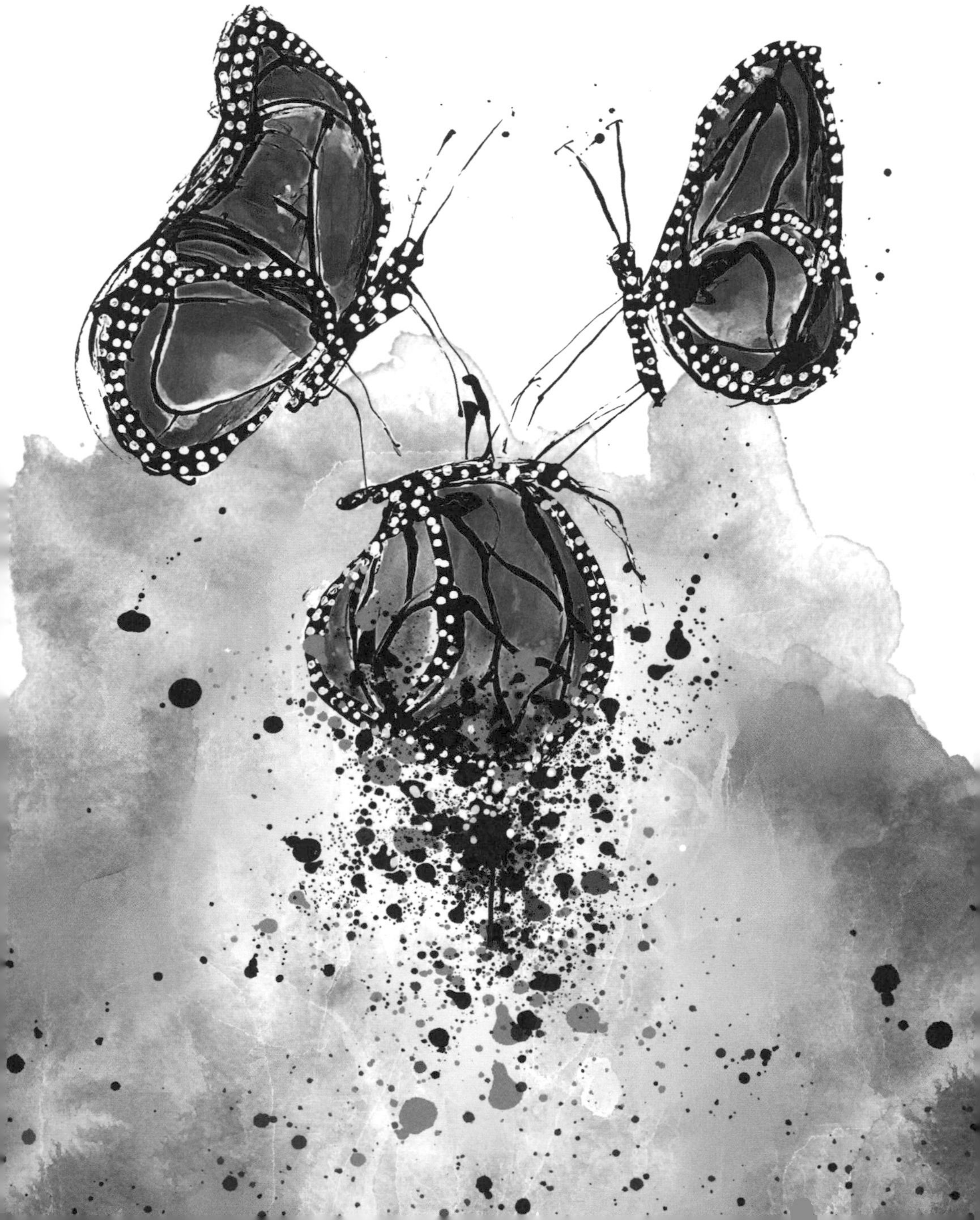

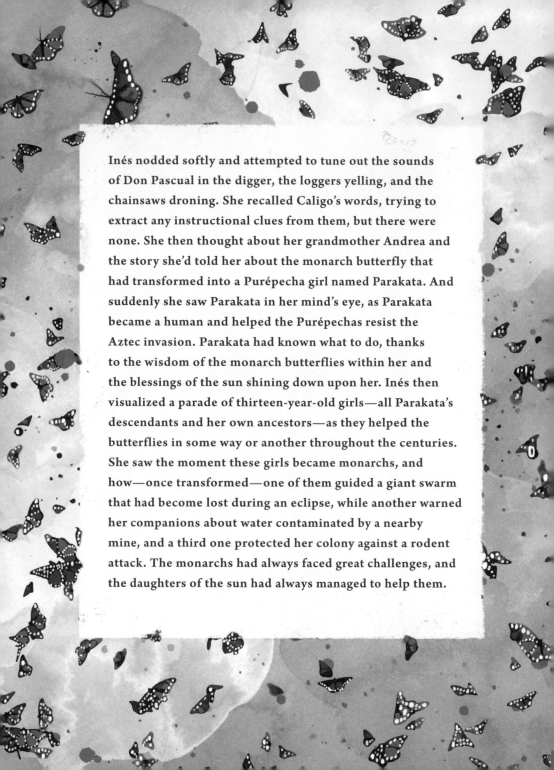

Inés nodded softly and attempted to tune out the sounds of Don Pascual in the digger, the loggers yelling, and the chainsaws droning. She recalled Caligo's words, trying to extract any instructional clues from them, but there were none. She then thought about her grandmother Andrea and the story she'd told her about the monarch butterfly that had transformed into a Purépecha girl named Parakata. And suddenly she saw Parakata in her mind's eye, as Parakata became a human and helped the Purépechas resist the Aztec invasion. Parakata had known what to do, thanks to the wisdom of the monarch butterflies within her and the blessings of the sun shining down upon her. Inés then visualized a parade of thirteen-year-old girls—all Parakata's descendants and her own ancestors—as they helped the butterflies in some way or another throughout the centuries. She saw the moment these girls became monarchs, and how—once transformed—one of them guided a giant swarm that had become lost during an eclipse, while another warned her companions about water contaminated by a nearby mine, and a third one protected her colony against a rodent attack. The monarchs had always faced great challenges, and the daughters of the sun had always managed to help them.

And then Inés thought back on the moment she herself had become a butterfly, and she remembered her grandmother's words about the butterflies being able to make tremendous things happen when they shared a collective goal—and she knew what she had to do.

Inés summoned all the strength she had and attempted to flap her wings. At first Josephine and Valerio looked at her with confusion—they'd been awaiting a verbal instruction and it was clear Inés couldn't fly—but within moments Josephine understood and she too began to flap her wings. Valerio then flapped his wings as well; and even with just her two friends joining in, Inés immediately started to feel stronger. Within moments the butterflies closest to them started to flap, and then the ones next to them. The monarchs that had been flying at the loggers scrambled to perch on trees or on the forest floor and began to *swoosh* their wings in unison as well, and soon the millions of monarch wings beating together created a sound that resembled the deep note of a pre-Hispanic flute. The note echoed through the forest in a rhythmic and circular manner, growing louder and then subsiding and then growing louder again as it wove its way amongst the trees.

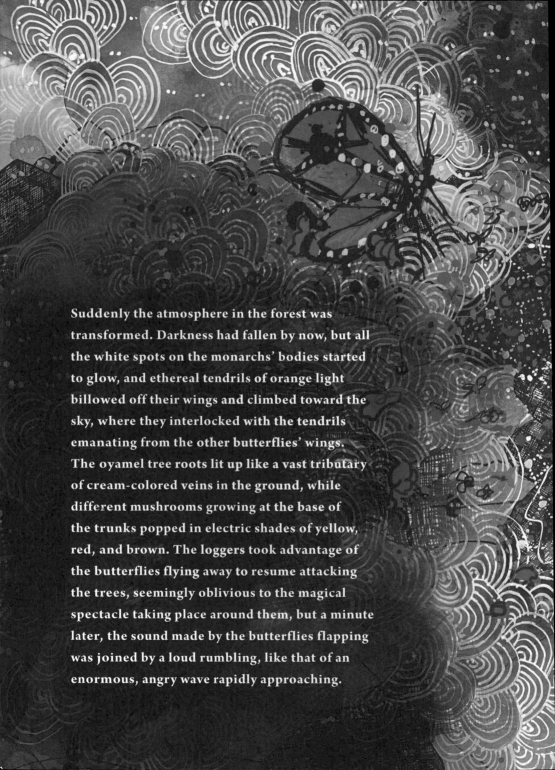

Suddenly the atmosphere in the forest was transformed. Darkness had fallen by now, but all the white spots on the monarchs' bodies started to glow, and ethereal tendrils of orange light billowed off their wings and climbed toward the sky, where they interlocked with the tendrils emanating from the other butterflies' wings. The oyamel tree roots lit up like a vast tributary of cream-colored veins in the ground, while different mushrooms growing at the base of the trunks popped in electric shades of yellow, red, and brown. The loggers took advantage of the butterflies flying away to resume attacking the trees, seemingly oblivious to the magical spectacle taking place around them, but a minute later, the sound made by the butterflies flapping was joined by a loud rumbling, like that of an enormous, angry wave rapidly approaching.

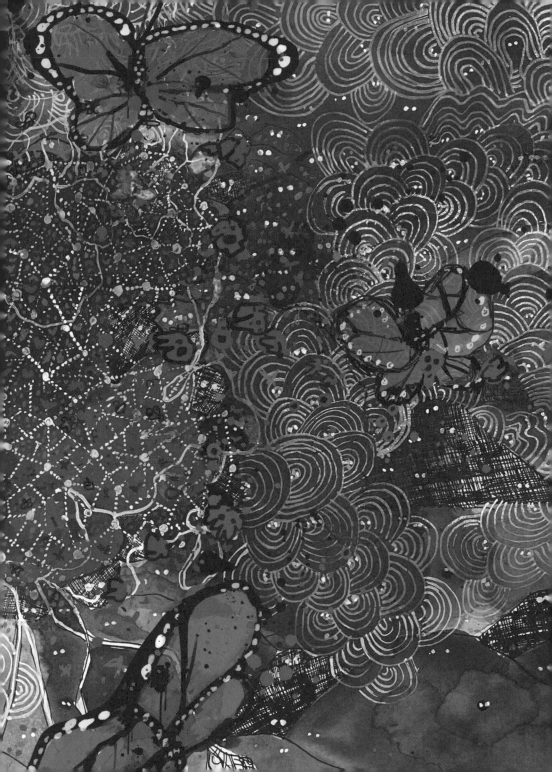

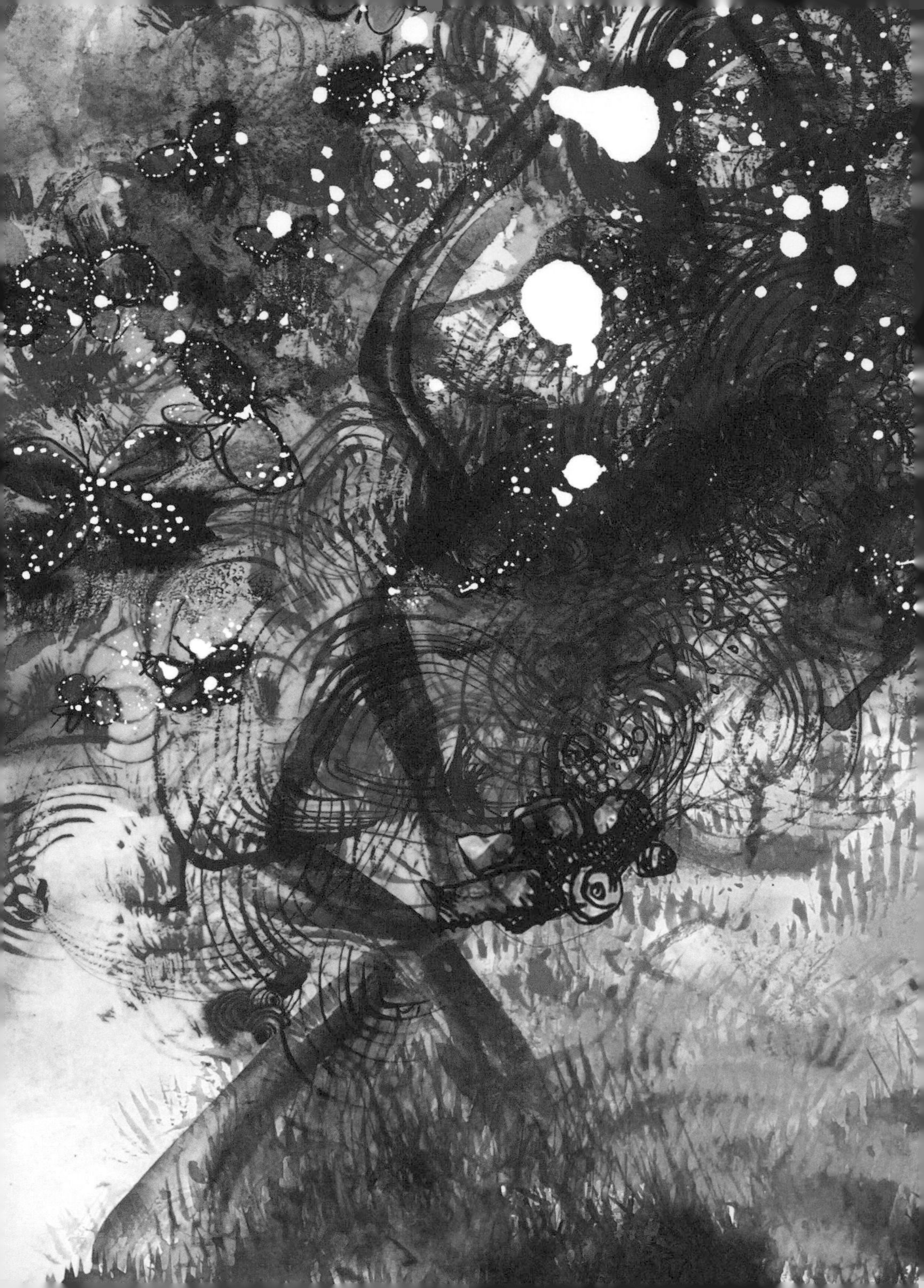

The earth began to vibrate, and the loggers dropped their chainsaws and ran toward their vehicles, desperate to descend the mountain and escape what they knew to be an imminent landslide. Don Pascual ordered them to stay put, but the men paid him no heed this time, clearly preferring to lose their jobs than their lives. Don Pascual, still sitting in the digger and still believing he had the ability to control nature, charged at a tree full speed with a demented look in his eyes. But the digger hit a bulging tree root and turned on its side, and Don Pascual found himself stuck inside and unable to climb out. Chaneque flew over to flap above the digger and shriek in distress, while the butterflies ascended to the tops of the trees and into the sky. Rodents and lizards of all sorts scrambled up the tree trunks toward safety, while birds and other winged insects accompanied the monarchs in the upper echelons of the forest they called home.

Inés could no longer fly properly, but Josephine and Valerio lifted her up into the canopy. The three had just found an empty spot at the crown of an oyamel when they saw a river of mud and rocks approaching from higher up the mountain. They looked around with panic when they realized that they had lost sight of Homero, but then they spotted him with a headlamp on, attempting to rescue Don Pascual from the digger. The metallic door facing the sky was too heavy for Homero to lift and the landslide was quickly approaching, so the boy clambered to the top of the overturned digger and stood on its highest point. Within moments the debris had completely covered the forest floor below, including the digger with Don Pascual sealed inside, but stopped just shy of Homero's shoes. The soil buried all the discarded chainsaws that the loggers had thrown to the ground, and their trucks could be seen and heard zooming down the side of the mountain, with the front of the landslide nipping at their tailpipes in pursuit.

And then suddenly everything settled and was still.

The only sounds that could be heard were the distant rumbles of the retreating trucks and the music from the Day of the Dead celebrations in the village. Not a single tree had been destroyed by the landslide, and Inés and the other butterflies realized that their sanctuary was now safe. The joy and relief felt by millions of monarchs—as well as the thousands of other plant and animal species who lived in the majestic reserve—were palpable, despite the darkness that enveloped the forest.

Inés asked Josephine and Valerio to take her to Homero and they floated downward, with her friends once again supporting her achy and weak body. Homero was cautiously descending from atop the buried digger, calling out "Don Pascual! Don Pascual?" But there was no answer or movement from within the mound of mud, and it appeared that the avocado kingpin had perished.

Homero looked up and saw the approaching butterflies illuminated by the beam from his headlamp. When they landed on his arm, he grinned and said, "We did it, friends! *You* did it!"

Inés lifted one of her front legs and pointed toward the town, and Homero nodded with understanding. "You want me to find your grandmother? And tell her you're safe?" Inés nodded with gratitude. Then Homero noticed that Inés was injured, and his face contorted with worry. "Shouldn't you come with me?

You're hurt. Maybe your grandmother can help." But Inés shook her head. She wanted to stay here with the butterflies, and she couldn't face the long journey down the mountain and through a village bustling with festivities and noise. And what could Andrea do to help her anyway? For now, she just desperately wanted to rest.

The three butterflies made their way back up to a tree and settled in amongst thousands of their exhausted sisters and brothers. Before long Josephine and Valerio were asleep, and it seemed Inés was the only butterfly awake in the whole forest. She watched for several minutes as Homero descended toward the village, the light on his forehead showing her where he was. When he disappeared from sight, she turned her attention to Chaneque, who was now perched on top of the digger watching over Don Pascual's inadvertent tomb, looking crestfallen.

Inés thought about the many events of the evening and felt tremendous pride in herself and all the other butterflies for saving their ancient and future home. She had fulfilled her destiny as a daughter of the sun, but protecting her monarch family had come with a cost. Inés felt a deep sadness over the death of the wise and beautiful Caligo, but she also suspected that his martyrdom was part of the prophecy, for had he himself not stated that he could see the future? And the fact that he had appeared in the forest at the very moment that Chaneque was going to destroy her . . . Yes, it was clear that Caligo's sacrificial death had been part of the plan—of his plan, of Mother Nature's plan.

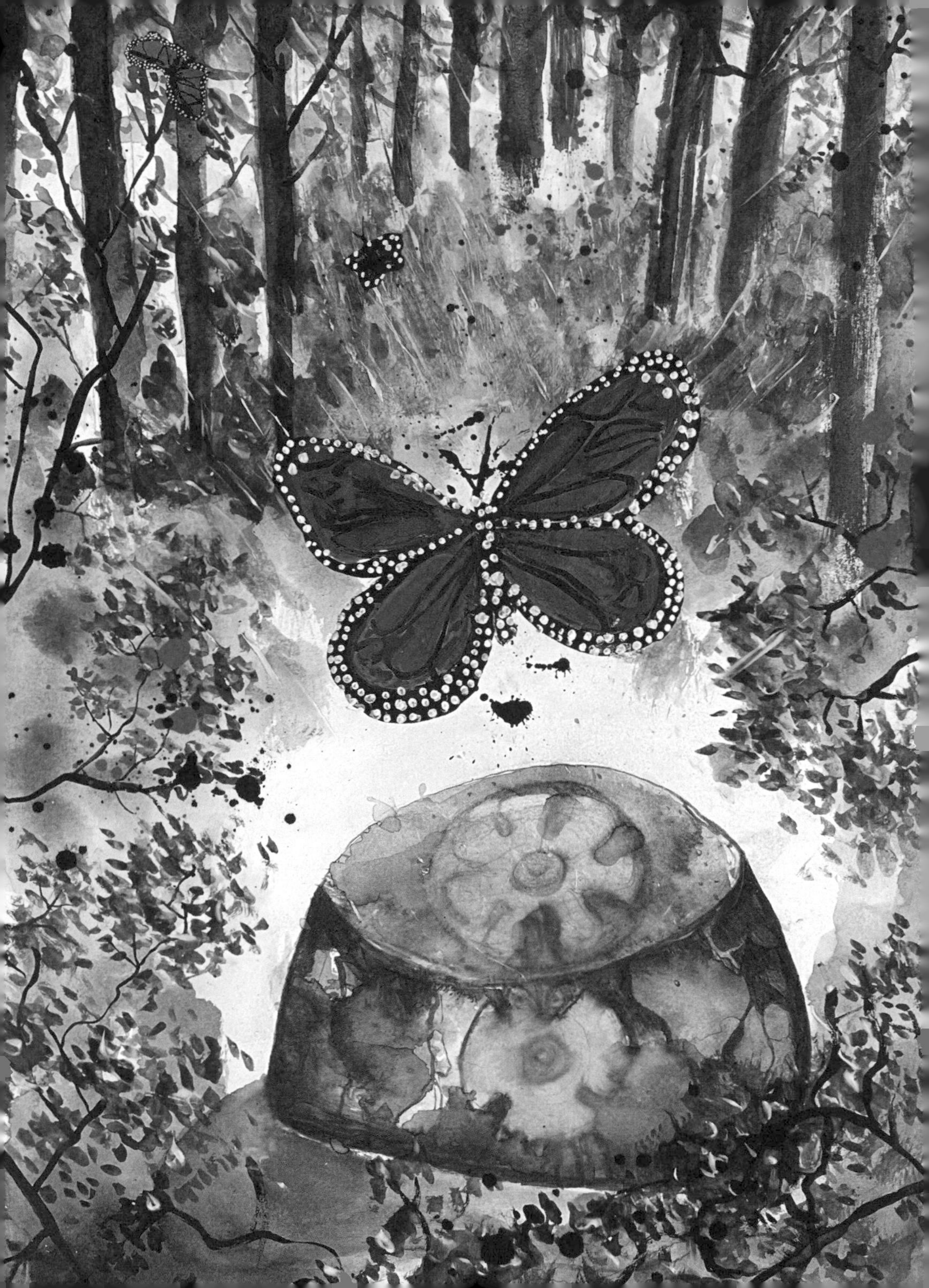

Then Inés's thoughts turned to her own situation. If she had accomplished what she was meant to accomplish, why was she still a butterfly? Would she ever turn back into a human? And if so, when? She particularly wished to do so now that her butterfly body was battered and frail.

Inés eventually fell into a dreamless sleep, exhausted by the physical and emotional exertion of the day. She awoke at the first hint of dawn, as the sun cast warm rays through the trunks of the trees and birdsong filled the air. Some butterflies around her began to stir, but most of the monarchs remained in their roosts. Inés looked down toward the forest floor and saw that Chaneque was still perched atop the digger, next to the twenty or so trees the loggers had managed to fell. Inés then noticed a large, round stone that had broken off the side of the mountain and been carried down by the landslide. The stone had a flat top with an image carved into it, and she felt a strong urge to go down and investigate.

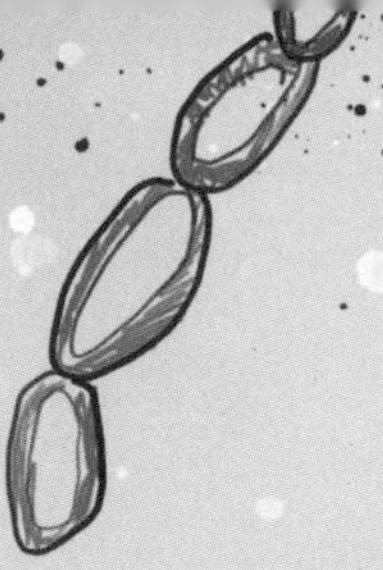

Inés asked Josephine and Valerio, who by now were also awake, to carry her down. As they landed on the stone, she was amazed to see that the carved image was that of a butterfly—the exact same shape and design as the butterfly pendant Andrea had gifted her on her birthday. Inés felt a terrible sinking feeling, and her head and antennae drooped with disappointment. "What's wrong?" asked Josephine.

"This butterfly matches an obsidian butterfly necklace I have back in the United States," replied Inés. "I'm thinking that in order to turn back into a human, I was supposed to bring it here."

Valerio shook his head. "I don't think so, Inés. How could a small butterfly like you carry a heavy pendant for three thousand miles? It doesn't make sense." Inés's heart brightened a little, as she realized

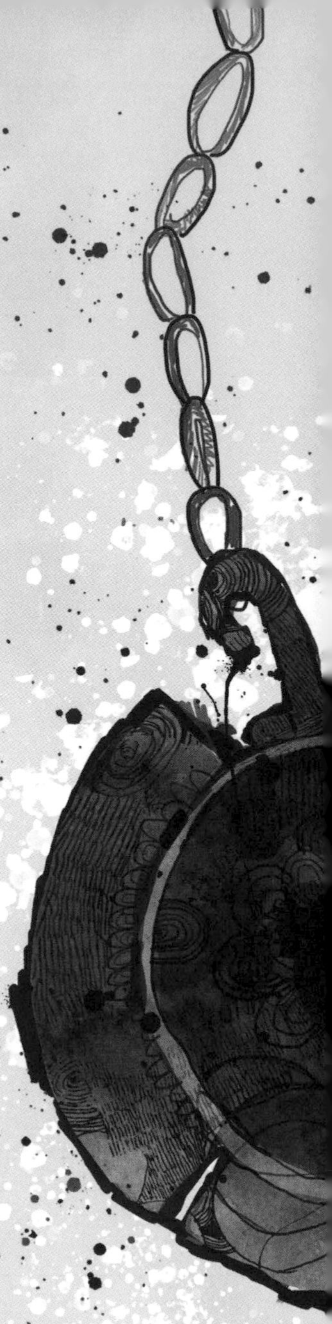

Valerio made a good point. But if she didn't need to have the pendant with her, what *did* she need to do? The pendant had surely been passed down from one daughter of the sun to the next for a reason.

Just as Inés uttered the word "sun" in her mind,

a brilliant ray of sunlight broke through the trees and illuminated the stone.

Inés opened her wings and—even though it hurt terribly—flapped them with the little remaining strength she had. She was able to lift herself into the air, where she hovered directly above the stone, positioning her body so that the sun was directly behind her and the shadow of her body filled the shape of the butterfly in the stone perfectly.

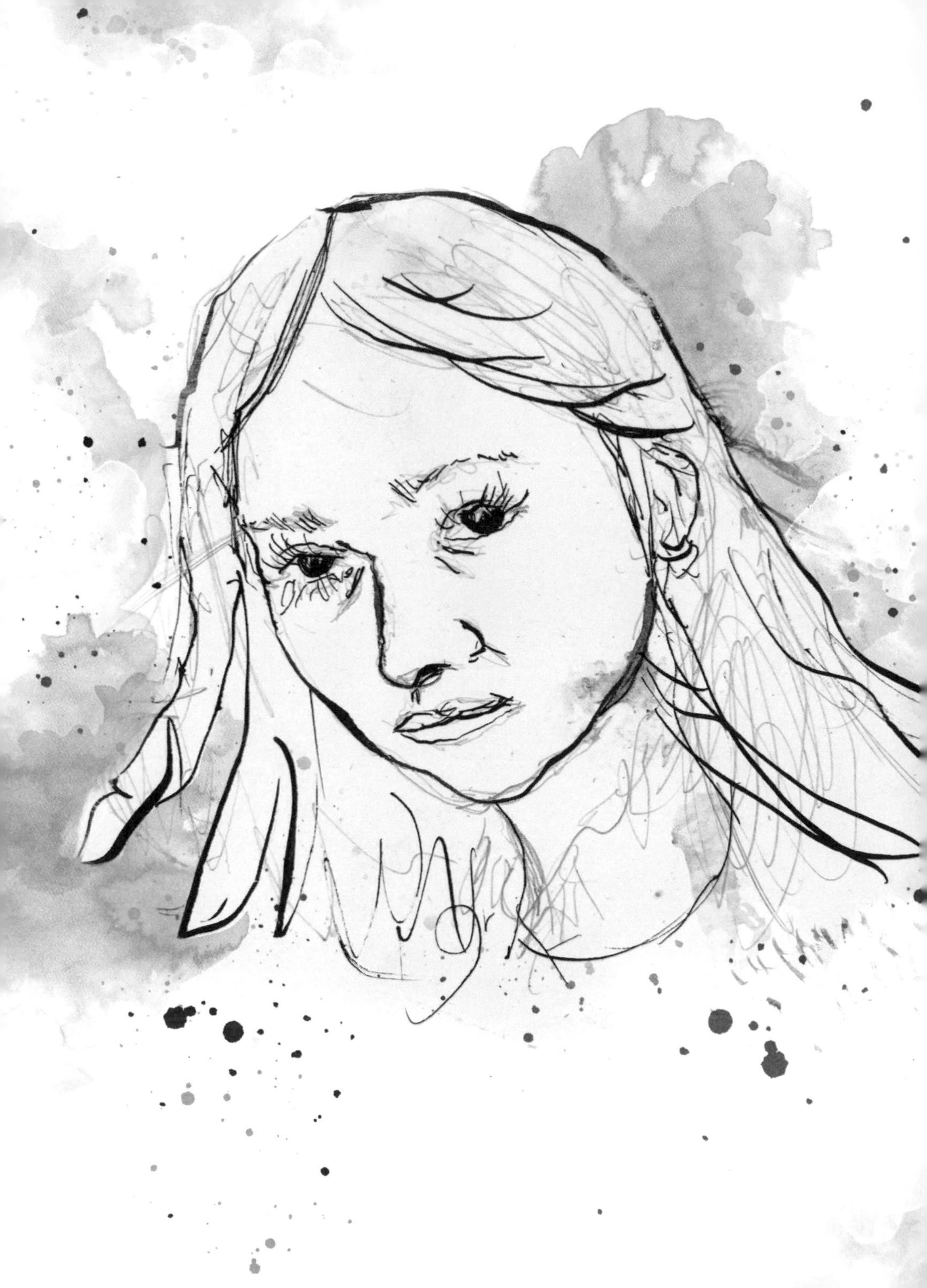

And then a miracle occurred, for Inés felt her body stretching painlessly as if it were filling with light and energy, and a barrage of memories and sensations struck her all at once:

Her birth as a human baby in a bright hospital, and seeing her parents' beaming faces for the first time.

Her first moments as a butterfly, looking down at a furry, spotted body and seeing Josephine smiling and speaking to her.

The taste of warm milk from her mother's breast, the taste of a milkweed leaf, the sweet taste of nectar from a purple aster.

The sound of pre-Hispanic drums, the sound of her heartbeat, the sound of a piano playing Satie, the sound of a million monarch wings flapping in unison.

The smell of Andrea's green *mole*, the smell of her brother's hair, the smell of the mud puddle she had gotten salt from, which she had smelled through her antennae.

And finally the softness of her bed at home, the feeling of a current of air carrying her above a verdant land, the warmth from other monarch wings and bodies next to hers, as they all roosted together on an oyamel tree.

Inés realized that she was back in her human form, standing on top of the stone, naked. She looked down at her feet and saw that they were perfectly nestled inside the contours of the carved butterfly's wings, like a ballerina's shoes in first position. She looked down at one leg and saw a thin streak of blood running down it. Like the monarchs, her sexual development had been paused during the migration, but now it had resumed. She looked at her honey-colored hands and lifted them to touch her face and her long, brown hair. Josephine and Valerio smiled with delight as Inés held out an arm to each of them, which they landed on. She stepped down from the stone, careful not to jostle her passengers, and again looked down at her body with wonder, still not entirely convinced that this was really happening. Millions of compound eyes were also on her: the monarchs watched in awe at the spectacle of metamorphosis, not thinking about the fact that they too had undergone one just as beautiful and magical.

A moment later Inés heard a car approaching and turned to see Homero and Andrea inside it, driven by Homero's mother. Andrea climbed out of the car and hobbled over toward Inés with a robe in her hand. As soon as Inés had slipped it on, they shared a long embrace. Homero and his mother then joined them, and as they discussed the incredible events Inés pointed out that Chaneque was still on the digger, clearly not knowing what to do now that he was masterless.

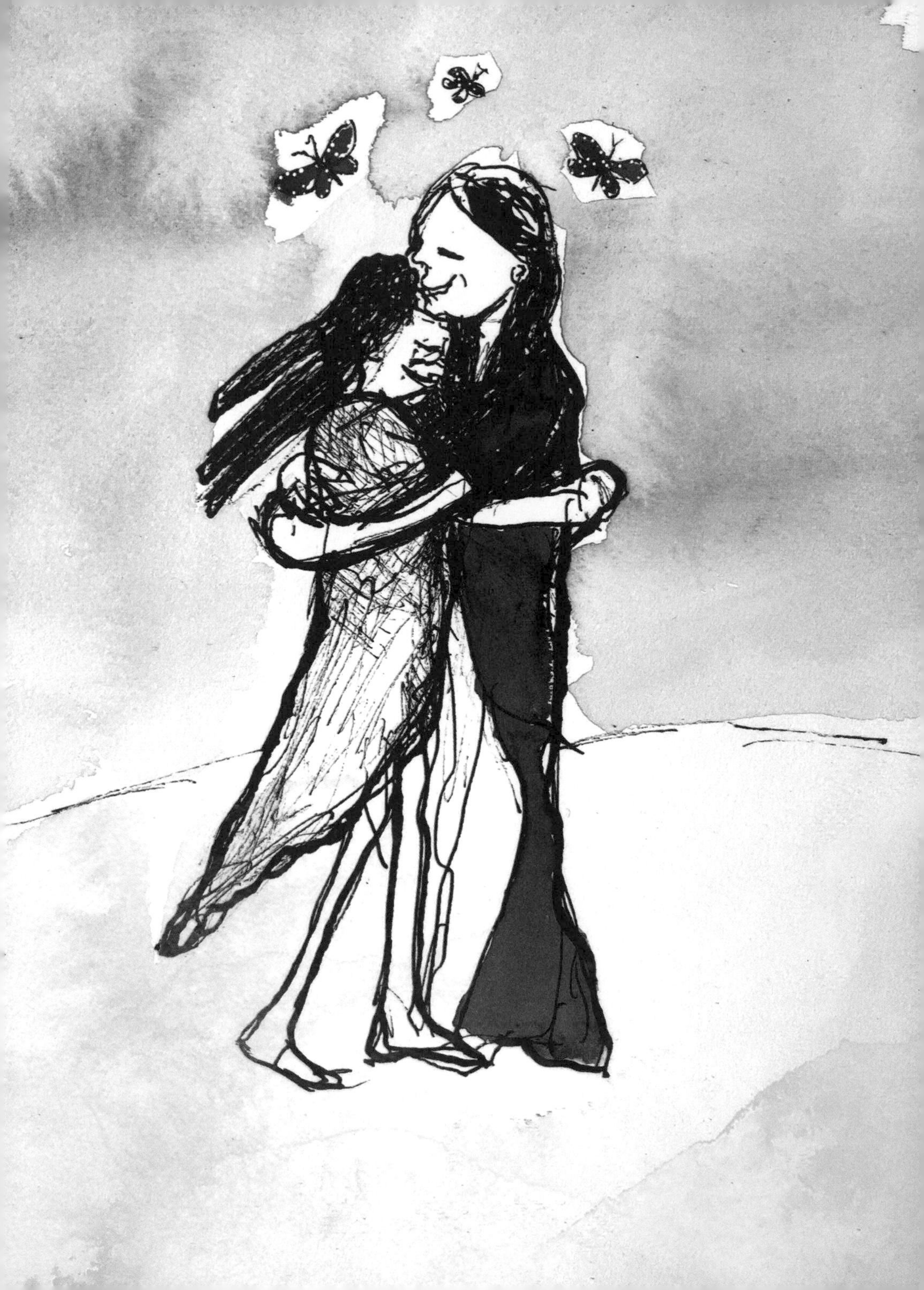

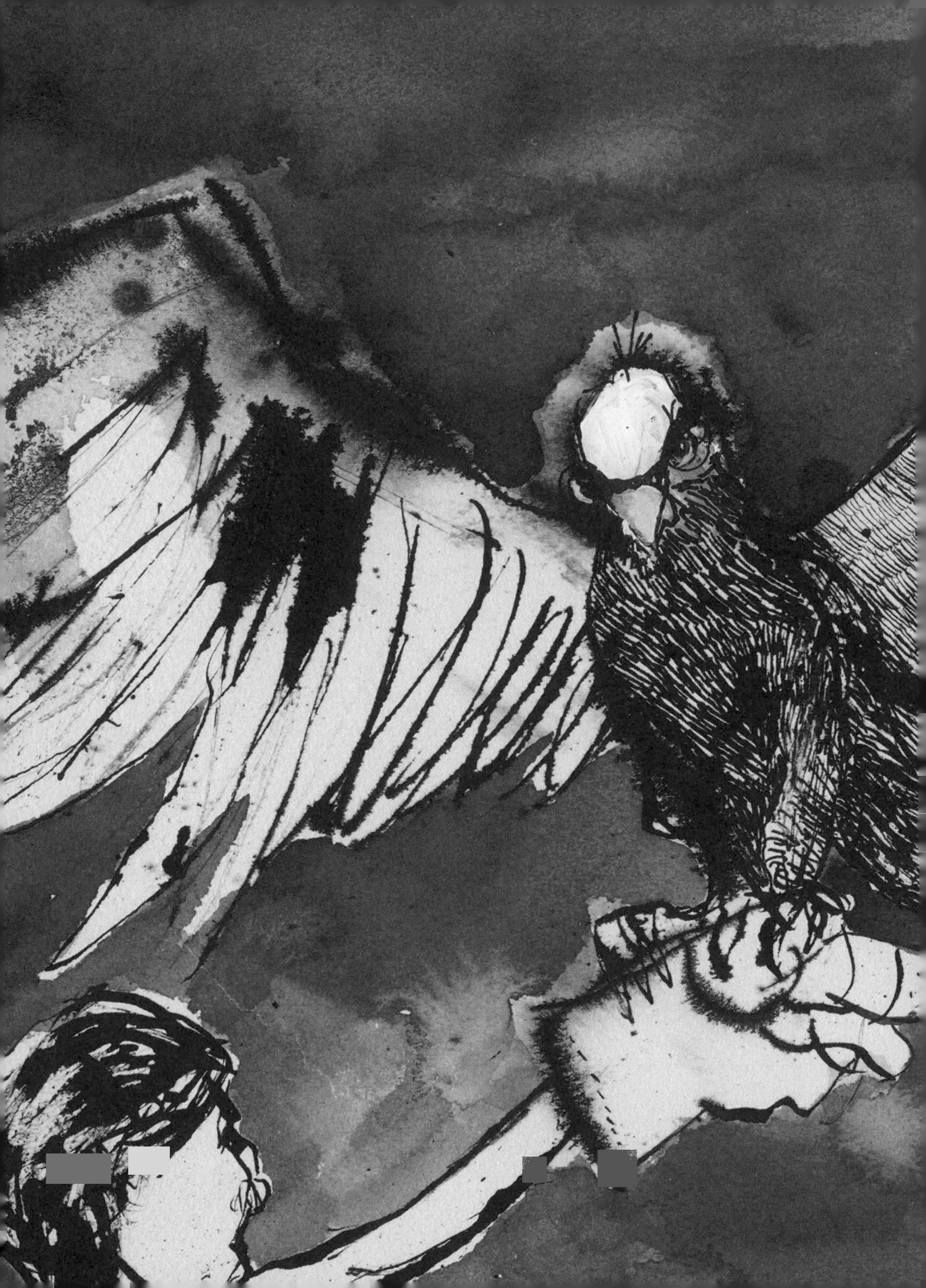

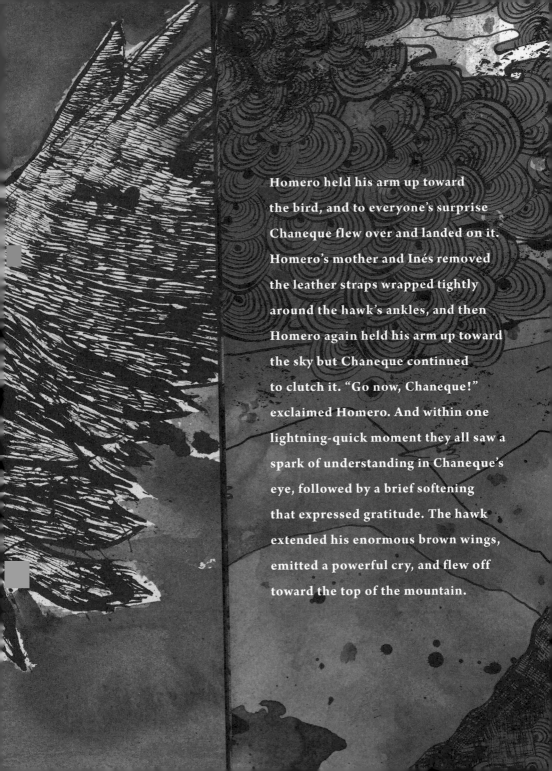

Homero held his arm up toward the bird, and to everyone's surprise Chaneque flew over and landed on it. Homero's mother and Inés removed the leather straps wrapped tightly around the hawk's ankles, and then Homero again held his arm up toward the sky but Chaneque continued to clutch it. "Go now, Chaneque!" exclaimed Homero. And within one lightning-quick moment they all saw a spark of understanding in Chaneque's eye, followed by a brief softening that expressed gratitude. The hawk extended his enormous brown wings, emitted a powerful cry, and flew off toward the top of the mountain.

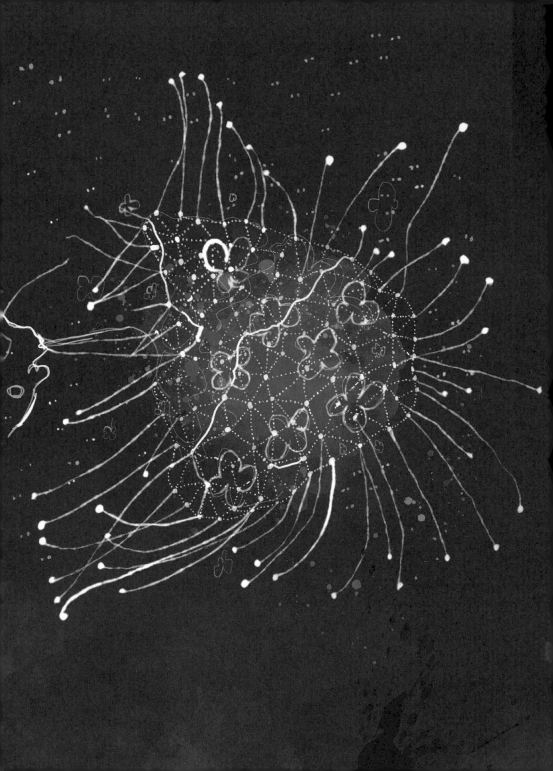

Inés spent a few days at her grandmother's house, and of course the first thing she did upon arriving there was call her parents in the United States to let them know she was safe. After her two months of absence, her parents and brother had assumed the worst, and they cried tears of joy and relief when they heard her voice. She explained that she had left willingly—it was nothing against them, she simply had to do something that entailed traveling to Mexico—and she apologized profusely for the pain and worry she'd caused them. They insisted on flying down to Michoacán to see her and accompany her on her journey back north, so soon Andrea's house was full of family, laughter, and warmth. Every day Inés would make her way up the hill to visit Josephine, Valerio, and the other butterflies, and every night she and Andrea would stay up late— waiting until everyone else had gone to bed—so that Inés could tell Andrea stories about her adventures with the swarm, or hear about those of her ancestors from Andrea.

During this time Inés also read everything she could about monarch butterflies, wanting to know what Josephine, Valerio, and the others in the sanctuary would be experiencing in the coming weeks and months. She learned that they would spend the winter hanging on the oyamel trees in a state of almost complete inactivity, as most of them had enough fat stored in their bodies to make it through the winter without feeding. And then in early March, with the warming weather and blooming flowers, the butterflies would begin their return journey to the United States and Canada. While traveling north they would feed and mate, their mating ritual consisting of an elaborate dance in the air that ended with the male enclosing the female in his wings and taking her to a secluded place. The male would then transfer a sperm sac from his body to the female's, and she would carry it inside her, fertilizing each individual egg before laying it. Both the males and females could have several partners each, and females could carry several sperm sacs at once.

But the butterflies would have to mate and find milkweed to lay their eggs on in a hurry, as most of them would die shortly afterward, somewhere in the southern United States or along the Gulf Coast. And then it would be their offspring, the first- and often second-generation monarchs, who would continue and complete the journey back north. It made Inés incredibly sad to learn that her swarm companions only had a life span of eight or nine months, but compared to the other generations of butterflies—who lived a mere two to six weeks—she realized they were incredibly lucky to be fourth-generation monarchs. Life was fleeting and they were blessed to have had the wonderful and magical experiences they'd had, as well as the three stages of existence that came before.

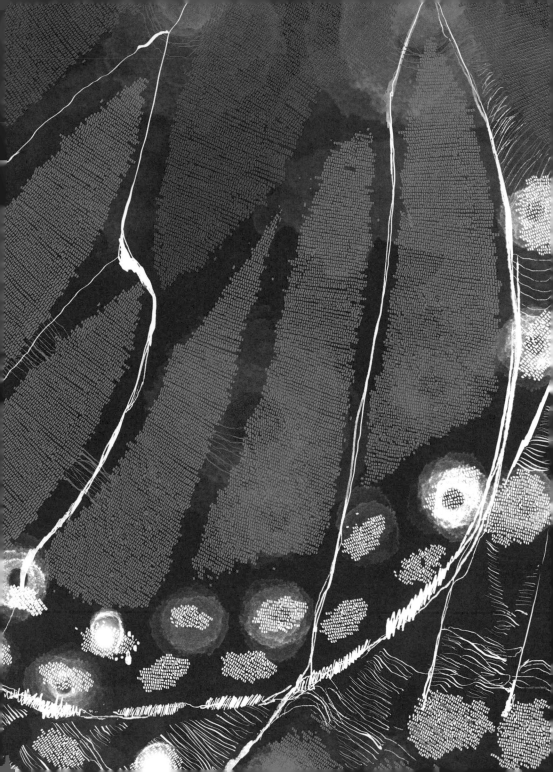

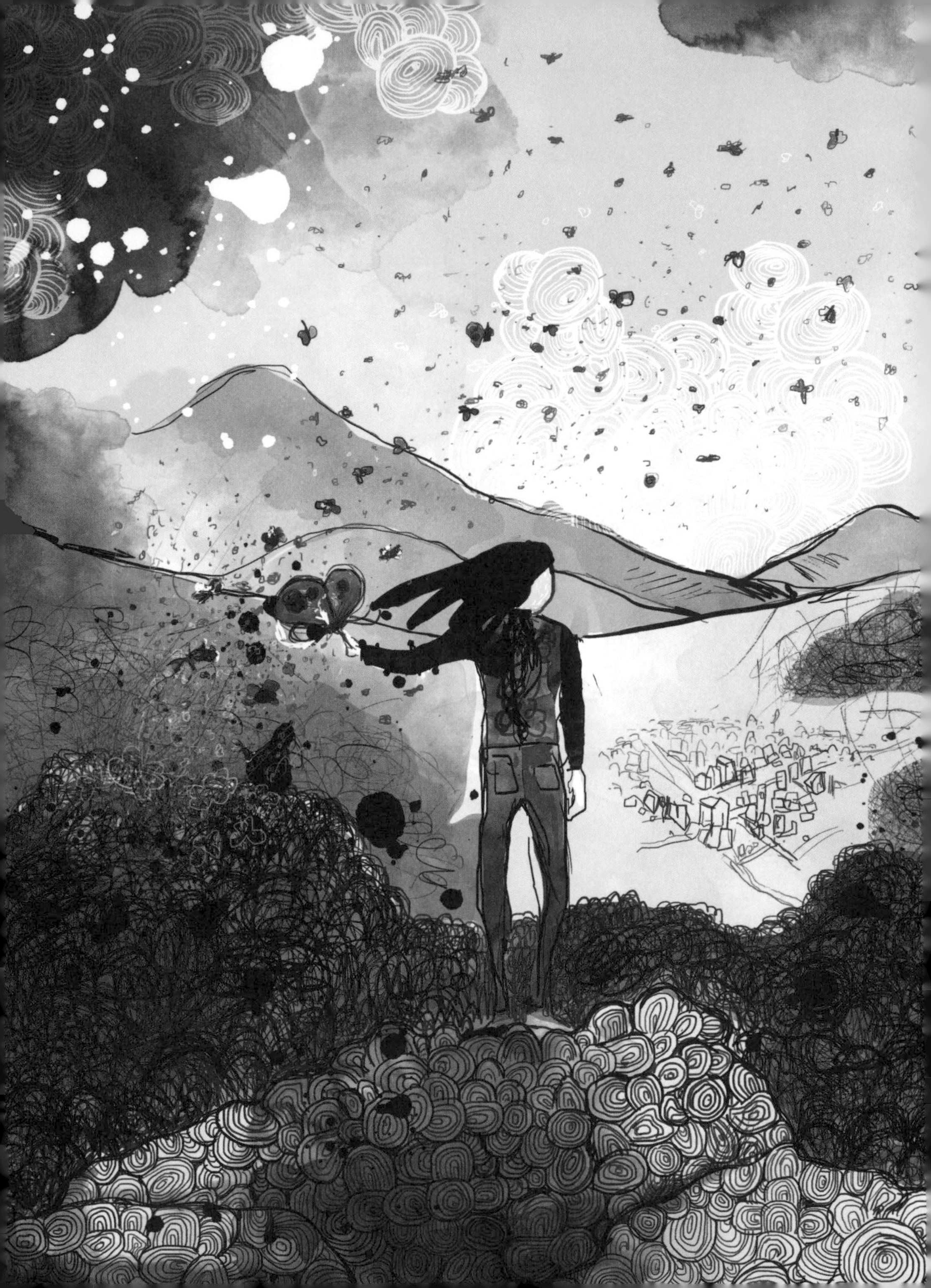

Finally the day came when Inés and her family were due to fly back to the United States. Inés made her way up the mountain to the sanctuary for the last time, with Homero and a large bag of oranges in tow. It was a sunny but chilly morning with not a cloud in the sky, and Inés felt a large lump forming in her throat as she reached the entrance to the reserve and looked up at the hundreds of trees blanketed in beautiful monarchs. Inés and Homero sat down and sliced open dozens of oranges with little pen knives, and they laid them out in a long row so that the butterflies could come down and feed.

Josephine and Valerio, who had been scanning the road waiting for Inés to appear as they did every day, flew down to greet them. Inés watched them drink from an orange and admired the hundreds of thousands of monarchs visible from where she sat, and she listened to the calls of different birds and felt the warm Michoacán sun caress her face. This majestic and perfect place felt like home to her, and it was going to be very hard to leave. And soon it was time to say goodbye, so she stood up and Josephine and Valerio each alighted on one of her open palms.

First Inés turned to Valerio. "Thank you, brave Valerio, for always reminding me of the significance of the migration, for teaching me about the incomparable value of community and the swarm, and for showing me that everything we do should be for the good of all butterflies, not just for ourselves or for the present. You helped me see how deeply connected we are to our ancestors and our descendants, at all times and in every way."

Inés then turned to Josephine, and her eyes filled with tears.

"And thank you, wise Josephine, for being my guide

in the magical world of butterflies, for being the first butterfly who spoke to me, for teaching me how to feed, sunbathe, and roost, and above all, for showing me how the natural world provides all living creatures with the sustenance and knowledge they need. You are like my butterfly mother *and* best friend; you always offered me the comfort of your words and the caress of your wing when I lacked courage or optimism."

Josephine responded first: "You are a beautiful and generous soul, Inés, and I will miss you terribly. I wish you happiness always, and I truly thank you for helping to save our swarm."

And Valerio added: "Yes, thank you, Inés, for joining our migration and for bringing the wisdom of your ancestors with you. You will live on as a hero in our monarch history forever."

Inés then addressed the two of them, and at this point she couldn't stop the tears from streaming down her cheeks. "Thank you both for being my companions on this journey—surely the most important experience of my lifetime—and for teaching me so much about the world. Good luck during the remaining winter months and with finding your mates, although I suspect you've already found that in each other. I love you and I will never forget you." And with that Inés gave each of them a soft kiss on their tiny heads, and she watched as they fluttered back up toward an oyamel tree, their bodies soon lost within the shimmering tapestry of orange, black, and white.

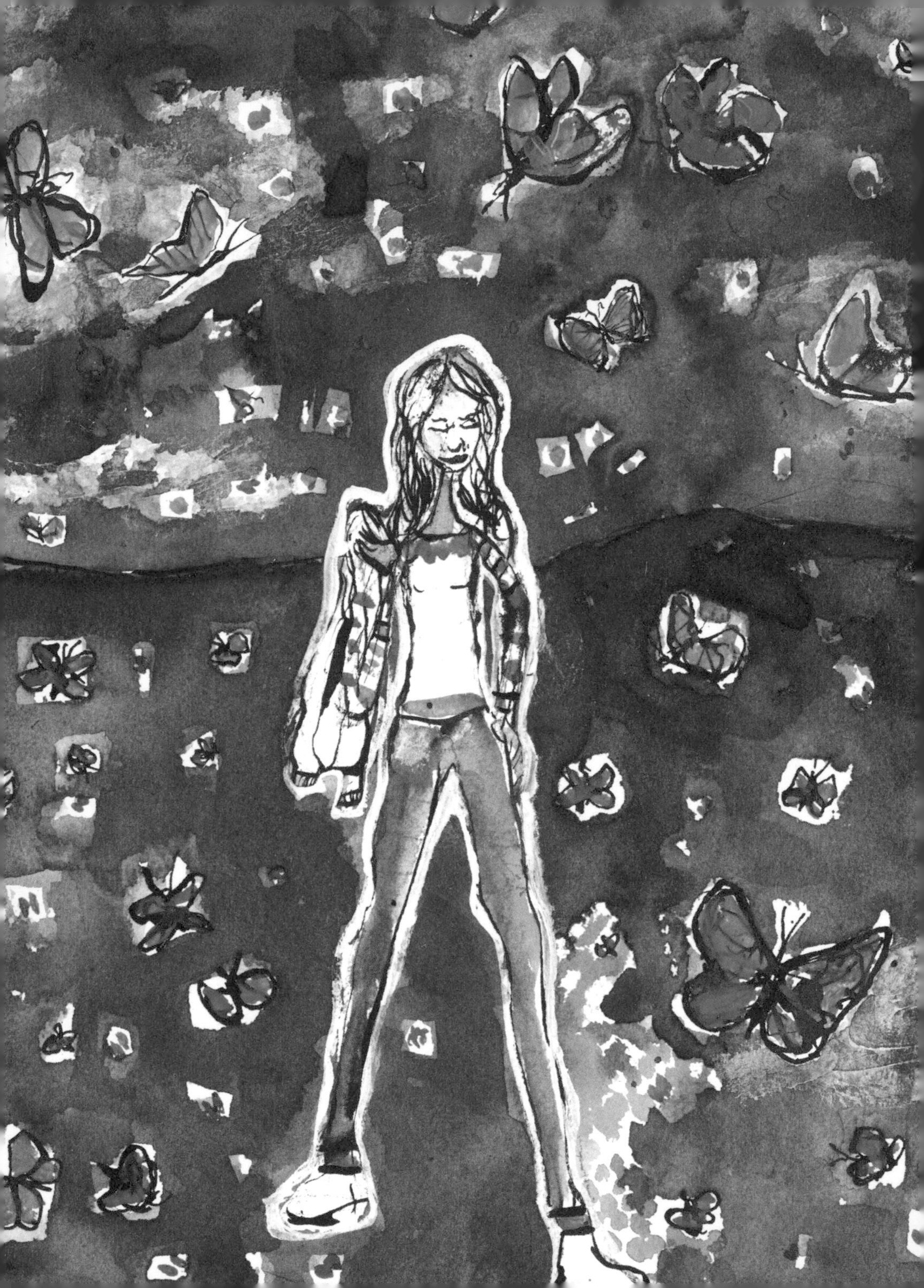

Inés then called out a final goodbye to all the butterflies, and that would be the last time she saw Josephine, Valerio, or any of the others.

As Inés and Homero made their way back down the mountain, Homero saw that Inés was still crying. He touched her arm gently, saying, "I promise I'll take care of them, Inés. I'll come see them every day, and I'll do everything within my power to make sure that the butterflies we love so much are safe. When I'm older, I'll make sure this sanctuary is better protected so that what happened the other night can never happen again."

"And I'll go back to my hometown and start a milkweed and wildflower planting program," said Inés, "to make sure that every monarch caterpillar or butterfly being born there or passing through is never wanting for nourishment. We may be young, Homero, and we may seem small and insignificant in the grand scheme of things, but if a few tiny butterflies can make such a big difference, I know that a few small humans can too."

And with these positive words and uplifting dreams, the two friends arrived back in the village, bid each other farewell until Inés returned to Michoacán again, and went home to their respective families. The next morning, when Inés said goodbye to her beloved grandmother, Andrea whispered the following words in her ear: "Even though you are a young woman now, remember that you are still a butterfly. And you will always be a butterfly, not only because you've had butterfly experiences and butterfly dreams, but because you've reached the butterfly stage of your development. You fulfilled your duty as a daughter of the sun, and you will now take all the wisdom that you gathered and share it with others. Goodbye, Inés—come visit again soon."

When Inés stepped back into her bedroom for the first time in months, the first thing she did was put on her butterfly necklace. The bag of seeds was still sitting on her desk, and of course Inés now knew what they were. She planted the milkweed seeds in her garden, and as promised, she next started a milkweed and wildflower planting program in her school, and then in her hometown. By the following summer, the whole area was teeming with newborn monarch caterpillars and butterflies feasting on the leaves and flowers that had cropped up everywhere.

Inés had changed since her migration, but her love of dance was as deep as it had always been. She choreographed her own ballet inspired by the flight of the butterflies, and called it *Daughter of the Sun*. Like all monarchs in the fourth stage of life, Inés was pollinating and leaving her mark on the world.

And then the fall arrived again, and Inés turned fourteen. One afternoon she was sitting on a knoll overlooking the backyards and sloping rooftops of her hometown, when a monarch came to rest on a fallen branch in the grass near her feet. Inés stared at the monarch and felt as if she knew her, but how could she? The butterfly took flight and alighted on Inés's bent knee, and Inés smiled when she saw that the butterfly had one crooked antenna and one straight one.

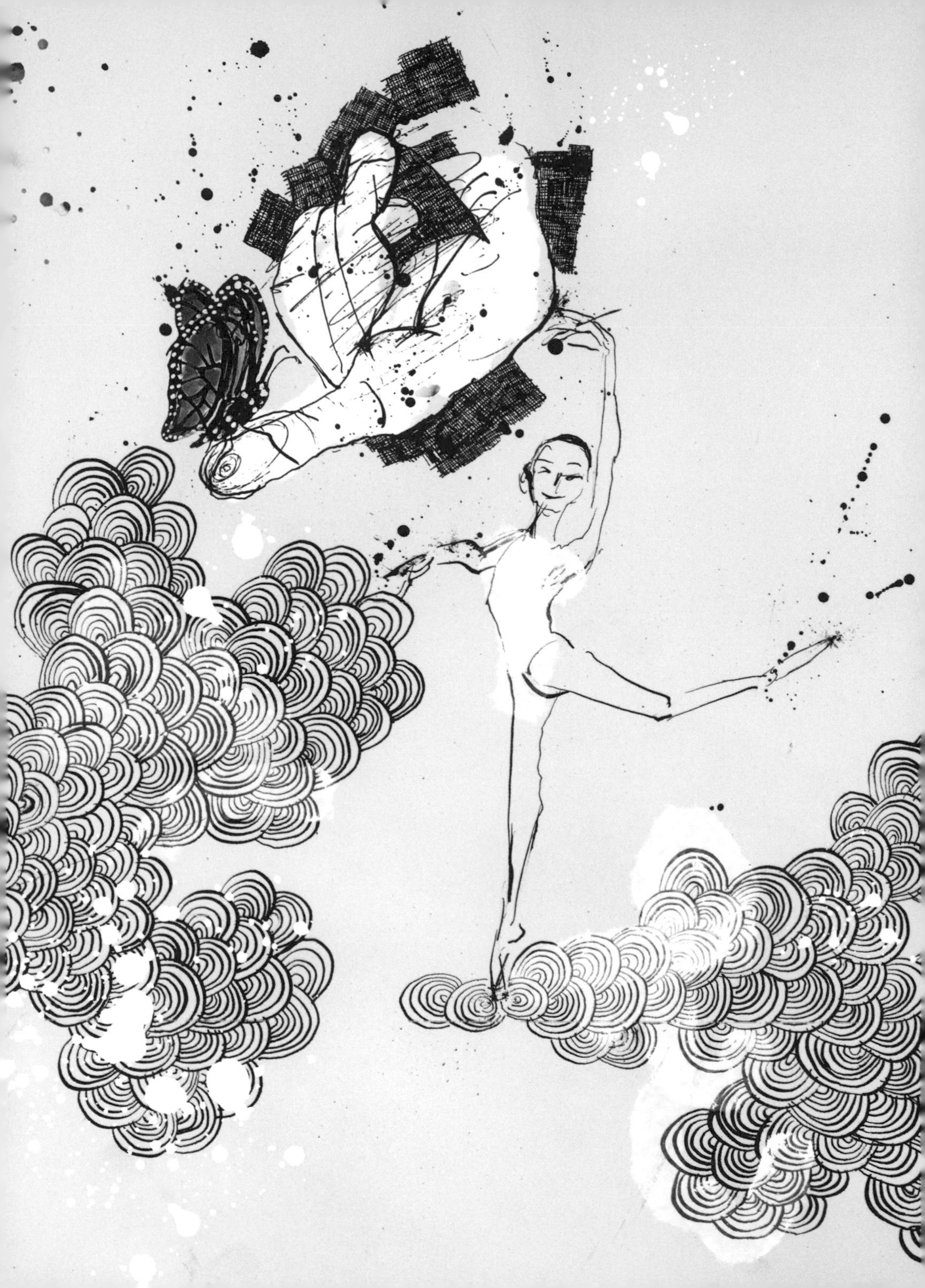

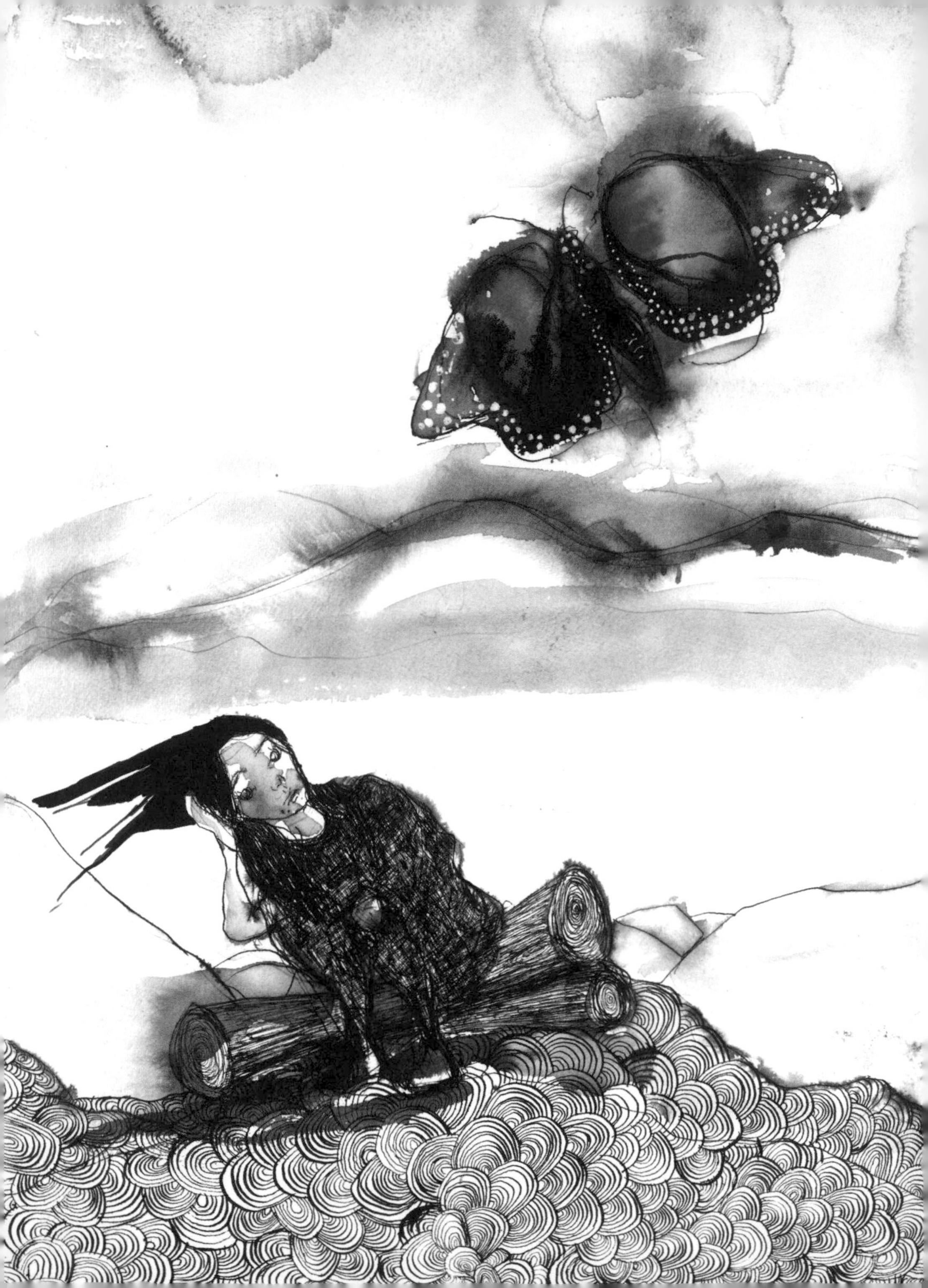

epilogue

Inés finished speaking, but it took her a few seconds to emerge from the vivid memories and visceral sensations she had just revisited. She turned to look at the butterfly perched on her knee, and for a moment she thought she was with Josephine again.

"And that's us, right now?" asked Jo-Jo.

Inés nodded. "I hope you see now, little Jo-Jo, that your great-great-grandmother Josephine was a very special butterfly, that you *will* know when to depart on your migration, and that a very small creature like a monarch butterfly or a young human can achieve great things."

"I do," replied Jo-Jo, "and I'm grateful. You've taught me about the four stages of growth and transformation and how, even though I was just born, I've already reached the last stage of my development and have a lot more wisdom within me than I realized. Not only am I no longer afraid of the migration, but I can't wait for it to begin."

Inés and Jo-Jo looked around and saw that there were dozens of monarchs in the vicinity now. Some were flitting about in the sky, while others were perched on trees, flowers, or blades of grass. Jo-Jo looked back at Inés and said, "Thank you, daughter of the sun. Thank you for all that you did to save my species, and for helping to make sure that the oyamel forest will still be there when I arrive, exhausted, after my three-thousand-mile journey. I will tell the other butterflies I encounter the tale you've just told me, so that they too will know about the adventures and teachings of Inés, Josephine, Valerio, Homero, Andrea, and all the daughters of the sun and monarch butterflies who came before us."

Inés smiled and responded: "You can tell them my story, Jo-Jo, but don't forget that you are about to create a story of your own. May Josephine's spirit guide and protect you, and please say hello to the beautiful forest of oyamel trees for me."

"I will!" replied Jo-Jo. And with that the young monarch gave her wings a good, long stretch and alighted into the sky with newfound confidence. A light but chilly breeze blew her body southward a few feet, and she turned and called out to the other monarchs, "It's time to go, friends!" The butterflies flew over to join her and Jo-Jo looked to the colorful lights in the sky, converging at a point far in the distance, and headed toward them. Her new companions followed, and thus the new swarm embarked on the journey of their lifetimes, guided by the sun, their ancestors, their inner compass, and instinct.

Inés watched them as they disappeared into the sunset, and then she stood up and stretched her arms as if she still had wings. She missed the sense of freedom and abandon that flying had provided, and part of her longed to go with Jo-Jo and her swarm. She had just relived her whole time as a butterfly while telling the story, and although that part of her life had lasted only two months, it had led her through all four stages of transformation, with her metamorphosis being not just physical but emotional, psychological, and spiritual as well. And now that she was focused on giving back to others—to the butterflies and the natural world, to her community and her family—her own dreams of doing well at ballet were materializing, and she felt happy and complete for the first time ever.

Another small gust of wind blew and Inés shivered.

She started to descend the hill and head home, ready for the next experience and journey of her own. She didn't need to travel to Mexico in order to have it; in fact, she didn't have to go anywhere. Inés was eternally an egg, a caterpillar, a pupa, and a butterfly. What unexpected moments would this evening bring? What dreams would she have tonight? What events would she encounter tomorrow? Every day was a new opportunity for growth, experience, and love, and each moment could be used for teaching and learning, for giving and receiving, or for simply sitting in quiet communion with nature or one's ancestors. One didn't have to be a daughter of the sun or a monarch to undergo a metamorphosis; one simply had to be willing and open, a dreamer or a seeker, and truly alive.

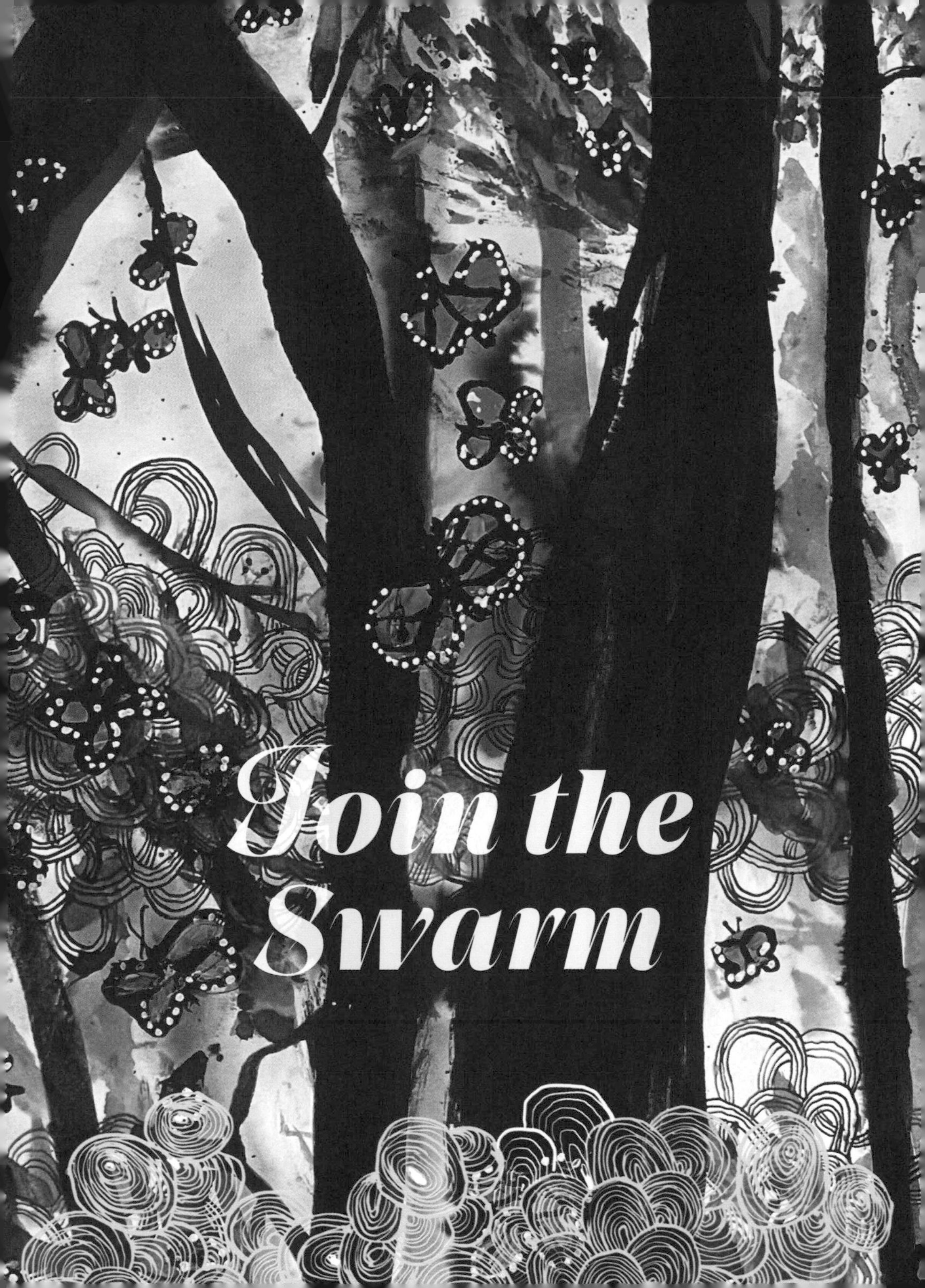
Join the Swarm

Many of the events depicted in this book are based on real dangers that monarchs face during their migration and upon arrival in Mexico. But in reality their situation is much worse, and environmentalists and biologists are calling for the iconic insect to be declared an endangered species. The North American monarch butterfly population can be divided into two groups: the much larger eastern population, which originates in Canada or the United States east of the Rocky Mountains and overwinters in Mexico, and the smaller western population, which originates in the northwestern United States and overwinters at two hundred roosting sites along California's Pacific coast, from the Bay Area down to Baja California. Both populations have been in steady decline since the late 1990s, with the eastern population's numbers dropping a staggering 85 percent from nearly 1 billion to fewer than 60 million during the past twenty-five years, and the western population's numbers dropping at an even more devastating 99 percent. In 1997, the number of butterflies overwintering in California was 1.2 million, but by 2019 it had dropped to 29,000, and in 2020 under 2,000 were counted. It is highly possible that this will be the western population's last year in existence.

Why are monarch numbers dropping so much and so quickly? As an insect that depends on food, weather, and habitat conditions in several countries, today's monarch butterfly is affected by a myriad of issues in the United States, Mexico, and Canada. The main issue in the United States and Canada is the loss of milkweed, the sole food source for the monarch caterpillar and the only plant a monarch will lay her eggs on. Habitat conversion (urbanization) and adverse land management have led to a steady decline in milkweed availability, with 165 million acres of monarch habitat—an area the size of Texas—lost over the past twenty years. Widespread use of insecticides and herbicides used to control both insects and weeds have destroyed milkweed plants in much of the remaining habitat. The glyphosate-based herbicide Roundup, produced by Monsanto/Bayer and used all over the Midwest, kills every plant doused with it except those genetically engineered to tolerate it. Some 850 million milkweed plants—representing 71 percent of monarchs' support infrastructure—have vanished from corn and soybean fields in the United States in two decades. Climate change leads to more forest fires and drought (particularly in California and other western states), and this also leads to less milkweed, while extreme heat waves can cause monarch eggs to never hatch.

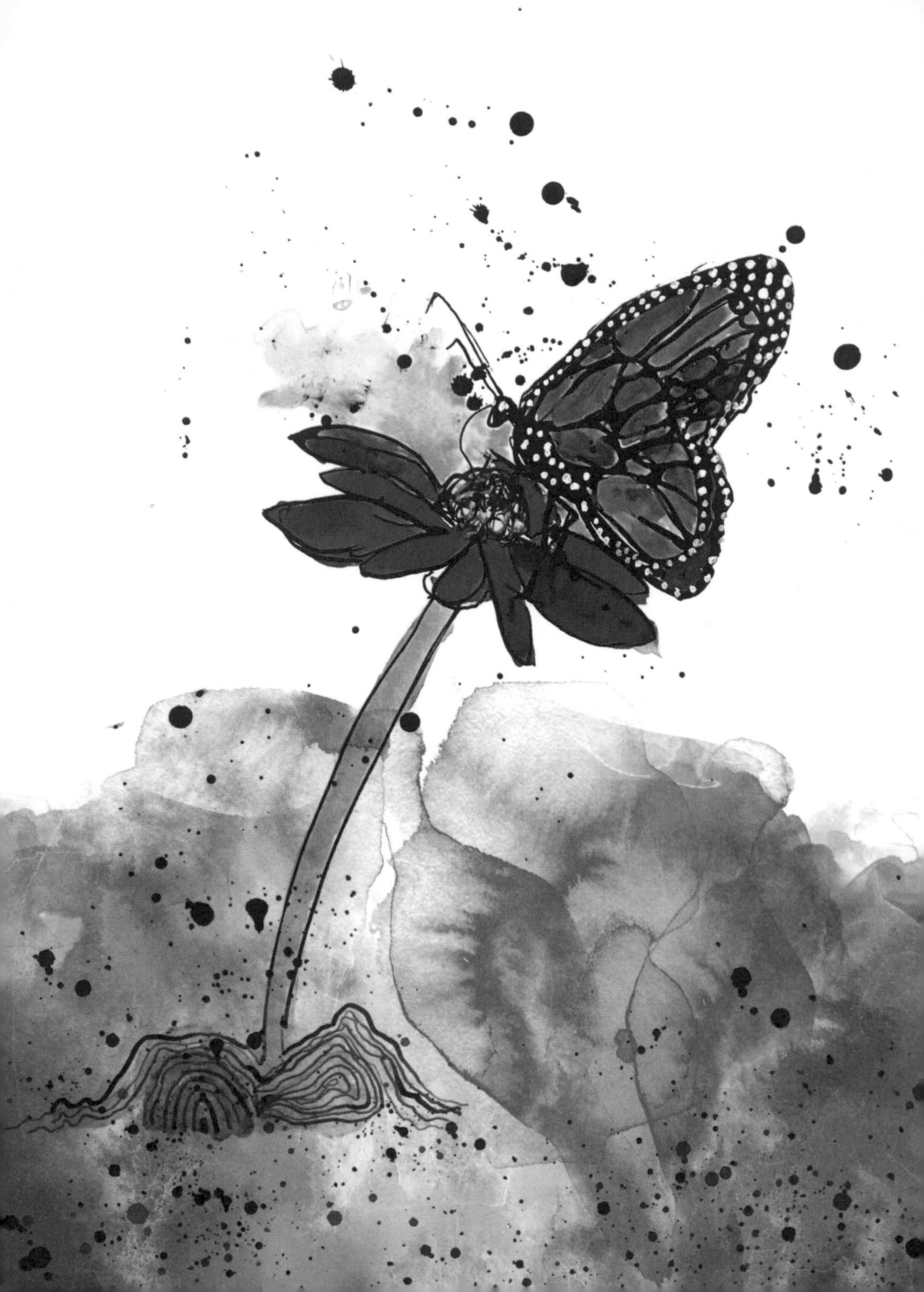

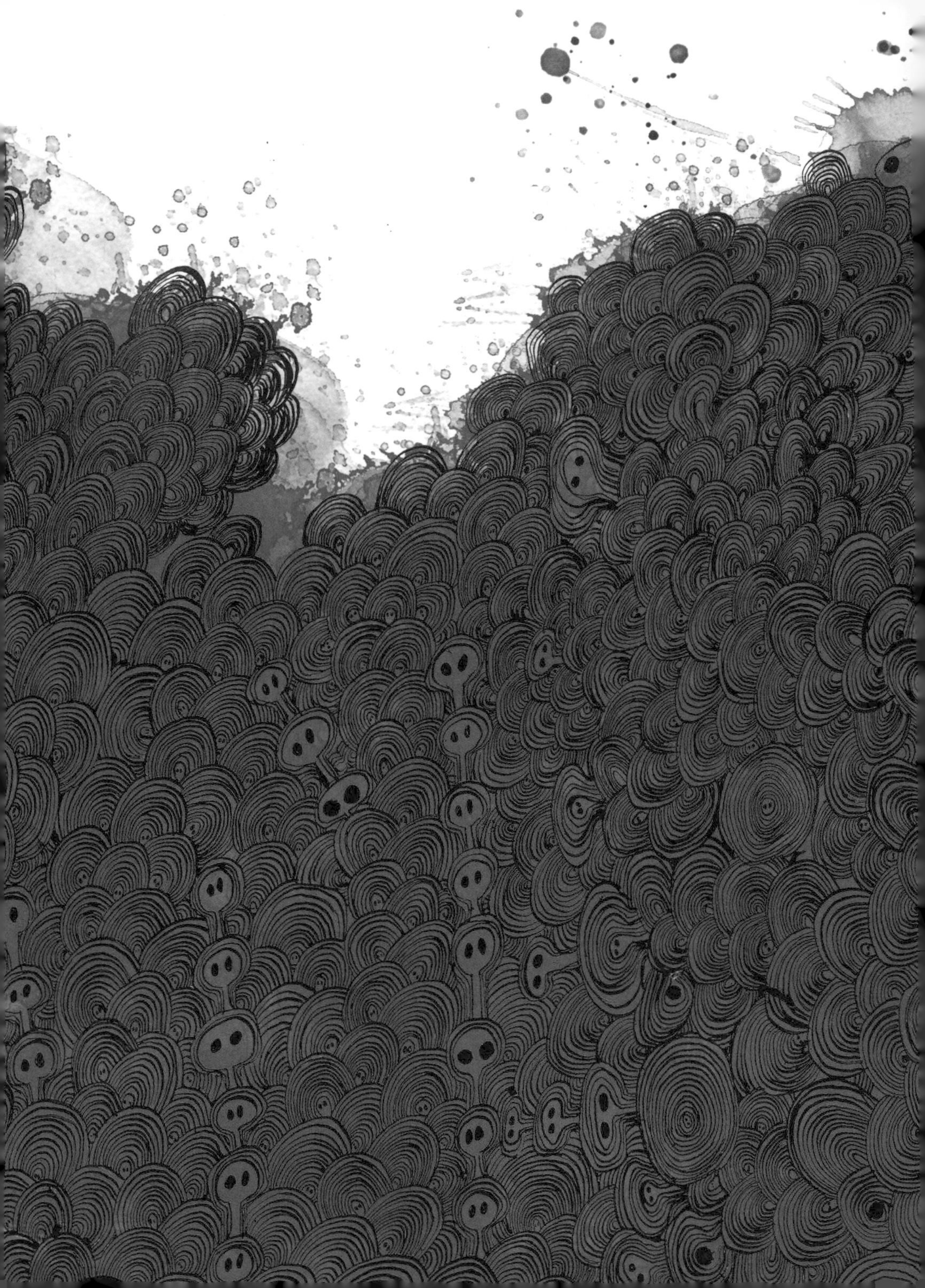

Monarchs encounter many physical obstacles during the course of their migration. Some drown while flying over the Great Lakes, others are killed in storms, and some are destroyed by wind while flying over the Eastern Seaboard. But the single-largest cause of monarch mortality when it comes to accidents is roadways, where some 25 million monarchs die in the United States and Mexico every year when they're run over by cars and trucks or get caught on windshields and in grills. Additionally, polluted runoff from oil and salt alters the quality of food sources for monarch larvae, and monarchs are stressed by vehicular noise.

As described in this book, once the butterflies arrive in Michoacán after their journey of up to three thousand miles, their struggles are far from over. An estimated 10 percent of the overwintering population are eaten by predator birds and mammals each year, while one bad winter storm can kill tens of millions. In December of 1995 it snowed for two days in the sanctuaries, killing as many as four million butterflies. But the biggest issue facing monarchs in Mexico is illegal logging and the destruction of their winter habitat. The tree-covered mountains of central Mexico provide the perfect microclimate for the butterflies, who spend the winter sheltered amongst the thick, needle-bearing branches of the oyamel fir trees. It stays warm enough for them to not freeze, but not so warm that they become active and resume their reproductive cycle (mating prematurely can prompt monarchs to migrate north too early and not find milkweed to lay their eggs on). And it is wet enough to protect the trees from forest fires, but not so wet that the monarchs become chilled. However, any threat to the trees is a threat to the butterflies, and the fir forests that once covered this whole region now represent less than 0.5 percent of the land.

In 1986, at the urging of Michoacán-born poet and environmentalist Homero Aridjis (Eva Aridjis's father), the Mexican government decreed the creation of the Monarch Butterfly Special Biosphere Reserve, encompassing five butterfly colonies on 16,110 hectares (39,809 acres) in the states of México and Michoacán. In 2000, the reserve was expanded to 56,259 hectares (139,019 acres). But logging has continued at an alarming pace in both the unprotected and protected areas, and during the year 2005 up to 461 hectares (1,140 acres) were depleted inside the reserve. The trees are felled by commercial loggers with sawmills and trucks, by locals using them for firewood or building purposes, and by farmers expanding their fields onto the slopes of the forested mountains, while their cattle trample and eat the fir seedlings.

Most recently, avocado farming has presented the biggest threat. Avocados originated in Mexico ten thousand years ago, and today 80 percent of the avocados consumed in the United States come from Michoacán, the only Mexican state authorized to export this fruit. Known as "green gold" due to the high prices avocados fetch and the soaring demand for them, the fruit's booming industry has been brutal for Michoacán's oak and pine forests. Both the forests and avocados grow at an altitude of five to seven thousand feet, and between 1974 and 2011 about 110,000 acres of forest across Michoacán's central highlands were turned into avocado orchards. This deforestation has accelerated with demand for the fruit (Americans eat seven pounds of avocado per capita per year, up from three pounds in 2008), and Mexico's environmental watchdog, the Federal Attorney General for Environmental Protection, often turns a blind eye to the illegal logging taking place. Powerful interests including drug cartels now have ties to this lucrative trade, making local officials fearful through threats or compliant through bribes. In addition to fueling the destruction of the forests that the monarchs depend upon for survival, avocado farming is also consuming much of the water supply.

So what can we do as individuals to help these magnificent butterflies? The first and foremost action we can take is to plant milkweed and wildflowers for them. This can be done in our backyards, local parks, school and church grounds, university campuses, museum gardens, and even on our rooftops or in balcony flowerpots. Butterflies and other pollinators like to bask in the sun, and some of their favorite wildflowers grow best in full or partial sun with some

protection from the wind. Research what varieties of milkweed and wildflowers are native to your area, as those plants will require less maintenance and be heartier; and decide whether you'd like to use seeds (cheaper but requiring more care) or plants. If purchasing plants, be sure to choose ones that have not been treated with neonicotinoids or other pesticides. Also, think long term: pollinators need nectar in the spring, throughout the summer, and into the fall, and monarchs love a variety of flowers: zinnia, marigold, aster, ava, goldenrod, Mexican sunflower, miss molly bush, Brazilian verbena, may night salvia, lantana, and more. Meanwhile, milkweed is essential for monarchs to lay eggs on and for caterpillars to feed on starting in early March and throughout the summer.

In southern states like Texas, where monarchs roost by the tens of thousands before heading into Mexico, nectar-bearing plants help fatten them up before their 120-day hibernation, during which most won't consume anything except water. Similarly, many monarchs lay their eggs in central Texas when heading north from Mexico, so an ample milkweed supply for them there is critical. But habitat restoration and plantings for butterflies are effective *anywhere* monarchs breed or pass through while migrating, and it is essential that privately owned farms and ranches between Canada and Mexico enroll in voluntary conservation programs, providing food, breeding, and resting spots for them. It is preferable to not plant milkweed and wildflowers right next to roads, but if this is the only habitat available, it is better than nothing at all.

The second thing you can do to help monarchs is to urge the US Fish and Wildlife Service to list the monarch butterfly as an endangered species. Monarchs need immediate protection, and this designation would lead to a comprehensive recovery plan and funding to restore their habitat and ensure their survival and recovery. In addition, please urge the Mexican government to protect the monarch butterfly reserves from the destructive avocado trade. There are countless petitions for both of these causes to be found online, and they should be signed and then shared on social media for greater impact.

The third thing you can do to support monarchs is to consume only organic, Equal Exchange avocados from Mexico (if you can find them and afford them). Produced by a farmer cooperative in Michoacán named PRAGOR, these avocados are grown by farmers who have been farming organically for at least six years, and in areas where they're not contributing to any new deforestation. PRAGOR members make up a mere 25 out of 17,000 registered avocado farmers in Michoacán, but the more they are supported, the more sustainable avocado farming practices in the area will become. Please urge your grocery store to sell organic, fair-trade avocados and boycott the commercially grown ones. Perhaps we could suggest that responsible avocado producers label their avocados "forest and monarch friendly."

Lastly, teach your children to respect the earth and its nonhuman inhabitants and to appreciate the wonders of the natural world. Children love following the life cycle of a monarch—from egg to caterpillar to pupa to butterfly—and spending time in and marveling at nature is both exciting and educational for them. How much of the natural world will still be here by the time they've grown up depends on *us*, and then it will depend on *them*. Like Inés, Homero, and their butterfly friends, we all have the capacity to make a big difference—both in our immediate surroundings and on the entire planet— no matter how small we might be.

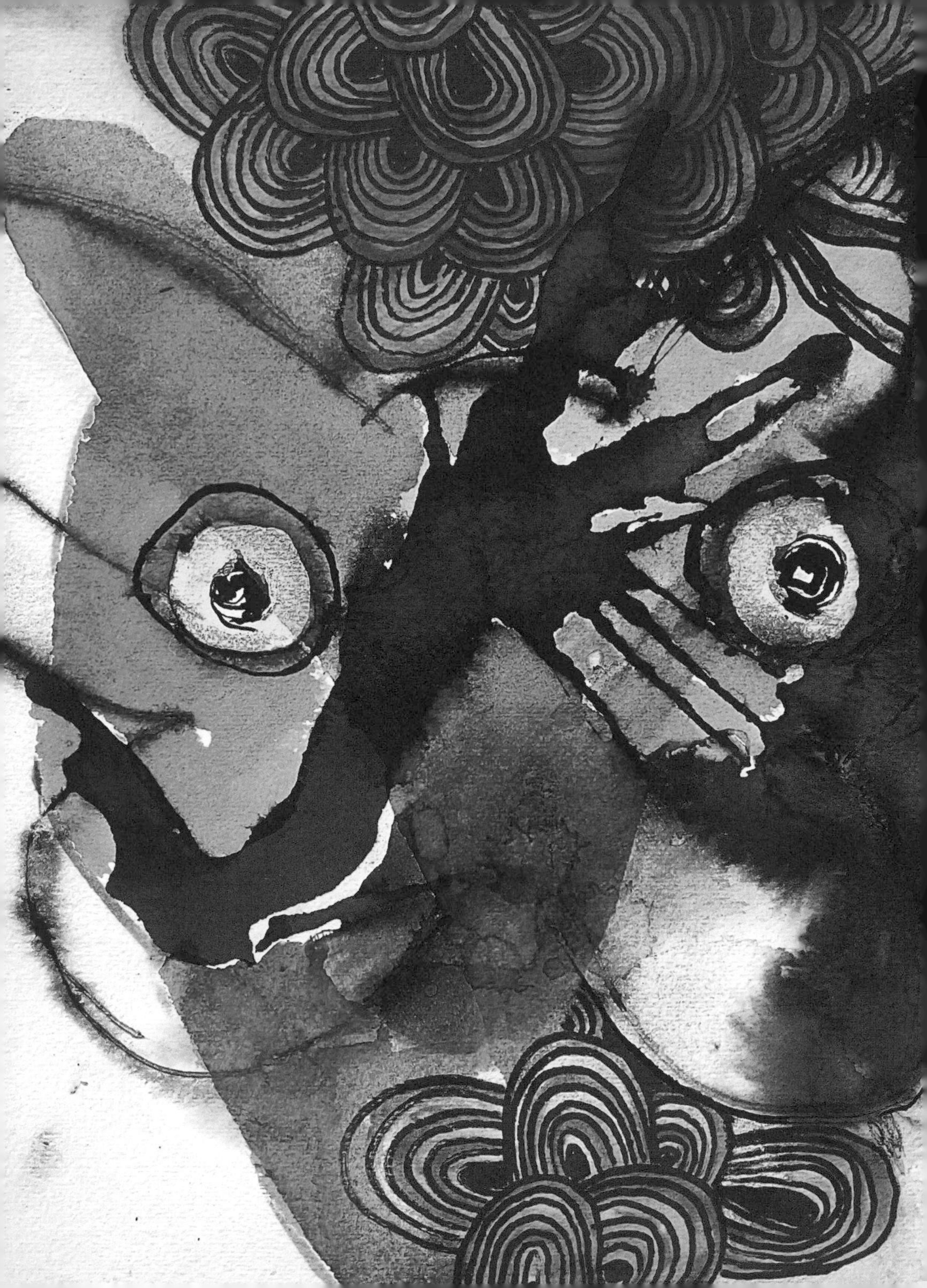

acknowledgments

The authors would like to thank our children, parents, and siblings, many of whom inspired characters in this book and whose love and support nurtured our creativity and our respect for the natural world. We adore you.

Enormous thanks to our wonderful editor, Anna Paustenbach, whose close readings and perceptive suggestions guided our rewrites and the ultimate direction of the book, and to our agent, Lisa Gallagher, for her commitment to this project from inception to completion and her valuable feedback at every step. And a very special thanks to the glorious Judith Curr, our publisher, who believed in this story from the moment she heard the first wing flap.

We are deeply grateful to James Manning for his wonderful creative contributions to the art, and to the whole design team for their beautiful work: Janet Evans-Scanlon and Yvonne Chan.

We would like to thank Emily Strode, Kathy Reigstad, Sun Paik, and Kim Nir for their meticulous work making sure the book reads flawlessly, and Makenna Holford and Maxwell Shanley for their invaluable help in getting it out into the greater world!

Muchísimas gracias a Ariana Rosado-Fernández for her passionate supervision and edit of the Spanish version, as well as our wonderful translator, Tatiana Lipkes.

Thank you to monarch butterfly experts Pablo Jaramillo and Karen Oberhauser for their generous help with the facts and statistics that appear in the "Call to Action" section of this book.

We send deep gratitude out to Andrea Valeria Grautoff and León García Soler, who are flying in their swarm at the edge of the galaxy . . .

Lastly we would like to thank Homero and Betty Aridjis for their tireless work defending monarch butterflies and their habitat in Mexico, and all of the eco warriors around the world who spend their days fighting to protect the countless endangered insect, animal, and plant species with whom we share this wondrous planet.

about the authors

Leopoldo Gout is a visual artist, award-winning author, filmmaker, and producer who believes that the arts can be a powerful driver of social change.

Eva Aridjis is an award-winning filmmaker, writer, and animal rights activist. Her films include *The Favor, The Blue Eyes, Children of the Street, La Santa Muerte, Chuy, The Wolf Man,* and *Goodbye Horses.*

leopoldogout.net
evaaridjis.com